# Electric Moon

A RAVEN INVESTIGATIONS NOVEL

## Stacey Brutger

This is a work of fiction. Names, character, places, and incidents are either the product of the author's imagination or are used fictitiously, and any resemblance to actual persons living or dead, business establishments, events, or locales is entirely coincidental.

All rights reserved. No part of this book may be used or reproduced, scanned, or distributed in any printed or electronic form in any manner whatsoever without written permission of the author except in the case of brief quotations for articles or reviews. Please do not participate in or encourage piracy of copyrighted materials.

Copyright © 2013 **Stacey Brutger**

Cover artist: Amanda Kelsey of Razzle Dazzle Design (www.razzdazzdesign.com)

Editor: Jennifer Bray-Weber (www.jbrayweber.com)

All rights reserved.

ISBN-10:1492232459
ISBN-13: 978-1492232452

## ACKNOWLEDGMENTS

I want to thank all my fans for their support and you, the readers, for giving me a chance.

A special thanks goes out to those who suffered through the first draft in order to make this book better: Madeleine Kenney, Melissa Limoges, Angela Rafuse, Jessie Teicher
You ladies rock!

And to my husband and family for believing in me.

Thank you!

Other books by this author:

BloodSworn

**A Raven Investigations Novel**
Electric Storm (Book 1)
Electric Moon (Book 2)

**A PeaceKeeper Novel**
The Demon Within (Book 1)

**Coming Soon:**

Coveted
Electric Heat (Book 3)

Visit Stacey online to find out more at www.StaceyBrutger.com

## ❧ Chapter One ❧

**TEN DAYS UNTIL THE FULL MOON**

 **I**n ten days, the conclave would decide Raven's fate and that of her pack. They just needed to survive that long. If that wasn't bad enough, the full moon would rip through the shifter community at the same time. Already the craziness they'd warned her about during the lunar cycle threatened to sweep over her.

 For she must be crazy to even listen to, much less agree to help, the two men who'd broken into her house. They would jeopardize everything she'd been working toward and possibly destroy the fragile pack she'd built. A hum of electricity licked under her skin, aching to be released, but she shook it off.

 She was a rare conduit, born with the ability to control pure energy. Maybe the only one of her kind. That meant she couldn't afford any mistakes, couldn't draw attention to herself, or others might discover the secrets she'd been concealing for years.

 Raw emotions had a way of wreaking havoc on her system, triggering her powers. Being in a room full of shifters demanded complete control. She couldn't afford to turn everyone furry because she had PMS.

 She'd learned the hard way to keep her emotions out of pack decisions when Jackson had been taken from her by the pack that had abandoned him. Her own fault really, because she'd hesitated to claim him when she'd had the chance.

 Dominic, the lone wolf who helped hold her small pack together, had the right idea to pack his bags and disappear when the full moon rose. He would've already been gone if it weren't for these two intruders.

No dealing with the conclave.

No slowly going insane with the desperate urge to touch as the moon madness spread from one shifter to the next. That her touch could kill if she didn't keep on constant guard merely made things a bit trickier. She shook her head, wishing it were that easy to clear her mind.

Dominic and London stood guard behind the two men. London stared at the back of Griffin's head. One wrong move and she had no doubt the bear would crush his skull like a watermelon.

"You need us." Griffin stood in the middle of the library like he owned the place.

His words were such a man thing to say, especially when they were the ones asking for help. Their agitation battered at her like war machines of old. Raven stiffened where she stood behind the massive desk, but the distance didn't help.

The alpha in her said leave them to their fate, but her conscience wouldn't let her take the easy out and turn them away out of hand. Not this man. Not with their murky past tying them together. They'd both been held prisoner, caged and awaiting death at the hands of a human psycho who thought it was his duty to cleanse the earth of paranormal filth.

Or it was until she killed him.

When she'd demanded help, the rogue had offered it without reservation. She owed it to him to at least listen. "Tell me again."

"If you want your wolf back, you'll need help navigating the shifter world without appearing weak." Griffin's chest expanded impressively, his hands on his narrow hips, all arrogance despite his exiled status. Ballsy, too, breaking into her home by just walking through the front door and making himself at home.

His brilliant green and yellow eyes drew her gaze, the combination disconcerting. Instead of being ringed by a second color, normal to most rogues, his eyes were completely splintered to show both man and wolf in full command.

The feat of control amazed her since most people would go insane being permanently stuck in such a condition. His all-wolf attitude reminded her of another.

Jackson.

She swallowed hard, remorse and betrayal too close to the surface for her to think rationally when Jackson trotted through her mind. She didn't question how Griffin had learned about her predicament. No doubt he'd seen the police cart Jackson away in chains, stealing him right from under her watch.

Apparently, she was the only one unaware that when a shifter was taken into custody, their alpha automatically received notification.

It should've been a mere formality.

Instead, his pack had purposely retrieved him before she could claim him for her own, and she had no one to blame but herself.

"And you want protection for yourself and Digger in return for your assistance." The slim, silent man who lingered in the shadows all but disappeared despite the daylight streaming through the windows.

"Just until the conclave ends." The hardness of Griffin's voice grated on her ears, a man used to issuing demands, but the brutal white-knuckled grip on his hips gave him away.

So much rested on her answer.

"Why didn't you disappear when you left the caves?"

Griffin clenched his jaw, refusing to look away or speak. Bruises dotted his face. The matching set London and Dominic sported were already fading. Stubble lined his strong jaw, shaggy dark hair fell into his eyes, both making him appear like a disreputable thug one would encounter after midnight on an abandoned street.

At his continued silence, Raven sighed.

Make that an obstinate thug.

There was something calculating about him that warned her not all was as it seemed. Being a helpless female and all, no doubt he wouldn't share it either, not until it came and bit her on the ass.

By avoiding her questions, he wasn't leaving her any choice.

"Because of me." Digger stepped forward, a painful limp to his leg. The man was dark, part Hispanic if she had to guess, and well past his prime. "I can be of value to you."

"Quiet." Griffin barked the one word.

She tensed at the lash of the command. The old man ignored the gruff order and stared at her levelly, a natural calm surrounding him. "I'm a doctor."

Raven's heart skipped a beat then dropped somewhere in the vicinity of her stomach to boil in acid. Fear burned over her skin, biting at her flesh. Though innocent enough, his words presented a real threat that said kill him now before it's too late. "No."

The expression on his face was that of a kicked puppy, but she refused to relent. No one was experimenting on her again. Images of the cold stone walls of the labs flashed through her mind, the sharp smell of chemicals, the repeatedly painful injections they used to try and alter her DNA until she'd learned to fight back.

She'd survived, a miracle in itself, one that a number of people wanted to reverse if they ever got their hands on her again. She was too dangerous to let live, not with all the secrets her body harbored.

"But—"

"We only need to stay long enough to heal," Griffin interjected, as if afraid of what his companion would reveal.

"Raven–"

"I'm fine." She waved away Taggert's concern, wincing when his chocolate eyes splintered yellow as his wolf rose with the call of her power. Despite her determination to protect him, with every exposure of her gift, the ties that bound him to her wound tighter.

Taggert had been a slave when she'd accidentally bumbled into an auction and claimed him. And until she could officially make him part of her pack, he was vulnerable.

Still only a slave.

He reluctantly did as bided, leaning against the wall, angled so his whole attention was centered on her. His eyes locked on her in a way that felt like a caress.

At the phantom touch, the animals at her core crept closer to the surface, battling to rise. Not willing to release its hold on her, the current thrummed under her skin. Breathing a little too fast, she bit back the pain as energy danced over her body in retaliation.

When her animals surface, her abilities as a conduit went on the fritz. She could have either one or the other, and she'd yet to find a balance to keep each side happy. The battle would only continue to worsen until one side won.

The energy finally relented, settling heavily in her bones in a way that ached, a punishment for daring to defy it. Though she worked hard at control, it remained elusive at times when her gift thought it knew what was best for them.

She was walking blind in the shifter world. She needed help before she got them all killed. If this man could guide her around the many obstacles, could she really turn him away?

Both intruders were malnourished, skinny to the point that their bones poked from beneath their skin. Each needed to gain at least twenty pounds. As she studied the two of them, she had no doubt Griffin passed what little food he could afford to Digger.

Griffin radiated distrust. He was vigilant, half-ready to pounce at the first sign of aggression. He could've continued without her aid, but he'd swallowed his pride and came to her for help because of his friend.

He would be trouble.

Danger increased for everyone when her developing powers were exposed to others. If they learned about her true nature and betrayed her secrets to the world, she'd be hunted in earnest.

A whiff of cedar curled around her.

His scent.

She stared hard at Griffin, wishing she could see through to the truth of him.

"Raven. Don't." Durant spoke for the first time, a tiger that seemed to take up most of the room even though he didn't move from his spot lounging behind her. He happened to be the last shifter who'd asked her for help, and she'd ended up claiming him.

She couldn't afford to add any more people in her pack. She was already too entangled in the shifter world for her comfort.

"They need help." Exhaustion pulled at her. She needed rest after burning out her power so recently. She needed peace to keep the beasts at bay. She had a sinking feeling she wasn't going to get either until after the conclave. "You can't ask me to ignore them. If they leave here, they're as good as dead."

Durant leaned forward in the chair, elbows on his knees, that intense stare of his hypnotic if she wasn't careful. "You have enough troubles with the conclave. If the council discovers you're harboring rogues, they could deny your petition."

She shuddered in response to his words. Not only could she lose her petition for pack status, she'd lose her claim of ownership on Taggert. He wouldn't survive going back on the market.

Everything was within her grasp...if she was careful.

Neither Digger nor Griffin spoke a word of protest, already accepting defeat.

"What information can you give me that none of the others can?" If they knew a way that could garner Jackson's freedom from his pack, they might be worth the risk. Her pulse leapt at the possibility of getting him back where he belonged.

Griffin lifted his chin. "My father is the leader."

Stifling silence descended.

Raven slowly blinked, then blew out a breath. "Well, hell."

"That only makes them more trouble." Durant glared at Griffin, a hairsbreadth away from physically reaching across the space separating them and ripping out his throat. "Any information you need on the council, I can provide."

"How?" The last thing she wanted was to pit the men against each other, but she couldn't let such an opportunity pass and he knew it.

"*Talons* has been selected to host the conclave." He clamped his mouth shut after he spoke.

The news surprised her, and she twisted to face him fully. Though it had to be a major coup, Durant didn't seem pleased to have his club chosen for the honor.

And the bastard hadn't told her, especially after his lecture to her about keeping secrets. Her fingers tensed as the beasts at her core flexed their claws. She eyed Durant, battling to keep her temper in check. "And when were you going to tell me?"

Her power rose then fell abruptly when the overwhelming smell of so many shifters buffeted her in such a crowded space. Their animals called to hers. The temperature in the room quickly became stifling as her animals clawed their way to the surface.

Fighting for dominance.

Fighting for freedom.

That loss of control scared her the most, and she clamped down harder to hold them at bay.

Durant raised one brow like an imperial lord, but Raven crossed her arms and waited, refusing to be intimidated.

"When the time was right."

The asinine little...she narrowed her eyes, imagining getting her hands on him, but part of her feared what her beasts' reaction would be if she dared touch anyone. She pursed her lips as another untenable thought struck her. "You were trying to protect me."

Durant didn't look away as he gave a Gallic shrug. "You would've found out eventually."

Raven dropped her arms, repressing a growl of frustration. How was she supposed to protect them when they kept secrets from her? And the sad part, they might not be wrong in their assessment. She was a danger to others until she could learn to bridle both sides of her nature.

They knew pack.

Who was she to argue that they were mistaken?

"As the host for the conclave, he is under contract not to trade secrets." Griffin's triumphant smile had her shifting her focus to him. If she didn't accept his offer, she wondered if the council would somehow learn of her situation just out of spite. Relief trickled through the other man's shields, the first real sign of emotion, though he quickly slammed them shut when he caught her staring.

She balanced all that she could gain and lose. One thing stood out. If she did nothing, she lost Jackson.

All else was just possibilities.

"You can come in now."

Dina darted into the office, a sunny smile on her face, no shame in having been caught listening at the door. "I knew you wouldn't turn them away. I have the rooms all prepared." The bright little fox practically bounced on her feet at the mention of having company. Raven grimaced as her stomach twisted, imagining the lavish food Dina would create. She just hoped it would be edible enough to choke down this time.

Durant towered over her when he stood. "Then I had best select my room before she gives it away."

Raven tensed at his declaration. Though his words sounded innocent enough, seduction and threat settled over her skin, wrapping around her as if daring her to refuse him. He wanted to stay and expected her to go back on her word.

His golden eyes fixated on her, the raw emotions exposed in them left her flustered. Speech deserted her, and she knew how mice must feel when caught in a predator's gaze. One wrong move and she had no doubt he'd pounce. Too bad her body liked the idea so much. His leather scent infused her, luring her nearer, daring her to close the distance between them.

It was easier to fight him than it was to fight herself. The damn moon madness shit was going to be the death of her.

When she made no protest, everyone vanished out the office, Dominic the last to leave. When he got to the door, he shut it with an ominous snick.

"I'm staying."

Part of her wanted to accept his offer, a large part of her, but Raven couldn't ask him to make the sacrifice. Dominic was their unspoken leader, shouldering most of the responsibility for them since escaping from the labs. He had always been the strongest of them. It unnerved her that he allowed her to see him so uncertain. "We'll manage. I can't ask you to change your plans."

"You didn't ask." He still hadn't faced her, tension hiking his shoulders up to his ears.

"This is your vacation. The time you use to get away from—"

If possible, his shoulders hunched further. "Do you think I have a harem waiting for me?" His harsh laugh bit at her ears, and he turned toward her. "My *vacation* consists of me traveling to a remote cabin in the middle of nowhere where I change into my wolf."

Raven blinked in astonishment. "For the full five days? Isn't that dangerous?"

His tanned complexion didn't hide the dark circles under his eyes of too many restless nights. His fists turned white on the door handle, his green eyes brimming with self-loathing.

This man prided himself on his control. It must drive him insane to be so close to the edge during the full moon that he was forced to concede control and escape into his wolf.

No thinking.

No feeling.

No having to trust anyone else.

"Dominic—"

"That man didn't come here for help, and I'll be damned if I leave you alone with him."

## ❧ Chapter Two ☙

**SEVEN DAYS UNTIL THE FULL MOON: SUNRISE**

Raven dodged the fist flying toward her face, the speed so incredible, she couldn't escape completely, and took the glancing blow to her upper shoulder that nearly knocked her flat. The hit numbed the right side of her body, similar to slamming into a wall at thirty miles an hour without the benefit of a car.

"Slow."

She grunted at London's grumbled reprimand, having no air to do much else. She clenched and unclenched her hands, still not comfortable being without the leather gloves she wore to protect others from an accidental touch of her power.

Shifters were programmed for survival.

Their fights primal.

Brutal.

He wanted her willing and able to use anything at her disposal. The training was to force her instinct to become second nature.

Attack and win.

She had no wish to hurt London and refused to call upon anything but her beasts when they sparred. Each blow she received only increased her annoyance. At least she managed to remain upright most of the time now.

She wanted to blame her irritation on the few hours of sleep she'd managed to eke out, but she wouldn't lie to herself. She didn't know what put her on edge more, the house full of strangers or Durant prowling the halls at night after he'd returned from the club.

When he'd paused outside her door last night, her breath halted in her chest, half-expecting him to enter. Disappointment struck hard when his footsteps continued past her door, revealing just how screwed up her thinking process had become.

Funny thing to feel lonely with so many people crammed in the house.

She'd been training for three days. Her body ached, she had bruises on bruises, and no pride left to speak of. Despite all that, she was glad to be fighting, the angst building under her skin needing an outlet that didn't have anything to do with the moon madness crap.

They sparred in the entryway, forcing her to learn how to fight in close corners. At least the others had stopped watching them from the balcony. Some had cheered at each small victory. Others had winced in sympathy. The constant rumble of Durant's tiger was a distraction all on its own, like he would lunge at London if he dared even breathe in her direction.

The large man who ran security for her dropped, swung his leg out and tried to sweep her legs out from underneath her. Not pulling his punches despite their size difference.

Swift.

Determined.

Deadly.

With no way to counter, Raven leapt back, surprising herself when she landed lightly on her feet. Using her advantage, she swung out with her own foot. But the big brute had already retreated.

"Too slow."

Her eyes narrowed. "Human," she spit out, panting to catch her breath.

"Dead if you don't learn better. Stop thinking. Trust your other senses."

Her chest constricted at his words, and she scanned her core. The animals that normally crouched close to the surface when danger threatened were nowhere in evidence. All that answered her call was threads of pure energy, eager to come out and play. She swallowed her unease and forced herself to ask the question.

"How?"

"Loosen your hold over them. They're animals. Treat them as such. They'll become dangerous if you continue to deny them their freedom."

Raven instinctively shook her head in denial, sweaty hair sticking to her neck. After three days, her reflexes were already quicker than a normal human. Though that was what London had intended, the subtle change left her shaken.

Each day, her beasts took over more of her life, consuming what little of her soul that remained. She caught the towel London threw at her head and wiped her face, ignoring the way her muscles quivered.

"You have the natural instincts. More importantly, you know how to get out of the way. For a human, you're good." London lumbered closer on silent feet, surprisingly light despite his bear counterpart, his thick brows drawn down in a straight line. He didn't bother to towel off his shortly cropped black hair. No need. The big bastard didn't even break out in a sweat. "But instinct is not enough. Stop thinking human. Until you can harvest your animal, you're nothing more than dead meat."

His words condemned her, but his eyes urged her to push harder. The ringing of the phone interrupted his scrutiny, and frustration bubbled up in her when he strode away. How the hell was she supposed to learn when no one could teach her?

"For you." Taggert slipped out of her office, holding a phone in his outstretched hand. Although she rescued him from the slave auction, he technically remained bound under contract until she could officially claim him at the conclave.

She rubbed her arms as his aura splashed against her body, her skin tightening almost painfully. Snatching up the phone, she backed away as if he were contagious.

Except distance didn't help.

Every nerve in her body was aware of him. She eyed his shaggy, sun-streaked hair and resisted the urge to brush it away from his face. His experience as a slave had jaded him that she sometimes forgot he was close to ten years her junior.

"Raven." She spoke into the phone, her clipped tone more abrupt than she'd intended.

"We have a case."

Scotts' voice rescued her from getting even crankier on everyone's ass. For a chance at freedom without the scent of shifters driving her batty with the need to touch, murder sounded like heaven.

"What have you got?"

"It's a mess. One of yours. It appears to be a bomb. I need you on this one. Consider this an official request. File the damn papers and get down here." Those papers were an application to join a national task force for paranormals. Until she filed, she couldn't officially assist the police as a private consultant as she had in the past, not with the new laws just passed.

The dial tone answered her before she could put up more of a protest. He sounded frustrated and overworked, much like any cop, except Scotts dealt with all the paranormal dreck that landed on the police's doorstep that even the paranormals refused to claim as their own.

It was also their first case on the new squad. They needed to close this one fast.

She walked in her office and sat. The large desk provided little protection against the future rushing toward her.

Ignoring the way her fingers persisted in shaking, she grabbed her gloves and busied herself working the leather over her hands The familiar action did nothing to relax her. "You heard."

"Sign these." Taggert handed her a folder.

Raven grabbed it automatically. When she saw the application, she hesitated. If she took this final step, there would be no going back. She'd be thrust into the spotlight, her whole life examined. But working with the police to help the paranormals was all she'd ever wanted. All she knew. After all the injustice she'd suffered from both humans and shifters, she never wanted anyone else to feel there was no one out there to help them.

"If you want to continue to work with the police, you need to sign the forms." He didn't put any emotions in his voice, tidying her desk as if he considered it his new den, taking over the hated paperwork she did for her cases. "Those who voted for you won't care if you take the job, but they will expect their favors returned whether you are able or not."

Stifling a growl of frustration, she flipped through the pages, noting Taggert had dotted every *i* and crossed every *t*, everything ever so legal like. No chance later for a loophole to come back and bite her on the ass.

She watched his hands as he picked up the pen and offered it to her. Those chocolate eyes of his regarded her with complete confidence, never doubting her or her ability to do the right thing.

The way he'd infiltrated her life scared the crap out of her. If she took one wrong step, they would take him from her. That she bit him, took his blood and claimed him, made little difference until she could prove her alpha status.

She snatched the blasted pen he held so patiently and scrawled her name on the line, sealing her fate. Tightness gripped her chest at making her position official. She just prayed she hadn't placed a bigger target on her back.

Taggert took the pages from her, his hand casually brushing against hers in a way that shifters frequently touched one another. Her heartbeat sped up pathetically at the barely-there brush of skin, and her wolf leapt out of the shadows in her mind so unexpectedly that Raven gasped.

The wolf was fully-grown, almost completely white except for a few distinguishing marks around the face, back and tail where the tips of her fur were dusted black. Intelligent blue eyes peered back at her.

Taggert's eyes went pure yellow in seconds, his wolf rising at the call of hers. And since he couldn't shift, pulling his wolf so close to the surface had to be extremely painful.

They both froze.

Taggert didn't react overtly. Delicious heat poured off him, all that tempting warmth soaking in her skin. Fur brushed against her mind, and her wolf lifted its head. The smell of woods, Taggert's scent, lured her closer. Urged her to grab the freedom he offered.

"Uh..." Very aware of her body and his, the act of pulling her hand away was a physical effort.

"It's the call of the moon. As an unmated alpha, you will be hit sooner and harder than the rest of us." Taggert calmly took the papers and placed them in an envelope, staring at her under his brows. Not a direct challenge, more like he couldn't take his gaze off her.

She could see the want in him, feel it tingling against her skin. It was all she could do not to leap across the desk and rub against him as her wolf urged.

Instead, she gritted her teeth and pushed to her feet. She had to get away from all the shifters that had somehow taken over her house.

She accepted the envelope, taking care to avoid touching him. Disappointment at her withdrawal didn't show on his face. It was there in the way his eyes lowered, the subtle stiffening of his body. His silence made her feel petty and frustrated all at once. "I better drop this off."

She beat a hasty path to the door, but halted when he breathed her name.

"It will only get worse. You have to learn how to control your response or you will have every shifter in a mile radius hunting you down to put in their suit."

Like the coward she was, Raven slipped out of the room. She leaned against the door and greedily gulped fresh air not tainted with his scent.

"Where are you running off?"

Raven nearly squeaked. She turned and pasted a smile on her face. Griffin's scruffy appearance had a more groomed cast today, but did little to tame the wildness that lingered just under his skin.

His expression said she didn't quite succeed in hiding how much even the smallest physical contact had rattled her.

She couldn't forget that he was dangerous.

Always watching.

She lifted the crumbled envelope clutched in her fists. "Delivering this document. I'm needed on a new case."

"Alone?" Griffin cocked his head, studying her like a riddle to be solved.

It settled her panicked senses, though the effort didn't go without cost. The door at her back opened. The smell of woods reached her, and every inch of calm she'd gained vanished like a wisp of smoke. She shifted her stance so she wasn't between the two of them, ashamed at herself for giving way to them.

If anyone else saw her so weak, they would mistake her for prey, and all her hard work would be shot.

"He's right. You shouldn't go alone. Being near another shifter will help." Taggert didn't offer anything else, still tightfisted with his words as if expecting a reprisal for daring to speak.

"That's not possible at the moment, and I'm needed at the crime scene." Though no one left her alone in the last few days, no one dared get close to her, either, for fear she would rip out their throat.

She couldn't say they were mistaken.

So they sat back and watched her like some toddler. "I'll be fine."

Griffin's brow furrowed over those brilliant eyes of his, slowly crossing his arms. "Take him."

Obstinate ass. As if he even got a say in what she did. The suspicion in his eyes let her know she wasn't going to get away with a pat answer. She understood. If anything happened to her, his meal ticket was gone. Taggert looked willing, but she couldn't take the chance, not until the conclave got their claws out of his hide.

Fiddling with the envelope, she blurted out the reason. "He's technically still a slave."

She carefully tugged a small cord of energy teeming in the walls of the house and twined it between her fingers. The energy doused the desire that had been creeping over her. If Griffin so much as lifted a finger against what was hers, she would rip away his consciousness and dump his unattended body on the pack's doorstep without a hint of remorse.

Griffin's start of surprise showed on his face, the first genuine emotion she saw since the hunt that nearly killed them. "But..." He lifted a hand and let it drop. "The collar."

Raven pulled more electricity from the house, the sting of it welcome as the last drop of mounting desire washed out of her completely. "I didn't like it. It caused him pain, and it was my job to protect him."

She didn't blink as she waited for him to process the information. When he just stared at her, all the energy she'd compiled slowly dissipated, and her wolf trotted to the surface in response to the curiosity of his animal. She nearly whimpered when the heat began to build under her skin again.

"He can't leave the house, not until we face the conclave. I can't risk losing him without ever having claimed him."

Not like she'd lost Jackson.

The scent of cedar intensified, drawing her attention back to Griffin.

His scent.

Wildness poured off him, a wickedness that urged her not to think, not to fight the demands of her animals. The temptation he presented was a dangerous lure for someone like her, someone who held more than one beast. She concentrated on suppressing her wolf as it fought to refuse her command.

That's when she realized Griffin was doing something that riled up her animals, and she didn't know enough to find out what the hell kind of game he was playing.

Her animals might be pesky, stubborn beyond belief, but they were hers. She couldn't allow Griffin to learn she held multiple strands of shifter DNA. The information was too valuable. According to the pack, she was an impossibility.

Well, she would be but for a little thing of being engineered.

He could trade her secret to get his pack status back, and she couldn't allow that to happen.

The shadows at the center of her core shifted, and all the animals vanished as coldness seeped into her chest. Her lungs felt weighted as crystals formed, her breath freezing her throat. A creature lifted its head, watching from the darkness, sensing something different about Griffin. Something almost feral. She was pathetically grateful when the creature didn't venture any closer.

Silence rang loud in the hallway, both sets of male eyes locked on her in an uncanny way that felt devouring.

"I'll go with you."

Raven blinked in surprise at Griffin's offer, and the spell woven around them snapped. "We already agreed that you should remain hidden."

The unwarranted offer only increased her suspicions. He was up to something. She scrambled to think of ways to change his mind. She hated that she had to rely on him and others for answers, not knowing if they had their own agendas.

She resisted the need to retreat.

She would not allow her ignorance to weaken her.

"I lose everything if something happens to you."

Something in his words didn't ring true, but she couldn't place her finger on it.

"We'll begin your lessons in the car." He grabbed his leather jacket and vanished out the door before she could protest. She had a feeling she wouldn't be able to pry him out of the car even if she tried.

She moved to follow when a large black wolf appeared on the doorstep. She stopped short, disconcerted to find such a large beast all but waiting to huff and puff her door down.

Then she saw the deep green eyes of her friend in the animal's face. The disorientation left her reeling. "Dominic?"

It had been three days since they'd spoken. She thought he'd left. Or maybe she shouldn't be surprised. Dominic was always one to take care of those he considered his.

She reached out to sink her fingers into the massive fur encased him, and his lips peeled up to flash his fangs. "Right. Not a pet."

He prowled inside, seemingly satisfied with her response. She glanced at Taggert and raised a brow.

Taggert shrugged as if having a wolf inside the house was an everyday occurrence, his gaze still glued to the doorway where Griffin had vanished. "Don't trust that man. He won't let anything happen to you, but you can't let him get close. He has his own schemes. Now that he knows some of what you can do, he'll be more dangerous."

He meant the collar.

Raven agreed and that's what terrified her. She couldn't afford to have anyone snoop into her past and search for answers. Especially not when it was her small pack that would suffer. She stepped outside, not feeling the sunshine as coldness crept through her gut.

Griffin thought himself safe here, but if it came down to choice, she would do whatever necessary to protect her people.

## Chapter Three

**AFTERNOON**

"The conclave is a collection of five council members. Currently one magic user, a feline shifter, one vampire and two wolves hold court."

"One who just happens to be your father." Raven struggled to breathe in the confined space of the car, fighting off the claustrophobia pressing on her chest, much like being held underwater. She rolled down the window, trying not to be too obvious. The awful stench of exhaust had never smelled sweeter as she drove through traffic.

Griffin grunted but otherwise ignored her clumsy probe for more information. "One from each race. They pride themselves on being purebreds. These men and women are not elected officials, they must earn their spots. A seat opens if someone steps down or dies."

The way he phrased the last part let her know which one happened more often. She took the corner on a busy street, two blocks away from the police station. "What else?"

"They hold court every month."

"Always during the full moon?"

Griffin's smile was more wolf-like than friendly. "Always. It forces packs to come together when the mating heat is high and pack is at their most vulnerable. The first two days are used for listening to petitions or offer challenges that can't be settled amongst themselves.

"The third day the council members are secluded to assess and change the laws. It's also a day of celebration. The day when new shifters crest. The full moon helps the transition and reveals the strongest of the budding pack. The last two days are used to answer petitions and claims."

"If this is about shifters, why have magic users and vampires on the council?"

Griffin gave her an assessing look, calculating if truth or lies would work best. "To keep the peace. Shifters have been at war with both. Witches had at one time ensnared shifters with their spells and used them as familiars. Our animals can withstand the abuse if too much magic is cast and the spell slingers can't control the backlash.

"Let's not forget the vampires. They claimed they created shifters as their daytime protection. Shifters swear they were enslaved. Vampires maintain a presence to show they are keeping with their part of the pact. The conclave is also the only place where all paranormals meet in peace. It's where they can keep abreast of issues with their fellow predators. A few shifters even hire themselves out to each group as mercenaries."

"Why are you being so helpful?" She studied his dark head, a devilish smile tipped his lips. She'd amused him.

"Payment for protecting us."

He lied.

After he'd made himself at home in her house, she'd swear that he had no intention of helping her, so why the spill of information? She'd love to be able to read him with her gift, but with his wolf so closely connected, she had no doubt he'd know what she was doing.

As the silence stretched, his smile faded. "You going in front of the council will be like blood spilled in a shark tank. You say what's on your mind. You have secrets in your eyes. What will they get by helping you?" He peered out the window, stricken, almost haunted as if he knew from experience what her fate would be. "You'll do anything to keep your pack. They'll use that against you."

His brutal honesty stung. She'd had no problems hiding herself until her friends had decided to make their stay in her life permanent. In the past, she only had to keep her distance from others to keep them safe. To become alpha and preserve the lifestyle of her people, she didn't have the same recourse.

She just needed to make the consequences of those who thought to take advantage of her known, so others wouldn't make the same mistake.

"So it's majority votes? I just have to sway three of the five to my cause?" Too bad it sounded a lot simpler than it was.

"Don't mistake them for puppets." Griffin sounded grim. "They twist the laws to suit themselves, changing things, tweaking petitions to maneuver people around like soldiers in war. They each have their own agendas. They work against each other to further themselves."

"But it can be done." She didn't ask the question. She'd find a way.

She parked the car, doing her best not to fidget under Griffin's steady stare. Then he gave a tiny nod. "Maybe for you."

A knock on her window startled her. She yipped and whirled. "Damn it, Scotts." She rolled down the window for the big black man standing on the sidewalk. "Don't do that."

He stooped and scrutinized the car, scanning the interior. She wasn't even sure he was aware of it, his actions done more out of habit. There was nothing to find, the car was new. Her last one had been totaled in an attempt to kill her and almost succeeding.

"You're late."

Without a word, she handed over the folder. Her fingers tightened on the envelope before she let go. "Here."

Scotts grunted, curled it up and shoved it in his pocket. "Let's go before they clean up the scene."

He walked away without giving her a chance to say anything.

"Friendly guy." Griffin cracked a small smile as they watched Scotts head toward his unmarked cruiser. Even his stride was no nonsense.

"A regular barrel of laughs." The tense set of Scotts' shoulders revealed his combative attitude, but Raven was sure she hadn't done anything to set him off this time. Pulling out in traffic, she followed the cruiser, stopping at the edge of town at a remote diner.

"Stay here." Raven got out, the hot air instantly mugging her. Only to find Griffin mimicking her. She eyed the branded rogue who stood so calmly before her, a wolf kicked out of his pack, all but dead except for the deed. "You being out in the open is not a wise move."

In response or defiance, Griffin put his hands in his jacket pocket to hide the symbol of his rogue status, which explained why he grabbed it in the first place given the warm weather.

He was the only branded rogue she'd ever seen, probably for the fact it was a death sentence that gave anyone permission to kill him on site without those pesky things called consequences. Though she might detest the rule, she had bigger battles to face in the next week.

"You being in danger is even less." Those eerie eyes of his didn't give anything away, but she doubted her safety motivated him in the least. Stubble already darkened his jaw. The leather jacket, the thick black hair and broad shoulders said more outlaw than lawman.

She opened her mouth to protest when Scotts yelled. "Over here."

She clamped her jaw shut, and narrowed her eyes on Griffin. The slight smile he flashed poked at her danger radar. "Cause trouble and I'll kick your ass."

He sent her a 'who me?' look that she didn't buy for a second. With more than a bit of trepidation, Raven followed Griffin back, behind the diner.

The old building was run down, the red and white motif a throwback from the past. Noise whizzed by from the passing traffic. Burnt coffee and hot grease clogged the air. The clean windows were sandblasted by age and debris from the highway, but you could still see the cracked vinyl seats and tarnished metal napkin dispensers through them, completing the picture of a fifties roadside diner.

Then the smell hit her.

Raw flesh.

As she rounded the corner to the back of the building, she saw the body...or what was left of it, anyway. Every surface in a ten-foot radius was plastered with remains. A particularly juicy section dripped down the wall to land in a splotch near one of the technicians. The splatters on his clothes said it wasn't the first time that'd happened. He grimaced and scraped it into a tub at his elbow. His muttered curse carried on the breeze along with a whiff of decay as decomposition encroached.

Her feet scuffled along loose gravel of the broken concrete as she adroitly avoided the rotten food overflowing from the dumpster. Wooden crates rested against the wall, offering them a tiny bit of privacy. The back door had three heavy metal locks. No one would enter or exit in a hurry.

"You called me for a bombing?"

Scotts didn't answer directly. "Tell me what you see."

Raven stepped closer to the scene, ignoring Griffin and Scotts when they stopped behind her. No large pieces of the victim remained, not even the skull.

The body had been pulverized.

The jeans and boots had contained some of the explosion, but the trajectory was off. The impact blew outwards, the detonation coming from inside the body.

Sliver of bones pierced the cowboy boots, the holes weeping blood. Inside, a pool of liquid swirled with bits of gore, the mixture already thickening as the blood clotted.

The concoction smelled darker, harsher than normal. Definitely a shifter, maybe a rogue, but there was something wrong with the blood.

As she drew closer, she saw bone shrapnel pepper the ground, the blast so powerful pieces had even pierced the cinder blocks of the building. The force needed to take apart a body that way had to be enormous. She continued to search, but she couldn't locate anything but body parts and clothing. She glanced at Scotts to find him staring at her.

"You see it, too."

Raven nodded. "No detonator or trigger. Do we know what did this?"

He ran a hand through his hair, obviously not for the first time today. "Witnesses said he came out here by himself." He pointed toward the mangled camera dangling in the corner above the back door. "The footage only shows him. No one approached. He appeared to have a seizure of some sort immediately prior. There wasn't just an explosion. The impact site was him. The footage stopped after that."

Hoping she was wrong, Raven turned to Griffin. "What do you smell?"

He glanced at the mess and shrugged. "Meat."

Raven crouched, absently waving away the comment. "Right. That's it. No ignition chemicals." Recognition set in. Pictures similar to this scene were documented in most medical journals. Though it happened infrequently, she was surprised no one else had made the connection.

She'd seen the aftermath of a similar murder years ago in the labs until they deemed the weapon too unstable.

She rose and strode toward the men. She'd seen enough. The pattern of blood and gore would forever be etched on her mind.

"You know what happened." It wasn't a question. Resignation lined Scotts' face at her words.

"How did I know you were going to say that?" He turned away and she followed his tobacco smell, Griffin at her back within eavesdropping distance.

What confused her was Scotts acted like Griffin didn't exist, especially since he put up such a fuss the last time when Taggert and Jackson had accompanied her.

Her hands curled into fists at the thought of Jackson, and her inability to demand his return.

Stupid politics.

She blew out a breath and focused on what she could change now. "Formaldehyde."

Griffin sputtered a laugh, but turned it into a cough when they both glared at him. A smirk danced about his lips, but he kept his head lowered, gazing at his feet. "Aren't you forgetting something?"

Both stared at him blankly.

"The smell. Formaldehyde has a very distinct smell. We would be able to scent it."

"But a small dose—"

Raven shook her head at Scotts comment. "The quantity needed for this extent of damage would be noticeable. He would have to be nearly submerged."

"But you're not changing your mind." Scotts slanted her a glance. There was no doubt in him that her conclusion was correct. "How was this done?"

Despite the difficulties between them on their last case, he believed her. "Formaldehyde creates a physical reaction when it comes into contact with shifters, a bomb, though usually not this extreme. The chemicals react long before they can infiltrate their whole system. It's one reason why shifters pick up their dead for burial or cremation."

Something that she said caught his attention. "One of them?"

Raven turned queasy at the other reason. "Some packs stick to the old customs and eat their dead, believing the strength of the deceased will be absorbed back into the pack. They consider it a great insult to the family if everyone doesn't...partake."

Even Scotts turned a pasty gray at the comment. She couldn't blame him.

"Plausible. Except for one small fact you forgot to mention." Griffin didn't look smug anymore.

Scotts glanced between the two of them when no one spoke. "What?"

Griffin finally looked away from her. "That the process is instantaneous."

Her mind spun with the ingenious and frightening possibilities. "I don't know how it happened, I just recognize the results. Suppressed poison. Darts. A skin bandage, maybe. Someone found a way to delay the response. Though formaldehyde is a gas, it can be turned into a liquid with a solvent. There can be any number of ways to create a weapon comprising it."

Griffin didn't appear convinced. "But there are much easier ways to kill. Why go through the trouble?"

"You think there will be more?" Scotts appeared resigned to possibly finding similar crime scenes.

"Don't you?" She gave both men a level stare. "It's the perfect weapon against shifters. We're lucky formaldehyde breaks down and bonds to the flesh, otherwise, every shifter in range would be infected."

"Were you able to identify him?" Raven tried to ignore the decomp as the pervasive smell invaded her hair and pores.

Scotts nodded to a man holding a bag of parts. "Everything on his person was destroyed."

"And no one in the diner recognized him?"

"The waitress said he was a shifter, but not a regular. He appeared to be waiting for someone, received a call then rushed out back." Scotts flipped open his notebook as if he searched harder, the pages would provide more information.

"I want to see the tapes. There are no void spots on the wall or ground, so no one was in close proximity. That doesn't mean he was alone." She normally would be invited to the morgue for review, but with the medical examiner officially missing, all requests for viewings were on hold. And although she technically didn't know where the body was buried, she had helped in his demise when she caught him experimenting and selling shifters for a twisted hunt. She thought it best to keep her distance.

Scotts reviewed his scribbles. "This was the extent of surveillance. I'll get you a copy, but the camera inside broke a few years back. They fixed it enough to have the red light flash, but nothing recorded."

"Great." Raven wandered to where the jeans lay, mostly in one piece if you could ignore the way the material was riddled with holes. She crouched without touching anything, noting a familiar rectangular bulge in his pocket. "You said he received a call. Think you might be able to retrieve anything from his phone? If the SIM card is still intact, we might be in luck."

Scotts gloved up and carefully pulled out the phone then held up the mangled black case. Bones shards pierced the hard plastic, almost making the phone appear like it was bleeding.

The efficiency of the explosion chilled her.

"I'll take it back to the labs, but don't expect much." Scotts sounded disillusioned as he waved over a technician and dropped the phone in the bag provided.

"You assume your theory is a forgone conclusion." Griffin lifted his face to the breeze, but his attention was fixated squarely on her. "How?"

"I've seen it before." She could've bitten her tongue, already regretting have spoken when both men stared at her.

"Where?"

"When?"

The men spoke in unison then shared a look that shot her senses into overdrive. "You two know each other." The men started like children caught being naughty. They avoided looking at each other. "How?"

For some reason, she felt betrayed by Griffin. He insisted he needed to come along to protect her, but what reason could Griffin have that he'd want access to her crime scene? She'd be suspicious he'd had a part in the crime except Scotts didn't appear disturbed by his presence. Her wolf gave a huff in disgust, and she agreed completely. "Don't make me ask again."

"Griffin and I have met." Scotts shrugged, but didn't say anything more.

Her skin prickled at the not quite lie. "You've more than met." She hesitated, but neither man gave an inch. Then she noticed their body language. "You've worked together." The revelation knocked her for a loop.

"She's good." Griffin spoke to Scotts while staring at her.

"The best." Scotts didn't even crack a smile. "I'll have a copy of the video and witness statements made available to you. Let me know what you find." He walked to the crime scene without confirming or denying her accusation, effectively ending the conversation.

And left her alone with Griffin. "You didn't think you were the only consultant, did you?"

Actually, she had.

Without another word, Raven spun on her heel and marched back to the car. Too bad getting rid of Griffin would be as hard as removing the stench from the crime scene. That smell permeated every inch of her and usually lingered hours after.

Griffin's solid presence suffocated the car, making concentration harder. "Tell me how to contact your father."

Griffin's expression didn't change, but the tension in the car ratcheted up to an inferno. "That would be a mistake."

"I need to know if they are involved, and if not, they need to be made aware of the threat. Someone may be trying to stop the conclave."

"They have their own checks and balances. Don't get involved."

"You mean Randolph?" Her body chilled at the mention of his name. He was like her, only his power had twisted and turned sinister. Her gut still carried scars when she deflected his attempt to kill her by absorbing the energy he wielded like a weapon.

It had retaliated by trying to eat her from the inside out.

All she got in return to her question was a look that was both dead serious and tinged with fear. "You don't want to tangle with him. He enjoys gobbling up little girls like you."

She shivered at his choice of words.

## ❧ Chapter Four ❦

Raven pulled up to the house, practically spilling out of the car to get away from Griffin. She slammed the door and strode up the walkway, the crunch of gravel under her feet echoing in the silence. She'd only gone ten feet when a tingle at the base of her spine pulled her up short.

She was being watched.

Very deliberately, she turned and scanned the landscape. Griffin paused at her side. He glanced at her then followed the direction of her gaze toward the tree line.

Nothing carried to her on the breeze.

No scents.

No sounds.

The foliage didn't stir. Clouds scuttled past, leaving pockets of darkness, almost like birds of prey circling. Despite all the evidence to the contrary, she couldn't pick out anything that should cause alarm. She rubbed her arms as her wolf rose under her skin as it, too, sensed something stalking them.

She reflexively reached for the electricity stored at her core to scan their surroundings. The animals snarled, quickly rushing to the surface in challenge. The tips of her fingers ached with the need to shed claws.

Something was out there, hunting them on her land. Neither she nor her animals appreciated the fact. When she got her hands on them, they would realize their mistake. She marched toward the grove, determined to eliminate anyone who thought to harm what was hers.

Griffin looped his arm about her waist and pulled her close until her head was tucked into his neck. When she tried to bring up her knee, he tightened his grip, squeezing the air from her lungs.

"Breathe, damn you."

Raven sucked in a greedy gulp of air and inhaled the fresh cut cedar scent of his wolf. Part of the mindless need to rent flesh from bone lessened. Rational thoughts returned in fits and starts. If anything happened to her, her people would be left vulnerable.

What caught her by surprise was the complete absence of attraction to Griffin.

Her wolf rejected him.

To know that she wouldn't mindlessly lust after any male in the vicinity left her lightheaded. Then the danger of the situation came slamming back to her.

Angered at her lack of control, she shoved away her wolf. She dipped into her core, actively seeking the full use of her power for the first time since the burnout a few days ago. Pure energy flooded her body. She gritted her teeth as pain seared along her flesh.

"Son of a bitch." Griffin's arms flexed a second when his muscles convulsed then he dropped his hold. When he pulled away, his eyes glowed.

Instead of shutting down, the power continued to build until the air crackled. Not wanting to draw more attention to herself, she reluctantly slammed all that delicious power into the ground.

The earth, in a five-foot radius, dropped two inches at the impact like a miniature crop circle, smoke rising like steam from the area. The action left her stumbling to remain on her feet and vaguely nauseous. All the power evaporated as if it had never been.

Whatever had been watching them vanished, and she could only blame herself. She tried to use her animals to search the vicinity, but the only thing she felt was Griffin's wolf demanding freedom to hunt. His condition only worsened as the very power she'd sank in the earth floated up to them, the ground too saturated to hold it all. The raw energy scratched at her skin, seeking entrance.

It had the opposite effect on Griffin.

It brought out his wolf.

"Go." The gruff word was a deep rumble from his chest.

She took a cautious step back, but hesitated at Griffin's obvious pain. His arms rippled as if he would shift then and there. "But–"

"I'm going to find out who was spying on us. Unless you want to see me in my skivvies, I suggest you leave." So saying, Griffin tore his shirt over his head and dropped it to the ground.

Raven gulped at the display of muscles. Though she felt no desire for Griffin, she could appreciate a man built with all lean muscles and tanned skin. While he still showed effects from his recent imprisonment, it was the old scars covering every inch of his torso that made her flinch. For a shifter to retain that much tissue damage after they'd healed, someone had to have tried to skin him.

When he popped open the first button of his fly, she inhaled involuntarily to catch his scent. The energy around her fluctuating wildly, slipping down her throat to sit like a warm glow heavy in her chest.

Not wanting to lose what little control she'd wrestled back, unwilling to absorb more of the power into her abused body after such a glorious failure to hold it all, she turned and hightailed it back to the house. His mocking laugh rang in her ears, but she didn't think he took any pleasure in taunting her.

The house was thankfully silent when she entered, giving a hum of welcome. The place was a home in the truest sense of the word. Part of her power had spread to the house, changed it fundamentally with the ability to store electricity.

The tug of war between the two sides of her soul left her exhausted. She inhaled then coughed at her own smell, desperately needing a shower before she tackled the next mess.

She plucked out the two chops holding her hair in place and peeled off her gloves. She headed up the sweeping stairs, the steps curving along the wall to the second floor to open up to a balcony. The grand open spaces, large rambling hallways might have been modeled from late Victorian architecture, but she and the old building suited each other.

She entered her room. The bed was still partially ruffled from this morning's fight with her dreams. The empty couch next to it mocked her.

Jackson's couch.

At night, alone in the darkness, she'd swear she could still heard his breathing.

A cruel trick of her mind.

She kicked her shoes off and had her shirt half-unbuttoned when she heard a noise that raised the hair on the back of her neck.

Instead of calling her animals, she reached for her core. She needed power she could rely on, not a mindless beast that just wanted to kill. Strands of energy slithered through her center, the blue cords springing forward at her call to swarm over her.

Much too strong.

"Shit." Electricity snaked down her arms, enveloping her hands in a light glow. Ignoring the burning of heat under her skin, she inched along the edges of the bedroom.

She cocked her head and listened. Then she heard it again.

Male voices.

Inside the house.

How had they gotten past Griffin...or had Griffin let them in?

Following the sound, she cracked opened the bathroom door.

And stopped stock-still.

The room was torn apart, only the shower and sink remained intact. Three men, shifters of some type, young and very fit, stood across from her. They straightened abruptly at her entrance, acting shocked to see her as if she'd walked into their bathroom.

They didn't look threatening, more curious.

Their reaction tripped her up, and she had to wonder what kind of picture she presented with her dark hair swirling around her shoulders, the prominent streak of silver near her temple, and the gilded tips.

A freak even amongst the paranormals.

She opened her mouth to demand answers when Taggert slammed into the room behind her. Raven whirled to face the new threat, angling her body to keep everyone in view. She lifted her hands, her powers amped and ready to blast anyone who dared follow him.

He pulled up short when he saw her.

When no one entered behind him, she reluctantly dropped her arms, but didn't release her hold on the building energy. "Would someone please tell me what the hell is going on here?"

"I tried to call you." Taggert gestured toward her hip, but his eyes were on her hair, his fingers twitching as if barely resisting the urge to reach out and stroke the strands.

She groped for her phone, cursing to find she'd sucked the energy out of the blasted thing.

Energy resistant her ass.

"We were hired to remodel the bathroom." The voice was low and respectful. The kid stared over her right shoulder, valiantly trying to avoid peering at the gap in her shirt.

"On whose orders?" Fighting a blush, Raven quickly covered the hint of exposed cleavage without removing her attention from the three men, who had to be related if their near identical looks were anything to go by.

The oldest of the three carefully pulled a work order out of his back pocket and handed it to her. He could be no more than forty, but she was learning the shifter world was deceiving. "Mr. Jeffery Durant."

"That son of a bitch." Raven made no move to examine the paper. The anger she'd been holding at bay built to a simmer, electricity crackling around her.

She turned toward Taggert. His eyes widened, and he hurried toward her, ushering her away from the others. That's when she realized her own eyes must be glowing blue as it did when her powers rode her hard. "Why the hell would he demolish my bathroom?"

"I think Durant is taking you up on your offer to make himself at home." Taggert scratched near his eye but refused to look at her. "He's ordered a connecting door and an extra-large tub."

"What?" That damn sneaky cat. But the image of Durant in the tub, rising out of the water, boggled her mind and left her anger floundering. "But all his crap is down the hall. Tell him to tear apart his own room if he must."

"I believe he didn't care for the room you'd selected for him. He packed some stuff in there, but found other accommodations more to his liking."

Heat flushed her face when she realized he'd set himself up in the master suite without saying anything to her. Too bad she didn't know if she was more angered or flattered that a man like Durant would go to such lengths to lay claim to her.

If Taggert so much as snickered, she wouldn't be responsible for her actions.

## ❧ Chapter Five ❦

**EARLY EVENING**

 Raven jerked open the doors to the club, not hesitating like she had the first time she'd entered just a few days ago. The industrial magnet snicked shut behind her with a finality of being sealed into a tomb. The stifling air only increased that impression.
 The walls were stripped bare of decoration, all except the prominent word *Talons* clawed into the heavy wooden panels. It didn't surprise her to find Durant's scent all over the carving.
 Heat and music crested over her first. While sorting and filing everything away, the many scents snuck up and swamped her. The spice of vampires, the stench of burnt magic and the more soothing, natural smell of shifters.
 She expected vampires, shifters and magic users, the usual clientele.
 What she didn't expect was to double over when a wall of lust slammed into her. Acting on instinct, she yanked a blanket of pure electricity around her. The air crackled and it took a minute longer to gain back her breath. Only when she was sure she had control did she turned down the wattage to a manageable level.
 If she kept the shield too high, she'd have the attention of every shifter and vampire in the club. Too low, and she might be caught up in the need to explore the rampant desire flooding the room. She rubbed her skin, debating the wisdom of pinning down the bastard in his own lair. One thing convinced her to enter. If she reacted this drastically just being around others, the conclave itself would be pure torture.

She needed to acclimate herself to the sheer amount of shifters and hoped to hell she could adjust accordingly before more trouble found her. Taking a deep breath, she opened the second set of doors and entered the club.

Red and blue lights flashed over the bodies on the dance floor, their sensual movements captivating to watch. The bar to the left was packed three people deep. The booths in the back were all occupied, shadows giving the occupants an impression of privacy.

She scratched her arm then stopped when she realized what she was doing. The presence of so many shifters was like a plea to let her own come out and play. The rushed shower she'd taken had done little to cool the lick of fire under her skin.

When Raven made eye contact with Cassie, the girl blanched.

"OhshitOhshitOhshitOhshit." Durant's assistant hurried forward, chanting under her breath as she shoved her way through the sea of people.

At the commotion, people turned toward the door then stopped to gawk. Whispers spread around the club like fire.

That's when Raven noted the surprised expressions. Another survey around the room increased her unease. Out of the few women present, she was the only shifter.

But it was too late to retreat. She straightened her shoulders, lifted her chin, daring them to approach. She refused to run and be seen as weak.

"What are you doing here?" Cassie reached for her arm, halting an inch from touching her skin, encountering the energy Raven used like a shield.

Her eyes immediately washed to black.

Fangs descended.

"Crap." Cassie's thirst beat at her like worms wiggling under her skin. Without being too obvious about it, Raven drew off a steady bead of electricity surrounding Cassie until the girl forgot to breathe.

Since she was a vampire, no problem. Cassie was new, the action more of a comforting habit than anything else.

"What the hell was that?" Cassie staggered, and Raven resisted the instinctive reflex to catch her.

No need to repeat what'd just happened.

The added power danced over her skin, threatening to escape. Shifters around them stopped, their eyes splintering to yellow or green as their animals surfaced, and she quickly swallowed down the extra energy.

She wouldn't be responsible for Durant's whole club going furry. An arm wrapped around her from behind, a large body cuddling up to hers, close enough his erection nudged against the small of her back.

"Taggert?"

The breath in her throat nearly strangled her.

He must have followed her.

When she would've turned and put distance between them, knowing physical contact between them had to be painful, he held her still and nuzzled her neck.

"Let me help." Power leached away slowly at the contact, his touch soothing the wild current enough for it to settle in her bones in a delicious ache. Lust and comfort was all wrapped up in his embrace.

Raven sighed of relief and faced him. "You shouldn't have come. It's too dangerous for you to be here."

His tense posture alerted her that something was horribly wrong. "What the hell did you do?" She reached for the collar of his shirt when he manacled her wrists with his fingers.

But too late.

Cold metal of the slave collar encased his throat, the beautiful threads of gold and silver doing nothing to disguise the terrible truth behind the twisted strands of metal.

"How could you?" Especially after they'd risked their lives to remove it.

He'd been free.

The back of her throat ached, and she couldn't bear to meet his gaze, see him forced back into the role of a slave.

All because she lacked knowledge of the shifter lifestyle and kept blundering into trouble.

Her stupidity had cost him everything.

If she wasn't careful, his relentless need to protect her would eventually get him killed.

"You needed me." Taggert shrugged as if his freedom meant so little when she knew it was everything. She tugged her hands away from him, unable to tolerate his touch after what she'd did to him, but he refused to release her. "It was the only way I could protect you without placing you in more danger."

"Bullshit. People already knew you had the collar off."

"There was no proof." Taggert stepped toward her, and she recoiled.

Hurt clouded his eyes, but the magnitude of his loss because of her stubbornness wouldn't let her unbend.

She was terrified she might shatter if he showed her any kindness.

"Uh, maybe we can discuss this in private?" Cassie nodded to the crowd, her eyes constantly scanning, braced for attack.

Raven glanced about the club. Way too many pairs of eyes were centered on them. It made her skin itch. "Lead the way."

Cassie cleared a path. The shifters gave the vampire wide berth, but they immediately crowded closer as Raven passed.

Damn touchy-feely shifters.

She picked up her pace, refusing to feel grateful for Taggert's presence at her back.

The door to the office closed behind them, cutting off nearly all sounds from the club. Cassie whirled toward the fridge, took out a bag and popped it into the microwave.

The smell of blood blossomed in the office.

The cool, natural tones of the room didn't lessen Raven's growing anxiety. The massive desk and matching set of chairs dominated the room.

They suited Durant.

A love seat rested against the wall, and she could all but envision Durant seducing a willing young woman on the overly plush cushions. The smell of leather only increased the rage building in her at thoughts of Durant with someone else.

Raven prowled the confines of the room. She'd come to confront Durant, both about his omission on hosting the conclave and his demolition of her bathroom. But once she stepped into the club, she felt blindsided by her wildly out of control emotions.

What worried her most was if she reacted so viscerally to them now, how would she be affected when the alphas entered the picture?

She'd be served up on a platter.

The microwave dinged twenty seconds later. Cassie popped in a straw, turned and leaned against the counter, settling in to watch the show.

Perturbed to watch her feed, Raven clenched her fists and stared at her hands. A sheen of blue rose from her skin. "Cassie, call Durant."

She mumbled behind her straw.

"What?" Raven slowly lifted her head and eyed Cassie. Barely twenty years old and a vampire of only a few days, she stood there like a seasoned vampire with at least ten years of experience, all thanks to Durant's uber potent shifter blood. The girl had taken a call at the club meant for Durant and had been attacked. If they hadn't turned her, she would've died from her injuries.

"He's meeting with clients to get the club ready for the conclave."

"Get him."

Cassie gulped then quickly hurried toward the phone without comment. Raven could hear Durant's brisk words across the club.

"Raven's waiting in your office. She's a little miffed, so you might want to come. Like now."

Miffed didn't even begin to describe the stunt Taggert had pulled.

First Durant and then him.

"Sit on her if you need to. I'll be there in five." The phone disconnected.

Raven saw the way Cassie eyed her. "I wouldn't try it." Her lips curled into a snarl, and Cassie lifted her hands in surrender, though she didn't back down completely. If Raven tried for the door, Cassie would do her best to follow through on Durant's order.

True to his word, Durant entered the door with a harried expression crouched in his eyes. He quickly scanned his office. When he spotted her, his shoulders eased.

"Leave." He barked the command at Cassie, and she skedaddled out the door like her panties were on fire.

Then he turned those golden eyes of his on Raven.

"I was two levels lower than the main room when I felt you enter the club. What the hell were you thinking." It wasn't a question. The dangerous, hypnotic tone in his voice was back. The one he used when he was either seriously pissed off or wanted something.

He stalked toward her, his gait all loose-limbed of a shifter on the hunt. Refusing to be intimidated by the bully, she lifted her chin. Nothing he could say would make her feel any worse. She was devastated at the steep cost Taggert had paid over her stupid little grievance with Durant.

And it was all her fault for being so damned stubborn.

She should've known he would've tried something. "Would you care to explain why you let three strange male shifters into my house without my permission?"

Durant halted on the spot, but his eyes lit up as his animal rose fully to the surface. It was incongruent to see him in his outfit, so pressed and perfect, with his beast staring out at her so boldly. "What happened?"

"Besides them seeing me half naked, you mean?" She took pleasure in the little growl of rage that rumbled from him. "How about a thing called invasion of privacy? I could've accidently killed them."

"Did they touch you?" He inched closer, his eyes roaming her body for injury as he prowled around her.

His perusal left trails of heat in its wake, potent enough to stun her out of her anger. He appeared genuinely concerned. "I'm fine."

"The three brothers signed a privacy contract. Besides their excellent work, their guaranteed privacy is what makes them the best in their field." He continued to hover over her.

The molten gold eyes peering out at her sent her back a step. He mirrored her move. There was less than a foot between her and the wall behind her. A snarl curled her lips at being cornered, and she planted her feet. He was a furnace, throwing off heat hot enough to singe.

And all she wanted to do was be scorched.

She shook off that thought. She would not be managed. If he took one more step, she would have him at her feet and enjoy every minute of seeing him there.

"You shouldn't have come alone." The danger in him was enticing, calling something deep inside her to come out and play.

"She didn't." Taggert stepped forward, a solid presence at her side and inching up the lust level to an almost unbearable degree. The men eyed each other, neither backing down. Then Durant caught sight of the collar and sighed.

Her palms itched to lay her hands on them, but it wasn't all her desire. The energy in the club infected her. She'd be damned if she would be forced into a situation she hadn't chosen.

All thoughts of scolding Durant for his impromptu remodeling paled at Taggert's sacrifice and the incessant desire trying to consume her. "How the hell am I supposed to fight this?"

Durant blinked and some of the unflappable club owner returned enough for her to breathe past his rich leather scent. "You're the alpha. You're the one who has the control."

"Why does everyone keep saying that? I don't understand. Contact is supposed to help, but every time I get close to either of you, the desire is ten times worse."

Before she could retreat, he snatch up her hand and pressed it against his chest. The fast beat of his heart thundered under her palm, heat radiated up her arm and raw lust nearly brought her to her knees. Taggert slipped behind her, his arm once more around her waist. His hand found its way beneath her shirt, his fingers splaying over her stomach. The heat of his touch, so intimate against her skin, caught her breath.

Power rocketed through her body.

His wolf.

He was close to the surface, reaching out for her.

She grabbed Taggert's wrist, her nails bit into his skin, unsure whether she wanted to halt or encourage him. The rumble at her back did delicious things to her body, reminding her of what his kiss had tasted like.

Instead of protesting her lack of control, he prodded her forward, only stopping when her body was caught securely between both men. Durant gritted his teeth, his breath hissed out of his mouth in a way that weakened her knees.

"You can increase the lust or soothe those around you with a touch. Without any control, you'll drive us insane before the week's out."

She brushed her hands over the front of Durant's shirt and the beast gave a rumbled purr. Taggert leaned down and nuzzled her neck.

She barely resisted the urge to give him better access.

"I don't think this is working." She swallowed hard, trying not to so much as twitch lest one of them broke.

She was terrified that it would be her.

Durant yanked up his shirt and shoved her hands beneath. They both inhaled sharply and didn't move. Fine hair just above his pants met her fingertips, urging her to explore further, and she couldn't resist stroking him. The hard muscles under her fingers flexed, begged for more, and he shuffled closer.

The tiger's near crazed need to be free and claim what it wanted pebbled against her skin. Instead of frightening her, her teeth ached to give him what it wanted. She leaned her forehead against his shoulder, a light current, different from the normal electricity, rose from the contact.

His animal.

"Shhhhh."

The tiger paused in its pacing and lifted his head. Time stopped dead. The beast was waiting for her to take what she wanted, what the beast so willingly offered. Taggert's wolf took advantage of her distraction and brushed against her back, offering and taking comfort. She didn't know how long they'd remained that way when she finally had enough strength to lift her head.

The tiger stilled, peering at her through Durant's eyes, but the restlessness and need had abated. Though he didn't look completely sated, he no longer appeared as rattled as when he'd first burst into the room. He continued to purr under her hands, but it was more a contented sound than one of lust.

"Touch." Durant smiled.

Raven couldn't prevent the heat of a blush from filling her cheeks at the men's obvious arousal. For some reason, what had just happened felt more intimate than sex. She reluctantly pulled her hand away, nearly sighing when Taggert dropped his as well and stepped back.

She nervously cleared her throat. "We should go."

Now that they weren't touching, the desire of so many shifters in the room beyond beat at the door, racketed the lust back up. Part of her calm evaporated in frustration. She'd hoped the effects would've lasted longer.

"It was foolish of you two to come here so close to the full moon." Gone was the contented man of a few seconds ago.

"It was better to face this now than be caught off guard at the conclave."

His lips tightened, but he didn't refute her claim.

"No female shifter is allowed out without protection for a reason." He ran a finger down her cheek. "If someone had touched you, I would've killed them."

Raven swallowed a gulp and resisted the urge to cross her arms. "I've managed to take care of myself for years." She drew up enough energy to make it spark between her fingers, unconsciously playing with the current in a show of nerves she rarely revealed. "Why is now so different?"

"You weren't a full alpha then. You had the DNA, but you only woke when you started to interact with other shifters. Most shifters will respect your position, but there are more than a few who crave what you can do for them more and won't ask your permission. If they attack, you will have to retaliate or be seen as weak."

A sickening sense of dread circled her gut. "Why are they so eager to throw away their lives?"

Durant snorted, his eyes darkening and a wave of heat snaked under her skin. Her breath caught. She had no doubt he did it on purpose to put her on edge. "I adore your confidence in your abilities, but you don't know how persistent weres can be, especially with something as precious as a female alpha." He crowded closer, his lips hovering over hers. "And if you don't leave now, I'll have you stripped and sprawled across my desk in less than minute, tasting every delicious inch of you."

Part of her hesitated, and a flare of lust grew in his eyes.

Her courage quickly faded.

Taggert captured her hand, pulling her against the hard planes of his body as if to protect her. The contact returned some of her rational thought.

She craved Durant's nearness, his taste, but she wasn't sure she was strong enough to survive what he would do to her, what he would make her feel. She left the office on shaky legs, glad for Taggert's support. Remembering his words of caution, she surveyed the crowd with a smidge of trepidation.

"Come." Durant crowded close to her other side, his large frame hunching protectively over her. Her skin tingled at the closeness of both males.

She took three steps in the crowd when a whiff of fresh cut grass whisked by her. She halted abruptly, her head snapping up to search the crowd, half-wondering if she was going crazy, imagining things. Durant tensed, surveying the club for the slightest threat. Taggert stepped back to give her room to move.

"You sense him, too, don't you?"

Jackson.

Taggert only nodded, his concerned thickened the air between them. "Whatever happens, don't react."

She turned away, not wanting to see his pity. Her eyes locked with that of a kid standing about fifteen feet from her, staring boldly at her with blue eyes so pale they appeared ghostly. She cocked her head, noticing the discord that simmered around him, but she couldn't place what bothered her.

Then the crowd shifted. A man stepped in front of the kid as if to protect him, and another pair of eyes met hers.

Familiar eyes.

Jackson.

Frost clouded Jackson's whiskey brown eyes as if rejecting everything that had happened between them. The reaction devastated her. Brutal pain struck fast, curling around her bruised heart like a meaty fist and squeezed.

She shoved her way through the crowd when a stillness to their right drew her attention. The too interested stare of a compact man of medium height sent a frisson of unease spearing through her. His analytical assessment of her stopped her cold.

Without being told, she knew this man had taken Jackson from her on purpose.

She sensed it then, the curiosity of his wolf. His aura shimmered without her even having to probe. When she blinked, she saw Jackson looming over the guy's shoulder. Any injuries he'd sustained from the fight had vanished. His light brown hair was styled, his clothes pressed. His whiskey colored eyes never warmed as they used to when he gazed at her. Instead, he looked ready to squash her under his boots if she so much as took a step in his direction.

The ogre was back and then some.

"You have to leave. Now." Durant tugged on her arm then growled when lash of energy leapt between them.

She immediately jerked away, but those nearest gawked at them in curiosity. "Who are they?"

"Jackson's alpha, and the kid is the alpha's heir." Durant sounded resigned, knowing he wouldn't be able to budge her without causing a bigger scene.

That didn't mean he went meekly.

He dipped his head until his lips rested next to her ear. "You will pay for this when we're alone."

Somehow, she didn't think he meant she'd get a good talking to. She refused to flinch under the golden glare of his animal. His hair was tousled, the barely-there strip of his tiger inviting her fingers to explore.

She slowly blinked and shook her head. "Don't try that mesmerizing shit on me."

She bit the side of her cheek to prevent herself from panting. Damned if she'd let him know how he affected her. Then he inhaled deeply and gave her a devilish smile. She had no doubt he knew what he did to her and relished her very intimate, guttural response to him.

Bastard.

Two could play at that game. She lifted her hand, trailing her fingers down his chest, over the open buttons on his shirt. She lightly brushing against the flesh beneath, enjoying watching his eyes dilate under her ministrations. "I wouldn't try that again unless you want to walk around aroused for the next hour."

A tinge of a smile tilted his lips. "Honey, all I have to do is think about you, and I'm in the same predicament."

Heat filled her face at his announcement, and she tried to ignore the wave of pleasure that tingled through her body. Her skin prickled, and she lost her smile, slowly turning to face the people heading toward them.

"Miss Raven, I presume." Jackson's alpha gave a small nod of acknowledgment. "I've heard much about you."

Raven refused to flinch as Jackson's betrayal dug its claws into her and gave a vicious twist for good measure. Part of the hope she'd harbored that he'd left her under duress shriveled a painful death.

Jackson hadn't been recalled.

He'd left with them voluntarily.

"How do you do." She couldn't believe her voice came out so steady when her insides seethed.

"I'd love for you to come and visit tomorrow for a job opportunity that might interest you." He handed her an embossed card blazed with his name and address. Kevin, owner of Pak Pharmaceuticals, a company renown for research and development.

And Jackson's alpha.

Her gaze flicked to Jackson, but he didn't acknowledge her in any way as he scanned their surroundings.

"I'm not sure you'd be able to afford my price."

A smile curled his lips. "I believe we can come to a mutual agreement."

Her eyes betrayed her and flickered to Jackson. Raven wondered what she'd have to do to get him back.

A commotion across the room put Durant and Jackson into motion. Jackson hustled the kid toward the door, while Durant stepped between her and the threat.

"I look forward to seeing you." With that, the compact wolf vaulted in the crowd to stand guard on the other side of his son.

Shouting erupted, but the crowd quickly dispersed. No one wanted to be banned before the conclave officially started.

"You will not go." Durant loomed closer, crowding her in the corner. "You are nowhere near ready for negotiations between packs."

"Did you notice anything odd about the trio?" Raven ignored his statement, staring long after the crowd had swallowed them. Something niggled at the back of her mind, something willing her not to give up hope, but she couldn't place what set off her radar.

"Raven, there's a call for you." Cassie reached between them with the phone, and Raven shushed Durant's little rumble of displeasure.

She grabbed the handset. "Raven."

"Get your ass downtown. We have another incident. Two victims." Scotts' harsh voice scratched across the line. Sirens rang in the background. She mentally took note of the address he rambled off, absently brushing her hand up and down Durant's arm without really being aware of the action until a light purr rumbled under her fingers. She froze at the sound then quickly pulled back.

"So soon?" That surprised her. "Give me ten minutes." She hung up the phone. Not in the mood to listen to more lectures, Raven dashed beneath Durant's arm and headed toward the door. His muscular body swiftly hugged her form as she followed Taggert to the exit.

"You can run, but this discussion isn't over."

Raven had no clue if he meant tomorrow's meeting or what had happened between them in the office, and she wasn't going to stick around to find out.

## ❧ Chapter Six ☙

"You knew that Jackson would turn on me, didn't you?" Raven stalked toward her car, the darkness welcoming her with open arms. The cracked sidewalk had crumbled in spots, matching her composure.

Taggert sighed. "You don't understand."

When he didn't say anymore, she pulled him to a halt. "Then explain it to me." She hated the quiver in her voice, wishing for all that wonderful anger.

"Shifters are loyal to their alphas. Absolute. Any hint of doubt, and they are punished or even killed."

Raven's fists clenched at the thought of Jackson being harmed by his own people because of her. Pack was permanent. His status made him valuable. It made a sick sort of sense. As an enforcer, he knew too much about Kevin's pack. He'd be too big of threat to just be dismissed. "But that's not all, is it?"

"He's protecting you. If he shows any sign of weakness, any softness toward you, the alpha will use that to his advantage." Taggert grabbed her, his unusually display of male aggression knocking her out of her funk. "As much as you both might want it, he isn't your wolf. You can't think of him as such. Not anymore."

They continued to the car, the silence heavy between them. She nearly missed the shadow leaning against the building, would have if her animals hadn't deserted her from one second to the next.

Raven stumbled to a halt. A chill crawled up her spine like the brush of thousands of spider legs. When her gaze finally broke through and pierced the shadows, she spotted Randolph waiting patiently, arms crossed, wearing a knowing smirk.

Upon spying him, she was too relieved to keep her secrets to mind that her animals had abandoned her.

Not when Randolph happened to be an assassin frequently used by the council. She swallowed hard at his pleased expression, wondering what made him seek her out.

She edged in front of Taggert. Randolph wasn't imposing, not much taller than herself. He looked ordinary, forgettable even. Until you peered deeper into his eyes to the devil waiting below the surface, a cold murderer who'd love nothing more than to strike at the least provocation.

His power matched hers in both style and strength. If it came down to a fight, she'd lay money on a draw.

Part of her wondered if that's what kept her safe.

At least for now.

"Randolph." She nodded and kept a healthy distance between them, steadily drawing a small current through the soles of her feet as unobtrusively as possible. Energy crackled under her skin, painfully pulling through her bones.

"You always get into the most interesting of troubles." His rough, unused voice prickled like a cat's tongue licking against her skin.

"Troubles?" Raven winced at the way her voice scraped her throat.

There went casual.

The street was deserted, the streetlights huddled in the darkness, few and far between, the warehouse where the club stood a good block behind them, nearly obscure in the shadows as if hiding from Randolph. If only she'd taken the hint instead of blundering into danger.

Randolph strolled forward, easily opening the locked passenger side of the car and slid inside. "Why don't we talk while you drive."

It wasn't a question. "Taggert—"

"Don't say it. I'm not leaving you alone with him."

"Brave pup." Randolph smiled, but there was nothing friendly in the mask he wore.

Raven flinched, silently cursing Taggert's stubbornness. Though he swallowed hard, he stubbornly stood his ground. Fear for his safety tingled on her lips. Taggert wouldn't be able to help her if Randolph wanted to harm her.

While she dreaded Randolph's curiosity, his indifference could get her killed quicker if she made the fatal mistake of boring him.

He was playing with her, a game that only he knew.

Raven took a steadying breath then drank down all the current. She couldn't drive with all the electricity seething under her skin. She'd fry the computer. She contemplated Randolph through the windshield. She wouldn't put it past him to crawl in her car on purpose to keep her vulnerable.

She reluctantly skirted the vehicle. "Don't react or interact with him in any way. Do you understand?"

Taggert immediately nodded, almost looking green at the prospect of getting into the car. The back of her teeth ached from clenching her jaw against ordering him to run and hide.

Raven's palms were damp as she pulled out in traffic. They were halfway to the crime scene when curiosity finally overtook her nerves. She had to know what she faced and broke the silence. "You mentioned troubles?"

"I wondered how long you would last. Most people babble within the first five minutes." He sounded impressed, which left her stomach a bit queasy. There didn't seem to be enough oxygen in the cramped confines of the car. "Remember the drug leak you told me about?"

He was talking about the woman who'd tried to steal Taggert from her by drugging him. The drug had weakened Taggert to the point he could no longer heal himself.

All to make the twit appear stronger.

Alpha.

The only thing that calmed the rage seething through her was knowing the woman would've suffered under Randolph's tender mercies.

Uncertain of Randolph's mood, Raven cast him a quick glance. Nothing in his expression gave him away. "Yes."

"You were right. The lead didn't have much information. She was a pawn. I've been tracking the escalating drug use in pack."

The words were half a question, half an accusation. "And found nothing. That's not why you came to me."

Randolph gave a short laugh that made her cringe. Absolutely no power resonated from him, his control phenomenal. She was almost jealous.

They were two blocks from the crime scene, and she found her foot resting heavier on the gas pedal, unconsciously speeding to reach safety. Not that a crowd of people would be able to stop him if he had his mind set on something.

"I discovered a more dangerous drug, a twin to the one you'd located."

"So the first was a prototype."

"I want you to help me find the people responsible."

Raven had to swallow twice in order to speak. "Why me?"

He ignored her question as immaterial. "The new drug is called Alpha, but it's a closely guarded secret between a select few. No one I question can find the source."

Tortured, he meant.

The news troubled her. It didn't make sense. "What does this drug do?"

"It gives shifters the ability to experience what it's like to be an alpha."

"What can I do that you can't?"

She didn't want to know what he was thinking. The safest way might be to work with him, but she had a feeling if she gave him even an inch, no one would ever find her body.

When he didn't speak, she turned to find him staring at her. "I've dug into your past."

Blood rushed to her head, and her vision wavered. Her grip tightened on the steering wheel, doing her best not to react. If he didn't know her secrets already, she couldn't have him know there was something to learn.

He was the type of man who would keep searching until he found everything.

"They say you are the person to go to if you want something done."

"So you want to hire me for a job?" She couldn't keep the disbelief out of her voice.

Randolph must have found it amusing but his smile didn't reach his too pale green eyes. "The council gives me leave to use whatever resources I deem necessary to solve my cases. You have the talent and connections that I don't."

Then Raven understood. "Because I'm now on the police force. You think humans are behind the sudden increase of this Alpha drug."

Randolph couldn't afford to harm humans. They were too fragile and easily broken. The shifters would hunt him down after the first suspicious death in order to protect themselves and keep the illusion that they could all live happily together.

Raven shivered. She appreciated why someone would crave power, but there were other consequences to being an alpha. The uncontrollable rage, bouts of violence, the need to dominate and protect against any threats...real or imaginary. Randolph nodded at her. "I see you comprehend the danger."

She wouldn't have a few weeks ago.

She didn't say anything as she parked. Lights flashed in the distance, police tape strung around a lone vehicle a few car lengths ahead of them.

"I'll let you get back to your work." Randolph exited the car without any overt threats.

No probes.

No tests.

So why did that make her more twitchy?

She followed his gaze toward the crime scene, her feet drawn forward against her will.

The first thing that caught her attention was the oddly red tinted car windows. As she drew nearer, her skin pebbled as her mind finally processed what she was seeing.

Blood.

In the next step, a familiar smell slammed into her.

Raw meat and rotten blood. Even with the car being sealed, she swallowed at the strength of the stench invading her sinuses. The conditions, coupled with the heat, had created a homemade pressure cooker. It took nearly a minute for her to control her gag reflexes.

"The doors were locked from the inside when we arrived." Scotts didn't say more as she studied the scene. She was barely aware of him and the techs.

Though parked under the streetlight, the car seemed to draw the darkness, reluctant to reveal its secrets. The police set up other lights, but nothing could take away the death hovering over the vehicle like a living thing.

"How do you know they weren't switched from the outside by remote?" Randolph appeared abnormally fascinated as he stood behind the yellow police tape. She was surprised that he stayed, drew attention to himself with the question.

Scotts ignored him. Raven peered closer at the car and answered. "The keys are still in the ignition. There are no smears. The gore on the side panels hasn't been disturbed." None besides the drips of blood and flesh as it slid down the interior.

Raven purposely avoided looking at the woman sitting in the driver's seat.

She was human.

Not the source of the detonation.

Similar to the last crime scene, the shifter was reduced to nothing much more than gelatin, pieces of him oozing from the interior of the car.

Raven did her best to breathe through her mouth. The decay told her that they had to have been there for a while, just in time for decomp to fully kick in with the late summer heat. That the other police officers didn't react to the smell told her that the other side of her nature had kicked in to help.

She wrinkled her nose, wishing it wouldn't help so much.

Tennis shoes lay discarded on the passenger side. They were red and twisted nearly inside out like they'd been through a dryer. She couldn't find enough of a shirt to swear to a color. The jeans had dozens of holes, the seams ripped apart where it couldn't contain the blast.

Nothing else remained of him, vanishing as if he'd never existed.

Same as the last crime scene.

The condition of the car surprised her. Other than some cosmetic damage, the interior remained relatively whole despite the force it took to tear a person apart from the inside out. The windshield was peppered with half a dozen chips. The plastic had what looked like speaker holes in odd places. A few cracks marred the hard dashboard. Tiny rays of light filtered into the side windows, like the glass was perforated, the shards traveling so fast it passed right through without even shattering.

The process of cataloging the car first helped switch gears in her mind from emotion to analytical. She crouched and got the first good look of what was left of the woman's face. "Do you suppose she was the target or collateral damage? What do we know about her?" She aimed her question at Scott's but didn't glance away from the scene.

"We'll have the whole vehicle towed back to the precinct to examine, but we were able to match her DMV records as owner of the car. She lived in the corner apartment building." He pointed the pen over his shoulder at a building cloaked in pale light of the streetlamps as he checked his notes. "We're checking with the super to find out more. According to him, the shifter is male and lives at the same residence."

Raven straightened, and walked around the vehicle, something nagging at her.

"What do you see?" Scotts was studying her and not the crime scene.

"She's been dead for at least six hours." Only a few hours after the original crime from just this morning.

Raven squinted to see under the gore, searching for a better angle. "Do you have a flashlight?"

Scotts barked an order, and one was slapped into her palm. She shone the light across the woman. Blood and tissue covered her body, the majority of it the shifter's.

Pieces of white bone flashed under the light.

After the brief scan, Raven reviewed the corpse from the head down. The woman's eyes had clouded over to a milky sheen. Half of her face had disintegrated, small splinters had shredded her features down to the tendons and skull. The heat had cooked her face, giving it a waxy appearance. Layers of skin and flesh were pealed back in stages, making her look like a plastic model in an anatomy lab.

Her torso appeared in little better shape. Blood saturated the female's blouse, obscuring the view, but Raven had seen enough.

Even if the woman had survived the trauma of the explosion, she would've bled to death by the hundreds of individual injuries that littered her body.

There was a stamp of some kind on the back of her hand, nearly obliterated by her wounds.

Raven didn't recognize the symbol.

"Well?"

Raven flicked off the flashlight and straightened. "The impact indicates she was alive when it happened. Most likely the same scenario as the last location. He suffered some type of pain. She turned to help him when the incident occurred."

Raven held out the flashlight. "Do we know if these two are the first murders?"

Scott's brows furrowed. "The only ones we've found. Why?"

"Shifters are gathering for the full moon. It's very coincidental that the murders have started now." Raven wondered if this could be the drug Randolph had mentioned.

Alpha.

The conclave would be the perfect place to spread chaos.

Kill off those pesky shifters.

There would be no way to test the shifters as they entered. Each could be a bomb waiting to happen.

When she surveyed the crowd, Randolph had vanished. She might not like being the center of his attention, but liked it even less when she didn't know where he was at all.

## ✌ Chapter Seven ✌

**SIX DAYS UNTIL THE FULL MOON**

A large boom jolted Raven out of the bed before she was fully awake. Power surged along her body in a massive wave, strong enough to bow her back. Current swirled in the air as if pulled from the nightmare chasing her, the heat blistering against her skin.

She cracked open an eye.

Sunshine slashed through the window and hit her full in the face. She flinched, squinting to preserve her sight, and swore she'd just laid her head on the pillow.

With bleary eyes, she scanned the room, half expecting the corpses from her dreams to lunge out from under the bed and clamp their clammy fingers around her ankles.

Nothing.

There was no threat.

Whatever she'd sensed had vanished with her dreams.

She slowly relaxed then bit back a curse when energy nipped along her arms and shoulders. As her surroundings filtered to her, she pinpointed the disturbance.

Damn Durant and his workers.

Her lips curled in a snarl at his high-handed ways. She didn't mind the remodeling, but it would've been nice to have been asked.

Then she remembered yesterday.

Jackson.

Coldness seeped into her skin, and a twinge of doubt stole over her. He looked very comfortable, even content to be back with his pack. His glacial eyes had her question everything that happened between them.

She reluctantly rose and fingered the heavy linen card from the dresser, the one she'd received from Kevin, knowing she would go to find out what he was offering.

She had to see Jackson one more time to make sure.

She wouldn't forgive herself if she just gave up on him until she was convinced he would be better off without her.

No one in her pack objected when she'd informed them of her plans to attend the meeting. That Durant had been absent was a non-issue. It was her decision, and she wouldn't back down.

Raven picked her outfit with care, selecting clothing that hid more than revealed. She couldn't have this lunar craziness affecting her at the meeting today.

As if his going was a foregone conclusion, London waited for her in the car, his bulk dwarfing the driver's seat. Raven shook her head. "We're going to have to go shopping for an SUV if people keep showing up."

He only grunted and slammed on the gas.

Tires spun.

Gravel sprayed.

No one could ever accuse him of being a talkative bastard.

"I think the house is being watched." She stared out the window. Shadows moved in the trees as they roared down the driveway, the place practically a hive of activity.

So far, no one had threatened anyone.

She was determined to keep it that way.

"Daily." He took a corner without braking, her poor car nearly going up on two wheels. Raven watched the side mirror, half-expecting to be followed.

Nothing.

"At least a half a dozen cars pass by the cameras every hour since you've been nominated as a Region and those are the ones that I caught." He drove like the rest of the cars should get out of his way.

Horns blared, tires squealed, and she opted not to look out the windshield to preserve her sanity. "Because of the conclave?"

When the traffic light turned yellow, instead of slowing, London gunned the accelerator until the little engine screamed in protest.

"Conclave. Unclaimed female alpha. Your election and subsequent job on the police force."

His ready answer made her blink. "You knew this would happen."

A shrug was the only answer she received. "It's my job to know. You had other things to worry about."

Once again, Raven gave silent thanks to London and his calm acceptance. She didn't say anything as they parked the vehicle outside the headquarters to Pak Pharmaceuticals. They made it in one piece and record time.

The business name was boldly stamped above the door in large white block letters at least as tall as her. It was not what she'd been expecting.

Research and development, the perfect place to create an experimental drug and conduct trials, so very legal-like no one would think twice.

Her mind flashed to her case, and she wondered if her leap of logic was a reasonable step or a way for her to unconsciously seek revenge on the people who'd dared to steal Jackson.

Raven craned her neck to scan the forty floors of the high-rise. The building was deceptive. Despite feet of concrete and granite, she could tell the place was teeming with shifters. From the quantity, she bet there were at least half as many floors located underground.

Sunlight sparkled off the glass. A level of pure concrete separated every few floors. The place was a fortress dressed in disguise for human sensibility. She had no doubt the place could withstand a full frontal attack.

To prevent aggression, meetings of pack leaders were limited to the alpha and a second. The rules to brokering deals were sacred. If she messed this up, she could be blackballed from working with other shifters in an alpha capacity, which would leave her pack vulnerable.

Nerves skimmed along her back as she stood on the sidewalk. Her animals shifted in unease, but surprisingly remained dormant, possibly understanding that they the need to remain hidden to protect her.

She took that as a good sign, but not enough to relax her stranglehold over herself. "Ready?"

London grunted, still clearly not pleased with the lack of security, even though he was the security. Since they were going into the wolves' den, she thought it best to be loaded with bear.

Literally.

When riled, London would turn into a full-grown Kodiak grizzly. That she suspected he was a hybrid, genetically engineered, merely increased his value in her eyes, though most saw it as a defect.

Her pack was raised in the labs where each breath was a struggled to survive. The shifter community fought amongst themselves, but they never really had to stand alone. They couldn't survive without the support of their pack behind them. That gave Raven and London a very important edge they needed to come out on top.

She took a deep breath and stepped up to the door, only to halt in surprise when a doorman opened it for her. Clearly they had money and wealth and weren't afraid to show it.

The thick glass was bulletproof. The doors reinforced. There was even a fall back door behind the main desk if the lobby fell in an attack.

Everything inside was marble. One would normally call it elegant, but the quantity tipped the scales to vulgar. The place would've been a beautiful piece of artwork if you could discount the awful décor.

"Status."

"What?" Raven continued into the lobby, grateful for London's presence when the smell of wet dog threatened to overpower her. Not appreciating the scent either, her wolf pawed the ground restlessly. The beast took advantage of her preoccupation to peer through her eyes and assess the scene.

The unexpected action startled Raven so badly, she stopped and scrutinize everything around her. The sheer quantity of information filtering into her brain nearly overwhelmed her. She didn't care if it appeared she was gawking as she processed everything.

Her wolf's vision muted the distracting colors of the human eyes. Movements were sharper, shadows disappeared, and every predator was noted, judged and found lacking.

"They're proclaiming their status amongst other packs."

His words broke her concentration. Her wolf retreated, dormant for now, waiting to be called at even the slightest sign of trouble. The disorientation lasted seconds. Vision restored, Raven snorted at London's comment. "More like screaming it at the top of their lungs."

She continued toward the front desk, resisting the urge to sneeze and clear her nose. Without waiting for her to speak, the man rose.

"If you would follow me, Miss Raven, they are expecting you." She tensed at the recognition, so used to her anonymity throughout the years that being identified on sight disturbed her.

Though slim and unassuming, the sidearm revealed the guard was prepared for trouble and would take care of it the most efficient way possible. Not surprising. He was a wolf, the scent of pack all over him in what smelled like itch weed.

London prodded her in the back, nearly sending her sprawling when her feet were reluctant to move. "Thanks."

Teeth flashed. "My pleasure."

"This way, please."

They were led down a series of corridors. After crisscrossing their own path more than once, she decided it was either a test or they were trying to make sure she couldn't find her own way. She was betting on the former.

"If you could wait here." The room was blindingly white, the walls, the floors, the flowers and even the furniture. She saw the refreshment, but wasn't tempted closer.

London stood to the side of the door, took the standard bodyguard pose, and just froze. His uniform of a white shirt and black pants did nothing to diminish his impressive size. Though he looked bored, she knew he would come to attention at the least provocation.

The room didn't really have a smell to it, everything new and unused. Cocking her head to the side, she closed her eyes and concentrated. The walls teemed with energy, the wires all but crackling with power. She couldn't resist the urge to probe further. She mentally hovered her fingers over the cables then stiffened when she saw where the electricity pooled.

The room was rigged.

They were being watched.

She withdrew slowly, careful not to trip any wires, leaving no trace of herself. Turning, she lifted her chin toward the camera artfully hidden at the top of the picture frame, another in the far corner and a third hidden in the fireplace.

"Most guests never discover the cameras." The boy from the club slipped into the room, his dimple flashing as he spoke. The jeans and shirt were casual, but not to be mistaken with cheap. They probably cost more than her car. "Mother's letting you stew."

"I suspected." Raven nodded, doing her best not to show her surprise at his sudden appearance. He'd been so well guarded at the club, she suspected no one knew he'd snuck in to talk to her.

He wasn't as compact has his old man, but he had a few years of growing left. Given time, she didn't doubt he'd outstrip his father in strength. Closely cropped blond hair stood in spikes around his head, and those ghostly pale blue eyes studied her with unnerving intensity. A twang of discord simmered around him, same as at the club, but she couldn't pinpoint what actually felt off about him.

"Should you be down here?" The boy didn't wander away from the door. When she shifted to sneak a glance at the cameras, she understood. He was out of range if he remained still.

A security breech? Or done on purpose?

Damn sneaky shifters.

She angled her body so she appeared to be speaking to London.

"Jackson's very protective of you."

She shrugged off the quick surge of hope, but could do nothing about the way her heart leapt. "As he is of you."

He shook his head in denial, never taking his eyes off her. "Not like you. You're different."

Footsteps sounded down the hall behind her, and she looked over her shoulder at the door. When she turned back, the kid was gone.

London came to her side, his chest an impressive expanse of muscle enough to discourage any inquisitive wolf. "Strange kid."

"Why do I feel like I've just been vetted?"

The door opened before he could reply.

"If you'd follow me." A different male approached, his suit impeccably pressed, his shoes shined to a polish, every piece of hair in order. The man looked so similar to the guard that if he hadn't smelled slightly tangier, she would've guessed he'd changed clothes.

They obediently followed him into the elevator and watched as the steel doors slid shut. "Is that normal?" She gestured toward their escort's back, and the building's *Stepford* husband look-alikes.

London's face was expressionless. Nearly a minute passed before he shrugged, and Raven's brow furrowed. "More status shit?"

She would swear she saw his lips twitch, but no smile formed. The ride shot upwards without warning. The confined space sucked out all the fresh air. With each breath, the man's scent crept over her skin, invaded her lungs.

The walls pressed closer.

Determined not to let her beasts out of their cage, she grabbed a tiny spark to ensure they remained tame, stepping back so she wouldn't infect the others.

And gasped when her back pressed against cold steel.

Electricity leapt at the contact, feeding her a steady stream of current. Her core greedily sucked it down as if starved.

Or threatened.

Lights flickered.

The motor to the elevator clunked ominously, and Raven nearly bolted into London as she put distance between her and the walls.

"That's odd." The guide pushed a button but seemed appeased when the ride smoothed out.

London didn't say a word, though a wrinkle creased between his eyes. He hadn't once removed his stare from their guide, and she wondered if he expected the man to hijack the elevator.

Raven studied the man as well. Nothing appeared out of normal. Benign even. But a tickle scratched at the back of her mind. She closed her eyes and twisted a strand of energy around his shields, shaking at the tremendous amount of control it took not to breach his control and touch his wolf.

And nearly strangled at what she found.

The man's aura was pure animal lust, his beast raging to get out. He all but panted at her nearness, desperately begging for her touch. The man's restraint was extraordinary, but if she so much as brushed against him, he'd have her up against the wall in seconds.

And she'd pay the price for poaching on another pack.

Another damn test.

She couldn't afford any transgressions before the conclave.

The machine stopped seamlessly, the doors gliding open. The guide stepped to the side, indicating they could leave. The wolf stared at Raven, hunger burning in his eyes, as if she were lunch and dessert all rolled up in one. He practically licked his lips when she took a step forward, but didn't move in her direction in any way.

It took a lot of will for her not to bolt. She stepped carefully between the men in what felt like a dangerous game of *Operation*. If she touched anything, game over.

Anger at the cheap trick burned away her nerves, and she entered the penthouse suite.

Her feet sank in lush white carpeting. Wide-open space greeted her. Fresh air filled her lungs and cleared her head. Raven and London fanned out to give themselves room, falling into the relaxed, lazy fighting pose London had taught her. With no sign of her beasts, the energy at her core took advantage of the opportunity and teemed around her. The tangled strands settling under her skin, just waiting to flare up at any hint of a threat.

Raven didn't know if she should be grateful or not. Any signs of the moon madness had been erased, but no one could be allowed to know how she'd managed the feat.

Kevin and a tall blonde woman entered the room. Both looked toward the elevator, and Raven turned in time to see the guide shake his head, his eyes locked on her ass.

When she turned back, Kevin was smiling and the blonde had her pinned with a scowl. Raven didn't need to be told she was the alpha bitch of the pack. It was written all over her attitude.

The perfect coiffure of fake curls and silk clothes screamed money. Too bad it didn't purchase taste. Cold blue eyes trailed over her person and the blonde snorted inelegantly. "So this is your idea of a solution?" She laughed, ran a finger down Kevin's face hard enough to leave a small bead of blood, marking him in front of her like Raven was a rival, and then left the way she'd come.

Kevin didn't once lose his smile as he brushed away the blood. He waited for the woman to vanish before he gestured back toward the elevator. "How about we go to my rooms for a little privacy?"

Raven crossed her arms. "How about we take the stairs?" No one was going to get her in that elevator with another male.

"Of course." He didn't have the grace to blush, but since he was doing what she asked, she didn't push the issue.

Two flights of stairs down, they entered a much more muted room, still expensive, but understated and lived in. "Please, take a seat."

Raven raised a brow.

"No more games, I promise."

"What do you want?" Raven ignored his suggestion, grateful to have London at her back. She didn't care if she was blunt. She just wanted to find out what the hell he wanted and leave.

"Your help. I couldn't ask for it until Vivian gave her approval." Anger clouded his eyes, but it was there and gone before she could be sure.

"My help with what?" Suspicions crammed into her mind.

"My son."

That was the last thing she expected him to say. Raven stilled, disliking being taken off guard. "What about him?"

"He's going to die unless you help." The man met her stare dead in the eye, worry stealing the confidence that seemed so much a part of him.

His comment baffled her. "What help could I give that you don't already have at your fingertips?"

Whatever she saw hardened, and the father disappeared in place of the businessman. "You want Jackson returned to you, yes?"

Raven remained mute, her eyes narrowing, not liking the way this conversation was going. His expression was almost feverish. "If you agree to my terms, he's yours."

## ❧ Chapter Eight ☙

"You can't do this." London paced behind her, showing his agitation for the first time since they'd arrived. She would've said he lumbered, but his footsteps were too light.

Raven gazed out the window, down at the streets so many stories below. Kevin went to fetch Jackson, leaving them alone. Trepidation froze her feet to the carpeting. Hell, half her body refused to move, and only part of it had to do with seeing Jackson again.

No, most of the dread stealing over her was because London was right. "What choice do I have? If I don't agree, he'll make it a point to never allow Jackson to leave."

"You don't even know what he wants, and you're already agreeing." London didn't sound angry but more resigned.

The elevator warned them of their host's return. The doors opened. The only thing she saw was Jackson's whiskey colored gaze. She didn't know what she envisioned, but his bitterly cold expression wasn't it.

Kevin walked in the room, his son trailing behind him. "I want to hire you to guard my son."

Raven blinked and eyed Jackson. He looked fit. If anything, he appeared broader, stronger than she'd remembered. "And what you have isn't sufficient?"

Kevin didn't deny it, his expression unchanging. "You want Jackson. They come as a package deal."

The feeling of being played hardened her resolve to get to the bottom of this visit. "What would I be able to do that you can't?"

"I believe he means my mother." The boy stepped forward, his dimple flashing. "I'm nearing my maturity. Since I'm an alpha, that means I could take over the pack and displace her rule. She won't give up her power willingly, especially since I'm not so easily controlled." He didn't offer his hand, but gave her a good-humored smile as if his mother trying to kill him was an inside joke. "I'm Aaron."

"And this is something you want?"

Intelligence sharpened his pale blue gaze, but she had no sense of his wolf. Absolutely none, which was odd since he claimed to be an alpha. "I want to live. Jackson said you could help."

Jackson flinched imperceptibly. Raven's heart bottomed out, pumping hard. She didn't allow herself the luxury of imagining what secrets he'd divulged for fear she would crack.

They had a type of truce between them, but now that he was whole and healthy again, he could be one of her biggest threats.

He knew too many of her secrets.

Energy wavered around her, dread threatening to topple her control. She turned away to preserve what was left of her composure. "Help you with what?"

Aaron cocked his head, his stare unnerving in its intensity. The discord around the boy increased, threatening to make her head explode under the weight. She rubbed her temple. "What are you doing?"

The teenager couldn't disguise his shock. The pressure immediately stopped. "You felt that?"

His question caused her mouth to snap shut. Neither of them said anything else, both unwilling to give away more of their secrets. Each eyed each other up, uncertain what to expect. Then he whispered a plea only she heard.

"Say yes." Genuine turmoil radiated from him.

Her gaze flicked suspiciously to Jackson, but his stoic expression gave nothing away.

Damned stubborn bastard.

"For how long?" London grunted at the question, clearly not pleased she was still thinking about their offer. It wasn't a yes, but it wasn't the no he demanded either.

Aaron gave a casual shrug that she didn't buy. "Until I crest and can be presented to the conclave. No one would question it as shifters sometimes foster their kids out to other packs as a type of learning tool."

Raven wasn't buying it. "No one would believe your parents would let you out of their sight, especially as you near your cresting. They wouldn't risk someone contaminating you."

"But they might if they thought there was a way to snag one of the few unclaimed alpha females in the area." There was something in his phrasing that put her back up.

"You have no romantic interest in me." Raven was too relieved to be offended. "Why do you wish to leave?"

Another shrug. "Is it not enough that my mother is trying to kill me? Does there have to be something more?"

No, there didn't, but she'd bet her life that there was something he held back. But was this wild gamble worth the risk to her fledgling pack? Yes, if it meant that she could get Jackson back where he belonged.

She couldn't let him go without a fight.

Not this time.

She owed it to him to at least try.

She faced Keith and took a deep breath. "What are your terms?"

* * *

Raven parked the car in front of her house and waited for the second vehicle to pull up behind her. The air pressed heavily against her, and she tipped her head back. A storm brewed on the horizon, the dark thunderclouds rolling ever closer as if drawn to her turmoil.

The pull of the storm was incredible. Like a living lightning rod, all the hair on her body stood on end. There was nowhere to go that it wouldn't reach her. She resisted the wild urge to draw down all that beautiful power waiting for her and just wallow in it.

Even now, her skin felt alive. Energy danced in the air, current pulsed around her, urging her to come out and play. She turned the key, heard to the engine die, but she didn't move as she battled to rein in her volatile mood.

London casted her a look, then left without a word, never once glancing back.

Smart man.

From the rearview mirror, she watched Jackson unfold himself from his black diesel.

For a fleeting moment, his shoulders relaxed.

Then it was gone.

Cold fury covered his expression, and she found herself faced with the imposing pack enforcer who would kill anyone that got in his way of doing his job.

She exited the car , her own anger burning bright. When he came closer, she gathered the agitated blue strands whipping around her core and wrapped them over her clenched fist. Without speaking, she swung as hard as she could.

Jackson didn't just go down, he flew back a few feet and landed flat on his ass. He lifted his head to peer up at her, but didn't do anything stupid, like try to get up. "Don't you dare disappear on me like that again. Do you understand me?"

She stalked closer to stand over his body. "And if I find out that you put anyone in my pack in danger with what you told them, you'll wish we'd never met."

The air around her throbbed with her fury, and his eyes splintered yellow under the influence. But instead of shifting, he meekly offered his throat in supplication. She didn't know what pissed her off more, that he just rolled over without a fight or that he didn't deny her accusation.

Weariness dragged away her anger. She had to leave before she did something she would regret. "Take the kid and find a room. We'll talk about our next course of action in the morning." Without waiting for a response, she stalked toward the house.

"Wait." Aaron loped to her side. "Jackson told my father very little about you and my mother even less. Only enough so as not to raise their suspicions. He risked his life to protect your secrets."

Dying light haloed him, illuminating the earnestness on his face as he trotted to her side. She saw a glimpse of the type of man he would become. "But he told you more."

Though his expression didn't change, the static hum around him increased. "He did what he could to protect you even knowing that you would never forgive him."

Something about the way he phrased his words raised her bullshit antenna. "What do you mean?"

They stepped inside the house, the shadows half covering his face. "He never expected you to come for him. He doesn't know how to react."

Behind them, Jackson picked himself off the ground, not even bothering to dust himself off as he trudged toward the house.

"If you were any other alpha, the punishment for betrayal would be death." Raven met Aaron's pensive gaze. "Please tell me from everything I've heard that I haven't misjudged you."

His words were not quite a plea or demand. Raven turned away from Aaron, unwilling to have him see her reaction.

Though Jackson might have tried to protect her, he had violated her privacy knowing it would destroy her. She felt exposed down to her soul. She tried to rationalize that she would rather have him alive, but her hurt wouldn't be forgotten so easily.

"I gave my word. You're both safe here."

Aaron didn't seem pleased by her answer, but didn't say anything more when Jackson stepped into the house. Jackson's whiskey brown eyes had thawed, leaving behind a hesitant, hungry expression as his gaze roved over her body. But he never lifted his eyes to hers, as if afraid of what he would find.

"Grab an empty room upstairs and make yourselves comfortable." She needed to get away from Jackson and the yearning to give him a hug.

She clutched her hurt in her chest, not ready to forgive.

Not sure if she could ever completely trust him again.

The situation threatened to break heart.

She took the stairs two at a time, eager to hide from their prying eyes and organize her scattered thoughts. By the time she hit the hallway, she was panting, having practically run to get away.

She was a coward.

But at least she knew it.

She entered her room and drew up short. Taggert sat on the bed with Digger holding a needle full of blood. Any pretense she had of control vanished. The shield around her fluctuated. Energy crackled, taking advantage of her hesitation, dumping into her core. Her control snapped. The strands of blue and white slashed through her insides.

Eager for escape.

Eager for the hunt.

Each lash of the whip left a singe mark scoring the underside of her skin, the pain an old friend that took over to protect her from the bad things that happened in the labs.

Taggert launched to his feet, standing between her and Digger, his head tipped to expose his throat in supplication. He shuffled closer, his hands open at his side. Concern darkened his face but no fear. "I asked him to take my blood. I wanted proof that you weren't hurting me."

She pushed away the horrors of the past, her instincts fighting her every step of the way. Memories, like flames, licked along her flesh, ready to consume her.

"Stand down." Griffin came through the balcony doors behind Digger, aggression radiating from him as he faced off with her. Heat from his wolf crashed through the room, aggravating her tenuous battle for restraint. The urge to attack burned along her arms as her powers gained momentum.

A sound came from the doorway behind her. Raven whirled in time to see Jackson charge into the room. He took in the scene at a glance, picked up on her fear, but misunderstood the reason. He hurdled himself at Griffin, going after the biggest threat in the room.

To protect her.

The two men crashed through the glass doors. The doorframe quivered but held.

Not so the men.

They slammed against the balcony, nearly toppling over the railing. They weren't just fighting, they were trying to kill each other.

She hesitated at the unexpectedness of the attack. The battle riveted her, their brutality equally matched despite Jackson being taller and heavier. Their savagery brought home just how much skill she lacked.

How lucky she'd been.

The storm overhead rumbled, a massive boom rattled the house. Neither of them even flinched.

Jackson virtually tossed Griffin in the middle of the room. But instead of cracking into the floor, Griffin rolled into a crouch, ready to launch himself back into the battle.

"Stop!" Neither man paused at her command.

The first hint of unease rose.

Something was wrong, like they were being pushed.

They had no intention of stopping until one of them was dead.

She had to stop them, but her animals were nowhere to be found, taking her alpha ability with them.

That only left her power.

Resignation settled in her gut.

The time for hiding had come to an end.

Raven allowed herself to be drawn to the window, the raw strength of the storm luring her onto the balcony. She planted herself by the railing and braced herself for what was to come.

Then she dropped her shields.

Power hummed low on the air, drowning out other sounds as it drew closer. Lightning slashed through the sky and struck feet outside the window. It crawled up the building, the wiring in the house guiding the wild electricity up to her.

Raven thrusted her hand over the railing, and the jagged bolt arched into her waiting palm. Pain and pleasure twisted inside her. Holding the massive charge ripped up her insides like someone had stuck her finger in a socket then tossed her out of a plane to add variety to her pain. Jaw clenched, she turned and waved her arms.

Jackson and Griffin flew apart. Their bodies slammed into opposite walls.

Absolute silence filled in the room. No one moved, not even bothering to pick themselves up from where they'd landed.

Raven refused to flinch under their stares or read deeper into their expressions. She already knew what they were thinking. She, too, was horrified at what she'd become.

"My power is amplifying your aggression. Leave." Even now, tiny particles circled in the clouds about the house, the current building for another strike.

And she had no way to stop it.

Wasn't sure she wanted to.

The storm called to her.

It was uncontrollable.

Wild and addictive.

But she could only channel so much electricity. She could withstand another strike, maybe two before burnout began to creep over her and shut her down, then she was going to crash, and she didn't want anyone to witness the aftereffects.

"Everyone leave the room."

When no one moved, she couldn't keep the roar from her voice. "Now!"

Digger didn't argue. He collected his bag and strode toward the door, calmly going about his everyday business. Griffin rose, followed Digger, all without turning his back on her.

Fierce need darkened Jackson's eyes as he stood. Despite his injuries, which were already healing, he closed the distance between him in the boneless, muscular way of his kind.

She held her ground, barely resisting the urge to run, the need to hide what she was becoming. When Jackson kept coming, panic caught her breath in her chest. She couldn't bear to have him touch her and discover just how little of her remained human.

Power cracked into the floor between them, nearly tumbling Jackson to his knees. Electricity leaked from her in a steady stream that she couldn't control, sending the charged air swirling in the room. The hair on his body stood on end. The next strike would go for him whether she wanted it or not. She could already feel it building.

She couldn't allow that to happen. "You can't stay. You have to protect Aaron. That's why you're here, isn't it?"

He pulled up short as if she'd struck him. His face hardened, and he left without bothering to look back at her.

What else did she expect? That he would stay and choose her?

"Raven—"

"No." She cut off Taggert's protest.

"You have to ground." He was calm, no sense of fear or self-preservation in him.

The fool. It would get him killed.

Before she could stop him, he grabbed her arm.

Then it was too late.

Electricity arced between them, wrapping around him like an

unbreakable band before it seeped into his skin.

His eyes didn't just splinter with color, they turned solid yellow, his wolf staring boldly back at her. Raven quickly pulled as much energy away from his that she could manage, desperate to keep him safe.

There was just too much of it to reabsorb.

She grabbed the railing, forcing the electricity through the metal and back into the house. The railing heated, the metal grew soft, bowing under the current. The skin of her hand burned at the amount of current. She could feel her palms crack and blood slowly trickle out from the wounds.

Despite trying everything she could think to protect him, it still wasn't enough. If she didn't do something soon, he would die in her arms. She struggled to dislodge his grip. Taggert only tightened his hold. Every time he was exposed to her power, it changed him, made him bolder and brought out his baser instincts.

The changes scared the shit out of her.

Unsure if it was her fear of hurting him or the lure of all that power being so near, the shadowy figure around her core shifted in the darkness. It uncurled itself and gave a lazy stretch.

Ravenous hunger unfurled through her gut.

Then its talons sank into the flesh around her core, pressing down on her chest like a physical weight. Her shields cracked as if the creature was trying to gain access to the current so deliciously out of reach. When the creature couldn't break through, she contented herself by wrapping around the vault, snuffing it out like it'd never been.

The lack of power nearly dropped her to her knees. A new terror took root. What would happen when the creature gained access? And it would only be a matter of time. It was growing bigger, feeding off her core, and she had no clue how to stop it.

She swayed with exhaustion. Without the heat of her core, frost crept through her chest until breathing hurt.

Taggert gasped, his eyes wide as he gaped at her. "What was that?"

She couldn't speak.

At her lack of response, Taggert engulfed her in his arms,

clamping down around her almost brutally as if afraid she would run. She didn't resist, didn't have the energy to spare, as she struggled for air.

Without her power, she was left vulnerable to the animals that inhabited her skin. They lifted their heads and roared in anger at the new intruder. The wolf emerged from the darkness. She dug its claws and teeth into her flesh, staking ownership.

She wouldn't be dislodged.

Would not be denied.

Alpha.

Something inside her eased, and the stranglehold around her lungs lessened. She gasped for breath, nearly lightheaded. She tentatively placed her hands on Taggert's chest. His heart leapt at the contact, and he cuddled her closer as if needing the connection more than her. She imagined her hand running over his wolf's fur, the action surprisingly soothing.

She didn't need anyone to tell her she was in deep shit. But she did wish someone could hand her a shovel, so she at least had a way of digging herself out.

## ❧ Chapter Nine ❦

Taggert lay sprawled across her bed, the demands of keeping her wolf calm knocking him out cold. Tremors still rocked through her at how everything could've gone so horribly wrong.

Taggert had risked everything for her by staying. Raven was amazed that he didn't suffer more for coming to her aid. Despite her worse fear, his touch had saved her.

At least bought her some time.

For everyone's safety, she normally locked herself away in the basement. She marveled at being able to witness the awesome ferocity of the storm for the first time in years. She watched the sky lighten as the storm began to fade.

Even hours later, her core remained inaccessible. Though her shields had wavered, they remained steady. Not wanting to push her limited luck, she remained in her room, restricting her exposure to the others until the storm cleared. But that was only part of the truth. She just wasn't ready to face the fall-out of tonight's latest fiasco.

She brought up the video that Scotts had sent from the first crime scene. She pressed play for the hundredth time in hopes that she could pick up something she might have missed. She watched the man grab his head then turned into mist before the cameras fuzzed out.

She searched the background for any witnesses, for any shadow that moved, but there was nothing to be found. She hit the pause button and sat back from her laptop, restless eating away at her calm.

"You found something."

Raven startled at the voice, swallowing hard when she spotted Griffin at her door. "Unfortunately not."

He didn't wait for an invitation, but sauntered in the room like a pesky brother intent on snooping, showing no hesitation approaching her. She concentrated solely on the frozen scene, not ready to face anyone's judgment.

"Show me."

His lack of fear shouldn't have surprised her, but it did. None of the shifters seemed leery of what she could do. They well understood the threat, but it was as if they recognized her as dominant and just accepted it.

Raven cleared away the tightness of her throat. "What did you find at the tree line? Any signs of an intruder?"

"Unfortunately not." Griffin didn't stiffen at her question, didn't react in any way. It wasn't lost on her he used her very words back at her. That's how she knew he was lying. What didn't he want her to know? He had been gone all night. He had no lover, so whom did he meet and why?

Raven blindly punched up the video again and studied Griffin as he watched it, unable to pinpoint his reason for being here. Unless he was there to see how big of threat she presented and determine if she needed to be eliminated.

None of the effects from the fight were visible on his body. His wolf roamed beneath the surface, but they both appeared to cohabitate in harmony with no animosity between the two.

"How?" She hadn't realized she asked aloud until he turned to face her. A blush of heat filled her cheeks, but she refused to back down. "How do you keep such perfect control?"

At first he didn't move, his dual gaze settling on hers like a weight. She thought he would avoid the question or just give a glib answer. Instead, he straightened and held out his hand as if he'd made some decision. "Let me show you."

Her heart thundered against her ribcage. Caution warned her to watch her step, not trust him, but the need for answers won hands-down. If she could keep her people safe, did it really matter what price she had to pay?

She inhaled deeply, the scent of cedar immersing her, and slipped her hand into his. Fire immediately crackled at the contact, burrowing up her arm as his beast pushed at her. Then he dropped his hold and stepped back, unconsciously rubbing his palms on his pants as if stung by the contact.

She stood and rubbed her arms. "Is it always like that?"

Those broad shoulders of his shrugged in a kind of answer. "Children of the pack are raised to know what to expect. Some packs are loving, some stern, but children are always kept separate from the public as they learn about their beast. They are guarded until they reach maturity. With so few born, they are precious and trained early to know what life in the pack entails."

"At the age of eighteen, they pledge their loyalty."

"The cresting." That's the word he and Aaron had brandied about.

Griffin smiled, quickly grasping she didn't have a clue what it meant. "Cresting is a rite of passage into adulthood. It's usually their first shift. If they are accepted, they pledge to the pack."

"And those who can't shift?"

"There are three options and none of them kind. There are those who still pledge. They show some promise or skill that will benefit the pack, but without the ability to shift, they are treated as secondhand citizens. The others, the weakest, are disowned."

"But they're just kids."

Griffin gave her a cynical look. "They're shifters."

"And the third option?" Raven wasn't sure she wanted to know anymore.

"The last option doesn't happen often." Griffin paced the confines of the room. "Someone in the pack has to vouch for them. That means both are held responsible for any transaction the kid commits until they prove themselves worthy."

She didn't believe for a second that he hadn't passed the test. "You vouched for someone."

Griffin stopped short and gave a bitter laugh, his stillness more unsettling than his pacing. "You're very observant."

Raven kept her questions to herself when she realized he was talking about himself. If she interrupted him, it would never happen again. With each step, his agitation increased, heat flashed in the room until his wolf filled the space.

"A younger man was brought into the pack. A brother. Father

had successfully mated with a human. When the kid had reached puberty, he became violent. His wolf was starting to emerge. His mother had no way to deal with the rage and dropped him off on Father's step to deal with.

"The pack wanted nothing to do with him. He was nearing maturity, so they just waited. When the time came to crest, he failed. He was impure. Too much human blood. They labeled him as worthless and voted to exile him."

"So you stepped in."

"He was my brother. He deserved a chance to prove himself."

"But something went wrong."

Griffin nodded, a curious lack of emotion of his face. "His first moon hit him hard. He became obsessed with a woman and lost control.

"He slaughtered her before I could stop him. It's an automatic death sentence. I vouched for him. I was responsible. For his crime, they chose to exile me." Exile for a true blood shifter like him was a fate worse than death.

"And your condition?"

"Came with the exile. Being rogue forces your animal closer to the surface. You have to be ever vigilant and brutal. The only way to survive was to merge completely. For the first few weeks, I thought I was going insane. Then everything settled."

It made sense. Evolution had forced his body to adapt. Shifter genetics accelerated the mutations. "It's your gift."

Griffin laughed abruptly. "I'm not sure I would go that far."

Raven jerked in surprise, seeing he really didn't understand. "Haven't you noticed that a few shifters have developed certain talents? I think yours is the ability to access both forms at once without serious side effects."

Griffin didn't look convinced.

"Some people who lack in one area have a special ability to adapt in others."

When he continued to gaze at her a little too intently, Raven shifted uncomfortably. Then he cocked his head. "And what is your talent?"

"Getting into trouble." She muttered it under her breath, and his deep laugh startled them both. Her lips unconsciously curled at his genuine humor.

"And what kind of trouble are you in now?"

She switched off the computer and walked toward the door. "I think it's time to meet your father and ask him some questions."

All amusement drained from Griffin's expression, but he didn't try to talk her out of it anymore.

"Tell me where I can find him."

* * *

Raven couldn't stop fidgeting as she entered the country club doors. Even with Griffin running interference, it had taken her half an hour to sneak out of the house.

He wasn't keen that she'd went alone, but disliked the idea of anyone else going with her, where his secrets could be exposed, even less. Despite their shared past, they danced around each other, neither ready to fully trust the other.

Dark and masculine, the club catered toward the rich and influential clientele. She'd bet her house the likes of her kind had never been granted access beyond the service counter. The ancient age of the building pressed down on her, the atmosphere terribly expensive, but surprisingly tasteful. Dressed in jeans, a long sleeve shirt, gloves and boots, she stood out like a scarecrow at a bonfire.

The uniformed man at the front counter wore a suit more expensive than all her clothes put together. He smiled as she neared. She'd give him credit when his smile stayed steady when he got a good look at her scruffy self. But beneath, she could all but see his wolf turn up his tail and dismiss her. "I'm sorry, but only club members are allowed—"

"Tell Mr. Donaldson that I'm here to see him."

"I'm afraid that—"

"It's about his son." Raven lowered her shields and allowed the heat and scent of the many shifters beyond the double doors to call her own. Her wolf rose without any prompting and peered out through her eyes. Wildness licked through her at the freedom.

The man stopped his protests, his face unreadable as he picked up his phone and dialed. "If you will take a seat, I'll see if he is available."

She expected to be kept waiting, but less than five minutes passed before an imposing man in a full-out tux came from the room beyond. The barrel-chested man was not what she expected. There were similarities to his son, the way he leashed so much power around him, the blank eyes that gave nothing away, and the purposeful way he strode forward, expecting everyone else to get out of the way. She stood at his approach, refusing to be intimidated by his hard expression.

When she opened her mouth, he held up his hand. "Follow me." He didn't even slow his pace as he walked past her and through another doorway to her right. She turned and obediently followed.

And found herself in a library of sorts. A few tables were discreetly set up around the room. Fireplaces brightened the area enough to give off a welcoming glow. At their entrance, a few people glanced up, took in Donaldson's stiff countenance, and quickly left. He faced her, lighting a cigar.

She wrinkled her nose and waved her hand. He immediately tapped out the embers, but the job was done. Her sense of smell was destroyed. Sneaky, though she should've anticipated that given Griffin's warning.

"What do you want?"

"I have a few questions I need to ask about the conclave." She met his regard directly, refusing to be cowed when his mind crashed into her shields with a clang. When another few moments passed at a standstill, she raised a brow. She refused to wince and show the pain, curling her hands into fists until her nails cut into her palms. "Done?"

"Who are you." The question was a demand, and the pain immediately stopped.

"That's not how this works. You answer my questions, and I'll do my best to answer yours." And try to keep as much of her secrets safe as she could.

There was a short pause before he walked toward the sideboard. She must have passed some sort of test. "Ask."

"Are you aware of anyone who would want to stop the conclave from taking place?"

Donaldson paused in pouring to study her. "Everyone. Your

name."

"Raven." She eyed him in turn, noting he didn't offer her a drink. When she opened her mouth, he waved a hand.

"I suggest you ask your questions with better care." Humor danced in his eyes, and she took him at face value.

"A number of deaths have increased with the coming full moon." Donaldson just stared at her, not denying or confirming anything. "I think the recent murders are tied to the approaching conclave."

Still no response.

"I want to know if you think this could be a grab for power from within the conclave or an attack on it as a whole."

"You're quick. I'll give you that." He took a calm sip of his drink, never taking his attention from her.

His comment so mimicked his son, it was uncanny. She refused to twitch under his formidable stare. Something in his gaze made it feel like he could see right through her shields and steal all her secrets in a single breath. A flutter of panic gurgled in her stomach, but she held her ground.

Donaldson raised his own brow then relented. "Either option is possible, though not likely. We bring too much influence to the shifters. If the power structure were to change, the shifters would not be as prosperous, and that would hurt everyone. As for an individual trying for a seat on the conclave, maybe, but the attack would have to be more direct."

Raven tipped her head at his response, her senses sharpening. "Direct approach? I never said how they died."

"I believe it's my turn to ask the question." He set down his glass. "Do you even know my son?"

The intensity in his eyes increased, snippy at the thought of being tricked. Griffin warned her to choose her words with care if his father asked. "I've met him."

Those eyes narrowed further. "Where?"

"You might say we were hunting the same killers." She didn't know why she said it, why she protected Griffin, but it felt right.

Donaldson sighed, seemingly eased at her confession. "He's still playing games, I see."

Raven thought about asking how he knew about the deaths, but figured someone in his position would have contacts. She didn't want to waste her question. "You know about the deaths. Does that mean you have an idea of who might be behind them?"

He laughed out-right, and she saw the charismatic man that had the ability to hold a room full of alphas if he'd wished. "You're a clever little thing, aren't you." He set down the glass and walked toward the door. "I don't, but I suspect you'll find out the truth soon enough." He paused by the door without bothering to face her. "Try to keep my son out of trouble if you can."

## ❧ Chapter Ten ❦

**FIVE DAYS UNTIL THE FULL MOON**

By the time she'd left the country club, midnight had come and gone. The moon beat down on her, its rays a cool threat of things to come. The exhaust smells of the cars had lifted, and she could almost taste the chill in the air. Raven walked a block to her car, her thoughts lost in what Donaldson had said and so artfully not said.

She unlocked the door when a shiver worked up her back. Not giving herself a chance to think, she threw her body sideways.

Most people hesitated for fear of feeling stupid if they overreacted.

Raven would rather be alive.

The baseball bat meant for her head cracked against her car window. A waterfall of glass hit the road. Raven whirled, stumbling to her feet. Two teens, hoodies raised, charge toward her. Menace pooled around them.

"Can we talk about this?" Their movements were faster than humans, almost a blur.

The guy with the bat wound up and swung again. She rolled over the back of the trunk and landed on the other side of the vehicle. Her car wasn't so lucky. The rear light shattered under the impact meant for her knee.

"You should've minded your own business, Region." The other boy hurried after her, a blade shimmering under the streetlight. Instead of running, she dropped into the fighting stance London had drilled into her. She lashed out with her foot, knocking the blade from his hand.

It was a tossup which one of them was more surprised, her or the kid. Unfortunately, he recovered quicker, swinging his fist. She weaved to dodge the blow, but his fingers grazed her jaw. That she could've handled, but she hadn't anticipated the brass knuckles.

Her skin split open. Blood spilled down her neck. Up close, she could see a shock of hair fall over his brow. His clean jaw indicated the kid was no more than fifteen years old. No animal blazed out from his hazel eyes, but the potential was there. His eyes widened when he caught her looking, fear turning them green.

She spun and without thinking, slammed her foot into his knee. A rumble of rage or pain ripped from his throat, but she had no time to find out which. The mini-league wannabe was up to bat again.

A metal bat.

A really stupid, totally irrational idea grabbed her. Running didn't even enter her mind. They'd be on her before she made it back to the club. Raven pretended to stumble. She pushed her back against the car, taking comfort from the cold metal against her spine.

When bat came down toward her head, she ducked. Metal thunked against the roof of her car. She reached up, and saturated the bat with electricity.

A hum filled the air at the sheer quantity of juice she funneled. Lights all the way down the street flickered as she drew the power from the city grid.

The jolt slammed into the kid with enough force to toss him back a few feet. He landed hard, skidding a yard before he stilled. Fear that she'd killed him curled through her. Then he coughed as he grasped for air, rolled to his side, but didn't rise.

Raven slowly straightened. The other kid hobbled over to his friend, practically picked him up and scurried away. She debated going after them, but reason asserted itself. If they turned on her, she couldn't guarantee she'd win the next round.

As adrenaline wore off, her chin throbbed. She probed the bruised area and winced at the pain, her jaw already swelling.

"Shit." She was so busted. There was no way to hide that. Though already clotting, she wouldn't be anywhere near healed before she arrived home. She scrubbed away the blood and walked around her poor vehicle.

Her once pristine new car.

London was going to kill her.

The roof had a huge dent, the window was gone and the rear light was not only broke, the bumper was crumbled as well. The kids had been stronger than she'd anticipated.

Because of the new Alpha drug Randolph had mentioned? But that made little sense. Why target her?

There had been a wildness to them, a lust for violence that seemed reckless. They reminded her of Griffin without the taste of alpha on them.

More rogues.

Scraping the keys off the road, she groaned and all but fell into the car.

The ride home dragged on as she riddled out everything she'd learned. Most importantly, why rogues had targeted to kill her when she was working to save them?

And she had no doubt that they would've killed her. She was faster than before, but still not quick enough. She needed to be better. Needed to train harder and trust her animals more. If they had sent anyone but boys, she doubted she would've come out on top.

By the time she parked the car and trudged toward the front steps, exhaustion had mugged her and won. All she wanted was a hot shower and a bag of ice.

Hand on her jaw, she opened the door and pulled up short.

Four men littered the hallway: Durant, Jackson, Taggert and Dominic in his wolf form. As one, all eyes riveted on her like she was a ghost. She could've kicked herself for not getting a clue when the house was lit up like a beacon. "Uh, what's up?"

She carefully kept her hand on her jaw, thankful the light spilling from the study didn't reach her. She angled her body to better hide in the shadows. Unobtrusively as possible, she wrapped the darkness around her to smudge her appearance. She dropped her arm to her side. If they looked at her jaw directly, they'd be able to see the injury. Otherwise, she should be safe.

Dominic reacted first, stalking toward her on stiff legs, his fur ruffled on end in outrage. Tags and a harness rested on the floor, the only way a shifter in animal form could go out in public. No one would've mistaken his beast for a pet.

Then there was Durant. "Shouldn't you be at work?"

"Where were you?" The calm, soothing tone of Durant's voice raised her hackles.

No one moved. Their extreme reaction alarmed her. "I went to meet a guy about the case I'm working. Didn't Griffin tell you?"

"He gave us some cockamamie story about you meeting an alpha on your own then proceeded to disappear. That was hours ago."

"It was for the case I'm working." So why did that sound like a lame excuse?

"Work is fine, but you are not just a Region. You're the alpha of this pack. Please tell me you're not stupid enough to endanger yourself by meeting another alpha without any type of backup." He stepped toward her, and his nostrils flared. In seconds, he was at her side.

She tried to turn away, but he had her face gripped in his big palms before she could so much as twitch. She sucked in a breath when his fingers swept ever so lightly over her injury as if brushing away the darkness she'd grabbed.

Stupid.

Of course they scented the blood.

"What the hell happened to you?" He tipped her face into the light. Jackson whitened, clearly holding himself responsible. Taggert's reaction hurt the worse. He stared at her with wounded eyes. Not that she was injured, but that she'd left without telling him and broke his trust.

Their expectations were too much. They treated her as a prisoner. "You're overreacting. You knew I had a meeting."

"But you conveniently forgot to tell us where. You can't go into a potential dangerous situation and not expect us to react."

"The meeting went smoothly. Why make it into such a big deal?"

A rumble of anger worked up Durant's chest, her question testing his patience. "You're the alpha. Even a male wouldn't have left his pack without protection. Until you achieve pack status, your situation is even more precarious. And to make it worse, you know what I'm saying is true. Look at you. You're injured."

"But not from the meeting." Admitting the truth was humiliating.

She was a fully-grown female. She could take care of herself, yet two teens nearly took her down. "I was attacked getting into my car."

Durant captured her wrist in his grip. When she tugged, his hold clamped down like a vise, and he dragged her unceremoniously toward the kitchen.

He slammed the swinging door open so hard it warbled and rebounded off the wall. She barely caught the wood before it thumped into her. Durant yanked out a chair, wood screeching across the floor, before shoving it under her ass. She plopped inelegantly on the seat with an oomph.

Everyone filed into the kitchen behind them. The wall of glass was dark, reflecting the too silent room back at her. The violence so prevalent in shifters lurked close to their surfaces, ready to erupt if she made the wrong move.

Jackson leaned against the wall, muscles tense, ready to explode. He crossed his arms as if he didn't trust himself not to toss her over his knee.

Taggert set about making tea, though he knew that she didn't drink the stuff. The action calmed him, so she kept her protests to herself.

"You've shown you can't be trusted with your own safety." Raven swiveled in her seat at Durant's comment. He opened the fridge, slamming around inside as he wrestled ice cubes free from the freezer. He piled the cubes onto a rag, forming a small mountain of ice.

"I—"

"You will never be alone without a chaperone." He roughly wrapped the towel and came toward her, a number of ice cubes escaping like mice to hide under the recesses of the cupboard. "Even if you have to go to the bathroom, one of us will stand guard by the door."

"That's not necessary." She thought he'd plunk the haphazard icepack in her outstretched hand. Instead, he placed it to her jaw with a gentleness that shouldn't have surprised her. The cold burned against her skin, and she clenched her teeth against revealing any reaction for fear she'd set them off again.

Durant lifted her face to his. "Isn't it? You're in charge of protecting that kid, Aaron. How can you protect him without being here? If something happened to you, everyone in this room would be at risk." He dropped his hand, but kept the icepack against her skin. "Explain to us how it's not necessary."

"Did something happen?" Dread tightened her chest.

His eyes flashed gold at the question. He leaned in closer, his jaw clenched so tightly, she feared he'd hurt himself. "No one could find you."

The kitchen fell silent. Raven searched their uncompromising expressions, and her shoulders slumped. They were in complete agreement. Part of her appreciated their concern, but another part found it stifling. A shiver worked down her spine at the possibility of being caged again. It didn't matter that their prison was made out of concern instead of hate. "You're treating me as a helpless female, not an alpha."

"Then damn well act like one!" The roar echoed in the room.

"Do not pretend like I'm just a shifter. My power gives me an edge. I will not stop working my cases because you fear I might be harmed."

"And I don't expect you to. All we're asking is not to take any chances until after your pack status has been approved by the council."

They weren't going to budge. To make it worse, a small part of her agreed. "Fine."

There was a pause of stunned silence. A contented rumble poured out of Durant now that he'd gotten his way. He angled her head in the light to get a better view of her injury. "Now tell us what happened."

"Two kids decided to have a little fun." Raven shrugged off his hold, ignoring the growl of upset. "My car took the brunt of the attack."

"What did they want?"

"They didn't say. Warning me off the case. What else could it be?"

"Which case?" Aaron opened the door and entered, a casualness to his walk that said he'd made himself at home and wasn't above eavesdropping. Though well into the night, he hadn't changed as if he, too, had been waiting up for her. "The police case or mine? Mother has a habit of hiring rogues to do her dirty work. Were they trying to scare you or kill you?"

Raven wondered that herself. It seemed almost too simple that his mother could be behind both. She was definitely capable of it. She had the ruthlessness for it and access to drugs. But the woman didn't strike her as being smart enough to pull it off without leaving some clue that would lead back her.

Raven kept her suspicions to herself. She needed solid proof first. "They called me Region, so I'm going to say the police case." She didn't mention that if she'd fallen, she had no doubt they wouldn't have stopped their assault until she was dead.

Aaron didn't appear completely convinced, but accepted her answer.

One important fact stopped her from arguing with them more.

If someone was after her, they could've easily gone after her people in order to teach her a lesson. The logic of it terrified her. Shifters were ruthless enough to do it.

Maybe the buddy system wasn't such a bad thing.

She would be able to keep them safe.

"Durant, get back to the club. Since I need to acquire more of a resistance to shifters, we'll be there tonight to absorb the pack atmosphere." The tiger didn't look happy, but didn't refute her.

He silently handed the icepack to Taggert, his golden eyes never leaving hers. He hesitated as if contemplating hocking his precious club and all it had cost him just to stay with her. She couldn't let him risk that for something as stupid as a tiny scratch. "You're hosting the conclave. They need you at the club. Go."

With a scowl, he turned and disappeared out the door.

"Aaron, go back to bed. I'll see you in the morning." He left without another comment, his eyes seeing too much.

Taggert took one look at her then Jackson. He dumped the ice in the sink and left on silent feet.

"And are you going to order me about like a lackey to do your bidding?" There was a snarl on his lips as he said it.

His continual silence since he'd arrived yesterday grated on her nerves, and she couldn't hold back a taunt. "So did you finally grow a backbone?"

His eyes instantly turned yellow, and he leapt toward her. Raven stood her ground and lifted her chin, silently daring him. She missed the old Jackson, not this lifeless soldier.

Only inches separated them when he halted. They just stared at each other, each too afraid to reach out to the other. His scent of fresh cut grass had haunted her.

She'd missed it.

Him.

He inhaled deeply, fighting for control or as eager for the scent of her as she was him. She didn't know which one she hoped for more and wasn't sure she wanted to find out.

She lifted her hand and placed it on his chest, nearly swallowing her tongue as delicious heat backwashed into her. The animals at her core gave a pleasant rumble.

"Don't send me away."

"You left."

"I didn't have any choice. I had to protect you."

"And did protecting me include spilling my secrets to anyone who would listen?"

A dull flush highlighted his cheekbones. "I told them enough to convince them that you could help. Nothing more. Are your secrets worth more to you than Aaron's life?"

His reply doused the last of her anger. He knew her too well and used it against her. She searched his face for a lie. And found none. "You could've asked first."

"Pack never asks another pack for help. It's a sign of weakness. A trade is different."

When he reached for her, she stepped back, not ready to concede yet. She needed answers first. He tensed at the rejection, her words hitting him harder than any blow. "Aaron seems to think he's here because of his mother. Is that the real reason?"

Jackson shook his head. "Only partially. Kevin is worried he won't be able to crest. No one can detect any evidence of his wolf. I explained your theory to the alpha that some shifters have certain abilities. Instead of being born with a defect that could cost him his life, the alpha is hoping that Aaron might have one of these gifts."

"I thought you didn't believe in that nonsense."

"I believe in you." The hoarse comment took her off guard and knocked her on her ass with the pure intensity.

Raven didn't confirm or deny what she'd uncovered about Aaron. The kid had a right to his privacy. If he wanted anyone to know, he would tell them. But it made a sick sort of sense. His gift could be a defense mechanism years in the works to protect him against a mother trying to kill him. "Then I guess we're lucky that the alpha didn't put spying on his son in the agreement."

She ignored the way Jackson's jaw clenched at being shut out. Jackson was the most honorable man she knew, but until his loyalties were decided, she couldn't afford to trust him.

She went to her room, craving to turn around, crawl onto Jackson's lap, and welcome him home the way her wolf urged. But she couldn't give into her emotions and lose him again.

She wasn't sure she was strong enough to let him go a second time without inciting an all-out war.

## ॐ Chapter Eleven ॐ

At seven the next morning, Raven rolled over, and opened her eyes to find Taggert standing next to her bed, a pile of messages in his hand. Groaning, she crammed the pillow over her head.

"Go away." This was his cruel revenge for disappearing on him while he'd slept.

Paperwork.

"Scotts called. You're to report at the station at ten." The bed dipped under his weight as he sat. The heat of him prickled over her skin almost uncomfortably, and she cursed as her beasts woke, eager to feel him up against her. She clenched her eyes shut. If she could just get back to that delicious dream, she wouldn't have to imagine what Taggert's body felt like touching hers.

As if by some silent signal, construction started in the bathroom. She tossed the pillow at the door. "Did you tell them to do that?"

"Durant gave them orders they weren't to begin until you woke." Taggert gave her a devilish smile, telling her that he knew about her dreams and wished to continue the torment. She had thought him innocent when she'd first took him home, now she wondered if he might not be the most devious of them all, slowly and insidiously slipping into her life.

"You're enjoying this." She glared at him.

Taggert grinned again, turning his face from handsome to downright sinful. "My room doesn't have any construction."

Why did that sound like an invitation?

She corralled her emotions and flopped back the covers. Taggert swallowed hard at the shorts and tank top, his eyes glued to her body. The total unexpected reaction for such a tame outfit tickled her.

Enjoying the little payback, she grabbed her clothes and headed down the hall to the guest bathroom. Still amused at Taggert's reaction, Raven hadn't noticed the room was occupied until she'd entered.

Jackson stopped toweling his hair and slowly lowered his arm. The flex and release of his tanned muscles as he finished drying was hypnotizing. The second towel was hooked precariously low on his hips, ready to slide to the floor any second. But she knew he wouldn't let it drop. He would not seduce. He would demand and take. The attraction was made sharper for the fact that neither of them could act on it.

Not while he belonged to someone else.

Maybe never.

She clutched her clothes like a shield, barely managing to scrape her chin off her chest. When she would've taken a step back, Jackson became unstuck.

"Almost done." His voice had a rough growl to it that spread goose bumps over her flesh.

Just watching him increased the burn of desire Taggert had ignited, something no cold shower would be able to fix. She leaned weakly against the wall and waited for him to gather his things.

Instead, he dropped the towel, stopping her breath in her chest. He grabbed his pants, slowly slipping them over his legs one at a time, and she couldn't look away from the muscular flex of his ass. All she had to do was reach out to feel all that warm skin under her hands.

A sharp shock from the wall startled a yelp out of her. She jerked away and rubbed her ass. She'd been so involved watching him, she hadn't noticed she'd been absorbing a charge. By the time she turned, Jackson had his pants fastened, covering all the important bits.

She nearly groaned and wanted to say 'no fair'. He must have guessed her thoughts for he gave a quick grin and raised a brow, silently asking if she wanted him to strip.

Desperation made her blurt out the first thing in her head. "You better go tell Aaron that we're leaving in an hour." She couldn't keep him a prisoner in the house, and what could be safer than a police station?

Jackson's intensity didn't dim after he left, and the promise on his face that this wasn't over kept her blood heated long after he'd disappeared.

\* \* \*

The police station was more active than Raven remembered. Jackson opted to stay outside with less people, while Aaron followed her to Scotts' desk. The kid's ghostly eyes flickered from one spot to the next, taking everything in with more than a casual interest, not missing much, as if he'd never been out of his tower.

Though slim, those shoulders hinted he'd grow into an impressive man. Coupled with a sharp intelligence, he would become an alpha to be reckoned with. He'd managed to escape his mother's machinations, so she didn't doubt he'd use the shifter's slyness to his best advantage. But as he walked before her, the oddness she noticed trailed in his wake like radio static.

"Aaron, what are you doing?" The strangeness instantly stopped.

He gave her a look over his shoulders as if completely unaware of his actions. Or maybe not used to other people being able to detect his unique gift.

"Sit." Scotts walked around them and planted himself behind the desk. The cracked leather chair cried in protest when he settled his heavy frame into the seat. Tobacco and sweat saturated the desk, telling her exactly how much time he spent there.

Aaron took a seat, while she leaned her hip against the desk and waited.

Scotts opened a drawer, slapped a gun, a loaded clip and a badge on his desk, along with cell phone, and then shoved them toward her. "Consider yourself sworn into duty."

Raven made no move to take the gun. The sharp smell of oil and spent gunpowder tainted the weapon. "No, thanks."

Scotts stopped searching his desk and met her gaze. "It's not a request. You have to be armed at all times. If the gun is not on you, it is expected to be in your trunk and within easy reach."

She raised a brow at his lecturing tone. "For one, I'm not sure it's such a bright idea to be carrying during a full moon. Not only will shifters smell the gunpowder, a gun won't kill them unless you have enough ammo to really do some damage. Also, not everything we run across will be the big, bad shifters. Silver bullets help on shifters, but silver and iron would be more effective on other races." She prodded the phone. "And these don't work so well for me."

"I'll requisite silver and iron ammo if we have any, three more clips, but the gun is not optional." Scotts rubbed his fingers between his eyes as if she gave him a headache. "Carry the phone. Your desk is there."

He pointed to the empty place across from his. Ancient and scarred, the desk had seen better days. She poked the heavy metal, half expecting it to rock, surprised when it remained sturdy. The rest of the furniture in the bullpen was in similar condition.

"I thought I would be assigned cases and work the streets. There's no need for a desk. No shifters would come to the precinct for help."

An evil smile crossed his face as he said one succulent word. "Paperwork."

Raven winced at his glee. "Bastard."

"That's 'boss' to you."

She blinked once then smiled. "Congratulations. You're the best guy for the job."

Scotts scanned the files on the desk. "I'm not sure it's much of a promotion." Then he got down to business. "You'll share the desk with other Regions when they're appointed. I expect you to show up at least once a week. When more are hired, you'll each pick a day to man the desk."

The idea of answering calls and being trapped in a room full of humans made her shudder at all the things that could go wrong. "Although shifters function during both day and night, a lot of the other creatures thrive by hiding in the darkness. They won't appreciate anyone ousting them. You might want to keep that in mind when working on schedules. As for the desk, shifters are very territorial and aren't known for sharing."

Scotts rubbed a hand over his scalp, his short, clipped hair undisturbed. "Let's hope the rest of the Regions don't give me as much trouble as you."

She pushed aside his chiding to latch on the unfamiliar word she heard so recently. The same word her attackers used. "Region? Is that our official title?"

He sat back, his old chair groaning in protest. "Regional Paranormal Liaison is a mouthful. The media dubbed the title Region." He held out his hand. "Welcome to the team."

That might explain the name, but not why two teens had targeted her. Raven accepted Scotts' hand, her leather glove protecting him from the static charge that was so much a part of her. He still jumped at her touch, and she suspected he was naturally sensitive to the paranormal.

"Do you have a lot of applicants?"

"I heard they were flooded, but only a small amount has survived the vetting. Less than one in a hundred. No one else has been voted through." He still seemed miffed that he didn't know who her sponsors were.

She couldn't help but agree. She didn't like knowing that there was some unknown benefactor out there. She suspected they hadn't helped her out of the goodness of their hearts.

"Tell me what you've found out on the case." Scotts' eyes sharpened as he asked the question, all the pleasantries over.

"I reviewed the video. It's like you said. Nothing."

Scotts shuffled through his stack of papers, pulled out a couple of files and tossed them to her. "They couldn't confirm what killed them, but your theory fits."

"Shifters gather during the full moon." Raven nudged the edge of the folders. "So the next few days are the perfect opportunity to hit them hard.

"The plan is ingenious. Just infect one shifter, and he'll go home to his pack. You take out the alpha, and you could potentially destroy the foundation of the pack. Until a new leader can be selected, shifters will be dangerous as they fight for status.

"Now multiply that by ten and imagine the chaos. Hundreds of shifters will run free with no one to keep them in check as they duke it out."

Aaron twitched in his seat, obviously uncomfortable with all the information she was sharing. She ignored him. What did the paranormals expect would happen when they voted in the Regions?

Lines bracketed Scotts' mouth. "And humans will be caught in the crossfire."

It stung that he accepted and dismissed the death of so many shifters, the destruction of such a fundamental way of life for them, and compared that to the loss of a few *normals* that might or might not be affected. "More than likely."

"Then why kill these two shifters now?"

"Practice?" Raven shook her head. "This is all guessing."

"Do you have any suspects?"

Aaron cleared his throat. "It could be anyone. An alpha thinking to get rid of his rivals, rogues who detest their bottom-rung status, slaves who live so precariously between worlds, vampires who want shifters to revert back to servants again, or even magic users who want to reduce the animals to nothing more than familiars. Let's not discount the humans determined to kill all the monsters. The list is endless."

Raven blinked in surprise, but she shouldn't be. Shifters were predators. They were trained to always be aware of all possible threats.

They fell silent at the daunting task of finding the killers before the full moon when shifters were at their most vulnerable. Raven grabbed the reports, determined to dig deeper.

She'd been contained in the labs during the first war ten years ago. Now war was coming to her, and she'd be dammed if she allowed anyone to steal what was hers before she even had a chance to claim them.

"Don't forget these." Scotts tapped his desk.

Raven curled her lips at the gun and phone. "A suggestion?"

"Can I stop you?"

She gave a tight smile. "Give the Regions Tasers or stun guns. They'd be more effective against shifters than a gun. The only drawback is that the voltage would have to be turned up a few notches, but not so high that a shifter might be forced to change."

Police had a right to use deadly force if confronted by an animal without a harness and tags. They were considered deadly weapons. "It would keep your officers safer than a gun as bullets would only enrage shifters into attacking."

Scotts didn't outright deny her. She'd take that as a small victory.

"I'll consider it, but for now, take the damn gun."

Raven reluctantly shoved the clip home and strapped the gun to her waist. The bulk settled awkwardly at her hip. The phone slipped easily in her back pocket, but she didn't hold out much hope it would survive the trip home.

"Here." She grabbed Scotts' files and shoved them at Aaron. "Let's bail."

Aaron obediently grabbed the papers and rose. Instead of his normal loose limbered gait, his shoulders were stiff as he dutifully followed her. "You told them too much."

"All Regions will be paranormal. I didn't say anything they wouldn't already have known." She gave him a side look as they wound their way through the maze of desks.

"These Regions will have a hard enough role to face, their job made more dangerous without someone to watch their backs. I shared as little information I could in order to protect them."

Aaron shook his head. "You sound so idealistic, but what are the chances that it will turn out that way?"

"I would say the same percentage of good and bad cops." They rounded the front counter when a prisoner, cuffed to the floor waiting for booking, lazily lifted his head. Raven's steps slowed, apprehension thickening the air as their gazes clashed.

Matted hair clung to his scalp. Dirt was caked to every surface of him as if he were allergic to water. Those eyes of his flashed when they locked on her then darkened with rage. He flexed and the chains binding him snapped like dental floss. In a smooth move only a shifter could duplicate, he sailed out of his chair and charged them with a roar so loud that the primal sound resonated in her chest.

## ❧ Chapter Twelve ☙

**D**ressed haphazardly in a weathered military jacket, the filthy man shot toward them with amazing speed. The odor of offal and vomit crashed into Raven first, the strength of it making her flinch. Shouts sounded, officers reached for their weapons, but no one would get there in time.

Raven turned and shoved Aaron behind the desk partition. That twang of discord around him increased and rubbed the inside of her skull raw like sandpaper. "Stay here."

Then there was no more time to do anything else.

The impact of a body launched her into the wall. Her spine cracked, her head slammed into the drywall hard enough that her vision blurred for a few panicked seconds. Her feet barely touched the ground then he was on her. Fetid breath clouded the air around her, stinging her eyes with its potency.

She twisted away from one fist, only to receive a blow to her ribs with the other. His fist, like lead pipes, cracked into her, and she lost the ability to breathe. But instead of dropping her like he'd intended, she snagged the edges of his jacket and refused to let go.

No way in hell would she allow anyone else to get hurt because she couldn't fight her own battles. She never expected anyone to physically confront her inside the police station. She only had her own stupidity to blame for letting down her guard. She'd been so confident, cocky that no one would attack them, that she'd become lax.

A police officer snaked his arm around the were's throat and received a head-butt for his trouble that knocked him out cold. Another officer quickly darted forward and dragged him to safety.

Using the distraction, Raven dipped into the pool of electricity that churned at her core, and slammed her palm against his chest.

The shifter's eyes widened as he stumbled backward. His arms windmilled to remain upright.

She'd shoved enough current into him to cook a human's heart to a dried lump of coal. As a shifter, the very least he should've been rolling on the floor in pain. All it gave him was a bad case of heartburn and pissed him off.

Damn indestructible shifter.

"Freeze." More officers piled into the cramped entrance, weapons drawn. No one took aim. They couldn't. They didn't have a clear shot.

Neon green eyes assessed her, ignoring the humans around them as of no importance. That's when she knew.

Rogue.

And he meant to kill her.

The discord around her increased, and Raven automatically glanced at Aaron, fear for his safety paramount.

The shifter followed her gaze. A satisfied smile kicked up his lips when his eyes lit on the boy.

The rogue bared his teeth.

Heat flashed through the room.

Then nothing.

He failed to turn furry.

Then she knew Aaron was doing something to prevent the change. The rogue figured it out at the same time. Those big hams at the end of the shifter's arms fisted. Another hit would cave in her ribs. She tensed for the attack, determined to just be faster.

Jackson burst through the doors at that moment. The police tried to hold the line, but he charged through and tossed himself at her attacker. The prisoner whirled to face the new threat, and both men smacked to the floor hard enough that the impact reverberated up her legs.

They twisted, struggling to gain control. Snarls echoed in the small space, the sounds vicious.

Jackson received a blow to his balls that loosened his hold, and the slippery man came at her on all fours.

"Use Tasers," Raven shouted to the officers as they watched the display.

One police officer was ready, and the snap of electricity sizzled as wires zipped through the air. The shifter jerked and batted at the cords like they were annoying bugs.

"Again."

Two more police officers reacted, and the unkempt man snarled as the darts hit true. He grabbed the live wires, the voltage nothing to him, and ripped out the cords without flinching.

Then Jackson kicked the man's legs out from underneath, preventing his advance. The rogue turned and slammed his elbow at Jackson's throat with enough strength to crush his windpipe.

Jackson barely blocked the blow in time. Raven was afraid to interfere. No way would she ever be able to win in a physical fight. It would be a quick way to get them both killed.

"Raven!"

Scotts tossed her a stun gun. The cool plastic stung her palm on impact. She pressed the button, enjoying the lovely blue and white sparks that crackled between the prongs.

But it wasn't enough.

The bastard was too strong.

Despite the fear of discovery, she allowed the power under her skin to gather. Jackson and the rogue quickly exchanged blows, the hits landing harder, doing more damage.

They wouldn't last much longer.

She had no more time to wait. The current she'd gathered had to be enough. She took a running start with no sort of plan in mind other than to save Jackson.

When she drew closer, she dropped to her knees and slid across the floor. She raised her arm, the stun gun firmly in her grip. The prongs landed on the corded muscles of the rogue's neck, and she took great pleasure in holding down the button.

The stream of electricity called her own, and they blended together seamlessly, her current amplifying the charge.

A gurgle emerged from his throat, those claws he called hands went for her neck. She felt a tiny prick of pain on her skin where he touched her when his body suddenly went lax.

That had been too close.

She only let up when his eyes rolled up in his head, and his body collapsed.

Now that the threat had been neutralized, her powers calmed as if satisfied. Carefully skirting his still form, Raven crawled toward Jackson. "You okay?"

"I've been better. You?"

Raven probed her ribs then grunted. "Bruised, not broken."

Scotts reached down, offering her his hand. She hesitated a second with a thought of what her power could do to him then took the proffered hand.

Nothing happened.

One on her feet, she closed her eyes in silent thanks, and then held up the stun gun. The prongs were tarnished, hot to the touch. She offered it to him with a shrug. "Sorry."

Scotts shook his head, shoving another toward her. "Your team will have their Tasers." Then he strode off to monitor the process of locking up the prisoner in the cages housed below the police station created to hold shifters.

Feeling self-conscious at being the center of attention and getting her ass handed to her in public, she ignored the gawking. "Call me when you interview him. I want to be there."

She needed to know why they were targeting her, why they wanted to kill her. Part of her wondered if they knew about her past, but dismissed it. Dominic had assured her that all the files from the labs had been destroyed.

All she received in acknowledgement from Scotts was wave that she took as agreement. His broad back disappeared out of the room, barking orders after the six officers it took to carry the now unconscious shifter.

Though some of the officers looked grateful not to deal with the shifters, others appeared resentful that they just couldn't up and shoot every last one of them.

Aaron drew closer, his face pale, his eyes never leaving hers. Fear and resignation drained him of his normal animation. The static around him was gone, vanished as if she'd imagined it.

But she knew she hadn't.

He'd managed to block their attacker from shifting somehow. Now that the threat was over, the animals she carried beneath her skin were back, acting almost fearful of the young man. They clung close to the surface, their fur brushing comfortingly against her, but otherwise remained silent.

"Ready to blow this joint?" She kept her tone light, half-fearing that Aaron might bolt if she gave him a chance. It was only when they arrived home that she spoke again. "Aaron, I want to see you in the study, please."

He acted like she were dragging him to the gallows, tugging at his collar as if a noose was already around his neck. When Jackson made to follow, she grabbed the doorknob and placed her hand on the frame to bar his way. "Not you." She wrinkled her nose at the smell that seemed to have transferred from the prisoner to him. "You need a shower."

No matter how much she wished she could stop it, her mind immediately flashed to earlier this morning.

Him.

Naked.

He must have read her expression, smiling a dangerous grin that lit a fire deep in her gut.

The animals woke with a vengeance, very much wanting to touch what was blatantly being offered. She licked her lips at the temptation then took the only defense she could.

She slammed the door in his face, wondering when her sanity had abandoned her. She thunked her head against the door, but she could still see the flames of lust in his eyes. "And tell Griffin I need to speak with him."

Sanity slowly seeped back into her body as his scent faded, but not without taking its pound of flesh as it sank into her bones with a heaviness that hurt.

When she turned, she drew up short. Aaron stood ramrod straight in the middle of the room, his hands behind his back in military precision, every inch a future alpha. Stillness wrapped around him.

And such loneliness her heart clenched in sympathy.

"What are you going to do?"

Raven stood in front of him, surprised to find herself peering up at his face. His hair no longer stood in spikes, resting limp against his head as if the starch had been taken out of him.

If she concentrated, the hum around him remained. Not as strong. Not as obvious. "About what? The attack?" She waited a heartbeat for his reaction. "Or your knack to null others ability to shift?"

Those husky pale eyes flickered to her before they went back to surveying the wall. His voice lacked any inflection, but the acidic smell around him sharpened suddenly. "I don't understand."

"Then let me make it clear. What you do is your business unless it affects my pack. I'm your bodyguard, not your jailor. I think we've both had enough of being locked away. As long as I keep you alive, I've fulfilled my part of the bargain. Understand?"

Even before she finished, his gaze landed on hers and stayed. "You really mean that, don't you?" He was talking more to himself than her. The sharp smell of worry that clung to him slowly lightened.

"My main concern was how did they know we were going to be at the police station? We weren't followed."

The boy's military pose eased, and she hadn't realized how tense he always held himself. "I didn't recognize the man. His scent was so offensive, I'm not able to place him. It also makes it impossible to track him back to his pack. It's a common practice for hired assassins." He rubbed his hand over the back of his neck, exhaustion placing dark shadows in his eyes. "This isn't the first attack made on me over the past few weeks."

"Your mother." Most people would be shocked a parent would kill their offspring, but it happened often in the wilderness. Even Raven's own mother sold her to the labs as a toddler. The painful truth behind her mother's abandonment still stung.

Aaron's arms came down to his sides, his posture relaxing more as if sensing the danger had passed. "I'm strong enough to threaten her reign. In a matter of days, I'll be asked to pledge myself to the pack. If I challenged for leadership and won, she wouldn't be the leader of a pack anymore. I would be allowed to choose my own mate."

"And she's not the type of person to give up something that's hers." Raven remembered the blatant display of ownership, the brutal mark Vivian took pleasure in delivering to her mates face. Vivian obviously saw her more of an obstacle than a threat.

"Is she aware of your gift?"

"She suspects something. If she knew, she would've used me as a weapon."

A normal alpha could help others in the pack shift, could force a shift. Others had the ability to stop a shifter from turning, but only in pack mates. None she knew of could cut off their animals so completely like Aaron.

"You are starting to understand my predicament."

Raven did understand, everything but one important fact. "But why come to me?"

"Father's done everything he can to protect me, but he can't take any overt action against Vivian. Other packs would see it as a weakness. My mother is too strong. If they fought, she would see him dead, somehow, someway when he couldn't protect himself. The pack needs him too much to risk it over me. Any protection he could provide from inside the pack would keep dying. The closer the conclave draws, the more desperate her attempts have become."

Raven closed her eyes, feeling stupid for not seeing it sooner. "So if she comes for you herself, I'm the only thing standing in her way. Another female alpha can kill without the worry of immediate extermination. You're using me."

He shrugged as if her death were of no consequence. "You accepted the deal. You're getting what you want in return. Besides, you're the only other alpha that might be able to win. We're just hoping it doesn't come to that."

Her shield pulsed in reaction to her emotions, increasing in intensity until the kid shuffled his feet. "Does Jackson know?"

Aaron shook his head. "No one would ever think to kill a female. Whatever he told you for the reason of me being here is the truth as far as he knows it."

Raven reluctantly stepped back, her fingers curling into fists as she resisted the need to use the energy sizzling under her skin. It bit at her, angry at being denied. She was coming to hate the convoluted pack politics and all their hidden agendas.

"You're different than I expected." He paused a moment, appearing stumped by her. "Genuine."

A harsh knock sounded on the door a second before it popped open. "I didn't realize you were busy." Griffin acted all innocent, but she had no doubt he'd been listening at the door for some time. How much had he heard?

"Liar, but come in anyway." Raven nodded to Aaron, secretly pleased when he returned the gesture so seriously before he left.

He would make one hell of an alpha with that type of power and control. She didn't know if she should be fearful or not.

As he left, the calm surrounding her all day vanished with him, and she'd realized he'd kept her sane. She'd thought she'd been gaining control over the moon's touch but it'd been him all along. The possibility of his gift boggled her mind.

No one could ever know or they would either enslave or kill him outright.

"I see you've made another conquest." Griffin watched Aaron's departure with interest. When she would've spoken, he lifted his arrogant chin. "You've summoned me?"

"With the increase of moon heat comes the need to have sex. How does the council monitor the packs?"

Griffin snorted then gave a tired sigh. "You're so innocent in the shifter world, they'll gobble you up." He rubbed the back of his neck. "If it's just sex, you only need your alpha's permission. If you're not a breeder for your pack, you're free and clear."

"And alphas?" Heat built under her skin.

"Females are required to mate. You can choose your own lovers, your own mates even, but since you are an alpha, you'll need permission from the council to take a Consort."

"And if an alpha doesn't give permission?"

"Then punishment is meted out. If the female isn't from the same pack, they could also end up paying a hefty fine in retaliation."

"Jackson mentioned I need to show proof of ownership for Taggert. What should I expect?"

Griffin smiled, openly amused for the first time. "You might want to consider petitioning for pack position first, then go back and fulfill your claim to Taggert. It will give you better leverage."

She acknowledged his words, but wouldn't be deterred. "And what can I expect?"

Those calculating eyes surveyed her, trying to read something. "Not to worry on that account. Since you are a rare alpha female, not to mention single, you will only be tested if you're challenged."

For some reason, his words didn't reassure her. "You have no clue what tests I'll have to pass." She tightened her lips, reaching for the gun at her waist and unclipping it. Opening a desk drawer, she let it drop inside, glad to have the weight gone. The stun gun followed. Her hand hovered over the badge before she set it and the clips down as well. She slammed the drawer shut then locked it, all the while never taking her gaze from his.

"The test is unique in each situation, tailored to the petitioner."

Raven hated the way he dodged the questions, brushing her concerns aside as if they didn't matter. "Then if you don't want to talk about the conclave, why don't we discuss about what you're doing in my house. We both know you are well able to take care of yourself without my protection."

Silence filled the room.

"Why don't we start with where you disappear to each night?"

## ❧ Chapter Thirteen ❦

**FOUR DAYS UNTIL THE FULL MOON: MIDNIGHT**

Hours later, annoyance still flickered through Raven the way Griffin had so craftily wiggled out of providing her any answers. Those green and yellow eyes of his had dilated slightly at her inquiries, but dammed if he hadn't managed to dodge her probes. She didn't toss him out on his ass like she probably should. He was too dangerous on his own. She would rather keep an eye on him than be blindsided later.

There was an edge to the night that warned of danger. Even with Jackson and Taggert in tow, walking toward the club left her feeling exposed.

She was being watched.

Again.

She could ignore the innocent curiosity. It was the cowards hiding in the shadows that were beginning to annoy the crap out of her.

In preparation for the visit, she'd shut down her shields to a tiny trickle. Pressure built up in her chest, the need to scratch off her skin to relieve the ache intensified as she drew closer to the club. She scanned her surroundings, but without her full senses, she couldn't even pry sounds out of the shadows.

Tension ratcheted up a couple of notches until the cool night air became stifling. She had demanded this visit. She must put aside her unease to make this work.

This was her last chance.

If she couldn't cut being around the shifters tonight, she'd fail in front of the conclave and lose everything that'd become so very important.

Raven allowed Taggert to lead the way as they entered the club, his leather pants so formfitting every muscle could be ogled at will. The black silk shirt caressed his body, all but begging for her hands to explorer.

He tossed a smile over his shoulder, confident he'd find her gawking.

And the bastard was right.

"Here." Jackson grabbed her arm, directing her to the table Durant had reserved for them. His touch drew her attention, and she glanced at his face.

Tension held him rigid, lines bracketed his mouth as he surveyed the crowd, but she had no doubt his annoyance was directed straight at her.

"Relax. Nothing's going to happen."

Jackson cast her a shuttered look, and it maddened her that she couldn't read him. All the walls between them were back. After their last conversation, his withdrawal left her bereft. Then he relented and gestured to the crowd with a small nod. "What do you see?"

The first glance revealed nothing out of the ordinary. If not for the damn moon heat, she'd swear it was like any rowdy club across America.

Then she noticed subtle differences. The males were more aggressive with other males. The women fewer and more protected. The excitement and lust sharpened to an almost frantic degree.

Not only were there more people in the club, the amount of bouncers had doubled. The clothes were skimpy, what little clothes there were, anyway. Raven's boots, long sleeve shirt and gloves felt downright matronly.

Anticipation infected the air. People brushed up against each other in complete abandon as they danced.

Other paranormals were there as well, but they appeared to be observing, plotting in preparation for the coming days. The atmosphere last week had been polar opposite. "Everything is harsher, the violence almost physical, as if brewing."

Then there were the stares that tracked her every movement.

"It's their beasts. They're hunting for a mate. The younger the shifter, the harder it is to control their baser needs. The older the shifter, the more desperate they are to find their mate." The words were bland as if they were nothing out of the ordinary.

"But that doesn't explain why it's so much worse tonight."

Jackson sent her a sharp look, his eyes splintering to yellow. "Being in the same room as an alpha can take off the edge of the moon. When these young ones are left to their own devices, their animal rises. You are probably the only alpha here tonight."

The rough quality of his voice had her breath catching at the back of her throat.

Jackson felt the connection between them, too.

Only he hid it better.

"With no clue how to help them." But maybe she could help Jackson.

Wishing to ease him, she grabbed his arm and pulled him to sit next to her. Muscles jumped at the contact, and she swore that he growled. Unable to help herself, she petted his arm. An unfamiliar current hummed under her skin, trailing over him with every caress. His wolf rose beneath the surface, sniffing to pick up her scent.

The animalistic sound that rumbled from his chest halted her movement. She didn't look up at him, half-afraid what she'd find. Taggert took that moment to sit opposite them. "The drinks are on the way."

Then he slowly slid around the booth until he was pressed against her other side. The heat of their bodies seeped into hers, and the desperate need that wrapped around them slowly eased to a manageable hunger.

"Here you go." Cassie had their drinks on the table before their seats were warm, a tight smile on her face. Taggert and she shared a look that had Raven opening her mouth to ask what was wrong when Taggert spoke.

"Dance with me." He threaded his fingers with hers and skillfully withdrew her hand from Jackson.

Only when she was on the dance floor did he take a deep breath, dragging her up against him. Her body came alive with the desire to touch him back, give herself over to the mood of the club, and she groaned in complaint. "Taggert—"

"Now isn't the time to distract Jackson."

She peeked over Taggert's shoulder. Jackson's hungry eyes devoured her, and she quickly jerked her gaze away. "I was trying to help. It worked with you and Durant."

"Because we're pack. Your touch impacts us differently than it does him." Before she realized his intent, Taggert yanked the clip out of her hair. The strands tumbled around her shoulders, and his eyes darkened as he stared at the silvery tips that shimmered in the limited light.

Ignoring his shenanigans, Raven concentrated on her latest blunder. She could just kick herself. "I didn't know. What did I do?"

The smile that lit Taggert's face did little to soothe her. "I'd say you just made yourself a target for one very determined wolf. And you know how they love to stalk their prey."

"Shit."

Taggert laughed, seemingly undisturbed. He drew her closer, moving them to the beat of the music. His body flowed around hers, making her feel inept and very much worshiped by his. Each light brush of his body lured her closer.

"You don't appear worried."

Teeth flashed as he smiled. "You'll make him pack."

"You seem awful sure."

"You claimed him when you first met him. You just didn't get around to sealing the deal." Taggert grabbed her hips, directing her with the music, pulling her snug against him. Their bodies moved in a rhythm that made her muscles turn to mush. "You like him too much to let him go."

The dance floor grew crowded, the air around them warmer. He stood a good four inches or more above her. His lips hovered over hers, and she curbed the irrational need to taste him.

"Do it."

She blinked, dazed by the heavy pounding of the music, the flashing lights, and the delicious tang of his lust as it swamped the air around him. "What?"

"Taste." He cupped the back of her head, drawing her inexplicitly closer until his body covered hers.

She found his leg pressed between her thighs, the movement of his hips heating her blood to boiling. Her lips feathered against his throat, and she inhaled deeply, enjoying the smell of forest. She licked her lips, accidentally brushing against his neck. He shuddered. A low groan vibrated in his throat, and he tipped his head to give her better access.

The slave collar gleamed, a reminder that he wasn't free. When she would've drawn back, he quickly distracted her.

His hips moved in time to the beat, and the need for more contact nearly drowned her under the onslaught. His hair was tied neatly at the back of his neck, the highlighted strands capturing the light.

Urging her to touch.

The angles of his face appeared harsh in his restraint. That he left her in control to do whatever she wanted only increased her need to ruffle him a little more and take what he so unabashedly offered.

That they were in public didn't matter.

"Do it again."

Raven lifted her chin at his plea, unaware she'd shuffled closer until her breasts rubbed against the muscular wall of his chest. His hands settle on her ass, seducing her, until they were both balanced on the delicious edge of what could be if she just stopped resisting.

She licked his neck again, enjoying the way his breath caught. Then she nibbled on his neck, her teeth nipping lightly at his tender skin. His pulse thundered under her lips, the power of his blood calling to her. His arms turned to bands around her, squeezing the air out of her.

Not that she minded.

She inched her hands down his back, enjoying the flex of his muscles under her palms, the way he shuffled her closer in invitation to take more.

Then he was ripped from her arms.

Jackson's hand settled on her elbow, his grip bruising, though she didn't think he was aware of it, and dragged her toward the table.

"What the hell do you think you're doing?"

Raven had to clear her throat twice before she could speak. "Dancing?"

In truth, she hadn't been thinking at all.

Jackson plunked her down in the seat then all but sat on her. "You are supposed to be here to find control."

Taggert took a seat across from her, the heat in his eyes a promise. When he reached across the table to tangle his fingers with hers, Jackson growled and pulled her hands out of reach Then refused to relinquish his hold as if Taggert would try to steal her from him. He leaned down until his lips brushed against her ear. "You are the alpha. Isn't it time you start acting like it?"

The reprimand smarted, all the more so because it was true. When dancing, she lost all thought of time and place. Sanity slowly trickled back, and some of the unrelenting heat washed out of her. Embarrassment stung her cheeks at the public display of what should've been an intimate moment between her and Taggert.

"Jackson, you're being an ass." Taggert's sexy smile had vanished. "She showed more restraint out there then most everyone else."

A muscle ticked in Jackson's jaw. "And you're not helping matters."

"Stop it." Their bickering would be comical if their attitude didn't annoy her so much.

Raven tugged her hand away from Jackson, but he refused to release her. A comical tug-of-war ensured before she conceded defeat. The way he brushed his thumb across her skin matched the intensity of Taggert's seduction on the dance floor. "How am I supposed to act when no one tells me shit?"

She scanned the club, taken aback to find so many hungry eyes locked on her table. At least they were keeping their distance.

For now.

"How about not making a target of yourself." Jackson grunted, and Raven suspected that Taggert had kicked him under the table.

"I can't hide myself away like a scared little mouse. That will only make me a bigger target." She shifted, trying to put some distance between them, only to have him follow. His hold tightened as if he felt her slipping away from him and couldn't stop it.

"Ease up before you break something." Jackson's hold on her fingers vanished, a faint color staining his cheeks. In a perverse way, now that he released her hand, she missed his touch. Instead of moving away, she let herself relax against him slightly.

He stiffened, not looking at her, but some of the tension drained from him as he scanned the crowd. Taggert nudged her foot with his, his knee coming to rest against hers, and shot her a content smile.

She shook her head at their actions and took a sip of her drink. As the night grew late, the atmosphere became more graphic, the mood darker and full of latent need. People vanished in the shadows or behind the curtains with their partners, and she turned away, feeling like a prude.

Others weren't so shy, all but performing for an audience. Then she realized she probably wasn't far off the mark. Their display was no worse than what she and Taggert had done on the dance floor.

With Taggert and Jackson both touching her, the frantic need surrounding the shifters didn't penetrate their shield. She allowed herself to relax and enjoy their company.

It wouldn't last, though.

She had to find a way to survive without their help.

As she finished her third drink, she stood. Both Taggert and Jackson rose as well. Humor tinged her words. "I'm just going to go to the restroom. I think I can find it by myself."

She slipped into the bathroom, grateful for a few minutes alone. She finished quickly then went to the sink to splash water on her face. It did little to cure the rising temperature from the club. By herself for the first time in hours, she closed her eyes and luxuriated in the peace.

The animals seemed content to be around others like themselves, with nary a peep from them. Even the electricity she carried was docile, which she couldn't help but be more than a little suspicious. Either the creature kept it occupied or vice versa. Neither scenario was comforting. Delaying as long as she could, Raven headed toward the door.

The hallway was shadowed, the light above the door too dim to penetrate the gloom.

Something about the darkness kicked her senses into overdrive.

Something was waiting for her.

She sent a light pulse through the air, aiming it at the inky blackness. When her power hit a target, someone sucked in a harsh breath.

Shifter.

Male.

She couldn't tell more without probing deeper and risking discovery.

Reaching into her pocket, she fingered the stun gun and stepped out into the hall. Instead of fear, the need to hunt urged her forward. Her eyes adjusted, and she saw the shadow shift.

By the time she pulled her stun gun free, he knocked it out of her hand and was on her. She found herself pinned face first against the wall, a hot shifter pressed against her back.

"More bombings are coming."

Raven ceased struggling. His hold didn't hurt, but her animals didn't care to be imprisoned. It was all she could do not to fight free. She needed answers more. "Where? When?"

"Your boy, Griffin, knows more than he's saying. You should ask him." His control wavered. Fear curdled the air around him for daring to approach, much less lay hands on her.

Wildness spilled over her body like a splash of cold water. He was a rogue. At the knowledge, things fell into place. "You followed me here to warn me. Let me help you."

His breath fanned her neck, a slight hesitation, as if he hadn't expected her offer. When leaned in closer, she braced to feel fangs pierce her shoulder. Instead, she felt a brief caress of his tongue, almost paying homage...or giving a pledge.

Then he was gone.

Raven whirled, but the hallway was empty. She inhaled, catching an elusive dark scent. Then it, too, vanished. She scooped up the stun gun and pushed out into the crowd, anxious to find any sign of him.

He could be the big break they needed on the case.

But she could detected nothing above the overpowering smell of shifters and sex.

After a few minutes of cat and mouse, she conceded defeat. She'd wandered further away from the table and Durant's office than wise. A hint of unease snuck up on her. She wove her way through the throng of people, taking care not to brush against anyone.

Too bad the touchy-feely shifters didn't take the hint. After the third *accidental* touch, frustration reared its head. The electricity around the club swept toward her, filling her core as if knowing she needed protection.

An insidious taint of panic slithering through her.

She couldn't lose control.

Not here.

Not now.

She coaxed the animals that normally prowled around her core to wake.

Nothing.

Not even a brush of fur.

Damn contrary beasts.

As the current grew, she hastily built her shields. Each time a shifter drew near, they bowed but held.

"You." She pointed toward a heavy built shifter, and one who happened to be reaching to touch her upper arm. The young male gave a start of surprise, his impressionable brown eyes flashing up toward hers. "See me to my table."

The dark-haired shifter lifted a brow then smiled in delight. That smile faded when his gaze moved past her. All the shifters in the area took a giant step back.

"How sweet, choosing a puppy to be your knight in shining armor to rescue you from us scary shifters." A bubble of caustic laughter filled the air, eating away the good cheer of the shifters around her.

Raven turned slowly, pasting a smile on her face and acted like everything was normal. She skimmed the entourage behind the woman, assessing the threat. "Hello, Vivian. I see you have your six-pack of goons to protect you from us little people."

The smug smile tightened at the insult. Vivian leaned closer and inhaled, tasting the air. "Your fear smells delicious."

Raven mimicked Vivian, crowding closer until the woman was practically leaning backwards to prevent them from breathing the same air. "Then you might want to get out more often. That's not fear you smell." She lied through her teeth, betting that Vivian couldn't scent shit from her. She'd practiced too hard to cover her scent in the labs. Even with her current fighting her, it wasn't something her body would forget.

A flicker of doubt entered Vivian's eyes, and Raven pressed her point home. "You haven't asked about your son." Raven tsked. "It's a shame that a mother can't guarantee her own son's welfare. But don't worry, he's safe with me."

Vivian's eyes narrowed, rage darkening the brown to nearly black. The smile she returned was all teeth. "What can I say? We hire the best." The woman crossed her arms, her barely there black dress pushed what was intended to be elegant into slutty.

Gaudy jewelry practically dripped off her. She was on the prowl.

"How is my son?" She glanced around, searching for him. "I hope he hasn't caused you too much trouble. The second you leave the boy alone, he gets into fights."

Malicious intent hung in the air. Vivian didn't expect her son to return.

Ever.

Unease burned the back of her throat. Could Vivian have sent men to her home? The energy ratcheted higher, the calming pool of her core now a raging storm that threatened to consume everyone in its path.

"Really? He's been an angel since he's been with us. He must have just needed a change of setting to feel at home." Raven spied Durant calmly walking through the crowd as if the people around him didn't exist. The paranormals scampered out of his way without a protest, and Raven breathed easier when he came to stand at her side.

"Is there a problem?" Durant asked Vivian, but Raven could tell the question was directed at her. He probed her battered shields, his touch like static.

"Everything is wonderful now that you're here, handsome. Why don't you escort me to my table?" Charm oozed from Vivian's pours. She looped her hand around Durant's elbow, the action crushing her breasts up against his arm.

Sexual tension vibrated in the air, and Raven knew the bitch was trying to influence Durant with more than just her body. Alphas were able to control lesser shifters, the talent usually limited to their own pack. She suspected that this was Vivian's gift, and likely how she managed to snag Kevin and get her way so often.

Raven detested the way her heart sped up at the contact between them. It was none of her concern whom Durant dated. She waited for his response, nearly ready to kick him the way his eyes trailed down the blonde's boney frame.

Jackson and Taggert stood, sensing the brewing trouble.

When those talons Vivian called nails came to rest on Durant's chest, Raven snapped. She allowed her power to slam into him, pleased at way he grunted at the impact. Vivian instantly stepped back, holding her hand as if singed.

Satisfied she'd proven her point, Raven withdrew her power. But Durant was having none of it. What started as a threat, turned into a caress as his cat bumped his big head up against her.

Those golden eyes of Durant's lifted, zeroing in on her. What caught her was the lust and playfulness in their depths. It dawned on her then that he'd been messing with her. Furious that he would play games, she was half-tempted to turn and leave.

The only thing that stopped her was the reminder that she was his alpha. She was supposed to protect him.

"Hands off." Raven turned to face Vivian. "He's not available for stud."

Vivian's calculating expression hardened. She smiled with sharp teeth, gazing beyond them both. "Then I'll just have to find someone else to occupy me."

Raven stiffened, not having to turn to know where her gaze fell.

Vivian sauntered around them, her attitude all smug. She cuddled up to Jackson's chest. She reached up, one hand resting at the side of his neck. They looked comfortable, that was if you ignored how her nails pierced flesh and the trickle of blood soaking the collar of his shirt.

Jackson didn't display any reaction, and Raven was horrified to realize it was probably not the first time he heard the command.

Repugnance that a shifter was left with no choice curled her lips. That they would compel others in such an intimate act.

Vivian must have seen the disgust, Raven made no attempt to hide it, and her eyes darkened with outrage.

"You're right, Vivian. Jackson's not my pack. But he is on a job appointed by his alpha. One he has neglected far too long." Raven gave an indifferent shrug. "You will excuse us. We must be going."

## ॐ Chapter Fourteen ॐ

The ride home was interminable, the awkward silences a suffocating presence in the car. Taggert sat in the backseat, Jackson next to her in the passenger seat after she'd wrestled the keys from him. Though she didn't look at either, their focus never once left her.

Durant followed them in his own car, never letting more than three lengths between them. As she hit the country road, the lights from the city faded, the moon a big globe in the sky.

The rays brushed against her like a warm caress until her skin tightened. She stretched, bones snapped, and she tried to settle back into her body.

It didn't work.

Her skin tingled with the ache to touch and be touched. She did her best to contain it, gripping the steering wheel to prevent herself from reaching for either man. She drove up to her house faster than necessary.

Tires skidded over rocks as she stopped and killed the car. Without waiting for anyone to speak, Raven bolted toward the house. A shadow parted from around the corner, darting toward her. She twisted and crouched, part of her spoiling for a fight.

Dominic, in his wolf form, stepped into the light. Disappointment struck, leaving all her pend up frustration over the evening to churned in her chest, locked behind clenched teeth. With a sigh, she straightened and reluctantly opened the door. The wolf darted into the house, but Raven hesitated, her throat tightening at the thought of being confined.

She shook off the feeling and swallowed hard. This was her home.

So why was it so difficult to step across the threshold?

The three men lingered outside as if sensing her volatile mood.

Hovering.

Plotting.

As she reached the top of the stairs, she heard the door open behind her. Raven turned, uncertain if she wanted to find out what they'd decided. All three men lifted their gaze toward her, each knowing where she stood without having to search.

"Don't." She didn't need more lectures.

She knew she screwed up.

"Raven—"

"No, Durant. Enough of this moon called bullshit. I did things your way. It didn't work."

"How about we try things your way, then?" Taggert placed one foot at the bottom of the stairs and peered up at her with soft, chocolate eyes so filled with compassion that her throat ached.

"And what way is that?" Raven crossed her arms protectively in front of her, refusing to apologize for the little flinch her words caused.

"You're not used to the shifter lifestyle, so why don't we give the human way a try?"

Nonplused at the proposal, Raven just blankly stared at them. She must have misunderstood. "What?"

Durant unbuttoned his cuffs, never once looking away from her. "He means that there are three days until the full moon. On each of those days, one of us will escort you—"

"I don't need a bodyguard."

Durant didn't smile, didn't do anything but waited for her to quiet. "One of us will escort you around for the day. We'll use that time to get to know each other."

"Like a date?" The last word emerged as a croak. She both craved and feared what they were offering. She hated the desire growing between them.

She wanted it to be her choice.

And despite what her mind thought it wanted, there was no denying that each of them enticed her in different ways. She needed to get to know them more, but feared the connections would only grow stronger.

How could she choose between them?

Maybe more importantly, did she want more?

Taggert smiled, a light to his eyes that had been missing earlier. He was looking forward to spending time alone with her as well. "Durant will escort you tomorrow since he'll be busier the closer we draw to the conclave. Jackson will be with you the next. That will give me time to make plans for our day together. We can each give you pointers on what to expect at the conclave since we've all been there in different rolls."

Raven shivered at the warm invitation in his voice. She studied each man, noticing the barely restrained emotions underneath. "What about my case? I need to be at the station tomorrow and question the rogue."

"We'll be with you every step of your day, but we get your undivided attention when you're done." Jackson spoke for the first time since the club. The hardness was still there, but the fragileness she'd witnessed the first time he stayed with her had returned twofold.

Like her answer meant everything to him.

"Do you agree?" Durant's brisk tone made her jump.

"I—" She cleared her throat then pushed past the sudden burst of nerves. "I'd like that."

Without another word, she hurried away. Excitement and dread chased her as if they were hounds from hell nipping at her heels. Going out with them as her protectors was antiquated. She thought their overprotectiveness would make her feel weak, so it took her by surprise to realize that she felt cherished.

Getting to know them better was wrong. Those who got close to her always suffered, but the selfish part of her wouldn't allow her to turn down this opportunity.

Once inside her room, the walls closed in on her. Dominic entered behind her, concern in his gaze. He claimed a spot by the balcony, circled and promptly sat, waiting for her to settle.

Needing fresh air, Raven swung opened the doors. "I don't think I understood what I was asking of you when I suggested you stay. If I'm already affected this much and it's not even the full moon yet,

I'm not sure how I'll ever manage to survive the conclave, much less convince them that I deserve my own pack."

As she walked onto the balcony, a movement near the tree line caught her gaze. Hardly daring to breathe lest she draw attention to herself, she waited. Three minutes and counting passed when she saw a familiar form skim low along the ground, the shape nothing more than a shadow.

"That shit."

Griffin was sulking around the property, his shape almost indiscernible from his surroundings. If she hadn't been staring off into space, she would never have seen him. Worse, he looked like he knew where he was heading, no hesitation in his movements.

Dominic edged forward and peered in the same location, his fur standing on end.

"What do you say about us doing a little hunting?"

Dominic glanced back at her from over his shoulders and tilted his head as if considering what she asked. It was uncanny to see such intelligence through an animal's expression. He placed a paw on the railing then leapt over.

Raven quickly followed suit. By the time she'd landed, Dominic was hugging the shadows, halfway toward the treeline. She followed swiftly, but both forms had vanished.

Following instinct, she ran through the forest. It was easier than last time, her footsteps surer, more comfortable in her body. Not wanting to lose Griffin, she pushed for a burst of speed.

And almost stumbled when the grace of her wolf answered. The joy of the run so distracted her that it wasn't until a man appeared in the path that she registered his presence.

Griffin.

Then it was too late.

He must have realized the danger at the same time. He sidestepped, and she twisted to avoid him. Their shoulders hit with enough force to knock the air from her lungs. She twisted and skidded to a stop, barely managing to remain on her feet.

"Hello, Griffin. Fancy meeting you here. Just out for a stroll?" Raven straightened, but didn't let down her guard. Not until she discovered the truth.

"I'm out for a tryst with my lady friend." He shrugged, completely unconcerned. "You're welcome to join us."

His story was plausible, but didn't ring true. "Sure, why not."

The smile dropped from his face. "You can't stay."

"I can't stay on my own property?"

"You need to mind your own business." He took a step toward her, and she quickly backed away. No way was she getting within touching distance.

Before either could break the standoff, a howl split the air. Answering yips followed, and Griffin swore. "You need to do exactly as I say. Don't draw attention to yourself. And no matter what, don't leave my side."

The urgency in his voice slapped her in the face. For the first time, she realized she might have misjudged him, and she wondered what her foolishness would cost them both.

"Don't look at any of them in the eyes. Don't offer confrontation of any kind."

Raven gritted her teeth, the muscles of her legs twitching to run as she fought the instinct of self-preservation. In a blurred move, he clamped his hand on her arm.

"You run and we're both dead." He got up in her face, demanding she obey. "Do you understand me?"

"Yes." She would not be prey.

Griffin slowly loosened his hold. "Cover your scent as much as possible. It would be bad if they find out you're a wolf, worse if they discover you're an alpha. There will be nothing I can do that will save you then."

"My scent?"

"Don't play the fool now, not when I've seen you do it. Hurry before they close in on us."

That meant he'd either been paying more attention to them than anybody knew or he'd been spying on them for a lot longer. She wouldn't put either past him.

She might not trust him completely, but she didn't doubt his assessment of the situation. She tried to force her wolf to retreat, but the beast growled and snapped in protest.

She was alpha.

She wouldn't run or hide from rogues.

"Hurry."

Some of his urgency spilled over onto her. Without giving herself a chance to hesitate, she grabbed a string of power and wrapped it around herself.

And groaned when the cords of pure energy tightened like she'd tangled with barbed wire. Metal knots bit into her skin like burs, burrowing deeper with each breath.

She was going to overload.

Power tore beneath her skin. The energy scraped the marrow of her bones clean then replaced it with ground glass, the agony nearly dropping her to her knees.

"Raven! Snap out of it."

A blow struck her across the face. The jolt snapped her out of the sea of pain that had swallowed her. He had gotten what he wanted. Her wolf was gone, taking half her soul with it.

"They're coming."

"Who?" She gritted her teeth to stop shaking.

"Rogues."

"Friends of yours?" Either way he answered, Raven was screwed. She toned down the juice to a breathable level and scanned their surroundings. She sensed them out there, drawing nearer. As long as no one got too close, she should be able to contain everything.

He gave her a look she couldn't decipher. "No."

Then there was no more talking as people poured into the small clearing. And in people, she meant at least a dozen or more men of varying sizes. They were a rangy lot, more than half of them not looking sane enough to be allowed out in public.

Their wildness buffeted her. She would never have been able to control her wolf around so many.

They maintained their distance, but she had a suspicion it was more out of fear of Griffin and the way he stood in front of her than any show of respect. They eyed her, their animal parts to the fore, all but licking their lips to catch her scent.

"What have you brought us? A gift?" A brute of a man swaggered forward, leering at her, his gaze never lifting above her breasts.

Griffin didn't smile, didn't move. "She's off limits."

The man snorted and groped for her. "You can't bring something like her and not expect to share."

Raven listened to Griffin's advice, restraining herself from acting and tearing this man apart. Fetid breath wafted toward her, pudgy little fingers wiggled at her face.

Then Griffin was there. He grabbed the man's wrist and twisted. Bone snapped. The man screamed in agony. Griffin spun and knocked the feet out from under the brute, slamming him into the ground with a heavy thump. The scream cut off abruptly, the air knocked clear out of him.

When Griffin straightened there was a crazy light in his eyes that worried her more than the pig rolling around on the ground.

She scanned the crowd, prepared to defend them, but none of the rogues reacted to the violence. In the back of the group, a familiar shape of a man caught her gaze.

The rogue from the club who'd sent her a warning.

She remembered her offer to help him and knew of only one way.

Not wanting anyone to grow suspicious of their connection, she turned and focused on those closest to her. "You are on my property. As long as you don't disturb me or mine, you will be allowed to remain. No attacks. No murders. No crime. Nothing you do will lead back here. Are we understood?"

No one said anything for a moment. A few appeared doubtful, a couple hopeful, but otherwise, they just continued to stare.

A lean man wove his way to the front.

"Do you believe you're doing us a favor?" He wore glasses, standing a few inches taller than herself, the smallest of the pack, but he exuded confidence that belied his size. The others quickly scrambled out of his way, terrified to bring notice to themselves.

One wasn't quick enough and tripped. He turned and slammed his fists into the thigh of the man behind him to draw attention to someone else.

The display made her regret her invitation. They weren't like her men. They weren't like pack. They were vicious as a group of wild dogs with no loyalty. Strength and might were the only thing that kept them in line.

"A favor? No, Professor. But you will be removed from my land, permanently if necessary, if my rules are not followed. And I will find out."

The man smiled as if he liked the moniker, but there was no truce behind his expression.

"Enough." A large man from the back pushed himself forward.

The very same shifter who'd warned her at the club.

He had a mop of wildly curly hair that defied a comb. With his pale complexion, light, almost reddish hair, she half expected an Irish accent.

He had a presence that demanded respect. If she didn't know better, she would say an alpha pretending to be something else.

"What's to stop us from killing you now and taking what we want?" He asked the question, menace in his voice as he prowled toward her. He appeared to be growing larger with each step.

He didn't look happy to see her despite the warning he'd given. When she didn't answer, he closed his eyes as if already regretting what he was going to do.

That's when she realized he was trying to give her an out.

"Have you heard of the infamous hunter employed by the council?" She masked the wince at the thought of Randolph learning about this incident. He would demand a steep price for using his name. "It seems he's fascinated by me. He wouldn't be pleased to find out someone else killed me before he got bored."

Dominic circled around the outskirts, upwind of the pack. Raven gave a small shake of her head to warn him to wait for her signal. Though his lips pulled back in a silent snarl, he obeyed and slinked back into the shadows.

Her vague threat proved effective. Everyone quieted, a few taking a couple of steps back. The leader gave a faint smile his pack couldn't see and bowed his head.

"We accept your proposal." He turned and howled an inhuman sound.

At the cue, the men scattered in the woods. Professor cast her a curious look, not in the least bit alarmed at her threat. He then walked into the darkness and disappeared from one step to the next.

\* \* \*

Griffin stalked back toward the house, not saying a word. Raven would not be put off. She refused to allow him back into her home without knowing what the hell he was up to. She would not have her people in danger. "Would you care to explain what the hell is going on?"

He whirled on her, not stopping until he was in her face. "What do you think would've happened had they caught you alone?"

His beast rose as if the thought of her harmed disturbed him. A snarl twisted his face, and a startling revelation came to her. "This is why you came to me for help instead of running after you were freed from your prison, isn't it? You didn't need my help. You needed access to my property."

"They're rogues. They're banding together, which makes them even more dangerous. Alone, they are vicious. Together, they are a brutal lot, a danger for any unmated female. To a rogue, a female is precious. That doesn't mean they would treasure her. There would be no mating. Each man would take their turn on her unless one was strong enough the keep her safe from the others."

Raven shook her head. "Not all rogues."

Griffin snorted, jerking away from her. "Yes. All rogues. A female grounds a male, keeps them from going feral, keeps their wolf and human sides sane." He paced away from her and studied the darkness. "It's worse for alphas. Wolves are pack creatures. If a rogue alpha had a chance to claim a female wolf, let alone a new and very vulnerable alpha female, he would leap at the chance."

"You included?"

When he didn't say anything for a long while, the hairs on the back of her neck rose. There was only one reason why a male alpha wouldn't react to a female near the full moon, the reason he has such control over his beast.

"Unless you're already mated." Something about his silence, the tense set of his shoulders, felt like mourning. "Who was she?"

After another lengthy pause, things fell into place. "She's the reason you went rogue." Then she swallowed hard as bile rose in her throat. "Your brother..."

"Sometimes, you just need to leave things alone." Griffin turned and strode away.

"You said he died."

His hands fisted, and he walked faster.

"Oh, Griffin."

"Just leave it alone."

"He killed your mate. He deserved whatever you did to him."

He whirled on her, the stark angles of his face red with rage. "He killed my woman. It was my right to demand justice, and I took it. I tore him apart with my bare hands." He lifted those hands between them as if they still carried blood. "Is that what you wanted to hear?"

Raven's heart ached at the pain radiating from him. "He deserved that and so much more."

Griffin didn't move, just stared at her. "Promise me that you will not travel alone anymore. You placed a target on yourself tonight. You are too important to risk yourself so needlessly."

"Too important how?"

He tugged a lank of her hair like a big brother. "You're smart. You figure it out."

She slowly trailed behind him back toward the house, his stiff posture telling her she wouldn't get anything more out of him tonight.

She just hoped she figured it out in time.

## Chapter Fifteen

**THREE DAYS UNTIL THE FULL MOON: DURANT'S DAY**

Dominic loped at Raven's side as they followed some distance behind Griffin. Though silent, she felt the sting of Dominic's reprimand all the same.

"I didn't have a choice. I needed to know the danger."

The little yip he let out made her groan. "I know enough. I trust that Griffin wouldn't willingly risk our lives if there were any other way."

Dominic's tongue lolled out, shooting a look at her that said he didn't believe that for a second.

"Did you know that he had worked with Scotts? His father asked about him as well. I'm starting to suspect that though his rogue status is legitimate, he is using it to work undercover."

She didn't know it was possible to do in animal form, but Dominic snorted. Thankfully, the house came into view, keeping her from dwelling on the new mess she'd practically landed in face first. As they reached the house, Dominic promptly sat.

When she opened the door, he whined and glanced back toward the woods. "If you're going to follow them, please be careful. Don't get caught. They're the type that will rip you apart if they get a chance."

With one last yip, Dominic took off like a streak.

Raven entered her silent room, already missing Dominic despite his animal form, or maybe because of it. In a week's time, her life had completely reversed. She wasn't sure it was a good thing.

How was it possible to become attached to more than one man in such a short time? Now that she ordered them out of her room, her contrary self just missed having them around.

Missed their scents.

Their voices.

Their heat.

Morning would arrive all too soon, and nervousness at going out with Durant sent her stomach fluttering.

Her first date.

She'd always thought it silly when girls mooned over a man like a lovesick fool, but now found herself in their very shoes. Rolling her eyes at her own folly, she quickly changed and crawled into bed.

Raven felt like her head barely hit the pillow when a sound startled her awake.

The construction workers.

Night had passed all too quick. Sunlight splashed across her face, and she groaned, curling away from the beams to get a few more hours of rest.

Until she remembered she had to go to the police station and speak with the shifter that had tried to kill her.

Then her eyes snapped open.

Durant.

Their date.

A small smile tugged at the corner of her lips, and she rolled out of the bed, unable to contain the thrill of excitement that shot through her.

She landed on her feet just in time to miss being squashed by the man who'd launched himself at the bed. Raven stumbled backward, slammed into the wall, and tripped over Jackson's couch as she scrambled to get out of the way.

Only then did she notice the second man enter from the balcony, the very door she'd forgotten to lock when she'd went to bed last night.

The noise she heard hadn't been the construction workers.

Wide-awake now, she recognized the man on the bed as the same rogue that Griffin had nearly killed for daring to touch her.

"If you value your life, you'll leave now." The power that all but glowed last night had dissipated. Her animals were in full force, the moon's call having lured them out while she'd slept.

As if he hadn't heard her, the second man strode around the bed toward her. Raven pushed away from the wall to give herself room to fight.

Two against one.

She might have been able to take them if she had her power available to her. Without it, she didn't stand a chance in hand-to-hand combat.

She widened her stance as London had taught her, kept her body loose, and managed to dodge the first punch. She weaved down and landed two light blows before dancing away.

"Don't mess her up too much. I want a piece of that before we kill her." The Pig crawled off her bed, angling to come up behind her and trap her between them.

When the Pig grabbed for her, she gave a quick jab to his weak arm, the one broken last night.

He screamed and grabbed his wrist.

Raven spun, kicking the other man directly between his legs.

He immediately dropped.

The Pig grabbed her from behind in a bear hug, his hands groping her breasts. His arousal was like a weapon pressed against her lower spine. She gritted her teeth and threw back her head, hoping to knock him out cold.

Only she hadn't counted on his head being harder than her own. Pain wrapped around her skull, stunning her. He laughed at her attempt, his hold tightening as she wiggled to break his grip.

Breathing became difficult.

The wolf at her core growled in outrage, rising toward the surface.

The man at her feet struggled to stand, cupping his balls. "Bitch. I was going to kill you quick, but I've changed my mind."

"Raven?" Taggert stepped into the doorway, taking in the scene at a glance. Without hesitation, he threw himself at Blue Balls. She slammed her elbow back and was rewarded with a wave of bad breath. It smacked her in the face with enough potency to set her coughing.

London's training kicked in. She switched her footing and threw her weight forward. The move was so unexpected, his hold loosened.

He tottered for balance and fought to keep his grip on her at the same time.

She grabbed the arm still around her chest and, with some help from her wolf, heaved him over her shoulder. The man landed on his back with a solid whoosh of air. Without giving herself time to hesitate, she slammed her foot down on his throat.

At the last second, he lifted his arm to deflect her blow. What should've crushed his windpipe only bruised him instead. He grabbed her foot and yanked, neatly pulling her off her feet. Her shoulders hit the carpeting, cushioning the blow.

The commotion drew attention, and the bathroom door opened. One of the workers peered out, the younger one, and his eyes widened at the scene. He cast a look at her, but no shifter would dare interrupt an alpha fight. Raven gave a silent prayer for those asinine rules when he charged through the door and grabbed the man struggling with Taggert.

Struggling but winning.

Then she had no time to worry as the Pig dragged her closer. Sweaty hands tugged her wrists down to her sides, leaving her defenseless. He crawled over her prone body, and she quickly wrapped her legs around his waist.

It immediately halted his forward motion.

The expression on his face would've been comical in any other situation. He released one hand to pry away her leg.

Raven thrust her hand forward, her palm striking his nose.

Bones crunched.

Blood gushed down his face.

Then she had both arms free.

Then she was presented with a dilemma. If she released her legs, he could easily overpower her. If she didn't get her ass moving, he would beat the crap out of her, and she doubted she would be able to stop him again.

A shadow fell over them, and they both looked up.

"It's about time that you arrived. I can use a little help here." Pig's voice came out as a nasal whine as he held his nose.

"You." Raven saw the rogue from the club gaze down at them. Her heart sank, and the fantastical notion she'd harbored that he was one of the good guys deflated.

The knowledge hurt.

Even if he were only following orders, he would die for this. Then she hardened her emotions when he reached down. She flinched, his actions more painful than the bruises the other two men had inflicted.

Only the pain never arrived.

The weight pinning her lifted. Her lungs greedily sucked in air, and Raven rolled to her hands and knees to keep them in view.

"Hey, stop." The Pig wiggled frantically, his feet clear off the ground. "What are you doing? We were ordered to kill her."

Raven surged to her feet. The rogue gazed at her, then with a very deliberate twist, snapped the Pig's neck.

He dropped the body at her feet and raised his hands, never once removing his gaze from hers. The men from the construction crew stepped next to her and reached for him.

"Don't." She jumped in front of her unlikely savior. "He's a friend."

Maybe she was stupid to trust him enough to give him her back, but she didn't think he'd hurt her. The workers gave her varying looks of disbelief.

When no one objected, she glanced at the two dead rogues sprawled across her floor. Pig lay in a heap at her feet, the other looked like he'd gotten mixed up in a blender. Blood saturated the floor in an ever-increasing circle. "I don't suppose you do carpets?"

The innocuous question caused the youngest, the one who had helped Taggert, to come forward. "We will have the mess cleaned by the end of the day." He paused, flashing a look behind her at the remaining rogue still standing. "I would suggest that you allow us to clean up everything."

The meaning was clear, but she shook her head. "He's come to my aid on two separate occasions. He didn't have to enter the house. He came to save me. I won't have him killed for that."

Then she eyed the three workers who'd come to her rescue. "What do I owe you?"

She would not have them demand a favor from her later.

The eldest waved away her question. "They are rogues. It's the duty of any pack member to put down those who have grown unstable. That they'd dare enter your house, a single alpha female...that's proof enough."

Their words were both comforting and disturbing. She shifted to keep them all in view. The rogue appeared impassive, not giving anything away. He might have noted the workers, but it was her that he watched.

Like he hadn't expected her to stand up for him.

Besides Durant, he was the biggest shifter she'd ever seen. Maybe it was because of his size that he didn't watch the other men for attack. He was large enough, strong enough to take them.

Or more disturbing, maybe he just didn't care if he survived.

Taggert came to her side and gently tugged on her arm. She opened her mouth to argue when she looked up. Blood was smeared around his nose, his eyes had already started to blacken, and his lip was split and swollen.

"Oh, Taggert." He easily caught her hand when she reached for him, maneuvering her toward the door. When she would've protested, he spoke.

"I came to tell you that Durant is waiting for you downstairs. Why don't you go and let us take care of this mess?"

"Not you, too."

Taggert didn't look away, didn't hide. "You risk yourself too recklessly. There are reasons they are rogues."

Last night came to mind, how the rogues turned on one another. As if might was right and brutality the only way to survive.

"He's right."

Raven's head snapped up, and she met the rogue's stare. That's the last thing she expected him to say.

"It would be better if I left."

Though she hated to admit it, Raven agreed with him. She wasn't sure she could keep him safe. But was that the right thing to do or just the easier way out? She owed him. When he saw her not quite winning the battle with the rogue, he intervened. He had to know that coming to her rescue would be his death sentence.

He came anyway.

"Will you be punished for failing to do your job?"

He only shrugged as if it were unimportant. "There is more going on than what you can see. If I don't return, the truly innocent will suffer."

The words could be taken as a threat or warning, but she knew. "You're protecting them."

He studied the tree line. "There is little that I can do anymore. I'm the second in charge and can't openly defy the alpha without consequences."

"But you try anyway." She knew she shouldn't offer, but she couldn't turn away from innocents. "What can I do?"

A slight smile tipped his lips then vanished in the next second. "Stay away from the woods."

"That's not what I meant, and you know it." Raven saw the hesitation in his eyes and waited. "Ask."

"There are three kids in the group without a pack. Their first moon is coming up on them."

One of the workers heaved sigh, and she glanced over. Him and another man lifting the first body. At her stare, he spoke. "Wolves only shift as they mature. First shifts are hard. The pack is usually there to guide them through the process."

Her rescuer leaned his shoulder against the balcony door. "They aren't completely rogue yet. Two didn't even know they were shifters until the darker urges of their animals presented themselves. As soon as they figured it out, they came to us for help. We're all that they have."

Raven was appalled things were allowed to progress so far. They were children. "Does that happen a lot?"

The first two workers had vanished through the bathroom with the body. A third had collected a tarp so not to trail blood over the floor. He was the one who spoke. "Children of the pack are precious. They wouldn't be given up willingly. Their parents were most likely rogues unable to care for them. The very few who manage to conceive are either abandoned or out-right killed."

Raven faced the rogue. "How many?"

"Two teenagers. I'm hoping being around pack will slow down the change and give them more time to learn. The other kid is older, but in worse shape. He's been fighting the change for years."

"He's going feral?"

He didn't say more, didn't ask or plead with her. They were used to relying on themselves for everything.

Raven took a different track. "Why fight the change?"

"They are worthless now. Once they change, they will have to fight for their place in the pack and prove themselves useful."

Raven closed her eyes, took a deep breath and slowly let it out. "If I do this, you will owe me."

"Agreed." He didn't hesitate to commit himself.

When she opened her eyes, his face was alive with an emotion she couldn't name. Swallowing hard, she turned away. "Fine. Bring them to the house. I'll meet them and decide. I won't take them if they pose a threat to mine."

"That's all I can ask. I'll send them before sunset." He backed toward the balcony. "Lock your doors. Post more guards. And stay away from the forest."

"Wait! Tell me your name."

"You may call me Jamie." With that, he bolted over the railing and disappeared over the side before she could ask more questions.

Like why they wanted to kill her.

Silence descended until the eldest worker spoke in a deferential tone, as if her decision had meant something to them. "We'll have your room ready for you before tonight."

Raven grabbed a change of clothes, dressing haphazardly before heading down stairs. This was not how she imagined her very first date, but she'd already been too long. She couldn't have Durant investigate until the rogue had enough time to make good his escape.

A tiny flutter of nerves struck, and she slowed before she reached the kitchen. She eyed her clothes. They matched everything else in her closet, and she almost wished she had something nicer, something womanly, to wear.

She grabbed the mess of her hair and pinned it up, futzing with herself. She tugged her gloves up then stopped. She hated the barrier between her and others. For most of her life, her greatest wish had been to touch others without the fear she'd kill them hanging over her.

With the moon calling her animals, she was being granted the chance of a lifetime. Slowly, ever so slowly, she peeled off her gloves and shoved them into her back pocket. Her hands felt exposed, sensitive to the slightest caress of air. She rubbed her fingers, marveling at the textures and wondered at her own daring. But if she didn't grab this chance, she would hate herself for missing the opportunity to be free.

Taking a deep breath for courage, she pushed open the door to the kitchen. She wasn't sure what to expect, but finding Jackson and Aaron eating at the table wasn't it. Dina bustled around the kitchen.

Her shoulders drooped in disappointment. "Dina, we're going to have three guests staying with us. Young teenagers."

"Shifters?" Interest brightened her eyes.

"Yes. Can you get the rooms ready?"

She was already bouncing on her feet before Raven finished speaking. "Of course."

Raven ignored the way Jackson narrowed his gaze. She turned to avoid his questions and nearly smacked into Durant.

"Were you looking for me?" Durant had stepped through the outside door, the wall of glass at his back haloed his body in sun, highlighting the barely there stripes in his hair. The manifestation could be a reminder not to forget or his beast's flat out refusal to hide.

When he stepped out of the light, her breath caught. She was so used to seeing him in his pressed clothes that his casual attire made him appear way too approachable.

Made him appear playful, Lord help her.

The jeans were custom made, if she had to guess, and fit him so lovingly she wanted to trail her hands over them to see if those muscles of his felt as delicious as they looked.

The sleeves of his shirt were rolled up to his elbows, revealing a light dusting of hair on the corded muscles of his arms. The collar of his shirt was opened two buttons, hinting at the powerful chest hidden tantalizingly out of reach. A lazy smile curled his lips at her perusal, but his eyes were all hunter as he studied her in return.

Then his eyes fell to her hands and stopped there. He swallowed once, hard, and quickly glanced up into her eyes. There was a vulnerability in his expression, as if she had offered him something he'd never expected.

"Come. I have a private breakfast prepared for us." He turned and held open the door for her to pass through.

She gave him a tentative smile and took a step forward when the phone rang. All the pleasure of the moment drained.

In response, he calmly picked up the phone and held it out to her. "You're not getting rid of me that easily."

Without taking her gaze from him, she accepted the phone. "Raven."

"There's a problem." Hope for the day fell when Scotts' smoke-roughened voice came over the line. The noise from the station filtered into the background, sounding as hectic as ever.

Raven tucked away all the expectations that had been building since last night and fitted her gloves back on her hands. She should've known better than to expect anything. "I'll leave now and be—"

"Don't bother. The shifter is dead."

"But I thought he was in a locked cell. How did they get to him?"

"He killed himself during the night. He was locked down. We had no cause to watch him."

"What?" His answer floored her. "But a shifter would never kill themselves."

He was silent for a moment. "They sent the body to the morgue. Meet me there."

## ಶಿ Chapter Sixteen ೊ

"The last place I expected you to take me on our date was the morgue." Durant's droll tone made Raven wince.

She fumbled with her badge to show at the new checkpoint, unsettled to be back in the building where she'd almost been kidnapped to further some lunatic's experiments. She gave a small smile to Chuck, the guard, as he waved her through.

She concentrated on Durant's words and the present before thoughts of the past, the things she'd done to survive, drove her insane. "I'm sorry. I—"

Durant laughed, waving away her words as they walked down the corridor to the morgue. "You don't bore me."

What should've sounded like an insult came out as a compliment. She smiled at him, expecting to see a teasing light in his eyes. Only, he didn't smile in return. His green eyes deepened, and she found her steps slowing as she drifted closer to him.

"Uhm-mm." Startled at the throat clearing, Raven whirled to find Scotts waiting for her down the hallway.

Heat filled her cheeks at being caught mooning over Durant, and she avoided both their gazes. "Are we in here?"

Scotts took pity on her, pushing open the door without a word. The room had been fixed since she'd been there last. The stainless steel refrigeration unit replaced.

Then she saw the doctor.

Even though she knew Ross was gone, Raven shivered, half-expecting the person in the white coat to turn and smile at her with cold, calculating eyes while plotting ways to vivisect her.

The cold chills she'd always thought was trepidation that she might accidentally make the dead walk was still there but less. She wondered if she somehow knew all along the horror Ross had intended for her.

A flicker of energy crackled between her fingers, more to calm her than any sense of fear.

The person turned, revealing a full figured petite woman. Blond hair was severely pulled back, showcasing a surprisingly young face. The little skip in her chest hurt, but her relief was too great to do anything but nod to the doctor.

The other woman ignored her and gestured toward Scotts. "I thought I told you cops only."

Raven bit back a retort at the attitude, and Scotts quickly answers. "She's clear. She's the new Region."

The doctor snorted, not pleased, but it was unclear whether because of the Region title or that she was a paranormal.

"And him?"

Raven glanced at Durant. "He's my escort. What have you got?"

The doctor paused for a minute longer then picked up her notes. "Male. Mid-thirties. Healthy. Died from asphyxiation."

"He hung himself?" Raven wandered closer to the body, and the doctor held out her arm.

"No touching. I want no contamination."

As if Raven were at fault for stealing all the air in the jail cell. Well, she did fight him not hours earlier, but that didn't mean she had anything to do with his death. The whole police station had witnessed and participated in the capture.

Raven turned toward Scotts. "Is she able to give us a full report without bias?"

A fierce frown lined the doctor's face. "I am a professional. I will do my job."

"You also hate paranormals."

The doctor didn't deny it. "I checked into my predecessors cases. This morgue seemed to be a hot spot of activity for *your kind*." And her observations were all the information she needed to cast judgment. "And you're at the center of it all."

Raven smiled, pleased to see the doctor taken aback by the action. "If by hot spot you mean a lot of death comes through the morgue, then yes. Since a number of people still believe being a paranormal is contagious, the cases are either shuffled around until they are lost or they get sent here.

"My involvement is because I'm on file to be called on problem cases. You must also be aware that your predecessor had been experimenting on the paranormals to further *human* well-being. He used his position and this office to gain access to the bodies. I mean, they're just paranormals, after all."

Raven and the new doctor eyed each other, both at a stand-off. Raven gestured toward the covered corpse on the table. "So he hung himself?"

The doctor hesitated a moment longer, still clinging to her anger, then finally turned down the sheet. "Actually, no. You would expect that, but it appears that he just laid down and stopped breathing."

The body on the table looked like he was ready to get up and walk away. His skin was pale, gravity having settled the blood in the lowest points in his body. There was no other marks on him, all the injuries from the fight having long since healed.

His death made no sense. Oh, shifters had the willpower, the total control over their body, so it was physically possible.

"Is that normal?" The doctor voiced the very question bothering her.

Raven shook her head. "I have no idea."

Durant cleared his throat, and Raven turned toward him. "Shifters don't kill themselves. Ever. But they would volunteer for missions where they either complete their tasks or die trying."

Raven waved a hand toward the table. "Even a rogue?"

"Rogue?" The doctor peered at the exam table as if the body would give her an explanation.

Durant ignored the doctor and spoke to Raven. "Some fringe groups contract themselves out for work. It all depends on the job and the price tag attached."

"Like mercenaries. So we need to find out who hired him then."

"What's a rogue?" Raven turned at the annoyed voice to find the new ME watching them with a frown on her face, clearly frustrated that she couldn't patch the cryptic conversation together.

Raven debated the wisdom of telling the truth. "It's complicated, but essentially, a rogue is a shifter without a pack to call home."

"You make it sound like a disease." She scowled at Raven and Durant, suspecting they were keeping something from her.

Very astute.

Durant remained silent, face impassive as if the doctor was of no concern to him. And he was right, she wasn't. But the doctor was Raven's concern if she wanted a place in law enforcement.

"In some cases, it can be a disease. Without a pack, shifters are vulnerable. There's a list of symptoms that affects them and could eventually lead one to going feral."

The ME quickly flipped the pages of her chart. "What are the symptoms."

It was a demand, one that Raven had no intention of fulfilling. "What is your name?"

"Dr. Shade."

"You're a medical examiner for the police. You applied and were given the position, so you're intelligent, probably one of the best in your field."

"Yes." There was no pride on her face when she answered.

"Humans are only half your job now. Everything you've learned about shifters from all your teachers…toss. Start over from here. As police are investigating more into the shifter world, you'll have to adapt or you won't make it."

Raven headed toward the door. Durant easily beat her to it without appearing to rush and held it open. "Let us know if someone claims the body. If not, have it incinerated."

She matched her steps to Scotts. "I need to talk to some shifters about what they know. I can't do that in the office. With the full moon, the best way to catch them is on their own turf."

Scotts nodded. "Do it. Keep me informed." He waved them off and headed back toward the morgue. "I'm going to see what else our Dr. Shade has for us."

"Let me know what you find."

Durant said nothing as they walked down the hallway. "You think I was too tough on her."

He gave her a quick look. "Not really. You only spoke the truth. A shifter would have told her less."

"But?" She stopped by the door leading outside, rubbing her arms, the static building under her skin crackling at the gesture.

The movement lifted her sleeve, revealing a line of massive bruises bracketing her wrists and higher. Durant grabbed her hand, his eyes splintering with gold. "What happened?"

Damn.

She'd hoped to keep the incident quiet. "There was a couple of uninvited houseguests this morning."

"While I was there? And you didn't call for help?" Outrage roughened his voice. He drew himself up to his full height, released her and stepped back as if affronted.

"It wasn't like that. They were there when I woke. I just reacted. By the time I thought about calling for help, the situation was resolved."

A muscle ticked in Durant's jaw, as if realizing for the first time that he alone wouldn't be able to protect her. "This is the third attack in as many days. Only luck has kept you alive this long. What happens when that runs out?"

Raven wished she could argue with him, but he was right. She was learning to defend herself, but not fast enough. If she didn't learn to survive without her powers, learn how to rely on her beasts, it would be too late. "I'm trying."

Durant whirled, stepping right into her private space. "Try harder."

She wanted to smack him, but her cool, unruffled tiger seemed so disturbed she didn't have the heart to argue. Instead, she settled her palm over his chest. He covered her hand and rested his forehead against hers.

His golden gaze locked onto hers. Funny enough, she felt no fear at being so near his beast. A rumble sigh escaped him as he finally relaxed. The big cat brushed his tail against her mind in a show of possessiveness, content with her touch.

At least for now.

"You have one weapon that will work every time."

Raven wished it were true. "Not during the full moon. When my animals surface, my abilities as a conduit go on the fritz. I can have either one or the other, and I have yet to find a balance."

Durant smiled, but there was no comfort in the gesture. "No, that's not what I meant. You're a strong alpha, especially for one so new. And as an alpha, you have power over anyone weaker than you."

Raven's brows wrinkled as she played the attack over in her head. She would have done things differently, but she didn't have possession of any weapon that could've helped. "I think I would know if I had power to stop them."

"I'll teach you."

That captured her attention. "How?"

"Lust." Durant opened the door and vanished outside without another word.

The door drifted shut before she could close her mouth. She shot outside, her strides quickly eating the distance between them. She wanted to blurt out her questions, but held back, not sure she really wanted to know. "I'm not going to like this, am I?"

She should've been more careful what she wished for.

\* \* \*

The Aston Martin purred as Durant started the car, the strong leather scent that so reminded her of him filled the confined space. Raven inhaled deeper, savoring it. She didn't touch anything for fear of leaving even a fingerprint on the pristine surfaces. "Kiss me."

Those were the first words out of Durant's mouth since they'd left the morgue, and she went rigid.

"What?" The word emerged as a croak, her mouth going dry at the thought of her leaning over and boldly kissing him. She tried to smile, only to have her lips wobble. "Aren't you moving a little fast for a first date?"

He put the car into gear, the tires chirping as he shot out into traffic with a casualness that shouldn't have surprised her. The car suited him.

Sleek.

Powerful.

Ready to pounce.

Traffic zipped by at an alarming rate. Her heart rocketed, but she didn't have any qualms of them crashing. No, he handled the car too smoothly for that. What made her nervous was the edginess to him that she didn't know how to tame.

"I won't force you to do anything, but you have to learn how to control those around you. The easiest way to begin is by physical contact."

Though his body was relaxed, his words casual, there was something between them that belied everything he'd just said. "Is that what you want? Me to control you?"

White teeth flashed as he smiled. "I have more mastery over my beast than anyone else in our pack. I'm the only one strong enough not to surrender to you."

She watched his arms flex as he maneuvered the car. "Won't that be painful?"

Durant's laugher filled the car. Warmth spread through her at the sound, but the slight edge to the heat had her shifting in her seat.

"It will be delicious torture." One he sounded like he would relish.

Unable to look at him for fear she would give in without thinking through all the consequences, she gazed out the window. She wasn't aware that she'd been fiddling with her gloves until Durant caught her fingers. He placed her hand on his thigh, uncurling her fist until her fingers were splayed over his leg. Muscles bunched at her touch. When she would've pulled away, he tightened his hold.

"You have to get used to touching us. You have to get used to using us. Let me do this for you." He released her and gripped the wheel like her hand wasn't nestled inches from his growing arousal.

When she didn't immediately reject the idea, he continued. "You can use lust against those who try to hurt you. Most alpha's learn the tool at an early age. It's subtle."

"It's manipulative."

He signaled and smoothly switched lanes. "It's pack. Even if you don't use it, you need to know how so you can recognize it in others. I can teach you. I won't touch you unless you bid me."

Why did that sound so deliciously dangerous?

## ॐ Chapter Seventeen ॐ

They arrived at *Talons* twenty minutes later, entering through the back door. With each step, Raven resisted the urge to turn and run. The thought of touching Durant made her tremble, and she couldn't claim it was all fear. "I'm not sure this is a good idea."

"We can stop at any time."

The energy that had risen while at the morgue had dissipated. The burn of the moon licked through her, whispering for her to brush against him. Logically, she knew what he said made sense. She needed him to teach her. She feared that once she started, she wouldn't be able to stop.

She'd wanted to get to know him, but not like this. "Tell me about yourself?"

Durant opened the door to his office. She went to step through when he quickly closed it on her, shutting her in the hallway with him. He crowded into her space, placing a hand on the wall by her head, blocking her avenues of escape. "How about we play a game? For every kiss, I'll answer one of your questions."

Heat poured off him, tempting her to give into him, anything to just be able to touch him. Thoughts became clouded. He leaned closer, his lips hovering so over hers. "Say yes."

She tore her gaze from his lips and met his stare. "You want this?"

She hadn't meant to sound so breathless. Hadn't meant to reveal her need. It'd been so long since she'd been able to be close to someone. She wasn't sure she could say no when she wanted that connection so badly.

"More than anything." Durant didn't smile, didn't move in

anyway. The power of him bunched under his skin, waiting for her to say no.

"And you'll stop at any time?"

His throat bobbed painfully, and he gave a curt nod.

She bit her lip, and a groan rumbled in his chest before he could prevent it.

"One question for one kiss."

Durant nodded again.

"And we'll put on a timer." It would keep her from getting lost in the moment. Prevent her from taking too much.

"Anything you want."

She closed her eyes, her breathing a little too fast, leaving her lightheaded.

Or maybe that was just him.

"Teach me."

The door shot open, and she was shoved inside in under a second. Raven whirled to see Durant very deliberately lock the door. She swallowed hard, her heart pounding as excitement and dread tumbled through her.

Durant rested his forehead on the door, struggling for control, presenting her with a very drool worthy line of his back and ass. She licked her lips, the sight of him so pushed to the edge, calming her. She no longer felt like prey.

"I need you to do something for me."

She traced her fingertips against her lips, still able to feel his breath on them. Could almost taste him. It solidified her decision. "Of course."

"In the bottom right hand side of my desk, you'll find a box of confiscated items from the club. Grab two handcuffs and bring them to me."

Doubts began to edge their way into her mind, cooling her thoughts. "Durant—"

"Please."

Raven hesitated, but the wealth of emotions in his voice changed her mind. He didn't ask anyone for anything. Ever. He just took or demanded and people obeyed.

She opened the drawer, hating the way her hand shook. She

trusted him.

Didn't she?

She pulled out two metal mismatched cuffs with the keys tied to them and walked toward him. "Here."

She thrust out the cuffs, half-expecting to feel cold metal slip around her wrist. Instead, he clamped them on his own. He caught her hand, pried open her fingers and gently placed the keys in her palm.

Her heart skipped a beat. "What are you doing?"

"Is that your question?" With cuffs dangling from his arms, he walked toward an old, antique chair and placed it in the center of the room. He sat then calmly cuffed himself to the chair's arms.

"Question?" Her eyes widened at the implication. "No."

She rushed forward to stop him. By the time she reached his side, he calmly held out his arm.

"Cuff me."

When she would've protested, she saw the slight tremor in his hand. A vulnerability he allowed her to see. She did as told. Her whole body warmed at the thought of him helpless to her. She couldn't meet his gaze when she straightened.

She should've been horrified, but that was the last emotion she felt.

"Set the timer then come back here."

Raven set the clock on his desk, reluctantly returning to stand in front of him.

"Crawl on my lap."

"What?" Her head snapped up, unaware that she'd been watching her feet. The raw desire on his face made her heart thump painfully against her ribs.

"So you can reach me better." He held up his hands, only to be caught up short. "And I need you to touch me."

Feeling clumsy, Raven stepped closer until her leg bumped his knee. Her stomach whirled at seeing him so defenseless. "Why are you doing this? I can feel your beast isn't pleased."

"We'll be fine once you touch us." Then he smiled. "I'll consider that your first answer. Kiss me."

His knee nudged her leg. Waiting only stretched out the torture, so she sighed and grabbed her courage before she turned and ran.

Raven placed her knees on either side of his thighs and scooted closer, balanced precariously at the very edge of the chair. At the contact, he relaxed completely into the cushions as if he wouldn't be anywhere else.

"You did this for me, didn't you?" He thought she would run, so he'd made himself vulnerable.

Smug, Durant settled his head against the back of the chair. "You owe me two kisses now."

Raven scowled. "Neither of those were questions."

"That's the only pass you will receive." His gaze slowly worked its way up her body, leaving behind a trail of heat that made her fidget. "What do you want to know?"

"You gave up leading your own pack to run *Talons*. You took in a human and treated her as your cub. You came to me for help, willing to pay any price for me to save her."

Durant gave a crooked smile. "Is there a question in there?"

"Why choose me?" She hadn't meant to ask that. She wanted to know more about his past, but the question had just slipped out.

"The most important thing to remember is touch. Shifters live by physical contact, the connections forged between pack members. It can be used as a reward and punishment. Put your hand on my arm."

Raven did as told, trailing her leathered-tipped fingers over his forearm, marveling at the warmth.

"What do you feel?"

"Skin. Heat. You."

Durant shook his head. "You're thinking like a human. Push deeper."

Raven closed her eyes and brushed her fingers over his arm again, concentrating on something she could only sense beneath the surface. "Your beast."

In answer, curiosity called her own animal toward the surface.

Only it wasn't a wolf that answered.

Feline. Big.

The smell of rainforest and exotic flowers whirled in the air.

Then she was there, waiting under the surface, observing her prey. Durant's stillness clued her in first. His eyes were completely gold with shattered emotions.

"A shifter is most vulnerable when they are between forms, when neither animal or human is in complete control." His voice was a rough whisper. "This is when an alpha can overpower the other shifter. If your beast shows enough dominance, your adversary will back down. If you're strong enough, you can take command."

Raven inched closer. "And if the shifter was bad and gave me a lesson instead of answering my question?"

Cuffs rattled. He lowered his arms and gripped the chair until his knuckles whitened.

"Naughty kitty."

She knew she shouldn't mess with him, but she couldn't resist having him completely at her mercy. She doubted she would ever have the opportunity again. She ducked her head closer to his, stopping short from touching him.

She didn't even think he was breathing. Raven placed her palms on his shoulders and slowly dragged her hands down his chest, her nails sharp enough to leave a sting in their wake.

Durant bowed under her contact, seeking more.

"Tell me."

Instead of a reply, he snorted. "You learn fast. I want my kiss."

Raven drew back an inch, and he growled. "You gave me a lesson, not my answer. Why me?"

"You were a temptation." Durant smiled gently, and Raven pulled back further, unnerved by the unexpected emotion. "Shifters are drawn to strength, and you were an alpha just growing into yourself. You foolishly fought for something when you had no reason to interfere. Because you thought it was the right thing to do. You have the power to touch a person too deeply and change them." He tipped up his head. "Now my kiss."

Raven didn't care for his explanation at all. She didn't want to change people. Changing people drew attention. She leaned closer, her face nearly touching his. "And why did you want to change?"

"Shifters are pack creatures. They don't do well alone."

Raven narrowed her eyes, recognizing he was holding something back. "We're not talking about shifters. We're talking about you."

A scowl marred his face. "You're like me. You're searching for something."

"And what are you searching for?"

"You." Without waiting for her, he leaned forward, sealing his lips to hers. Her eyes slid shut as he devoured her mouth, begging her to open and return the kiss.

Under the onslaught, Raven was helpless to deny him. His need fed her own. As soon as she surrendered, the kiss gentled. But gentle was more devastating. He took his time to learn her taste. He wasn't just taking. He was seducing her with his mouth, making her crave him so she would come back for more.

Frightened by the strength of the desire he stirred, she pulled back. They both stared at each other for a few seconds before she realized that the buzzer was ringing on his desk.

She rose without looking at him, turning off the clock.

"Set it again. There is more you need to know."

It was a demand and it made her smile, but she was afraid to discover more. His answers were too revealing. She wasn't sure she wanted the brutal truth about herself exposed. The lies she told herself were the only comfort she had. She was afraid she wouldn't be able to live with the truth.

"Ask me a question."

The taste of wildness and seduction lingered on her lips.

Just one more taste.

What could it hurt?

Raven set the clock for fifteen minutes.

"Now come here."

She lingered behind him, relished teasing him too much to obey quickly. Who would have thought the delicate nape of his neck would be so attractive? She trailed her fingers down the strip of flesh. "You're a bit bossy for the one tied up."

"I want to see you." He twisted to catch a glimpse of her. "Please."

Raven circled the chair and stopped a short distance away to clear her head.

"You need to learn how to mete out punishment."

All thoughts of lust evaporated, and she retreated a step. "I don't want to hurt you."

Durant raised an eyebrow as if to say that was even possible. "I'm alpha. I can show you control. And you need the practice. If you slip, I can manage the pain. Do it."

"Bossy." But he was right. She needed to learn, if not for herself, she needed to know how to keep her people safe. That included him.

But if he wanted to do this, she wanted to actually feel him this time. She missed physical contact, missed the feel of another living person beneath her touch, skin to skin.

She lifted her hand and watched him, ready to stop at the least sign of trepidation. His gaze dropped to her hands and didn't lift again as she worked the leather off her fingers, one at a time. When she finally pulled off the gauntlet glove and tossed it to a chair, his breath caught.

It shouldn't amuse her.

It was just her hand, but she adored his reaction. She de-gloved the other hand slower, watching him watch her and couldn't believe how much the small act made her feel daring and sexy as hell.

When she walked toward him, she kept her hands away while she straddled his lap. She leaned in close and inhaled his scent.

"Ask a question."

Her lips twitched, brushing against his neck ever so lightly, and he trembled.

"Raven."

"Have you ever been in love?" She could've bitten her tongue as soon as the question slipped out. He stiffened beneath her, and her whole body froze in horror.

"Don't ask questions you don't want to know the answer." The harshness of his voice sent a flash of hurt through her, and betrayal quickly turned to downright pissed-off.

Fury bubbled up her chest, and the creature at her core woke. Menace pooled in her blood, and sped through her system like a virus. Raven should've been terrified, maybe she would be later, but it wanted answers and so did she.

Her hand shot out and encircled his throat. His pulse pounded under her grip. The heat of his skin burned. Unwilling to give up her prey, she tightened her hold. "Am I some sort of game to you?"

Durant stilled as her fingers dug into his neck. "I will never lie to you. I was in love a long time ago."

"And you still love her." Jealousy curled through her, but Durant was theirs now. And they wouldn't give up what was theirs.

Durant leaned forward despite her hold. "I deserve my kiss."

Raven slammed him back into his chair. Her lips curled into a snarl, and the creature clenched her talons, ready to rip out his throat. "I will not play second fiddle to anyone."

Durant snorted, amusement dancing in his golden eyes, in spite of her painful hold. "I was a different person then. If I'd loved her still, I wouldn't be here with you."

The creature seemed satisfied with the answer and went back to its slumber. Some of her anger eased but not the sting of betrayal. The coldness in her chest lingered. "That's why you accepted the position as owner of *Talons*, why you gave up your right to form a pack. Because of her."

"My kiss."

"What am I to you?"

"That's another question." Durant eased back, sensing the worse of the danger had passed.

She was almost grateful he didn't answer. She didn't know if she would be able to handle the truth. She leaned forward, but couldn't bring herself to kiss him on the lips. Instead, she set her mouth against his throat and licked the base of his neck where his pulse pounded, revealing that he wasn't as unaffected as he wanted her to believe. He tipped his head back to give her better access, but she wasn't done with him yet.

He shivered when she pulled back. Before she could ask her next question, he spoke.

"You have the threatening part down, but now we need to see if you can go through with it."

"But I wasn't done with my questions."

Durant didn't smile, didn't move. "If you kiss me again right now, I can't guarantee I will be a gentleman."

Raven wasn't sure she wanted him to be one either. But he was right, she needed to focus on surviving the conclave first. In order to do that, she needed his help.

"Fine. What do I do?" She wiggled to put more distance between them, then stopped when a rumble filled his chest.

"First, don't move like that unless you mean it."

Heat filled Raven's face. "Right."

"Then let's begin. Touch me and allow your beast to rise."

Raven hesitated and scanned her body. The creature lay like a block of ice, curled tightly around her core. It couldn't be allowed to wake again.

What decided the issue was that she needed an edge before she went in front of the council. She couldn't let her fear cause her to lose everything.

She gently brushed her fingers over his arm, and a grumble of displeasure rose from him.

"Unbutton my shirt. You can reach more of me that way."

His words were innocent enough, but him being without a shirt was so not a good idea. "Durant—"

"It will be fine. It's not sexual. Unless you can think of another way to make your beast rise?"

No, she couldn't. His nearness befuddled her mind too much. Her fingers fumbled with the buttons. His shirt parted, exposing his very well developed chest.

And what a chest.

Smooth, tanned skin lay bare, her fingers itching to explore. A light dusting of hair rested lower on his abdomen, arrowing downward as if inviting her to delve lower.

Realizing a few minutes had passed with her drooling over him, she glanced up. Instead of teasing she'd expected, she saw a dark pool of desire on his face.

"Touch me."

Not taking her gaze away from his, she reached out. A tremble shook her finger as she lightly brushed his chest, marveling at the texture of pure male. He inhaled, seeking a firmer touch. After one more stroke, she forced her hand to still, ignoring the desire to explore further.

Like he said, this was business.

"Now reach below the surface for your beast."

Raven closed her eyes, waited for her animal to rise. Only this time, it didn't work. Then her brows lowered in understanding. "You're locking your beast away from me."

"Do you think others would just allow you access?" Durant's

voice rumbled around her until only the two of them existed. "Fight for it."

Raven drew in a deep breath and concentrated. The first thing that came to her was his leather scent. Following the smell, she leaned closer until she nearly had her face buried in the crook of his neck, stopping just short of touching.

Heat poured off him, and she grabbed the trail back to the source. His core. And was rewarded by a warm brush of fur. "I feel him."

"Now show him you're the stronger alpha." His breath fanned the side of her face, causing her to shudder.

"Am I?"

"It's possible. Test yourself. You won't hurt me."

"Won't or can't?" The darkness behind her eyelids allowed her to hide and be bolder than normal. She brushed her lips along his collarbone then did her best to concentrate on the lesson. Trepidation burrowed under her skin as she waited for his answer.

"Either you do this now or we need to leave. I can't take much more and not have you beneath me."

Raven shivered at his delicious words. Too bad they weren't more of a threat than they were intended. But he was right. She wasn't ready for the commitment he would demand if they took that step.

"How?"

"Think about control. Keeping it. Demanding it. Let your beast free."

Raven wanted to protest, but maybe he was right. She'd never allowed her beasts free reign, letting her fear get the better of her. But maybe during the moon's call and Durant's help, things could be different.

There was only one sure way that had ever worked to call her beast.

Touch.

Close, physical contact.

"I hope you know what you're asking." Taking her courage in both hands, Raven laid her lips against Durant's neck.

"Uh, Raven? Not that I mind, but what are you doing?"

Raven rubbed her cheek against his jaw. "The fastest, surest way to call my animal is by physical contact."

Cuffs rattled against wood.

Callused fingertips brush against her waist, possessiveness in the gesture. "More."

Raven shivered at the rough demand.

Unable to stop herself, Raven let her hands drift lower to trace over his pecks. Muscles flexed, and he scooted lower in the chair, tumbling her across his chest with an umph. When she straightened, she inhaled sharply to find his arousal press so intimately against her.

"Kiss me like you mean it." Durant lifted his chin, the demand clear, but he let her take the lead and set the pace.

Temptation beckoned, but so did his beast. If she kissed him directly, she would become lost. Instead, she ducked her head and licked the strong column of his throat. Only the angle was different, forcing her breasts to brush deliciously against him.

The cage at her center wavered and the large cat prowled forward. Relief was instantaneous. It lasted only a second, then darkness swallowed her. The creature at her core slowly unfurled. All the lovely warmth vanished like ice seeping through her veins.

The need to taste intensified.

The little nibble became a nip.

Durant arched up into her, a hiss of air escaping through his clenched teeth. Then his beast was there, growling a warning.

Raven tried to pull back, but she wasn't the one in control. A scream of fear and rage locked in her throat. Desperate to keep Durant safe, she grabbed a string of electricity, burning herself in her rush. She sent a blast directly toward the creature.

Her whole chest felt like it was being torn apart from the inside out, but the beast would not be stopped.

Not until it got what it wanted.

Only when the taste of blood spilled into her mouth did control revert back. The luscious taste of Durant curdled in her mouth as the horror of what she'd done shot through her. The creature encircled her core, a physical weight on her chest, then went back to its slumber, content with the taste she'd stolen.

One second Raven was in his lap, the next she was near the door, her heart pounding so hard she could barely catch her breath.

She scrubbed her mouth with the back of her hand, unable to take her eyes from Durant. "I'm sorry."

Maybe worst of all, she hadn't wanted to stop.

## ❧ Chapter Eighteen ☙

"Un-cuff me." Metal clanked against wood as Durant lifted his arms.

Raven could only shake her head.

"You don't want to leave me locked up for others to find."

She hadn't realized she'd backed away from his damn hypnotic voice until her shoulders hit the wall. It knocked some sense into her. She fumbled with the keys as she fished them out of her pocket, nearly dropped them when she pulled them free.

She haphazardly tossed the keys at him, grabbing for the door when she heard wood groan then splinter.

The lock slowed her down.

Before she could crack the door open an inch, he was there. His palm came to rest near her head, oh so very casually cutting off her escape. The cuffs from his wrist dangled inches from her nose. "Our date isn't done."

Raven couldn't stop herself from shaking, couldn't make herself turn to face him and the truth. "You need to get away from me. You're not safe."

He spun her around, slamming her back against the door. She glanced up in surprise. Anger darkened Durant's face. "Let's get something straight. If I wanted to leave, I could've at any time. You didn't hurt me."

Her gaze dropped to the bright splash of blood that stained the collar of his shirt.

"The need to bite is instinctual." He tipped up her chin. "A bite from an alpha is a strong aphrodisiac. You're supposed to enjoy it. You denied me the first time you tasted me." He closed his eyes and inhaled. "I can still recall the smell your arousal."

"Crude."

"Your fear is eating you alive. You can't let it. I'm not sure what creature took control, but I'm glad you have her. It means that if push came to shove, she would protect you. She knew I was yours. I believe she was staking claim. If I wasn't good enough for you, the result might have been different."

"But she tasted you before, that first night."

"And I lived both times." He seemed almost cheerful, not scared shitless like he should be.

"You're missing the point. That thing is in me. It's stronger than my powers. Stronger than my animals. And it's growing. I have no control over it. Eventually, if it ever wakes completely, I'm not going to be me anymore, and no one will be safe."

Durant cupped her face and kissed her forehead. "We are introduced to our animals at puberty. Your animals are young, yet. You missed the step where you and your animals grow together. They are testing and challenging you like any teenager. What took us years to master, you are experiencing in weeks."

Raven so wanted to believe him that she didn't pull away. "You really believe that?"

He gathered her close until she was pressed against him, her cheek against his bare chest. The steady beat of his heart soothed her. Oh, she knew he was doing it on purpose, but she didn't care.

"Let's get you home." He snagged the keys from the floor and pocketed the cuffs with a devilish smile. "I think I'll take them with me in case you want to try that again."

Red welts marred the skin of his arm, but they were lightening even as she watched. She turned her back when he buttoned his shirt.

"Here." He handed her gloves to her over her shoulder.

Grateful for something to do, she put them on. The ride home was silent but for his amusement and ragged need he made no effort to hide. She almost gave in and reached for him, but it was too soon after what happened at his office. She couldn't afford a repeat until after she'd had time to cool down.

They pulled up to the house sooner than she'd expected. The instant her door opened, Dominic trotted around the side of the house, keeping to the shadows. He inspected them both, but seemed satisfied with what he saw.

Then he turned toward the woods. Only when her attention was on the forest did Jamie step from the shelter of the trees.

"Why don't you go in the house. I'll take care of this." Durant took a step when she caught his arm. Power crouched beneath the surface of him, ready and eager to leap out.

"That rogue saved my life this morning. I invited him here." Durant studied the other man, clearly not pleased at the turn of events, but conceded to her.

"I think I'll accompany you."

Raven didn't argue. She wouldn't win. She crossed the lawn, stopping with ten feet between them. "You could have come up to the house. They knew to expect you."

The large man only shrugged. "I trust you."

He gave two short whistles and three boys slowly emerged from the trees, their focus divided between her and Durant.

Raven held out her hand to the eldest. "I'm Raven. Welcome to my home."

The young man was painfully thin, but healthy enough. He carefully wiped his hand on his jeans then looked toward Jamie. At his nod, the boy held out his hand. "Jase."

One of the other boys snorted. Jase whirled and smacked him on the back of the head. "Show some respect."

"This is bullshit." The kid stomped away, hugging the shadows, a slight limp to his leg. Something about him nagged at her. She could almost put her finger on it.

"Kyle," the other kid, who could pass for a double, whispered in shock and whitened at the blatant disrespect.

Raven held up her hand. "And your name?"

"Brant." His voice cracked.

She looked between the two brothers, noticing subtle differences between them. Kyle was maybe two years older if she was generous. His dark hair was longer in the front, the bad boy if she had to guess, while Brant had his hair trimmed more for practicality. Both had hazel eyes, but Kyle's were more cynical and untrusting. "Kyle, do you know why you're here?"

"Some crap about you being able to protect us." He snorted at the thought of a girl protecting him was ludicrous. As if being a shifter made him indestructible.

Jamie growled, and the kid straightened so fast she could all but hear his spine snap straight.

"So tell me this, Kyle. You fear Jamie, yes?" The kid only glared at her. She took a gamble. "Jamie, if you and I came to a fight, who would win?"

He didn't hesitate. "You."

That had Kyle lifting his head to study her closer.

"Do you know why?"

"Because you're alpha." Raven was surprised when Jase spoke.

"My ability is not fully developed yet, but an alpha is still stronger and faster than a pup who hasn't yet turned. You don't have to stay here, but Jamie risked his life to give all three of you this chance. Come or go, the decision is yours. You'll never get another chance to see how pack lives."

Raven dug into her pocket and pulled out a business card that just had her number printed on it and handed it to Jamie. "You're welcome back anytime. Call if you need me."

He bowed almost formally then vanished into the trees. She wanted to tell him stop, ask him why his alpha wanted to kill her, but instincts warned her not to say anything in front of Durant. She and Durant strode back toward the house. She heard one set of feet follow.

That would be Jase.

There were some harsh whispers and soon another set trailed behind them.

As they neared the driveway, she heard the last set finally shuffle forward.

"Would you care to explain?"

Raven studied Durant's impassive expression as he scanned the house. "He saved my life. In return, he asked for a favor."

"Asked? Or did you offer?" Durant shook his head. "You give away too much."

Raven marveled at his reaction, the same reaction as every other shifter. "They're kids. They have no one else."

"Shifter kids are much more dangerous than you can even imagine. Have you ever considered he planned the attack?"

"He wouldn't." Jase cringed, obviously expecting a blow for speaking out of turn.

"Jase is right. He wouldn't. In fact, I suspect he's been watching for a while, protecting us from the rogues camping on the state land behind the house."

"But something changed."

Raven was unsure how much she wanted to share in front of their audience. "A number of rogues have died in the last week. No one seems to care."

Before they entered the house, Dominic stepped from the shadows, his gaze on the woods where Jamie had last been seen. Raven hated that he spent so much time on his own. She hesitated to place him in danger, but he would do what he wanted. "Watch over him. Just be careful."

The wolf disappeared in the darkness, his black fur making him all but invisible, and she quickly lost track of him. She lagged behind the others as they entered the house and headed toward her office. "You three in here."

Durant gave her a narrowed look but didn't protest. "I'll see you later."

Raven stepped to the side, allowing the three boys to enter, watching Durant retreat up the stairs. That was not the way she'd pictured the evening ending. Maybe it was for the best. Things had gotten very intense between them too fast. It made her doubt what was her emotions and what was the moon's call.

When Durant disappeared from view, she turned and entered the office. Jase stood in front of the desk, staring straight ahead at attention, his arms behind his back like some soldier.

The other two boys appeared out of place as they lingered behind him, their eyes darting around the room, but not landing on anything more than a second. Their hair was too long and though they were clean, it was the clean of a quick scrub without benefit of a full shower and soap.

"The rules are simple. This is my home. These people are my family. Treat them as such, and you will be treated the same in return.

Don't and you will have to deal with me. Understood?"

Jase and Brant immediately nodded. Kyle took his time, but finally gave a lazy shrug in agreed as well.

"The food is in the kitchen. Help yourself. Your rooms have been prepared. If you require something, ask either Taggert or Dina and they will get you what you need.

"The rooms are considered yours. You can share or claim your own. I don't care." She noticed they brought no luggage. Their clothes were worn, maybe purchased from second-hand shops, but relatively clean for living in the woods. She rubbed her brow. "Taggert has one of my credit cards. Go to him in the morning and order new clothes and whatever else you need."

No one even moved, all their attention was on her with unnerving intensity. "Do you have any questions?"

Still not a peep.

"Jase, you will be in charge of your small group."

"What do we have to do to earn such rewards?" Jase's face was rigid.

"Rewards?" Raven contemplated them, trying to decipher what they weren't saying. Then she finally comprehended the question. Rogues had demanded payment for everything, their own type of pack. "Stay out of trouble and learn."

"I don't understand." Brant broke the silence.

"Are any of you registered?" If they weren't registered yet, they could still become pack.

Muscles flexed in Jase's arms, his answer a long time in coming. "No."

"In a few days, I'm going to petition for pack status. I'm also on a hunt for a killer targeting rogues. Things could become dangerous. Stay close to the house, and I'll do my best to keep you safe. Use the time to decide what kind of life you want. Understand?"

They all nodded like bobble heads.

A lank of hair fell over Kyle's forehead and recognition finally flashed into her mind. Raven peered toward the exit. "They're ready."

The door popped open as if her words were magic. Dina pranced in, her hands clasped before her in excitement. "This is going to be so much fun! Let me show you to your rooms."

"Kyle." Raven waited until he turned toward her. "A word with you first."

All four shifters paused. Dina took the hint and ushered the other two out the door. "We'll wait at the top of the stairs."

The door shut with a click, and the cocky kid from the forest was back. He crossed his arms and plopped down, his ass landing in the chair beside him with a bounce. He smirked and planted his feet on the chair opposite.

"I'm glad to see your leg is healing."

Those hazel eyes of his washed to green with fear. His expression froze, his body jerked, giving him away. "I don't know what you mean."

"Then let me refresh your memory. I recognize you from the night you tried to kill me. You were in the gray hoodie carrying the knife and brass knuckles."

He blanched, his body tensed, all but quivering under her gaze, but he didn't run.

Then Raven understood.

Because of his brother.

She'd bet everything he'd done had been to protect his younger brother.

"I propose we keep that incident between us. I will assume you were coerced into the job. That's fine. We've all done things that we're not proud of in order to survive. But that stops now. If you're in trouble, come to me. Do this and we'll pretend nothing happened." Raven stood and walked toward the door, remembering nights in the labs where a desperate few shifters had snapped and turned on their own for a chance at freedom. They'd become jailors, almost worse than the white lab coats. She pushed the memories away. This time would be different. This time she could stop it. "Do we have a deal?"

He rose slowly to his feet, the brash teenager knocked out of him. "My brother—"

"Is safe and will not hear a word of it from me. My pack knows of the attack but that's it. If you decide not to stay, he will remain safe. I don't punish people for crimes they didn't commit."

He looked troubled. His dark brows lowered as he walked toward her.

"If you stay, I will assume you've agreed to my terms."

Kyle nodded and passed her.

"One question, though."

He paused, not looking at her.

"Who hired you?"

He slowly lifted his head and gave her a blank stare, his eyes a light green, almost washed of color.

"I'm guessing your alpha gave the order. Do you know if he ordered the hit himself or took it on as a job?"

"I don't know. They just told me what I needed to do." His voice was a rough whisper.

And no doubt was punished when he failed. "Good enough. Use your stay here to learn from the pack. Teach your wolf how to survive."

As they headed up stairs, Raven turned out the lights and followed them. She lingered outside her door, talking herself out of why going down the hall to Durant's room would be such a bad idea.

She liked him.

She was attracted to him.

It only made the situation all the worse.

She could well imagine women throwing themselves at his feet. She wanted to use his past to put distance between them but for one important fact. If Durant loved a woman, he would never let her go.

She cast one last glance down the hall, mourned the loss of her goodnight kiss, but accepted that it was for the best. She entered her room.

Only to have her feet freeze to the carpeting.

It wasn't that the room was clean, the bodies gone. No, it was Durant lying in her bed waiting for her. He was stretched out on her quilt, his hands behind his head, wearing pajamas bottoms, a concession for her, no doubt, looking way too at home. Her heart lurched. "What are you doing?"

"You gave us one day each. My date doesn't end until my twenty-four hours are up."

Heat prickled her skin at the thought of lying in the bed next to him. Touching him. Being touched. Her throat went dry. "But—"

"Sleep only. You have my word." He rolled over to his side, propping his head up on his hand. "It will help you sleep through the moon."

She had no reason to think that he was lying, but the way his pajamas rested low on his hips distracted her from voicing the questions she should be asking. His stomach was ribbed with muscles, not an inch of fat on him. Her fingers itched to explore and see if she was right.

Running more from her betraying thoughts than him, she grabbed her clothes and hurried toward the bathroom. Changing didn't take long enough. She smoothed the leather material of the gloves on her discarded pile, debating the wisdom of her choice. They'd been a part of her life for so long, it felt wrong to be without them.

Durant was on the other side of the door waiting for her. She rested her head against the wood, clenching her eyes shut, half debating if it wouldn't be wiser to flee before things went further.

A knock sounded. Startled, Raven gave a girly squeal and leapt away, tripping over a pile of stacked rubble. The door thudded open, and Durant charged into the room, ready to rip apart anyone he found.

Even as she teetered, he grabbed her arm and hauled her toward him until she was flush against his naked chest.

She couldn't say she hated the way he cradled her so close. She should have pulled away, but his warmth and leather scent drew her. Despite the tension in him, Raven relaxed.

"Was it a mouse?" A teasing smile curled his lips.

"Ass." Her reply was muffled against his chest, but his amusement was infectious. He rubbed his large palms down her arms until he came across her exposed hands. He stepped back, stealing all that delicious warmth.

"Come. Tomorrow will be here all too soon." He retained his hold on her hand, but left the choice up to her.

Raven's fingers tightened reflexively on his, trusting him to pull her out if she started to drown. He drew her into the bedroom, her tension building walls between them.

Durant didn't seem to notice.

Or refused to take heed.

"Crawl up into bed. I'll lock up."

It was easier to get into bed without him in it. She dove beneath the covers, pulling them up to her chin. Durant chuckled, and her gaze jerked toward him.

His smile was gentle when the lights flickered off. The bed dipped, and she lay rigid. Five minutes later, Durant sighed.

"Come here."

His arm reached out of the darkness, dragged her closer. The coldness that'd encased her since the creature had made itself known began to thaw. It was only when he arranged her over his chest that her chaotic thoughts shut down. Unfamiliar peace settled over her.

The scent and heat of him slowly seeped into her skin. He tangled his fingers into her hair as if to keep her tied to him and gave a contented sigh of pure pleasure. Despite the repressed lust cocooning them, she couldn't be more surprised when she woke the next morning, completely relaxed with the first good night's sleep in ages.

"You're awake."

She turned, stretched, and encountered an empty bed. Rolling over, she spied Durant walking out of the bathroom. She wasn't sure how she should feel. But she knew one thing. "You were right. Thank you."

Tension dropped from his shoulders, and he smiled. "My pleasure."

"You're leaving."

He gave a short nod. "My time was up fifteen minutes ago. I need to get back to work and make up for the time I missed yesterday. I'll be back tomorrow night." He strolled toward her, dressed in the work clothes he wore like armor. His face softened when he peered down at her, taking pleasure at seeing her disheveled in a bed he'd just left. "Call me if you need me."

"Not much of a date, huh?" She fiddled with the covers of the blanket, suddenly insecure.

"I wouldn't change a thing." He pressed his mouth to hers, a barely-there brush of his lips that left her tingling from head to toe.

She shivered when he straightened, nearly pulling him down on the bed with her to finish the promise in his kiss.

"Don't forget me on your next date." With that, he turned and walked out of the room, all confident and too sexy for her own good.

## ❧ Chapter Nineteen ❦

**TWO DAYS UNTIL THE FULL MOON: JACKSON'S DAY**

Feeling more than a little trepidation to face Jackson again, Raven trailed down the stairs. Things haven't been right between them since he'd returned. She didn't want their strained relationship pushed to the breaking point.

She pushed opened the door to the kitchen, only to deflate when she found no one.

Again.

Part of her was relieved to put off their next confrontation. She wandered into the kitchen. Aaron stood at the counter, building a sandwich, his movements agitated. "Aaron?"

He barely glanced up at her. "Jackson's in the bathroom getting ready."

"Oh?" Raven walked further into the kitchen.

"Just be careful with him, will you?" He slammed the condiments back in the fridge one at a time.

"What's wrong with Jackson?" Her heart gave a nervous leap at the thought of the indestructible enforcer being hurt.

Aaron whirled on her, his face set in angry lines, but he paused before he spoke. "You don't know."

"Know what?"

"Ask me to go with on your date."

Raven's brow wrinkled at his abrupt about-face. "It's not safe for you to be out in public."

"I'll be safer with the both of you than here alone."

It didn't sound like a threat, but Raven was leery. "Are you sure that's wise with your mother?"

"She'll try to get at me either way. At least out in public, I'll have the two of you to protect me. You'll be expecting her."

"Would she really try to kill her own son?"

"The sooner the better." He didn't show any emotions. He took a bite of his breakfast sandwich and chewed, studying her with a calculation frightening for one so young. "I can guarantee you a day with Jackson without the moon's call interfering."

His generous offer stunned her. Temptation whispered her to grab the offer and quick, before he changed his mind. Instead, Raven walked around the table, unable to place the worry that niggled at the back of her mind. There were always consequences to any route she chose. "Are you able to hold your power all day without any ill affects?"

Aaron shrugged. "Nothing I can't handle."

"Tell me."

"Headaches. Extra tired. I need to consume more calories to stay balanced. Jackson is vulnerable to you, and he doesn't know how to react. Not with you, not while being an enforcer of another pack. He's wound tight. All the distance between the two of you is driving both him and his wolf crazy."

The door opened behind them with a whoosh, and Raven whirled. Jackson had halted on the threshold, stunned to find her there, like he hadn't expected her to show.

Fear and possessiveness whirled in his eyes.

His hands clenched until his knuckles whitened, but otherwise, he gave no other reaction. Raven was shocked to realize that Aaron was correct, and a little jealous to realize that the kid knew Jackson better than her.

She made him vulnerable. If she wasn't strong enough to hold Jackson to her pack, she wasn't sure he would survive. Not the Jackson she knew. But she could do one thing. She'd show him what it could be like to be a member of her pack and demand that he fight for a chance to be with her.

Pack.

Fight for a chance to be with her pack.

Raven mentally flinched at the slip. "Aaron is going with us."

As if she said a chant, the raw emotions plaguing her, made her second-guess her every decision, immediately toned down before it finally dissipated.

The relief was instantaneous.

What surprised her was that she missed the little hum her animals emitted at the back of her mind. She hadn't realized they were awake and aware, helping her get through the day.

Jackson swallowed. "Agreed."

"Aaron, why don't you get ready. We'll meet you outside."

The boy left without a word, scooting around Jackson to escape the kitchen. Raven walked forward, stopping right in front of him.

She had one more thing to do before she forgave him.

She drew back her hand and slapped him. Her palm stung. His head whipped to the side, and he rubbed his face, working his jaw as he turned toward her.

"Don't you ever scare me like that again. If you leave me, at least have the balls to tell me to my face." She couldn't bear to have him vanish on her again.

He gave a brief nod.

Unable to help herself, she closed the distance between them and wrapped her arms around him. He stiffened in her embrace then very slowly hugged her in return, almost afraid that if he touched her, she would vanish.

He ducked his head next to hers and inhaled slowly, and some of the strain finally peeled away from him.

"Are we ready?" Aaron swung open the door then backed out.

As reality intruded, Raven pulled back. His arms took longer to drop, but when he drew away, some of the Jackson she recognized was back.

"Are you ready?"

He grabbed her hand, his eyes so intense that she had to force herself not to pull away. "I think so."

Why did that phrase sound so ominous? Not wanting to ruin their date with a fight, she put it behind her and smiled. "Where are we going?"

\* \* \*

They rode to town in Jackson's black diesel. The loud rumble of the engine suggested some kind of programmer had been added for extra power. The inside was pristine, the seats a supple gray leather. The care he took of his truck surprised her, and she suspected he would treat his woman the same way.

She watched Jackson maneuver through traffic, sitting so close, yet the distance between them was greater than ever. The vents circulated his fresh cut grass scent, one that had haunted her through the long nights. She never expected to be granted a second chance, and she wasn't going to squander it. "Do you travel a lot with your job?"

Jackson glanced at her briefly, the first look he sent her since entering the vehicle twenty minutes ago. They were almost to town.

"Depends on the job."

When he said nothing more, she turned to stare at him. Annoyance at his behavior began to dig its way under her skin. "Either you can't tell me anything because of your pack rules, or you're being an ass. If you don't want this date, turn around."

The truck didn't slow down. If anything, it sped up as if he thought she'd jump out of the vehicle.

"He can't talk about some of it." Aaron popped his head between the seats, his eyes urging her to be patient.

"Then tell me, what does an enforcer do? London does my security, but I let him handle all of that."

When Jackson remained mute, Aaron rolled his eyes and nudged him.

"I solve any issues that prevent the pack from running smoothly."

Now that her animals were securely locked away, her power gradually increased with her irritation. "The purpose of the date is to get to know each other. I asked a question. Did you want to ask me anything?"

There was a slight hesitation, like he didn't want to inquire but needed to know. "Why did you come back for me?"

Raven's brows furrowed. "That's what you want to ask?" She heaved a sigh. "You're pack. *My* pack. Why wouldn't I come?"

His hands clenched on the steering wheel. He turned and stared at her so long, the truck veered into the other lane. Horns blared. He jerked the wheel, easily keeping the vehicle under control. He didn't look at her again, but there was a cocky curl to his lips that had been missing since he'd come home.

That's when she knew they'd be all right. In under five minutes, they hit the edge of the city.

They pulled up to a deli just as a parking spot opened. "I'll be right back."

Jackson jumped out of the truck and disappeared inside the small building. The mid-morning was surprisingly busy, people swarming the shops along both sides of the streets. Five minutes passed when he emerged with a basket in his hand.

"Shit." Aaron hopped out of the vehicle without warning.

"Wait." Raven tore her gaze from drooling over Jackson's muscular form, cursing herself for being so easily distracted, and threw opened her door. She scanned the crowd, trying to locate what'd set Aaron off.

The sidewalks were crowded. People pressed in on all sides, their stink nearly stifling with the lack of breeze. Jackson must have sensed her unease. He hurried forward, placing her in between himself and Aaron. With his large body, people automatically veered around him.

Then Raven recognized the woman who'd exited the store three doors down.

"Shit." She unconsciously echoed Aaron's earlier sentiment.

"Hello, Son." Vivian smiled sweetly, mockery coating her greeting as she strode up to them. "I was worried that she was keeping you prisoner. I almost sent some men to make sure you were being treated all right."

The area around them immediately cleared of humans, only a few *normals* brave enough, or maybe stupid enough, lingered to snap pictures in hopes of capturing an altercation in all its digital glory.

The tension in the air was palpable. Though Vivian's words were a veiled insult, Raven curled her hands into fists to stop herself from reaching for the strands of energy that begged to be used. She wanted to avoid an incident if possible. Aaron had more than enough experience to handle his mother.

Jackson appeared torn, uncertain who he should protect. If he thought she was in danger, he would risk everything to protect her.

Vivian was no fool. She wouldn't go for the direct approach, much less openly attack in public.

"Not to worry, Mother. I couldn't be safer if I was in the bosom of my loving family." The boy she'd recognize had vanished, in his place stood a young man on the cusp of becoming a very powerful alpha in his own right. One that should make any mother proud, if she were anyone other than Vivian.

While they traded barbs, Raven tracked the movement of the three wolves spread out behind Vivian, watching for any signs of aggression. Jackson wouldn't be able to go up against his own pack without consequences. She and Aaron had to keep him out of the fight if things went south.

"I expect you are taking good care of my son. If anything happens to him, I will hold you personally responsible."

Raven nearly snorted at Vivian's machinations. "No worries. The only way anyone would be able to touch him is over my dead body."

Vivian's smile hardened. "Then we are in agreement."

Without a goodbye, she strode past, walking between Raven and Jackson as if to divide them. The stench of sex wafted off the woman, strong enough to crawl down her throat and choke her. Her goons followed, though they stepped more carefully. None of the three gave any indication that they knew Jackson or Aaron. Raven would venture a guess that they were Vivian's personal guards. She had a feeling that they'd find out soon enough.

The meeting was timed almost perfectly. Too perfectly. They were watching the house. She expected that, it's what she would've done, but why the staged meeting?

"She was testing our defenses." Jackson guided her toward the truck with a hand on her back. He went into protective mode, stuffing her and the basket into the truck. He was so distracted that when he reached over and buckled her seatbelt, the back of his arm brushed her breast. He went rigid, realizing what he'd done.

She grabbed his wrist before he could retreat. When he turned his head to her in question, their faces halted inches apart. "There are three of them and three of us. If it comes down to a fight, I would put money on us."

"She thinks she can take you." Jackson grinned, both of them knowing what would happen if they were challenged in a fair fight.

Raven matched his smile. "Won't she be surprised."

He slammed the door to the truck and circled around. Aaron slipped into the back, and she glanced at him for an explanation. "He's different."

"He had nothing to lose before."

"So how do I get my Jackson back?" Maintaining her distance wasn't cutting it anymore. It was too late to prevent either of them from getting hurt.

Jackson scowled when he entered the vehicle. "Why don't you try asking me?"

He pulled away from the curb with a chirp of tires.

"Maybe I would if you would stop dodging my questions."

"I'm trying to do my job." He weaved through traffic, stomping on the accelerator.

"Does that entitle you to being such an ass?" Getting more than a little pissed, Raven felt the bite of power build under her skin. She welcomed the distraction, surprised at how much she'd missed the burn of it.

"Give me your gloves."

The abrupt change in subject threw her. Suspicions wormed their way into her mind, and her immediate response was to deny him. "Why?"

He only held out his hand. Deciding to trust him, she slowly worked the leather off her fingers. "I hope you know what you're doing."

## ৵ Chapter Twenty ৶

**T**he park Jackson picked was off the beaten path. The term *park* being used loosely. Trees crowded the small grove. The grass was overgrown, the undergrowth and deadfall slowing their progress.

"Where are we going?"

Jackson merely nudged her along. "It's only a little further."

Grumbling under her breath, she pushed forward, ducking away from a swarm of bugs that torpedoed pass her.

She heard water first. Unaware there were any streams in this area, she veered away and followed the sound. Trees thinned. The rough terrain smoothed out. She came to a stop atop a small bluff that overlooked their own personal lagoon.

The small pool rested less than ten feet below them. The water kissed the grass, the surface absolutely calm. The trees kept their distance, giving her a good fifteen feet on either side to keep watch for trouble.

Everything was a green so bright that her eyes hurt. The wind blew the smell of cut grass to her that reminded her of Jackson. Pleasure warmed her face, and she turned to ask how he'd found this place.

Her voice dried up to see Jackson charge toward her.

Raven tensed as she scanned the surroundings, frustration bubbling up in her chest when she wasn't able to detect the danger.

Then Jackson was there.

He bent like a football player and hit her low. Her legs cleared the ground and then they were flying through the air.

She caught sight of Aaron's laughing face seconds before she hit the water. Raven came up sputtering, her hair coming down around her face as she treaded water. "You bastard. What was that for?"

Jackson dove under the surface, his body cutting through the water with ease. The shadow of him circled below her like a predator closing in for the kill. A hand brushed her hip, another trailed up her spine. She narrowed her eyes, then pried off her shoes and tossed them to shore. She whirled to keep him in view, half expecting him to surface.

Instead, there was a tug on her ankles, and she found herself submerged in the water. She spotted Jackson a few feet away, grinning ear from ear. The smoothness of his movements drew her attention to his body, the flex of all that muscle tempting her to linger and just watch him move.

Thankfully, he couldn't access those damned senses of his underwater and use her attraction against her.

She launched herself forward, but by the time she closed the distance, the spot he'd occupied was empty. The thrill of the chase tempted her to forget about her troubles and just enjoy. A hand brushed her ass, and she twisted. But instead of moving, Jackson wrapped his arms around her.

They slowly sank to the bottom of the pool, a hazy light drifting down to them. Her hair floated around them like a cloud, and he carefully brushed the strands away from her face, his fingers lingering on her skin.

Raven grabbed his wrist, and his gaze shot to hers. She smiled then shoved up off the bottom. Jackson was so startled, she slipped through his hold and broke the surface.

He quickly followed. When he reached for her, she allowed the current to drag her away. Laugher bubbled up in her chest at his befuddled expression. Then he grinned and dove after her.

After another twenty minutes of playing and ducking his pursuit, Raven finally surrendered. She crawled to the shore and fell on her back, panting for air. Eyes closed, she basked in the bright rays of the sun on her skin.

When a shadow passed over her, she shivered and cracked open an eye. Jackson. The sight of his wet clothes plastered to his body sucked all thought from her head. The man had been built to bedevil women. He grinned and shook himself like his wolf counterpart, sending a shower of cool droplets raining down on her.

Raven squealed then took her cue from him and knocked his feet out from under him. He landed with a heavy oomph. Before she could scramble out of the way, he rolled, taking her with him until she lay partially under his large form.

He picked up a strand of her hair, flipping the silver tips through his fingers, studying the ragged edges. "I'm not the only one who's changed."

"Changed?" The enjoyment of the afternoon faded, cold seeping into her gut. Yes, she was changing. Old fears and doubts rose again like they'd never left, and the fragile shell she built around her cracked.

"You're becoming an alpha."

"Yes." There was no denying it. She had no choice if she wanted to survive. Though uncomfortable under his scrutiny, she refused to run away from the truth anymore.

"You're good, but you're not strong or fast enough yet. You're adapting to your animals amazingly fast, but the conclave is in two days."

He fell silent, words locked behind his lips.

She cupped his face. "Tell me."

"I won't lose you again. I can't."

"So you brought me here to..."

"Aaron is holding back your animals. Even now, I can feel your power building, reaching for me."

Raven let her hand fall away from him. "You planned this whole thing."

"Yes."

Well, at least he didn't lie to her, but how could she be mad that he would throw away their one chance at a date to protect her. "Where do we go from here?"

He rose, and she shivered without his warmth. He offered her his hand. Raven hesitated then set her fingers in his palm.

He yanked.

Raven flew into the water with a splash. Her head went under the water, and she came up sputtering. "What the hell?"

"I've been reading up on electricity. I suspect you can handle a lot more than you believe if you just trust yourself."

He was so confident that she didn't know how to answer him. "I burned out that night Taggert and I were being hunted. With the moon call following so quickly, I haven't had the chance to test anything."

"But you can now. You have to use everything you possess to survive and thrive in the pack. You can't hesitate. You must learn to master the two sides of yourself."

"You don't know what you're asking." Raven waded toward the shore, fine sand shifting beneath her feet.

Jackson waved her back. "Don't make me throw you back in."

Raven instantly halted, placing her hands on her hips. "I'd like to see you try."

"Do you know what you're problem is?"

Raven raised a brow. "I only have one?"

"You need to trust others. You need to let go." Jackson slicked back his hair. The action pulled tight the wet shirt he wore. The sight of all the muscle made her swallow hard. It took her a second to realize he was still speaking.

"And I'm going to show you how to follow through on your threat. Durant helped you with your animals. I can already see the difference."

"You have no idea how dangerous my power can be without control."

"But I do. It was your power, along with your wolf, that healed me." He stalked along the banks. "You must think like an alpha if you have any hopes of keeping your pack. You must be ruthless. Stop worrying about hurting us. We're grown men. We've made our decisions. We can't lose you now. So we need you to fight for us."

They wanted her to give up all pretenses of control. They couldn't possibly understand the consequences. But they were correct in one respect. She wasn't acting like a shifter. They would slaughter her if she didn't learn. "What do you think you know about my condition?"

"You're standing in water. It's a conduit for electricity. Let loose your power and learn how to control it."

Raven debated the wisdom of his request, but what did she have to lose?

"It's a hot spring. The water in the pool comes from an underground reservoir. There are no animals or plant life."

"So that's why the water is so warm." Everything was so very well thought out that it eased some of her trepidation. He'd obviously put a lot of effort into planning today.

She gave him a stiff nod then closed her eyes.

And hesitated, realizing that she'd never called upon her full power when there wasn't a need. She wasn't sure what to expect, especially after all the abuse last week. The burnout. Part of her feared she might have done her gift permanent harm.

Taking a deep breath, Raven dropped her shield. The energy eagerly escaped its cage and forked through her body. All but an ugly black void in her gut where a spark had burned too bright for too long. Even with her animals accelerated healing, there was no reversing the damage.

Electricity slithered under her skin, her body adapted quickly, welcoming the heat. Despite her turbulent past, she didn't want her gift gone. She only wanted control.

Then she did something she'd never done before and let her power loose on the world. Water swirled around her like she'd been dunked into a fryer. Her skin heated to near blistering, ready to burst under the pressure. Her toes curled into the sand. Gritting her teeth, Raven widened her stance and took the agony. Current sloshed around in her gut, slowly clamping down on her insides.

When her throat began to ache from holding back her screams, the pain finally eased. She opened her eyes to find Jackson standing at complete attention, preparing to rescue her despite the fact that it would almost certainly kill him.

Aaron sat by the basket, a forgotten apple in his hand. He met her gaze and gulped the mouthful of food. "Holy crap."

She gave a brief smile. "Yours just might not be the most dangerous talent out there, kid."

"I hid something in the water for you to find." Jackson seated himself next to Aaron and began removing items from the basket. "You better hurry before the food gets cold."

"Do I get a hint?"

"That would be cheating. You have to earn your present."

Jackson didn't even bother to turn.

"Present?" Her belly flip-flopped at the word. Part of her wanted to find what he went through all the trouble to hide. The rest of her wanted to leap out of the water, half expecting the gift would come with strings to tangle around her feet and drown her.

Taking a deep breath, she dove beneath the surface. Every inch of her skin felt sunburned, the current twisting and rubbing against every inch of exposed skin. She'd never been so completely submerged in her gift.

She had to surface for air three times before her body adjusted to the new denseness in the water. On the fifth dive, she hit bottom. There were no weeds. The whole area was covered by tiny granulates of sand and stone that time had eroded.

She circled twice before she ran out of air. "There is nothing down there."

Jackson smirked. "You're using your eyes. Did you think I would just leave it lying around for easy pickings? Use your power. That's the whole point of this exercise."

He took a big bite out of his chicken wing, his white teeth making short work of the meat, and she could easily picture him feasting in his wolf form.

With another breath of air, she dove under. When she called on her power, the whole pond responded. The shock was so unexpected, so sudden, she gasped. Water immediately filled her mouth, spilling down her throat.

She shot to the surface, choking as she sloshed toward shore. On her hands and knees, she waited for the press of panic to fade.

Jackson and Aaron remained seated, watching with unblinking eyes. She scowled at them, hating that they'd witnessed her failure. And it wasn't like they could help. This was something that she had to do herself.

Pushing to her feet with shaky legs, Raven turned, splashing back into the water and dove under. Knowing what to expect didn't lessen the jolt of pain, like being wrapped in frayed wire that gave off a nasty shock, but she braced for it.

Just when she thought she'd run out of air, the pressure on her lungs eased. She used the energy to search for something man-made.

Three plastic beer rings, a pair of sunglasses and thirty-seven cents later, she came up for air. She tossed the items on shore.

Since that wasn't working, she decided to search for something recent. Only the whole floor lit up in a blue glow, thousands of individual pieces of sand twinkling like her own private galaxy. The unexpected beauty stunned her. She hadn't realized how many granulates had dropped from the current.

She pushed off the bottom and treaded water. Jackson had fouled up the water when he dove in with her, so she couldn't trace his movements. There wasn't any scent to follow under water.

But what could she see? With another deep breath, she settled on the bottom. She pulled the electricity around her then sank it into the sand. Little whirls where she and Jackson had frolicked spun through the water. She also saw her power build in a light blue color where she herself pushed up the bottom or dug for treasure.

A light pure blue illuminated a large rock. Or more specifically, underneath the rock. Swimming forward, Raven gave the small boulder a shove to get it rolling. Beneath rested a small black bag.

She picked it up; caught off guard by the lack of weight. Wanting to make sure it was what Jackson had secreted away for her, she opened the tie strings and tipped the bag over.

A cord of silver slinked out, the metal cutting through the water in a way that caught the fractured light and sent it sparkling. She pulled out the chain until it pooled into her palm.

A large tear-shaped stone slipped through the water, floating down into her waiting hand. The bright blue stone was encased in a swirling silver lace of vines and leaves. Once the stone landed in her palm, it warmed to her touch. It had to be the size of a quarter, and no doubt very real.

If she accepted the gift, the lace would rest right below her collarbone. When her lungs finally protested the lack of oxygen, she shoved toward the surface.

Lights danced along the edges of the pool. But a foot away from air, the water darkened, offering resistance. It was actually a physical effort to break topside.

She opened her mouth to call out to Jackson when she spotted that they had company. Three men faced off against Jackson while a fourth hovered near the tree line to observe. She immediately recognized him from Vivian's entourage.

She swam closer to shore, walking when her feet finally brushed the pebbled bottom.

That's when the shifters noticed her.

Raven halted when the water lapped her thigh, afraid to venture further with all her power sunk into the pool and her animals tamed. "Problems, everyone?"

The shifter nearest Aaron took a step back at her arrival. "No one told us she'd be here. I didn't sign up for this."

Trailing her fingers in the water like a stirring stick, Raven pulled at the power. Energy seared up her arm, the coolness of the liquid dropping away. Blue sparks similar to a flint being struck snapped around her hand and up her elbow.

Two shifters launched themselves at Jackson. Aaron didn't wait and threw himself into the fray. She imagined a ball, wrapping the blue cords tight.

"Down!"

Jackson and Aaron immediately dropped as she drew back her hand, so did the one shifter that had protested. When she let loose the ball, it crackled like static. The power shot out, the cords unraveling like a weed whip. The raw energy plowed into the two shifters that remained standing. They flew backwards, their momentum only stopped by a tree. Wood groaned in protest at the impact, and their bodies thumped to the ground.

They didn't move.

Raven slowly walked out of the water, each droplet clung to her like a lover's kiss, delivering a charge of power before slushing off. She eyed the two remaining shifters. "You were following orders. That's done now. I suggest you pick up your men and leave."

She rubbed her fingers together until electricity crackled. "Or I will take care of you in a more permanent manner."

Their movements were slow so as not to startle her as if she were a dangerous animal. They picked up their comrades and backed away, never taking their eyes off her. When they put two hundred yards between them, they turned and disappeared into the forest.

"You found it."

Raven followed Jackson's gaze to the necklace still tangled in her fingers. He gently pried the metal from her grip, walked behind her, and lifted the pendant over her head. When the stone came to rest on her chest, the lace holding the stone in place curled up and over her collarbone.

"Where did you find a sapphire this size?"

"It's a rare blue diamond. It matches your eyes when I first saw you." He meant when the power was riding her hard. "It's nearly indestructible, so anything you do will not affect it."

He gathered her hair out of the way, carefully spreading the wet strands over her shoulders. When he stepped in front of her, the tips of his fingers were red and blistered from the silver. "It suits you."

"It's bad ass." Awe coated Aaron's words, excitement thrumming through him.

Raven's brows furrowed, his comment completely lost on her. "What?"

"When the other shifters see that you can stand that amount of silver directly against your skin, it sends a message."

She hesitated, wondering if advertising her differences was such a good idea, not if it would lead them to dig further into a past she didn't want revealed.

## Chapter Twenty-one

**B**y the time Aaron and Jackson packed up the basket, Raven had wrestled on her wet shoes. A pall had fallen over the afternoon. The secluded paradise no longer felt safe. Maybe it was for the best. She wasn't sure how she should act around Jackson and his too generous gift.

Though the men meant well, she felt like the one with the rough edges. She didn't fit anywhere. They were right that she hated relying on others. She only accepted their training grudgingly, when it had come down to survival.

She just hoped it wasn't too late.

Jackson got them back to the house in record time, the sunlight beginning to fade from the sky in a ball of orange fire on the horizon. Despite the turn of events, Raven had enjoyed herself. Jackson's confidence in her gave her the courage to push herself.

She never would've thought using a smaller amount of electricity would be harder than just allowing her power free rein. The aftereffects of burnout were still evident, but they were less. The last two days gave her hope that she'd ultimately be able to find a balance between her two worlds when she had though the only outcome would tear her apart.

"Here." Aaron accepted the basket Jackson handed to him. While he disappeared inside, Jackson came around to her open door, stopping her from exiting.

"If things don't go right with Vivian—"

Raven kicked him in the gut with both feet. He shot from the cab, nearly landing ass over teakettle. Raven jumped from the truck, storming toward him. "What the hell was this afternoon about if you didn't think I could handle all of this?"

When she would've left him in the dirt, he rolled and snagged her ankle. The ground rushed up to meet her. She would've face-planted into the gravel if her reflexes hadn't taken over.

Her palms stung as she slammed into the earth. Before she could contemplate more, she was dragged backwards. Feeling no pity, she tipped to her side, bent her knee and aimed for his nose.

He easily deflected the blow then grinned and pulled her under him. She managed to hit him with her elbow to his jaw, missing his temple and the chance to stun him.

He pinned her wrists to either side of her head. Without Aaron being close, the moon's heat crept over her.

Slow.

Insidious.

The fight turned into foreplay, both wanting to be caught.

Once he had her immobile, he leaned forward and rested his forehead against hers. "I have faith in you, but Vivian won't rest until she has what she wants. You are in the way of that. If it comes to a choice, I will choose you and my life will be forfeit. They will put me down like an animal."

Raven twisted his thumb toward his wrist, pleased when his grip broke. She grabbed his face. "I forbid it."

"You don't get it. I was sent here with the knowledge that if I did my job and protected Aaron, I was a dead man. I don't protect him, I'm dead. I can save him from the men she might send, but if she wants him killed bad enough, she just has to walk past me and murder him, and I can't do a damn thing."

Her hand fell back to the ground, stunned by his logic. She'd missed it in her conversation with Aaron, or had ignored it because she didn't want to face the truth. Since he was the enforcer, she'd thought he would be exempt. Fighting his own pack was bad enough, but she never expected this. "Then why?"

"I'm incentive."

"For me." Then it made horrible sense. "Bait."

He heaved a sigh, rolled on his back, throwing his arm up to cover his eyes. The part of damsel in distress sat ill on him.

Jackson would do his job...even if it meant his death.

Part of her had to wonder if the whole thing had been a set-up, or if Kevin had just taken advantage of the circumstances when the opportunity presented itself.

They were using Jackson to lure her into settling the war brewing inside their pack. Kevin refused to give up his son, but realizing that more people would be killed, the pack destroyed from within, if something wasn't done.

That's where she came in.

Clever bastard.

She'd call him on it if it weren't for two reasons. Aaron really did need protection.

And if they survived, Jackson would be hers.

Raven leaned up on her elbow. When Jackson didn't move, she leaned over and brushed her lips over his, stealing the taste of him.

Jackson seized up, afraid to react lest she pull away. His eyes, not quite hidden under his arm, had splintered yellow and whiskey brown. He feathered his fingers across the smooth skin where her necklace had rested. "Amazing."

Not willing to delve too deeply into his comment, uncomfortable under the admiration she'd done nothing to deserve, she leaned back and hesitantly stroked the necklace. "Why doesn't my body react as everyone else?"

Jackson sat, not bothering to dust off. "I'm not sure. There are many things about you that are different." Then he turned toward her with a suddenness that took her off guard. "Promise me you will not remove this necklace until after the conclave."

Raven studied him, trying to read past the demand, but couldn't riddle it out. "Why?"

"It's silver. If a shifter comes after you, it can be used as a weapon." He grabbed her wrist in an unbreakable grip, expecting her to deny him. "Promise."

The piece was beautiful and obviously cost a fortune. What meant more to her was the thought and consideration he put into his gift. Even though it would raise questions, she couldn't refuse him. "Until after the conclave."

His face relaxed a fraction, and he bounded to his feet. "I'm starved. Let's see if they saved us any food."

Raven accepted his hand, surprised when he didn't release her as they walked toward the house. She brushed off her clothes as they entered.

The low level of smoke in the room made Jackson groan. Raven couldn't help it, she laughed. "You're wish was granted. There will be plenty of food remaining. Must have been Dina's night to cook."

His hand gripped hers almost reflexively, maybe remembering when she abandoned him to his first meal here. She took pity on him, not wanting the evening to end. "Why don't you see if there is anything left intact. It's still our date. We can have an alfresco in my room."

"Give me ten minutes." Jackson strode away, full of purpose, a contented whistle on his lips now that they had a plan.

By the time Raven finished her quick shower and a change of clothes, Jackson was back. He pilfered the blanket from the bed and arranged it before the opened balcony doors. The evening air held a soft breeze. He turned off almost all the lights, so that the stars were spread out before them.

A bit nervous being alone with him, Raven hesitantly crossed the room. Jackson had his back toward her, a rare beer in his hand. Shifters didn't usually drink, their metabolism running through the alcohol too quickly.

He changed into a pair of jeans. His black t-shirt fitted him like it had been finger-painted on him. In a fight, no one could grab your clothes and use it against you. The effect on him was stunning.

But what caught her attention was his bare feet. It changed his appearance to someone more approachable, made him not so indestructible. Then it dawned on her what made him look different. It was the first time since his return that she'd ever seen him relaxed.

"Any trouble?"

He raised a brow as if anyone would dare stop him. And he was more than likely correct.

"How is your room with Aaron?"

"More than adequate." He purposely didn't look at the couch where he'd slept on his previous stay, but he had to notice that she hadn't removed it.

His couch. Just waiting for him.

The meal went quickly, Jackson attending her by keeping her plate full and sharing entertaining stories. When Aaron peeked his head in the door, Jackson's face shut down as he stood.

Raven gained her feet slower, suddenly anxious as she waved Aaron into the room. "We're ready for you."

He headed to the couch, his hands full of bedding.

A snarl rose from Jackson, his wolf tracking the kid's every movement, waiting for the chance to lunge for his throat. A sudden bout of nervousness shot her speech all the crap. When Jackson tensed to leap, she blurted out her invitation, her face burning at the awkwardness. "Aaron volunteered to be our chaperone for the night."

Jackson pivoted toward her so fast, she nearly retreated a step. One did not run from shifters unless you wanted to be chased. The ferocity on his face had her wonder if she made a tactical error. "If you want."

He gave her a short nod then bent to pack up the supper. When she went to retrieve her pajamas, his gaze trailed after her, every inch the wolf stalking his prey. She prayed she hadn't made a big mistake.

\* \* \*

Raven woke to movement. She cracked open one eye to find Jackson with his head resting on his hand, staring down at her. The dead serious expression on his face stopped her smile short. That was not a look of a contented man.

Trouble had found her again.

She jerked into sitting position, the hope for a few moments of peace shattered. She scanned the room, noting they were alone. "What's wrong?"

"Nothing. Aaron went down to breakfast twenty minutes ago."

Raven's brows furrowed, and she stopped scooting toward the edge of the bed. "Then why..."

"My day is almost up. I didn't want to miss even a second of our time together."

A half smile tipped her lips, some of the tension easing as Raven pulled the blankets back up. "You'll be back in the pack soon enough."

He nodded, but didn't appear appeased.

"Are you doubting me?"

He didn't blink as he stared. "You don't know how persistent Vivian can be. She gave up too easy. She's planning something."

Though Raven didn't know Vivian like Jackson, she agreed with his assessment. "All we can do is be prepared."

"I want you to promise me that if anything happens, you will do whatever necessary to keep safe."

Raven realized his expression now, the one he'd worn since he'd been returned to her. He didn't expect to survive. "You worry too much, Jackson. I know I'm new to shifter protocol, but I'm a lot harder to get rid of than you might expect. I'll do whatever's necessary to keep my pack together." And if he didn't know it yet, that meant him. She caressed his jaw, the stubble prickling her fingers.

He closed his eyes and leaned into her touch as if relishing it for the last time. Raven didn't understand how shifters could live with the constant uncertainty in their lives.

Once a shifter entered a pack, it was near impossible to break the bonds, no matter how desperate they might want to escape servitude to their alpha.

Jackson caressed the warm stone of her necklace. The clock revealed they had ten minutes remaining before their date officially ended. Likely the last few minutes they would have alone until after the conclave.

When she opened her mouth to ask him a question, he lunged forward and kissed her. This was no light brush of lips that they'd shared in the past. He devoured her, unable to get enough of her taste. Tongue and teeth dueled. He cupped the back of her head, pulling her closer.

His arousal pressed against her, and Raven groaned. In the past, she would've pulled away. This time, she only wanted to get closer. When she shifted restlessly against him, Jackson slipped his hand down her side, his thumb brushing at the edges of her breast, before trailing his fingers lower. He cupped the back of her thigh and pulled her leg over his hip.

She gasped at the intimate contact, and he took advantage, sliding his lips against her throat. Only to hiss when he encountered the necklace.

Without a word, he left the bed. She instantly felt bereft. Before she could gather her wits to protest, he disappeared out the door. Raven fell back against the mattress and sighed.

Then his reaction hit her.

A kiss goodbye.

He thought this would be his last chance, so he took and savored what she normally wouldn't have offered.

He was so convinced that he wasn't going to survive, her heart turned heavy with dread. She rolled out of bed and shivered, vowing to make sure he didn't slip out of her hold this time.

## ❧ Chapter Twenty-two ❧

**DAY BEFORE THE FULL MOON: TAGGERT'S DAY**

Raven fingered the necklace, the stone a warm presence under her shirt. Today was her last date. Her last day of freedom before the conclave. A part of her wondered if it would also be her last day with Taggert if she wasn't able to gain alpha status.

Taking a deep breath, she pushed into the kitchen. Only to find she'd been stood up for the third day in a row. She refused to feel disappointment at not finding Taggert waiting for her. She hadn't realized how accustomed she was to having him near.

"Have you seen Taggert?"

Aaron shoveled a spoonful of cereal into his mouth. He shook his head, then tipped back and spoke around his food. "Hasn't come down yet."

Something was wrong.

Taggert always woke early. He'd been looking forward to his date. He wouldn't be late.

She took the stairs two at a time then veered down the hallway toward his room. She knocked but received no response. Concern grew into alarm. Shoving open the door, she scanned the room.

What she saw stopped her cold. The room was bare, stripped of everything but the furniture, as if he had no intention of staying. A bubble of pain rose in her chest at the thought of him deserting her. Her hand tightened on the knob as if, by her will alone, she could force him to choose her.

She backed out of the room, hurt tightening her throat. He was hers. She refused to let him just walk out of her life without confronting him.

She turned to find Jase standing in the hall waiting for her. She licked her lips, her heart beating a little too fast. Could he already be gone? "Have you seen Taggert? We were supposed to meet."

Jase pointed down the hall. "He's with the boys ordering some items."

Raven slowly released her breath, but the fear of losing Taggert wouldn't be dismissed so easily. When Jase didn't move or say anything more, Raven pushed away her concern and focused on him.

He appeared preoccupied, his complexion sallow, not the intent soldier from the night before. "What's wrong?"

"You're giving us too much."

Raven didn't understand. "Explain."

"We're rogues. The bottom rung. We're not allowed to own possessions. If a bigger shifter comes along, they will claim everything. None of us are strong enough to protest without getting killed."

She hadn't known the situation was so stark. "What would you suggest?"

That seemed to stump him. He rubbed his chin, the movement lifting his shirt. Massive black and putrid green bruises covered his torso.

The decision was easy. "Order what you need. Use this time to decide what type of future you want. Being a rogue is not the only option for you."

Raven nodded toward his injuries, not willing to believe one of her people laid a finger on him. "Tell me who hurt you."

Jase clutched his ribs then immediately dropped his arm. "It's nothing."

"Let me help."

He lifted his chin, pride keeping him quiet. "Then let me earn my keep. Give me something to do."

She understood the need to feel useful. If she assigned him a job, they could keep watch, find out who's beating on him and take care of it. "Go to London. He'll teach you how to fight. You'll be paired and added to the rosters to do nightly rounds of the grounds."

Jase straightened, not expecting to be selected for something so important as their safety. "Thank you."

Raven snorted. "You haven't met London yet."

Taggert hurried down the hallway in their direction, the slightly harried expression relaxing when he saw her. "Sorry I'm late."

"Not at all. You were busy." Like a sliver burrowing under her skin, it bothered her that he'd made a place for himself in her life when he had no intention of staying.

Raven gestured toward his room. "Do you mind if we talk?"

His face smoothed out until all emotions vanished. "Of course."

He entered first, his presence a stark contrast to the abandoned room.

"Do you want to be here?"

His head snapped up, tracking her as she stopped by the window. "Yes."

"I don't understand. When Durant decided to move into the house, he remodeled two rooms without a by your leave. Yet, you haven't done anything to claim yours."

"I'm waiting until after the full moon." His hair was pulled back and tied at the base of his skull. The sunlight filtered through the window, highlighting the natural streaks that tempted her to run her fingers through the strands. All the passiveness melted in his eyes, the sharp hope there painful to witness. And she realized he was allowing her to see it.

It took her a few seconds to understand what he was saying without words. He wanted back into her room. Heat filled her face. "Oh."

Pack slept together, usually in twos or threes, touch an important element to their culture. It bound them together. It could be used as a sign of favor or a punishment.

It was nothing special.

But it didn't feel that way to her.

Sensing her unease, he gave a sudden smile. "Why don't we head downstairs?"

Glad for the reprieve, Raven accepted his overture. They walked into the hall together, the silence awkward. She hadn't gone two steps when Taggert slipped his hand into hers. Surprised by the move, she nearly tripped over her own feet.

"I read up on what humans do on dates."

Raven gave a half smile, a queer little turn in her stomach leaving her feeling half a step out of sync. "Holding hands."

"Did I do it wrong?"

His question caught her off guard, made her realize how little life he had outside of being a slave. "Not wrong. Just unexpected. What do shifters do on dates?"

"Hunt. Run. Have sex." Taggert shrugged. "Humans go on dates to search for their mate. Most shifters have their mates chosen for them. Since you wanted to get to know us more..."

"Right." They resumed walking, his shoulder's brushing hers. "So where are we heading?"

Taggert tugged on her hand, pulling her toward the kitchen. "Food first. You've lost weight. You need to eat more or your power will start cannibalizing those closest to you. Shifters are similar in a way."

She learned about her power the hard way, but the shifter thing was new. "So if I don't eat enough—"

"Our animal grows more aggressive, the need to hunt more insistent." They entered the kitchen, and Taggert hauled her toward the fridge.

He removed a large amount of food, either handing it to her or placing it on the cupboard. "What are we making?"

"A quick breakfast."

Raven rubbed her mouth to smother a smile. "Quick?"

There was a slight hitch in his movements before he caught onto her teasing. "Wash these."

She automatically grabbed the vegetables. Peppers she didn't remember being in there yesterday. "You purchased these for today."

He didn't even bother to turn around as he cracked eggs. "Wash."

The preparations went faster than expected, Taggert's efficiency sexy to watch. "Who taught you how to cook?"

"My father."

The water drained down the sink as she stood staring at him.

He pointed the whisk at her. "Wash."

When she did as told, he pulled out a few pans and tossed in some butter and spices. "Did you think I was born without one?"

The amusement made her wince. "Of course not. But you're a rogue. I thought that..." She didn't know what she'd thought.

"He wanted better for me. Made me promise that when he died that I would try to gain pack status."

That meant five years ago Taggert was left on his own as a teenager, pledging himself as a slave to just survive. She turned off the water, and he handed her a knife.

"Thin slices."

She didn't take it, studying him instead, marveling at the courage it took for him to just survive.

"The sharp, pointy end goes down."

Rolling her eyes, Raven did as told and prepped the peppers and onions. "What was your childhood like?"

"Good." He expertly lifted a pan and tossed the contents. "He wasn't able to shift either, so we lived as humans."

But that didn't make sense. Why would they turn their back on the life they'd built just to be marked rogues? "What happened?"

"Humans found out. I was in school. There was an incident." He heated more butter in another pan. "I was small for my age. I was defending myself, but it didn't matter. I broke a kid's arm. It was reported and those type of claims are investigated. When the pack found out that we were living in their territory, they gave us an ultimatum. Leave or die."

Taggert poured the eggs into the skillet. A small sizzle filled the room. "We packed up what we could in a few hours, but it was never the same. Dad had never recovered. This town was our last stop. He had some good memories here. A few months later, he died."

She was glad that his father had fought to give him a normal childhood. "And you applied for pack status by becoming a slave."

"I knew I would never be anyone. I'm not strong enough to challenge and win, so my Dad trained me early on what someone like me could expect." He nodded like it was no big deal. "Veggies."

She silently handed over the cutting board with all the rows lined up in a sloppy pile. He deftly dropped them into the pan and closed the omelets. Then glanced at her from the corner of his eyes to gage the danger level before speaking, still not used to addressing anyone directly.

"Ask."

"You could have left me." At her blank look, he continued. "At the slave auction, you could have left me at any time. You didn't. You understood."

When he didn't continue, Raven busied herself by washing the knife she'd used, hating the small tremor in her fingers.

"Who hurt you so badly you'd foolishly risk yourself for a nobody?"

"Stop." She dropped the knife and shut off the water. "You are somebody to me."

Taggert didn't flinch, didn't move away from her anger as had had in the past. He didn't fear her wrath. She wasn't sure she was grateful or not. "You're aware of where I grew up. The labs are not a place for a child, let alone a girl.

"The smallest act of kindness is worse than the experiments and needles. It gives you hope. After a while, hope dies and you know not to expect anything."

He began to set silverware on the table. The sharp spices and rich buttery smell had her mouthwatering. "At the club, you still had hope."

Taggert carefully crafted the food on the plates then served them. "Only until I saw you standing there as if waiting for me. I smelled it on you and...hoped." He pulled out a chair for her. "Sit and eat before things get cold. Afterward, I'll show you how to scent smells."

"Your gift." Raven watched as he ducked his head, but a small smile played on his lips, pleased by the attention.

\* \* \*

"We're being followed."

"I know." Raven didn't bother to turn. The two teen rogues weren't very good at being covert. "Did you want me to send them back?"

Raven could tell he was torn, his knuckles whiting on the basket he carried. This was supposed to be their date, but he ultimately shook his head. "Let them stay. It's something they need to learn as well."

Raven trailed him as he led her across the back lawn. "So when did you guys decide to use the dates to train me?"

Taggert gave her a half look, gauging her response. "Not really training. The conclave is tomorrow." His voice was stiff. "There are things you need to learn sooner rather than later."

She suspected it had been his idea. He was a master at working behind the scenes to get what he wanted. She couldn't be mad at him for all the trouble he went through to keep her safe. Raven slipped her hand into the crook of his elbow. "Thank you."

If she hadn't been close, she might not have noticed the slight blush to Taggert's cheeks. It charmed her that he reacted so readily to her weak attempts at flirtation. Being near him kept her desire at a slow simmer, and she savored his closeness.

He cleared his throat nervously. "Here's fine."

Raven detangled her hand, and he spread the blanket. While he was busy, she faced the tree line. Though hidden, she spotted the kids in seconds. "You might as well come here. You won't be able to see very well from there."

Nothing happened at first. When she crossed her arms and waited, two people emerged from the woods. The younger one had his eyes downcast, while the elder led the way with his chin high.

"I made him come along."

They expected her to punish them. "You are not a prisoner in the house. Since you're already here, sit and join us. Taggert is going to give me a demonstration of what his wolf can do."

"Him?" Kyle snorted and received an elbow in the gut from his brother for his trouble.

Raven stepped right into his face, not willing to let him get away with disparaging Taggert. "This is your one warning. You will want to step carefully."

Taggert stood calmly on the other side of the blanket, unconcerned at the drama. "Let me show you. Sit and face the tree line."

Raven did as told, taking the furthest seat so the boys could remain together.

"Close your eyes." Raven hesitated, uncomfortable not being able to see a threat approaching. The boys seemed just as leery, looking at her to gauge what she would do. Trusting Taggert, she did as told.

"When you take away one of the senses, the others are

heightened. You'll be overwhelmed if you try to sort all the smells. Let your beast do that.

"I'm going to open each container one at a time. You will tell me what's inside. The catch is that you can't use taste, touch or sight. I want you to concentrate on finding this one scent."

The almost twins quivered with curiosity, their bodies twitching at the possibility of using their wolves. Raven heard the lid pull free.

"What is it?"

Whatever he expected, he was doomed to be disappointed. She had no clue. The other side of the blanket remained just as silent. "Tell me what to do."

"You need to raise your beast. Let the animal do the work."

Raven called for her wolf and waited.

Nothing.

Damn contrary animal.

She cleared her throat. "How?"

She sensed movement and opened her eyes. Taggert knelt in front of them, a frown between his brows. "You should sit between Kyle and Brant. They haven't crested yet. You'll be able to help them."

She squinted up at him, alarmed by his words. She had a piss-poor track record for touching others without consequences. "Are you sure that's wise?"

Kyle snorted and cast her a dismissive glance. Brant took the opportunity to knee him. Kyle grunted and dropped his eyes along with the attitude.

"They haven't been through their first turn yet." He reached down a hand to help her rise. "They haven't been around a true alpha. Not someone like you. You can show them what they can expect."

With a bit of trepidation, she accepted his hand. Once everyone was resettled, she nodded for Taggert to continue.

"Remember how you healed me when we first arrived?"

Raven thought back, vaguely recalling that she'd manipulated his aura, forcing the energy around him to heal his body. "Yes."

"You can pull up their wolves that way."

"And my wolf?"

Taggert didn't answer for a while. "Your wolf is different than any others I've known. I've only seen her when danger threatens or when you're around other wolves."

He was so very observant that it frightened her. She couldn't help be curious at what other things he'd picked up from her and knew it was better not to know. She wouldn't like the answer. "Then let's do this."

She lifted both of her hands. Brant flinched while Kyle just looked grim. She didn't reach for either of them. They had to make their own decisions.

Slowly, they came forward and accepted her hand.

There was nothing at first.

She allowed a snap of energy to grow and let it soak into the boys. They fidgeted, their energy spiked, and then their wolves were there, tripping over themselves as they rose.

Taggert opened the first container. The smell was barely there. She cocked her head as she heard movement. "It's liquid."

"Holy shit." Kyle whispered the words, but everyone heard the awe.

Brant spoke next. "Raw egg."

Raven opened her eyes to see Taggert grin in triumph. "Correct."

Kyle scowled. "Do another."

Excitement and fear threaded through both kids, their breathing growing rough. Both boys had their eyes open wide, their pupils normal except for a few slivers of yellow encircling them, their wolf not strong enough to bring on the change.

Even as the second container opened, their scents grew sharper.

Overwhelming.

The stink of the enemy clung to them, same as the two men who'd attacked her. Heat washed through her, and her wolf snarled to the surface, begging to be let free. She craved vengeance, wanted to dominate the other two so they wouldn't forget she was alpha.

Raven's hands shook with restraint, her fingers curling into claws, and she quickly broke her hold on them before she did something irrevocable...like hurt them.

Both kids dropped like rocks to the blanket.

"Shit." Raven reached out with trembling fingers to check if they were still alive when Taggert grabbed her hand.

"Don't. They're just exhausted. It takes a lot out of a pup after their first brush with their wolf."

Oxygen rushed into her lungs at his words. Both had their eyes closed, so terribly still that she feared she'd killed them. Only when their chests rose and fell in deep sleep did she finally nod.

To prove his point, Taggert shook Kyle. The kid's eyes flickered as he battled to remain awake.

"Go back to the house and rest."

Kyle obeyed without question, struggling to stand, half dragging his brother to his feet. What shocked her more was the nod of respect he sent her as he passed. She watched them, Kyle nearly carrying his brother, until they disappeared into the house.

"So I can raise their wolf, but the desire to tear into them..." She still shuddered at the need to follow them and rent them apart.

"They're rogues living in your house. You're feeling territorial."

"But I asked them here. Why would I want to kill them?"

Taggert snorted. "You wouldn't have killed them. You would've shown them who was alpha, and they would've respected you for it."

Disturbed by his explanation, she bent to help collect the items to their little experiment. Taggert waved her away.

She thought about the last few days, trying to riddle out what bothered her the most about someone targeting her and came up with no satisfying answers. "Why am I being singled out by the rogues?"

Taggert took so long to answer that it chilled her to realize he had to sort out so many possibilities.

"You made yourself known at the club when you defended me, you're also working with the police. You brought down a ring of humans hunting shifters. It might not have made the human news, but it spread like wildfire through the shifter community. Not to mention rogues are living on your land."

"But nothing that deserves their retaliation."

Taggert paused in folding the blanket. "They could be testing you."

"By trying to kill me?" She brushed away his reply. "I mean, I understand that rogues hire themselves out. I understand territory and fear. I can even understand the self-preservation of Vivian's attack, but my death won't really gain them anything. Someone else will just take my place. It makes no sense."

"At the core, shifters are animals. They react and trust instincts."

"So they see me as a threat?" She hated politics. They twisted things about in a way that she had no hope of navigating.

"You're an alpha. They might have enhanced your abilities in the labs, but you're a natural born alpha. You instill a terrible hope and a devastating fear in all rogues. Their beasts will want to please you. You can control them and for that, some rogues will hate you on sight."

Her cellphone rang, startling Raven. The phone so rarely worked, she'd forgotten she worn it. She fumbled to answer it.

"Hello?" No one replied. She listened, using her other senses, and heard labored breathing. Not like a prank call, but more like the person couldn't gather enough air into their lungs. "Speak to me. Give me something to help find you."

"Injured." Jamie's voice cut in and out, distorted by the background noise.

Raven gripped the phone, hurrying toward the house. He wouldn't be calling unless there was trouble. "Where are you?"

"Old Lake Front Street." He panted from pain...or the middle of a shift. Neither option was an acceptable alternative in public. If caught in beast form without a collar and tags, he would be arrested, if not outright killed. If he was so injured that he wasn't healing, it could only mean the worse.

"I'm on my way." But he'd already disconnected...or fell unconscious. Taggert followed her to the house. "Grab my weapon and badge."

It took them twenty minutes, even with her speeding, to reach the far side of the city. The new car London had purchased ate up the miles quickly. She pulled up to the abandoned street. The windows of the worn-down buildings were boarded up, the people kept clear, knowing better than to get involved in something that could be detrimental to their health...like a police investigation.

She pulled out her phone and hit the re-dial. No one answered.

"Call again." Taggert rolled down his window.

She did as told, and Taggert held up his hand. "He's near. I can hear the ringing."

Raven veered to the curb, slammed the vehicle in park and hopped out before the engine stopped rumbling. A chime sounded.

Distant.

Muffled.

Raven cocked her head then took off running, Taggert hot on her heels. She turned the corner to the alley and skidded to a stop. Jamie lay sprawled in the shadows where the falling sun couldn't reach, only his shoes visible from the sidewalk.

"Jamie?" She hurried to his side when Taggert placed a hand on her shoulder to halt her.

"I smell blood. Be careful. An injured animal can react to the pain before they're aware of their surroundings."

Raven nodded and carefully knelt. Jamie was unconscious when she rolled him onto his side. It was only then that she spotted his injuries. From the grievous wounds all over his torso, she was amazed he'd managed to stay conscious long enough to call her, let alone remain breathing.

Then she recognized the wound pattern.

The same injuries that the woman trapped in the car at her last crime scene had carried. Her head shot up, and she peered into the shadows.

Liquid saturated the stone walls of the buildings.

Raven nearly jumped out of her skin when Jamie grabbed her arm. His mouth moved, but no sound emerged. She leaned forward.

"He wasn't rogue. If the shifters believe rogues are behind the deaths, they'll purge all rogues to protect themselves."

The news was shocking. Then another thought threatened to knock her on her ass. "Where is Dominic? The big black wolf I had trailing you. Did you see him?"

Jamie cracked a smile, revealing blood stained teeth. "Caught him the first night. Left him to watch the rogues."

He coughed heavily, blood speckling his lips. Raven grabbed his hand when it trembled, and she noticed the same tattoo on his hand that the woman had worn. "Where did you get this?"

She received no answer. He'd already fallen back into unconsciousness. Concern clutched at her chest. She concentrated until she heard the beat of his heart pounding reassuringly if a little unsteady. She glanced at Taggert for confirmation of her diagnosis.

"His wounds are severe. He needs all his energy to heal."

"So he'll be all right?"

Taggert hesitated, his eyes stark with the truth. "He's still alive."

But not for long went unsaid. Raven pulled out her phone and snapped a picture of the stamp on his hand, then stood. Her first priority was to get Jamie to safety.

He was alive. He would stay that way until she could get him to the privacy of her home and the help he needed. "I want you to take Jamie and leave. I need to call the police and stay until they arrived."

"I haven't driven a day in my life." Taggert crossed his arms. "And I'll not leave you alone at the site of a murder."

Raven cursed, having forgotten that as a slave, Taggert wasn't allowed behind the wheel of a vehicle. "Jamie can't be found here. The police will take him into custody. Since he has no affiliations, I'm not sure how long they'll detain him. With his injuries..." She trailed off. Nothing more needed to be said, they both knew he'd never see another sunrise if taken into custody. She pulled out her phone and snapped a dozen pictures of the alleyway.

Taggert conceded her point, but not enough to relent. "I'll take him to the car and park around the block. We'll wait for you there."

"He needs to be seen by a doctor."

"Then hurry. I'll call Digger and put him on alert." Taggert bent and lifted Jamie with an ease that surprised her as the man was nearly twice his own weight. Before she could protest either of his commands, they were gone.

Taking a deep breath, Raven dialed Scotts.

## ❧ Chapter Twenty-three ❦

"Why didn't you call before entering the scene?" Suspicion coated Scott's voice, the same suspicion that had shown up when she'd first started hanging around the wrong *group*, as he put it.

He'd meant shifters.

Raven bit back her response and nodded toward the alley. Without the falling sun, there was nothing but shadows. "What do you see?"

Scotts rubbed a hand over his scalp. "Point taken." Pale light from a few flashlights traced across the stained bricks, the techs still setting up their equipment.

Scotts scraped the tip of his toe over the spot where Jamie had lain, a pool of his blood still discoloring the cement. She waited for him to question her, but he didn't say a word.

"What did you see?"

His question caught her off guard. "Nothing. Once I knew it was a crime, I secured the scene. I didn't want to ruin evidence before forensics arrived."

"And how did you come to find," he waved his arm toward the slaughter, "him?"

His attitude was beginning to piss her off. "A tip that came through." She gave him a tight smile. "Someone smelled something and called. They didn't leave a name, but I suspect it was a shifter."

She wasn't necessarily lying. Jamie did call, and he was a shifter. What she didn't admit was to taking pictures of the crime scene. She needed answers now instead of waiting for the police to analyze everything and decide what they wanted to share with her. She wasn't sure when she'd stopped trusting Scotts, thinking of him as a *normal* instead of a cop.

He looked doubtful but took her words at face value. "Then let's look now."

Scotts was a big man. She wasn't able to fit her steps into his without looking like she was trying to play a game of *Twister* with shoe print. What remained of the body was spattered over a five-foot diameter. Tatters of a shirt lay scattered everywhere, half hidden in the gore. The jeans were harder to destroy, remaining mostly intact, including a pair of boots that were a little worse for wear.

The team snapped pictures, set lights and secured samples. After twenty minutes, Raven couldn't take it anymore. Jamie needed a doctor sooner rather than later. "I need to speak with a few of my contacts to see if I can find any leads."

Scotts waved her off, not taking his attention away from what one of the techs was unearthing. "Don't forget that you have to take your turn to man the desk at the office as well."

Taking that as permission, Raven shot out of the alley at a near run. She turned the block, relieved to find the car still waiting. Taggert was leaning over the front seat, tending to Jamie.

"We should hurry."

His voice sent her heart skipping a beat and fear crawled up her spine. Not waiting to confirm his condition herself, she shoved the car into gear. The ride home seemed interminable. Each second, she expected to hear the raspy breathing cease.

When the lights of the house finally came into view, she didn't take her eyes away from the beacon of hope.

They would make it.

Even as they pulled up, the door opened and Digger rushed toward them. All that was missing was to see his coattails flapping. He opened the door and examined the patient like any seasoned ER doctor. She hadn't even seen London follow until he nudged the doctor out of the way and extracted Jamie's too still body.

The line to the house reminded her too much of a funeral procession for comfort. "What can you tell me?"

Digger's shook his head. "I won't know until I can examine him closer."

Raven follow them into the house, and Digger waved her away

from the basement. "We'll inform you of any changes."

"But—"

The door snicked shut in her face, leaving her staring at the wall with a helpless feeling she knew all too well. She clenched and unclenched her fists only then noticing Taggert had remained at her side.

"It's a good sign that he's still alive. Digger will keep him that way."

She didn't know why she cared. He was just a rogue. He didn't matter. Or that's what everyone kept telling her. "Where the hell was Griffin? He was supposed to be watching the rogues. I want to know what happened."

She whirled, her beasts rising with her agitation, and she had no idea how to calm them.

"I'm here."

She crossed the floor to Griffin and grabbed him by the neck before he could react. He seized her wrist, but couldn't force her hand away without ripping out his own throat.

Raven dropped her beasts. She wouldn't be able to win that way. They were both too alpha to give way. Electricity poured over her in welcoming waves. She took Jackson's advice and didn't try to control current, but let it wash over them.

Griffin grunted as if she'd struck him, and he dropped to his knees. The grip on her wrist tightened, but the expected pain never came. She felt nothing but rage at the thought of him betraying his own kind. That he would betray her. "What game are you playing at with these people?"

His brilliant green and yellow eyes stared up at her. Sweat beaded his hairline as her energy snaked around him seeking answers. "No game. Trying to save."

The scar on the back of his hand reminded her of all that he'd lost. "You're an alpha in your own right. Why bother with these rogues? You're not one of them. Not really."

"You're right. Partially right." His smile was more of a grimace. Despite her control, he struggled to his feet, surprising her with his will not to be seen as weak. "I volunteered to infiltrate them and find out who was hunting shifters. Then, when rogues started to die," he raised his fist to show his scar. "I decided that I might as well make use of this."

She dropped her hold. The energy reluctantly retreated, leaving a sting in its wake. She'd almost swear that the lash was more of a caress.

As if the creature sensed her watching and listening, it settled down content just to be noticed. No matter how much she wanted to explore this new phenomenon, she had more pressing issues.

"And the story of how you became a rogue? Was any of it true?"

Every emotions shut down. "Every word."

"And Jamie?"

"He was following a lead."

"So he was helping you?"

"You might say we had an unsteady truce." Griffin paused, debating what to share. "He knows little of my past, but he also knows that without help, the rogues will suffer."

"Maybe it's time you tell me what's happening." It wasn't a question.

Griffin did smile then. "I know little more than you. There is a drug on the market that's making shifters act like alphas, but there are side effects. I'm not sure if they're caused by the drug or if the addicts were targeted. Maybe both. I'm trying to narrow it down."

"And getting nowhere." Raven couldn't help be suspicious if he really wanted the drug shut down or if he just wanted it for himself.

He didn't say anything more.

"You have an in with the rogues, but you are also limited on what you can do. I'm not. In the morning, we will discuss this further." Raven paused to push home her point. "The shifter who died tonight wasn't a rogue."

Griffin flinched, the action barely noticeable. He must have come to the same conclusion as Jamie. If the shifters thought they were being targeted, they will remove the threat.

They'll destroy all rogues.

\* \* \*

Raven trudged up the stairs, each step heavier than the last. Taggert followed her, ever silent, and she was grateful for his quiet presence.

Dating three men at one time was insane, but it didn't feel like she was cheating by being with the others. She didn't understand the bonds forming between them, and wondered how much her animals were influencing her decisions.

"Why don't you let me run you a bath?"

Raven turned toward him and smiled. "It sounds lovely except that my bathroom is currently under construction. I'm lucky I still have a shower."

Though no expression showed, she couldn't help sense his crestfallen emotions. "I'm sorry our date didn't turn out the way you wanted."

Taggert eyes brightened, a smile tipping his lips. "I had time alone with you. It was perfect."

When he turned to move away, she grabbed his wrist.

He inhaled sharply, a small whimper in his throat. She immediately dropped his arm, the sound more effective than if he'd slapped her. "You're hurt?"

He whirled on her, stepping right into her personal space like it didn't exist, backing her up until her ass hit the wall. Lust poured off him, but he controlled himself, not touching her in any way.

"Do it again." He placed his hands against the wall on either side of her head. His voice was part plea, part demand.

Only when she was able to tear her gaze away from the yellow glow of his eyes did she realize what she'd done.

The scar where she bit him stood out pale against the tanned skin of his wrist.

She should've been horrified to see her mark on him, know that she'd scarred him. Her wolf trotted forward, pleasure and possessiveness shivering down her spine. He was hers. Now and forever. "Will it always be so sensitive?"

Taggert inhaled deeply, breathing her in. "Only your touch."

She knew what he craved. What her wolf wanted. And if she was truthful, she was curious at what it would be like to indulge in touching him again.

Eyes on his, she leaned over and licked his wrist. The taste of him hummed through her.

As if she'd flipped a switch, he flattened her against the wall with his body. His lips sought hers, the hunger in them almost desperate as he kissed her. The wildness of him called her own, and she returned his embrace.

But concern edged out desire. It was harder than she thought to pull away from him. "Taggert?"

He jerked away from her as if she kneed him in the groin instead of said his name. "I'm sorry."

Raven was confused. What the hell was going on here? "Why are you sorry?"

He wouldn't face her. When she reached for him, he ducked away in panic. That only served to piss her off more.

"I shouldn't have touched you without permission." His voice was a raw, a barely-there whisper.

His reply gave her pause. "Because I'm an alpha?"

Raven knew he'd enjoyed their exchange, his arousal proof enough. Her gaze landed on his clenched fists, and the truth dawned on her. "Have you ever kissed anyone without being ordered?"

He glanced at his feet, never lifting his head. "No."

"Does it feel wrong to touch me?"

He shook his head then nodded. "Not without permission."

"So, the only way you'd feel comfortable being near me is if I ordered you." Raven was talking more to herself, their treatment of him horrifying.

The way they'd trained him.

She hadn't realized how deeply integrated he was into the submissive life.

"Orders are the only things that keep us alive."

His logic made sense in a sickening way. Any move he made without approval was a death sentence hanging over him. One she wasn't sure she was prepared to lift if it meant opening herself up and giving him permission to touch at any time.

It was too dangerous.

But she could give him one thing that no one could take from him. "You are part of my pack whether the conclave agrees or not." Then she licked her lips, suddenly uncertain. "If you want it."

His head jerked up at that. "I would be honored."

"But I'm not used to all the romantic attention. I'm used to blending into the crowd." His sudden smile gave her pause, and she eyed his sudden cheerfulness. "What?"

"You are an unmated female. Even with the best shields, shifters will seek you out."

Raven scowled at him. He was right but that didn't mean she had to like it.

His humor faded. "The system is not something you should try to fix. Not all rogues are worthy of being pack. If you intend to move forward and claim pack status, you need to get used to taking charge in all things. Even sex."

She could never order someone to service her like some animal. As if reading her thoughts, he shook his head.

"You're evaluating the situation like a human. A shifter would see selection as an honor."

Raven wasn't ready for that type of thing. "There has to be a compromise." She entered her room, but Taggert held back, hovering by the door. It brought home how rigid the slave lifestyle really was. "Enter."

Taggert opened his mouth but hesitated.

"Say it."

"Use me as practice. By giving me demands, you'll become comfortable to our ways."

Raven paced the room. "But it gives you no freedom."

He stepped in her way, blocking her so un-expectantly that she nearly ran into him. "I don't want freedom. If I wanted freedom, I could have become a rogue."

Raven plopped onto her bed, his reality finally coming home to her. "You really prefer me ordering you around."

Taggert tipped his head forward in agreement.

Her stomach launched up into her throat at the thought of ordering him to kiss or touch her.

"How about a compromise until you become more comfortable."

Raven shot Taggert a suspicious look.

"If I want something, I will ask permission and you can grant it or not. As the size of the pack increases, so will the demands on your time. You will have to get used to giving orders. Consider me practice."

Raven ignored the part about growing her pack. She had enough trouble keeping her people safe to even think of adding more. She eyed him skeptically. "And you will speak up instead of hovering?"

It was his turn to hesitate. "Yes."

It cheered her that this process would be similarly uncomfortable for the both of them. It was long past midnight and tomorrow was going to be even longer with the conclave and her petition.

"The other two spent the night in my bed. To sleep. If you want—" Even before she finished speaking, Taggert had his shirt off and crawled across the mattress behind her. The slave collar gleamed against his throat, but he didn't seem to mind, truly content in his role.

She just couldn't peg him down. He was so young in age that she sometimes forgot about his past.

Raven readied for bed...or more like delayed getting into bed until the last moment. Exhaustion pulled at her. She turned out the light, relying more and more on her beasts, almost able to see as well in the darkness.

They both lay rigid, the silence loud to her ears. Two awkward minutes passed before she gave up and rolled toward him. Taggert took that as a signal and wrapped his arms around her. He buried his face into her hair and inhaled. Whatever tension held him melted away. His fingers trailed lazily over the sensitive back of her arm, lulling her under the spell he wove. With her head on his shoulder, his heartbeat in her ear, sleep finally took pity and claimed her.

She woke to sunlight and an empty bed.

Why did all the men sneak out of her room as if ashamed?

She sat, tossing back the covers and stopped to see a box with a bow on the dresser.

Raven searched but saw no card. Inside the box rested a blue set of gloves that ended at the wrist, secured with a button. "Taggert."

She fingered the supple leather, feeling a bit foolish at the thrill over such a small gift. Gathering the armload of her items, she walked in the bathroom.

And stopped short.

Taggert was in the shower.

As in naked.

He noticed her the minute she'd entered, but instead of acknowledging her presence, he continued to wash. The drag of his hand down on his body slowed. Suds played peek-a-boo with her imagination. His chest was completely smooth, and she had an irrelevant thought that he must've shaved himself in preparation of her walking in on him.

Then Raven saw his erection and knew without a doubt that he was showing off. And despite herself, it took a good minute for her brain to kick into gear. She whirled, her face heating, and she wished she could say it was in embarrassment.

Part of her mourned not being able to see where his hand ended up, the animal part of her tried to get a better angle in the mirror. The shower turned off within a minute.

"I'll finish getting ready in my room."

Without an ounce of shyness, Taggert strolled out of the room. She expected him to be wearing a towel. He was in a way. He used it to dry his hair. She watched him walk, fascinated with the smooth expanse of his skin, the liquid way his muscles moved.

Who would have thought she was such an ass woman?

Once he left the room, she was finally able to close her mouth and blink her dry eyes.

She wouldn't put it past Taggert to have orchestrated that display to get her mind off the first day of the conclave. A smile played on her lips.

She'd have to hurry and shower if she wanted to check on Jamie, head toward the station to get in her mandatory desk time, and still make it to *Talons* and the conclave before nightfall.

## Chapter Twenty-four

**FIRST DAY OF THE FULL MOOM: WAXING MOON**

Darkness cloaked the basement, and Raven hesitated on the threshold. The antiseptic odors, the smell of blood and pain, brought unpleasant memories of her past.

She clenched her fists and descended into hell. It took her a few moments to locate Digger sitting on the other side of the prone figure. She braced herself to find Jamie tied down.

She'd been so focused on the image that it took her a moment to realize there was nothing sinister in the room.

"Did he wake?" Jamie was a shifter with all the benefits of accelerated healing. Part of her expected to see him up and about at the very least. Instead, he appeared just as tattered as last night. Dried blood had been removed, revealing exactly how many injuries he'd sustained. The right side of his body took the brunt of the injuries as if he'd tried to turn away, offering a smaller target.

Digger stood and walked over to the bench he'd commandeered for his needs. "The shifter in him will try to heal the worst of the damage first, which is the internal injuries he'd sustained. He is on the mend, but he'll be unconscious for the rest of the day, if not longer."

Raven wanted to offer to heal him, but refrained for two reasons. All his energies were already tied up in healing. There was nothing for her to redirect without putting his life in further danger. Not to mention she feared that her efforts would bind them together and leave her in possession of another shifter.

"Did he take that much damage or is there something else

slowing down the process?" She feared the transfer of so much blood from the other shifter might have somehow infected him as well.

Digger gave her a peculiar look. "It is possible. If you have an idea what it might be, it could speed up his recovery time."

"Do you still have the clothes he'd been wearing?"

Digger gestured toward a pile of neatly folded clothes on a chair near the wall.

"Not all the blood is his. If you can separate and analyze the blood types, it could tell us what's killing these shifters."

"But you suspect something already."

Raven gave him a considering look, suspicious to find him so open and unthreatening. He watched, noticed things, but she didn't sense him studying her.

She pulled out her phone and showed him the pictures of the crime scene. His face changed. "You see it, too."

"Formaldehyde."

"All the symptoms match. Despite what the others have said, I can't imagine this many shifters would kill themselves in such a gruesome matter. For what purpose? This last victim was pack."

She flipped through the pictures on the phone until she found the one of Jamie's hand. "Have you seen this symbol?"

Digger shook his head. "I saw the mark when I cleaned Jamie's wounds."

"Doc's too old." Aaron walked into the room behind her. "It's a rave stamp, a place where shifter kids that have yet to crest can mingle and make future connections."

An idea percolated in the back of her mind, but first, she needed to get to the office and study the case reports to see if they were able to find anything on the other victims. "Keep me informed of his progress."

Aaron doggedly followed her up the steps. "I want to go with you."

"Where?" Raven answered distractedly, a vague plan forming.

"I'm not allowed at the conclave until I've crested, but I can get you into the rave."

"I can manage." She refused to drag him into danger.

"You can't go alone. Not only will it look suspicious, it will be too dangerous for a single female. Kids usually go in packs. Use me. I've been there before and know what to expect. Everyone else is too old."

"And it's too dangerous for just the two of us with your pack hunting you."

"Not if we take Taggert and Jase." There was no smile as he argued his proposal in a businesslike manner.

Raven paced away from him, agitated to be dragging kids into her murder investigation. Aaron sensed her refusal, leaned against the wall and crossed his arms.

"You have three problems. Only the kids know where the rave will be held. Cops will be spotted within a hundred yards of the building."

Raven narrowed her eyes, expecting a trap. "And the last one?"

He gave a broad grin, displaying what a handsome man he would become in a few years. "Getting there is only half the problem. You have to get someone to talk to you. If you go, I go."

Neatly cornered.

They wouldn't find the killer there, the kids were the targets, but maybe she could lure out the dealer and set a trap of her own. She couldn't afford to lose her one lead. She trumped his demand with one of her own. "Only if you can get Jackson to agree. I won't have your safety compromised."

Aaron pushed away from the wall. "Tomorrow at midnight. I'll let the others know."

* * *

Raven pored over the case files, but didn't see any similarities between the locations or people. Except that they were all rogues with one exception. It looked more and more likely that the rogues were being infected by something at the rave. It was too coincidental that two of their victims bore the same mark.

The big question was if the rogues were the true targets or if they were the test trials for a potential hit on the conclave. And she didn't have a damn clue on how to prevent any of it.

Scotts paused in his walk to his desk when he saw her, then went back to reading the report he held. "Made yourself at home I see."

She refused to feel guilty for removing the files from his desk.

The sweet tobacco smell she associated with him increased when he sat across from her. "So tell me what you found."

"What makes you think I found anything?"

"You're here. That means you're searching for something." He tossed a file on his cluttered desk. "Tell me."

Raven leaned back with a sigh. "It's all speculation. I'm not able to confirm or deny anything."

"But..."

"I think I found a common thread." Raven refused to give up more until she had something tangible. She wouldn't have them hunting shifters down like animals without something concrete.

"You have no intention of sharing."

"Not without proof. Not after last time." Last time meaning when the police had arrested Jackson after killing the man trying to murder her. And she lost him when his pack came to claim him.

Scotts grunted, clearly not pleased. "We're supposed to be a team, yet you hardly set foot in this office."

"You know as well as I that no shifters will come here. I have a hard enough time getting them in the same room with me." All except the ones trying to kill her.

Scotts didn't say anything more. They both knew it was the truth. Not wanting burn bridges, she made the only concession she could. "I'll call you when things get heavy."

The conversation ended when the phone rang. He put his hand on the receiver but didn't pick it up. "Just make sure you don't wait until it's too late."

After another hour, she called it quits and headed home to get ready for the conclave. The animals prowled beneath her skin, restless, as if they understood what tonight meant for them.

When she pulled up to the house, the last thing she expected to find was Dominic wearing a collar, tags and a leash. She was too relieved to see him safe to scold him for worrying her.

Even though Taggert stood at his side, she had no doubt Dominic was the one in charge. "He insisted on coming."

"So it will be just the three of us."

"Four." London walked out of the house, passed them and sat in the driver's seat without saying another word.

"Until your position is accepted by the council, it could be dangerous to show too much support." Taggert walked down the steps. Dominic picked up the leash in his mouth and followed.

"Wait." Dina hurried out, a pair of boots and a jacket in her hands. "If you're going to battle, you need to be dressed appropriately."

Raven automatically accepted the armload. In seconds, she had knee-length high-heeled boots on her feet and strapped into a tight fitting leather jacket that left little to the imagination.

"Are these really necessary?" She stood, tugging on the jacket. At least the material allowed her to move easily.

"Oh, yes. Most definitely." Dina cast a critical eye over her, surveying and judging every angle. With one last twist and a tug on the leather, she straightened. "You'll do great."

Raven was shoved toward her ragtag group, uncertain what to expect out of tonight. She did the only thing she could. She got into the car to face her biggest challenge.

Claiming her pack.

## Chapter Twenty-five

**R**aven entered *Talons* just as night fell, taken aback at the press of people, the place near bursting with the numbers. The draped booths offered privacy between the different packs. Black material clung to the walls, making the room appear more spacious.

An empty dais was at the opposite end of the room, five seats waiting for the council members.

Smells burst over her, sharper and stronger than usual at the quantity of people. The combination of shifters' natural scents, the vampires' spice, and the overly sweet tang of magic users overwhelmed her nose. She tried to breathe through her mouth, but she only ended up tasting the combination as well. "How can they stand it so crowded?"

"The place will become even more so later when the council arrives." Taggert inched closer, his presence easing some of the claustrophobia slithering over her skin, and the need to let loose her power to give them more breathing room.

Thoughts of Jamie's brutalized body lingered in her mind, along with the photos from the crime scene. She scanned the room for Durant, the urgency mounting when she didn't spy him. The attacks were escalating, and she couldn't quell the dread that it was connected to the conclave.

That put Durant directly in the path of a killer.

As if her thoughts conjured him, Durant entered the club from his office. His eyes locked on hers, and he walked through the crowd like they didn't exist. Everyone either scampered out of his way or was yanked by their companions.

She really needed to learn that trick.

"We need to talk."

Durant ignored her words and lifted her hand to his mouth. His lips brushed and lingered on the back of her blue gloves. He traced his fingers over her pulse and gazed up at her with such hunger, her breath caught. Memories of them together nearly had her shuffling forward to touch him in a way that was much too inappropriate for public.

Her animals were observant but silent, assessing the possible threats around them. She expected the moon's call to be worse but the effects were muted. She was either learning control or her desire was reserved for her pack alone.

The revelation was a huge relief.

"Let me escort you to your booth." He straightened and tucked her hand into the crook of his elbow. The rest of her group preceded them to one of the few remaining tables.

Not willing to be distracted, she surveyed the bar. The normal bouncers so familiar to the club were gone, off with their packs. No one stood guarding the doors. "The club is vulnerable to attack."

Durant increased his step, hustling her toward the corner booth, most likely to tuck her out of the way before she created a scene. "Take a look at the club. What do you see?"

Her gaze swept the room and landed on the last man she ever thought to see.

Rylan.

He stared at her, hunger and want gleaming in his eyes before he could cover it.

The vampire was her pack. They'd survived the labs by trusting each other, but their shared past pushed him away. It was her blood. It'd changed him. To most vampires, her blood was like a drug, the power in it offering them an illusion of life.

Despite the precautions, Rylan had become addicted and kept his distance to protect her, or some such bullshit.

It broke her heart.

Rylan gave her a nod of recognition then disappeared as the crowd swallowed him.

His appearance rattled her. He avoided his own kind like the plague. His presence here made no logical sense.

Unless he expected trouble.

She blindly searched the room, trying to regain her composure.

And spied Randolph studying her with a little too much intensity. That sobered her. She had to step with care or he would ferret out all her weaknesses and use them against her.

She fought her instincts and turned away from him. Her eyes were sightless as she stared at the corner. That's when she saw Jackson and Aaron lean forward slightly from their hiding positions, partially protected behind the bar.

They both gave her a nod, then melted back into the darkness. The damned fools. They could get themselves killed for sneaking in the club.

That they risked their safety just to show their support should've made her furious. Instead, warmth spread through her chest that they would risk everything just to be there for her.

Raven glanced at Durant and suspected he'd arranged the whole thing.

"Well?"

She shook off her discoveries and concentrated on the defenses, or the lack of them. "Vulnerabilities. No one is watching the doors. No one is checking the dancers. The shifters and vampires, not to mention the magic users, were all eyeing up each other as if expecting trouble."

"Exactly. The whole room *is* the extra protection. No one is going to get in here that doesn't belong. Not if they want to live."

"But that's what worries me. The shifter won't even know—" He swung her around and seated her, brushing off her concern.

"Sit. Observe."

His dismissive attitude stung. When he strode away, she glanced around the club, wondering which one of the hundred or more shifters in the room could already be a ticking time bomb...literally.

Cobwebs brushed against her skin as magic skittered along her arms. "I thought shifters hated associating with magic slingers. Why are so many here?"

"They sell their wares to the shifters and forge relationships with packs. A partnership protects them both."

Understanding struck. "So the conclave isn't just for shifters but for the whole paracommunity."

Taggert nodded. "The council regulates the many groups and metes out justice before anything can spill over into the *normal* world."

"And the police force?"

London spoke for the first time. "It's all about control. Right now, we take care of our own problems. The humans are trying to get a foothold into our community."

Raven swallowed her automatic protest at his ominous announcement, but what he said was true. "Up to a point. Paranormals came out ten years ago. There is no more hiding in plain sight and sweeping things away as superstitions. Humans might be poking in where they don't belong, but you can't expect them to sit back when the battles between paranormals spills over into their world, not when there are casualties on both sides.

"Regions were created to be a go-between. The humans just made the first move...on their terms. That was a mistake on the conclave's part." Time was the enemy, closing in on her, forcing her to make choices that could affect her future, both personally and professionally.

"Is that your official opinion?"

Raven turned, surprised to find Donaldson at her back, the leader of the paraconsulate and Griffin's father. But she would not back down from her opinion, not when she was right. "The paranormal community lost an important edge when they allowed humans to take the lead and set the boundaries on how things should be done."

"Yet we get a vote in who's elected."

"Only after we follow their rules." She hated that she couldn't read anything about him. "Their rules limited us to following human laws without consideration that the people they're patrolling aren't human."

"We've heard about the rogue you've recovered from the last crime scene."

His meaning was clear. Pack wouldn't concern themselves with the welfare of an average rogue. He was asking about his son. "Jamie is safe and recovering. The rest of my team is investigating the incident."

He gave a nod and moved away without an ounce of emotion. He held everything so close to his chest, she couldn't make heads or tails of him.

As he moved through the crowd, he was joined by four others. The room fell silent. Donaldson seated himself at the center of the dais. The others claimed their spots in an orchestrated move that they all appeared to sit as one. "Welcome to the conclave. We will begin with the petitions. We ask all the alphas to stand and present their claims first."

Raven was astounded at just how few alphas stood. Less than fifteen people rose, and only a handful of them were female. These were the upper crust of the pack.

She anticipated a display of power, and there were a few that showed off. Those were not the ones that worried her. It was the ones she couldn't sense anything from that she needed to watch.

Taggert gave her a nudge.

Showtime.

She took her cue and rose. A murmur swept through the room.

"Objection." Vivian didn't show her normal smirk, though Raven could almost feel the smugness pour off her.

If Raven thought her presence had shocked anyone, an uproar now shook the room. Everyone spoke at once, but she refused to back down like some pup. She would not allow this woman to discredit her without a fight. Raven faced the council as they were the ones she needed to convince. "I ask permission to organize a pack."

"We received no official paperwork for your request." This was from the large male at the end with graying hair. A wolf if she had to guess, a position he earned by removing his predecessor in a challenge no doubt. Even at the distance, his displeasure beat at her shields, trying to get her to back down.

Raven wouldn't be dismissed by the mangy old wolf so easily. Now that they were questioning her right to form her own pack, she realized how badly she wanted this. It may have started against her will, but they were hers now. "That's why I'm here. I want to petition for my position."

"And what about your position as Region?"

Raven nodded her head at him. "As you are aware, a Region is an elected position. I did not campaign for it. I was offered the job after the fact."

"And you've accepted it without our consent." The vampire at the other end of the table spoke. She expected a quintessential vampire. Instead, he looked no older than a teenager.

Vibrant and alive.

Human.

Maybe that's what made him the scariest.

"Not at first. I waited. Delayed. But a murder case takes precedence. Shifters were being killed. That is not acceptable."

"Rogues." The older wolf shook his head, dismissing her protest.

"And as of last night, pack as well. Four murders that we know of so far and more will die unless someone can stop them."

"You."

She nodded to Donaldson. "Me."

"She is not claimed. She has no consort. If she'd survived this long on her own, she deserves the chance." The male who spoke was slender, but not thin. All of him was pure muscle. His pose was lazy, but there was no doubt he saw everything. A cat of some sort if she had to guess, but he wasn't the same breed as Durant. "Let her stay but double the fine."

The lone female studied at her a full minute before responding. "I agree. She is too rare."

The wolf scowled, not so easily put off. "What about territory?"

No one wanted to lose territory to another alpha. To her. Her mind raced for answers. She wouldn't lose her men now that she had two votes. "I have no desire to claim more than what's already mine. The land I own and the government parcel behind it are mine."

Someone in the crowd stood in protest. "That's public land."

Raven scanned the crowd, her gaze resting a second on Randolph. Malice shown in his eyes. If she lost the vote, any ephemeral protection would be gone and he would come for her. It brought home how much more she had to lose.

Swallowing hard, she tore her eyes away and found the man who'd spoken. Instead of avoiding her gaze, he defied her and refused to back down. "You talk like a *normal*. Pack has no public land. It's mine."

The man narrowed his eyes at the slur. A snarl curled his lips, revealing a hint of fang at her insult.

Then Donaldson spoke. "She's right. The land is unclaimed. And more importantly, none of the alphas will need to make concessions."

Each time a new alpha petitioned for alpha status, the current alphas lost land. They all ruled with heavy and sometimes brutal hands to keep what was theirs. Public land had always been sacred. Now that she'd claimed a large portion, the rest of it was up for grabs around the state. It gave the shifters a bigger prize to focus on other than her.

The vampire smiled. "Your land borders both the clan and magic practitioners. It is a delicate strip to own."

"And we have all lived there in peace for years." He wouldn't be appeased that easily, and Raven needed one more vote. "But if you prefer, we can choose an intermediary."

He revealed fangs when he smiled this time. "Who would you suggest? One of your shifters?"

Raven wasn't sure if he was repulsed or eager to taste whomever she selected. "Actually, one of your own. Rylan Pryor." May he forgive her for thrusting him back into his old life.

Rylan rose to his feet and met her gaze with an impassive expression. "I accept."

The vampire stilled, taken by surprise. "Then the clan approves your petition as well."

Donaldson nodded. "Congratulations. Be—"

"Objection." Vivian was now openly scowling. "I demand proof. She was not born pack. She's a were, not a pure breed."

A growl rumbled from Dominic at the blatant insult. Even the rest of the room fell silent. Ignoring the woman, Raven remained standing and waited for the council to decide.

They were clearly not pleased at having their decision challenge, but Vivian seemed blind to the danger.

"What is this proof?" Raven whispered the question to Taggert.

"You must demonstrate that you're an alpha, strong enough to hold your own and protect what's yours."

Donaldson let the silence stretch as he stared at Vivian. Only when she sat, jerked down by her husband, did she finally lower her gaze.

Silence stretched for a minute more, the air growing heavy, when Donaldson continued. "Do we have a volunteer?"

## ❧ Chapter Twenty-six ❦

**D**urant's golden eyes met hers as he threaded his way through the crowd to reach her side. A show of support. Taggert whispered toward her. "No one in your pack or the challenging pack is eligible to perform the test."

The thought of another alpha challenging her woke her wolf. If Raven allowed her to show, granted her any freedom, they would be considered weak. Thankfully, her power remained dormant, possibly sensing nothing would get her killed faster.

A man rose to his feet after only a slight pause. He was older, his hair mostly white. Though shorter, he had a strong build suitable to shifters. Then she spotted someone familiar sitting at his table. The youngest carpenter, the same one who'd come to her rescue a few days ago.

Though the alpha appeared congenial, he hadn't become an alpha for being nice.

"He doesn't have a female alpha for his pack. This way, he can get the first close look at you without competition." London was assessing the other man even as he spoke. "He's also one of the oldest alphas here."

Oldest meant more powerful. Would that make the challenge easier or harder?

"Acceptable." Donaldson stood, a slight frown between his eyes. "Please step forward."

She passed through the tables unmolested. Vivian sat with her arms crossed, clearly pleased at the turn of events. Raven refused to give into the need to rip out her throat.

Not yet, anyway.

She stopped only when she came face to face with her challenger. "What are the rules of the test?"

"No rules. The test is simple. All you need to do is call my wolf." The voice was gruff as he watched her. She detected no antagonism from him, a nice change for once.

But simple would not be the word Raven would've chosen. She'd spent so much time denying her animals and locking them away, she had no clue how to use her wolf to call his. She'd done it before to protect her pack but that had been with her power.

Despite all of the training in the last few days, the only way to call to her animal was by physical contract. "May I touch you?"

A light scowl creased his face. "Yes."

She could tell he wasn't happy, but conceded to her request. Talking a deep breath, she placed her palm over his heart. The heat he kicked off nearly burned. Instinct said he was canine, but what stunned her was that she couldn't sense his wolf at all.

Then the particulars of this test came home to her. He was an alpha. The more alphas there were, the less land and power they would have. His job was to prevent her from achieving her goal.

The touch of another male, an alpha outside of her pack, lured out her own wolf. The beast was inquisitive in whom Raven had allowed so close, but not dumb to blindly charge forward without gauging the threat.

But there was a barrier, like a hazy mist, that prevented her from reaching his animal. Every time her wolf neared, he whirled away into the ether, dark particles of him swirling around to reform a few feet away.

After the second time, Raven didn't give chase. Her wolf wouldn't catch him that way. There must be some alpha power crap that she was supposed to know.

It took a concentrated effort to call back her wolf. She knew of only one way to proceed. Though reluctant to call upon her power, she would do whatever was needed before conceding defeat. Then she remembered how Aaron knew where his pack was before they'd been visible. The first time it'd happened was at his home, the second when his mother arrived on the day of the picnic.

Instead of focusing on his wolf, she studied the energy around him. It immediately branched off in a dozen directions. She followed the fork, and her mind immediately shot in the direction of the nearest connection.

And shoved in front of a young wolf. Young, but dangerous, if the sudden display of fangs was any indication. At the presence of the animal, her own charged forward and snarled. Confused by the sudden change, the wolf backed away, a whine caught in his throat.

Raven sensed that she could grab control of this young beast if she wanted. A fast way to get herself killed. She carefully retreated. She turned to see at least sixty-some threads connecting the alpha all over the city and further.

The process was fascinating. Could this be an alpha trait? A response to blood being exchanged? Raven reached for the power, rubbing the unusual texture of it between her fingers.

Suddenly yanked from the other world, Raven dropped back into her own mind with a nasty thump that left her stomach reeling.

The alpha knocked her hand away from his chest, his wolf in complete control. Raven stood her ground, unsure if this was part of the test or not. She feared she might have made a tactile error and done something that should've been impossible.

A snarl rose from the alpha.

He grabbed for her throat, the intent to kill her clear in his yellow eyes.

And encountered her necklace. Silver warmed her skin. The alpha inhaled sharply and jerked away, coming back to his human self.

A flush filled his face, his breathing rough as he struggled for control. He reached out, lifting his hands in the universal show that he meant no harm. The palm of one hand was latticed with welts. Though she sensed wariness, she didn't feel any immediate threat. Funny, since just seconds ago he tried to kill her. Raven gave him a nod of permission, and he slowly tugged aside the collar of her jacket.

The silver necklace Jackson had given her gleamed in the dark lighting of the club like a splash of stars.

Someone whistled low in their throat.

"There's your proof." Vivian rose with a triumphant smile and faced the council. "I demand that she be taken into custody."

Donaldson gazed impassively at the alpha who'd performed the test. "What say you on your findings?"

"She's an alpha. I'm not sure of her beast, but with some training, she could hold a large pack." He dipped his head toward her in a sign of respect, but circled around her so they wouldn't accidently touch when he walked back toward his table.

Not that she blamed him.

When most people touched her, they only made that mistake once. She had no idea how she'd passed, what he'd learned, but her secret was safe for now.

"You must be wrong." Vivian glared at Raven.

People quieted, and the alpha halted.

Kevin rose to his feet at his mate's side and forcefully pushed her down in her seat. He'd finally had enough. "We apologize and accept the council's decision."

The other alpha pinned Vivian to the spot until she paled and lowered her eye in deference, maybe realizing for the first time what she'd done.

"Accepted." The alpha growled the words, clearly not pleased at being challenged. He settled into his seated, never once taking his attention from Vivian.

Donaldson showed no reaction to the tension crawling through the club. It was a full minute before he spoke. "Your petition has been granted and dually recorded. Let the conclave begin."

With that, talk sprang up again like excited chatter monkeys. Half of it was directed at Raven, the other half at Vivian.

People rose from their tables and began to mingle, while others went before the conclave to be heard. Raven turned to find Durant before her, his face pale and set.

Then he embraced her for the whole room to witness. "They would have killed you."

His whispered words made her shiver. The nerves she held at bay churned through her stomach at everything that could've gone wrong.

At everything she could've lost.

A fine tremor shuddered through him when she ran a finger down the side of his face. "Pack."

He pulled back and smiled. "Pack."

They made their way back to her table where London and Taggert stood waiting.

In lieu of congratulations, London nodded to her and scanned the crowd. "You are one of the few females that are able to hold a pack on your own. You just made yourself the biggest attraction and target for every male in search of a powerful mate. A seductive combination."

Raven took her seat then allowed herself to be nudged further into the booth to make room for all four of them. She sat in the center curve, a place of protection, one similar to almost all the other alphas in the room.

The only exception was Dominic. He sat, fully wolfed-out, at the front of the table, a gatekeeper for the unwary.

Most of the gazes cast their way were a combination of respectfulness and curiosity. She glanced at the corner for Jackson and Aaron. Only they had disappeared. The last of the tension dropped away to know they were safe.

"I need to get back to work. I'll see you back at the house." Durant lifted her hand and kissed her palm. "I never doubted you."

Then he was gone.

Rylan approached when Durant left. The large cat still hadn't forgiven him for turning Cassie, even if it had meant saving her life.

"I never thought to see you here."

"You didn't think I'd miss it, did you?" His smile was genuine, the friend that she thought she'd lost. "Congratulations."

"I'm not sorry I volunteered you." Raven lifted her chin, refusing to hide from what she'd done. It was selfish, but she wasn't ready for him to disappear out of her life without a fight.

His eyes darkened. "We'll figure something out. I'll meet you on the last day of the conclave to discuss where we go from here."

He lifted her fingers to his mouth. Instead of a press of lips, he nipped at the back of her hand, stealing a drop of blood. Then he, too, was gone.

The lover's kiss shared between vampires stung, heat spreading in its wake. Blood lust and desire were intertwined for vampires and a powerful aphrodisiac for those trusting enough to leave themselves vulnerable to their lovers.

Not wanting the others to see the effect he had on her, she

cleared her throat and gestured toward the crowd. "Do we need to walk around like the rest?"

Taggert shook his head. "Not tonight. They will come to us. After an hour or so, I'll make the rounds for you."

Raven wasn't sure of the protocols, but her relief at not having to parade herself about was too great to object.

Over the next few hours, a steady procession of people came to the table and introduced themselves. She made it a point to memorize faces and pack affiliation, but names blurred together after the first hour. Midnight came and with it, the press of shifters increased. Her skin itched with the need to get out and ease the ache resting below her skin.

Taggert sensed her growing unease and returned to the table. "We've stayed long enough. We can leave if you want."

"Yes." Raven stood, grateful for the reprieve.

The men guided her toward the door. Dominic led the way, the big, black wolf kept people at a distance. Bringing him was no different than brandishing a cocked weapon. She nodded to the few people she recognized, trying not to be bothered by the gawking. No one approached them.

"We can go over the petitions you received in the morning."

"My petitions?" Raven almost missed a step at Taggert's comment. They were almost to the door.

"Now that you're pack, it's time to build your connections. You'll receive petitions, requests for favors, and propositions in forming allegiances."

When she didn't answer, Taggert took it as incentive to continue. "It's commonplace practice at the conclave. You'll want to be selective, not let yourself be swayed by someone else's trouble. You need to make connections that will strengthen the pack. I handed out your cards and received a number in return. The first notices will start arriving tomorrow."

The unforeseen revelation poleaxed her. It was the last thing she expected. She burst outside into the fresh air, closed her eyes and inhaled, trying not to panic. "But I'm new. I have nothing to offer."

London unlocked the car and scowled at her over the roof. "And too naive if you think that. You're too attractive of a prize for anyone to pass up."

## Chapter Twenty-seven

**SECOND DAY OF THE CONCLAVE: WAXING MOON**

Raven had spent most of last night staring at the full moon spilling into her room. She hadn't slept a wink, the moon's call wreaking havoc on her body. She'd half expected an attack from Vivian, especially since Aaron would be joining the other teenagers in their first cresting tomorrow night.

Nothing came.

It made her suspicious.

They drove to the club in silence, the sun's dying rays barely tinged the horizon. In less than an hour, she would be claiming Taggert. Raven's stomach dipped at the possibility of being denied. Yesterday had been cutting it too close.

As they entered the club, she marveled at how relaxed Taggert appeared. He walked through the packed crowd with a confidence that she'd never seen in him. The place was crammed with more people than last night if that were possible. All the seats were taken, more than half the crowd standing along the walls.

The noise level dipped as they made their way to their table, like a novelty to be studied. Some were curious, while others sized her up, determining if she were a threat to be removed. She filed those faces away to remember for later.

Her ass barely hit her seat when the council members slowly filtered into the room. They were all pristinely dressed, each resuming the same positions on the dais as the previous night. "Let the petitions begin."

No one moved. Raven took her courage in both hands and stood.

"You again." The older wolf on the council scowled in disgust.

Raven would not be deterred. "I have a petition."

Someone on the council snorted, but Donaldson was the one who spoke. "Why am I not surprised. Let's hear it."

"My claim is on the slave named Taggert." The rest of her speech vanished as Taggert stepped out of Durant's office. When he'd left to ready himself ten minutes ago for inspection, the last thing she expected was to find him parading through the crowd like some Chippendale dancer on display for all to see.

Taggert held his head high, and she realized he was showing off for her. This ritual meant that he had been chosen. That someone had found him good enough.

The collar sparkled under the light. Though slim, his muscles drew her gaze, gleaming with oil that urged her to touch.

He was hers, and she disliked having to share him that way.

Then he came to stop in front of the council.

"What about the rumors that you'd removed the collar?" The lone woman on the board rose. She wore a flowing skirt, not appearing to walk but glide as she circled Taggert.

Her dark hair was neatly pulled back, drawing attention to her light coffee skin. Despite the faint wrinkles that dared to crowd the corner of her eyes, her exotic appearance easily captured the audience.

It was only when she pinned Raven under her gaze that she understood the power of the woman.

Her eyes were a dark brown, almost black.

Shadows moved in them.

The age of the woman pressed down on her, dragging her back to when voodoo priestesses ruled. If she peered deep enough, Raven could see tortured souls withering for mercy.

A warning.

Raven barely felt the undercurrent of magic. A moment ticked off before she recognized it and brushed aside the sorcery. The woman's eyes changed to just plain brown again.

The experience left Raven shivering.

It'd been a spell.

But what version of the witch was the truth and which one the lie?

"I was under the impression any tampering with the collar killed the host." It wasn't exactly a lie. She had removed the collar, but Taggert took it upon himself to wear it again to protect her. From the suspicious nature of the practitioner, Raven grudgingly admitted he might have made the right decision. "Yet, he's wearing it."

The woman inclined her head. "Indeed."

The curmudgeon wolf from yesterday rose and approached Taggert. After a short inspection, he shook his head. "Weak. Unable to shift."

Taggert didn't give any overt sign he heard but for a flinch around his eyes that made Raven want to smack the old man.

Abruptly, the old wolf leaned forward, caught a scent, and inhaled. His head jerked up, and he whirled on her. "You claimed his blood."

Raven relaxed her tense body, half expecting him to spring at her throat. "His life was threatened. He was under my care. I took measures to ensure his safety. The methods I chose were my decision."

The wolf didn't move as he continued to stare. Without a word, he resumed his seat. There was something in his eyes. Respect or foolishness, she wasn't sure.

"That might explain this one, but what about Durant." The cat's green eyes had been staring at her unblinking, his feet up on the dais until then. Now, he pinned her under his gaze like she were prey.

She studied the group of people before her. This was much more than a request for Taggert. This was an inquisition, and she stepped into it without warning.

The trick pissed her off. "What does my petition have to do with Durant?"

Trying not to leap to conclusions, feeling like she was called to the carpet to be reprimanded, she battled with the sudden suspicions that they wanted to take Durant away from her.

Unacceptable.

"Indulge us."

"No." Raven didn't even hesitate. "My decisions are my own. Durant is mine, claimed by blood."

And she had no intention of releasing him. A slight murmur ran through the crowd at her blunt refusal. More people paid attention to her conversation than conducting their own business.

The cat straightened. "Durant is—"

"Not part of my petition. If you have any questions, you can direct them to me at a later time where we can discuss your concerns in private."

"She's right." Donaldson brushed away the rest of the protests. "Any objections to her claim?"

A brush of magic curled around her much like walking into a mess of cobwebs. The practitioner spoke, a ruthlessness in her tone. "I don't have an objection, but I do have a stipulation. Spend one week at the coven after the conclave ends, and you may keep your wolf."

The sudden silence in the room was deafening. Even the stoic Donaldson appeared alarmed by the request. Then he sent her a pointed look and raised an eyebrow as if daring Raven to accept the challenge. The paranormal community had a long memory. To them, a few hundred years was not enough time to dull the harsh truth of their dual past. Magic users had enslaved shifters as familiars to escape the consequences of expending too much magic in a short amount of time by using the animals as proxy.

The truce between all races was shaky at best. She suspected the only thing holding it together was the humans. They needed to provide a united front against them. If the truce failed, the humans would have them declared monsters and hunted.

"I will agree." She held up a hand when Taggert whispered her name. Even if he managed to survive the last few weeks of his five-year term as a slave, the witch would make sure Taggert would either be claimed by someone else or killed long before then. "But only if you agree that my stay will be as your personal guest."

The witch narrowed her spooky eyes. There was only one reason she could think that they wanted her. They must smell magic on her. Practitioners were possessive of magic, fewer people were born with the gift every year. When one was found, they claimed the person as their own...if they were willing or not.

Raven felt cornered and didn't care for it one bit. But there was a dangerous lure to their proposal as well. What if they could teach her how to use her powers? Or maybe more importantly, what if they couldn't?

The witch finally gave a regal nod. "Very well."

She walked toward Taggert and cupped the collar. Raven didn't know what was supposed to happen, but nothing wasn't it. A frown creased the witch's face, and she closed her eyes. Magic thickened the air, clogging her lungs like breathing through water.

A tremor rocked the witch's long, boney fingers. By the time the lock disengaged, the witch was pale and sweaty. Taggert dropped to his knees, not looking much better, and Raven locked her legs to keep from going to him.

"There was no need to harm him. I gave my word."

The witch's eyes darkened. That was when Raven understood. The witch knew someone had tampered with the collar.

"You owe me one week." The witch whirled and stalked back toward the dais, her long, multicolored skirt swaying with her agitated movements.

Raven wondered if she'd overstepped and created an enemy.

## Chapter Twenty-eight

There was no time to celebrate Taggert's emancipation. They had a rave to attend. Lights of the city glowed in the distance, leaving the area with a wide-open feeling of being exposed. The closest cover was the old steel factory two hundred yards away. Music reverberated in the air, the pounding of the bass sounded like tribal drums calling warriors to battle. Energy poured off the place, a powder keg just ready for the match.

Raven just hoped she wasn't the flame.

Griffin stood at her side, his expression impassive.

"You didn't need to come."

He'd opted to tag along when he learned where they were going, claiming she couldn't go alone. More likely to steal her viable lead, but she could use the backup.

She had decided not to call the police. She justified her actions by saying it was nothing more than a lead, but even she didn't really believe that. The cops were human, their presence would be too obvious.

But that was only part of the reason.

The police couldn't be allowed to see the shifters so vulnerable. They couldn't be allowed to see them as a threat.

"I'll keep my distance, but if you suspect they are running the drugs through here, you have to be careful." Hands on his hips, Griffin stared unblinking at the building, lips tight as he imagined all that could go wrong. "If you even hint at shutting them down, they will not hesitate to remove the threat. For someone helpless, the chance to be an alpha, not to have to bow and scrape for every little bit...they would kill for it."

"Even if by taking the drug, they die?"

"Better to die free." Jase mumbled, assessing the laughing teenagers that entered the building.

Raven wasn't sure how to take his comment. As if aware of the attention on him, Jase turned toward her. "The drug isn't real. It gives power to people who don't deserve it and can't control it."

She was surprised someone in his position would understand, but maybe he comprehended it better than most.

They ducked behind the thirty-foot sliding garage door, the walkway opened enough for them to squeeze through single file. The smell of urine and rats indicated the place had been abandoned for some time. It made her miss the subtleties and comforts of *Talons*.

The dirt path guided them through the maze of plastic sheets that hung from the exposed rafters. Each step increased the decibel of the music. A babble of voices rose.

After passing through the third plastic sheet, color lasers flashed through the room. Taggert halted and lifted his face. "Booze and smoke."

"Nothing else?"

He shook his head.

It was too much to hope that it could all be over so quickly. But what if she found the drug? Did that really prove anything? They needed to find someone to lead them to the source.

The main dance floor was packed with shifters, ages ranging from fifteen all the way to their upper twenties. They were all relaxed, some laughing and talking, others moving in beat with the music. There was an edge to them, everyone hyped up on the energy of youth and high shifter metabolism. A dangerous combination if the mood turned ugly.

Aaron flashed her a mischievous smile, grabbed her arm and pulled her into the fray. Bodies brushed against hers, and she quickly lost sight of the others.

"Wait." Aaron either didn't hear or purposely ignored her. She suspected the latter. The kids threw themselves totally into the moment, the rave the only real freedom they had until they crested. Living under the shadow of the pack made everything a matter of life and death despite their age. Even here, the shifters roamed in packs, small groups of threes and fours.

A surprising number of women were present.

They were on the other side of the warehouse in no time. Aaron halted and surveyed the crowd. Without Taggert to stabilize her, she braced for an overwhelming surge from her wolf, a demand for freedom.

Nothing.

Understanding hit, and she tightened her hand on Aaron. "You're protecting me."

"Only a little. The animals of the younger ones are mostly dormant. A strong alpha might be able to call them out if they are close to cresting, but the effects of the moon calls to them differently. They meet here to form their own alliances, some strong enough they remain throughout their lives."

"And the women?"

"They are allowed their freedom now, kind of like sowing their wild oats if you would. They practice their wiles. They also know their worth and wouldn't risk their alpha's ire if they overstep themselves."

"How'd you get Jackson to let you come?"

"The rave is sacred. If I'm hurt here, it would be investigated by the conclave. Mother would be caught, held for trial, and torn apart by her very own pack."

Cheers erupted from the side of the room, and Raven raised a brow.

"They're fighting for dominance."

They found themselves jostled by the crowd, pushed closer to the fight. "What about the rogues?"

"They are tolerated, more so than what the adults normally allow." He pulled her out of the wave moving forward. "They can pretend they are someone else for a few nights a month."

"That's cruel." To taunt them with what they could never have.

"It's their reality. They have a chance to make alliances if they are smart and strong enough."

"Soldiers to be sold to the highest bidder."

"Better than going feral. They are allowed at the perimeter of the pack. It keeps them sane."

Another cheer rose, and Aaron allowed them to be jostled closer. People moved out of his way, some even going as far as to bow. That's when she realized being the son of two strong alphas made him kind of like royalty in their world.

As they drew closer to the commotion, Raven felt the building power coming from the center of the group.

Alpha power.

Not waiting for Aaron now, she pushed her way through the crowd. People grumbled, but quickly stepped out of her way when they recognized her as an alpha.

At the center of the circle, two teenage boys who should know better swung at each other, their nails sharp enough to cleave flesh down to the bone with each strike. The fight was brutal, blood flowing freely.

When she would have stepped into the ring, Aaron grabbed her arm. "They are fighting for alpha spot in the pack. A practice for the future."

As she inhaled, she recognized the smell that she found on the bodies, light, barely there. Urgency notched up with each blow. "You and I both know this is something more."

Aaron sighed as if she were overreacting. "You're not going to let this go."

Raven winced when the dark haired boy landed a hard blow that nearly took out the throat of the other kid. Some people gasped at the near miss. If the other kid hadn't twisted and taken the blow to his shoulder, he would've been dead.

"They're just kids."

Aaron shook his head. "Do they look like kids playing a game?"

The two kids circled each other, snarls harsh on the air, each wounded but refusing to back down. The rest of the crowd quieted, noticing the change, too. "They look like they plan to kill each other."

He heaved a sigh at her prodding then glanced at the fighters. He narrowed his eyes, immediately noticing something wasn't right. A muscle clenched in Aaron's jaw, and he stepped forward.

There was no overt signs that Aaron did anything, nothing that she would be able to pin back to him, but the fighters suddenly stopped, clearly confused at what prompted their need to shed blood. One swayed on their feet, desperately working to staunch a nasty wound to his side. The other dropped to his knees and hung his head as if it were too heavy to hold upright anymore.

No wonder Vivian so feared her son. Instead of using him to better the pack, she wanted to destroy the power that she couldn't control. If he ever challenged his father, he would gain possession of the pack, and dear mother would lose her standing.

Raven stopped watching the action and scanned the crowd. She didn't have a clue what she was searching for until she saw one man scowling. She nudged Aaron, but there was no way they could cross the room before he disappeared.

Miraculously, out of the crowd of people, their gazes clashed. The man blinked then stumbled back. He shoved into the crowd, never once taking his eyes off her.

Like he knew her.

Or was told to keep an eye out for her.

Raven shot into the crowd after him.

"Wait!" Aaron charged after her, but she didn't slow. She followed the bob of the guy's hat into a group of teens. It disappeared in seconds.

Raven stopped and spun.

Nothing.

The large plastic sheet separating the warehouse waved from an invisible wind. He'd ducked behind the wall into the part of the factory housing the machinery. As she neared, the hat she had been following lay trampled on the ground.

Not hesitating, she slashed through the plastic. From one step to the next, she was plunged into darkness. The smell of dirt, old metal and rust permeated the place. Sounds faded, muted by the plastic.

As if waiting for her, the man she'd been following tossed a fifty-gallon drum at her. The blasted thing was too large to dodge. Metal slammed into her with the force of a cannonball. She flew backwards, her body smashing into the barrels like a demented game of bowling.

By the time she struggled to her feet and navigated the forest of barrels, the man had vanished.

Again.

"Raven?" Plastic crinkled when Aaron entered behind her.

The bright blob of the rave barely lit the plastic behind him.

He took in the scene at a glance. "What way did he go?"

Hands on her hips, Raven surveyed the maze of stalls before them. "I have no clue."

But she had an idea. "Stay behind me."

With a room full of shifters, this was either the best or the worst idea she'd ever had. All she knew was she couldn't let her lead go without trying.

She called up her powers. It rose eagerly to her summons, and she let the energy build. She sent out pulse. Like a ripple in a pond, the wave expanded.

Aaron sucked in a breath, holding out his hands as if he could feel the current in the air. "Holy shit."

There was a ping.

"There." She pointed to the right.

Only, they didn't make it two steps before three more pings sounded. "Damn it. There are more people in here." She skidded to a stop at the first spot and found a couple hastily pulling on their clothes. "Get back to the rave."

She watched them leave and heaved a sigh of frustration. "We'll never be able to check all the spots before he disappears."

"Raven?" Taggert's eyes glowed as he walked toward her through the darkness.

"I lost my suspect. Can you scent him? His trail led back here, but there are too many people for me to find quickly."

"You're hurt."

Raven rubbed the back of her hand over her mouth, surprised to find blood. "I'm fine, but we need to find him."

Taggert inhaled, his chest expanding impressively. He turned toward the left, a maniacal gleam in his eyes that wouldn't be extinguished without tasting vengeance, and shot into the darkness.

"I want him alive."

When Raven moved to follow, Aaron grabbed her arm. "He's trapped. There is only one other exit from this side of the building. We can go around the outside and head him off."

That meant heading in the opposite direction instinct urged her to go.

But Aaron was right. Taggert would flush him out.

The outside air hit her like a fist to the gut. Smells died and the excess pressure from all the energy the shifters exuded vanished as well. They ran full tilt around the shed, but she knew they would never make it on time.

Griffin came up to her side, moving fast. He took one look at her face and shook his head. "You really aren't very good at staying out of trouble, are you."

Raven winced at the comment. "Anyone come outside?"

"Not from this end." They rounded the last corner to see Taggert and Jase emerge.

Alone.

"How could we have missed him?" Taggert swiped a hand through his hair. "I was following his scent, but it just disappeared ten feet from the door. I can try to pick it back up again, but with so much contamination, it would take a while."

Her lead had slipped right through her fingers, slapping them in the face on the way for good measure. "No sense backtracking. He'll be long gone by now."

"But he dropped these." Jase lifted his hand to show a clear strip of plastic between his fingers.

She held them up to her nose, smelled chemicals but no formaldehyde. Could she have been wrong? "He probably took a hit to cover his scent and dropped the rest in his haste."

"Let's head back home. There's nothing more we can find here. I want to see what we can learn from this drug."

As they drove home, Raven came to one reluctant conclusion. "Vivian isn't a viable suspect. She liked being in control, liked being the only alpha female. The drug was engineered to do the complete opposite."

Aaron nodded, as reluctant as her to give up his mother as a suspect. "No amount of money would entice her to relinquish her power over others."

"So where does that leave us?" Griffin's voice held no inflection. He'd already come to the same conclusion days ago. That's why he wormed his way into her household. He needed more leads.

"Without Vivian, all we're left with are the rogues." The very same rogue pack that she'd allowed to live behind her house. She'd insulted their leader, stole his people, and now she was trying to steal his miracle drug.

No wonder he was so determined to kill her.

Jase didn't confirm or deny anything, but his worried gaze latched onto hers as if troubled that she'd hold him personally responsible. She gave him a small smile. Instead of being reassured, he flinched and turned to stare out the window.

Taggert remained silent, his expression grim, clearly deducing what her fate would be if they didn't catch the rogue first. Any hope that she could continue her case without involving her pack evaporated. Taggert would make sure the rest discovered the truth.

She would have to work fast to keep them safe.

If it wasn't already too late.

* * *

"Can you tell me what's in this?" Raven debated whether to send the samples to the police to do the analysis or not. Her hesitation stemmed from the fear that what they found would go on record. Shifters couldn't afford to have the drugs reproduced or distributed. To eliminate them that way would prove too high of a casualty rate for everyone involved.

The peace between humans and shifters was too volatile. She ignored the little voice of her conscience that said she was part of the police and supposed to help them, not withhold information. Her only saving hope was that if she solved the case, it wouldn't matter.

Digger peered up from his work at the table, his eyes owlish in the dim light. "It will take me a few hours to run a couple of tests."

When he wandered away, Raven heaved a sigh of relief and hurried up the stairs. She knew she should ask what he'd learned about the tests he ran on Taggert, but it was too soon after the claiming. She wanted to remain oblivious for a little while longer in case she had to send him away to keep him safe.

She was half way across the foyer when she spotted Jase lurking in the shadows, haggard and pale.

"Can we talk?" His adams apple bobbed when he spoke.

"Of course." Raven walked toward her office. He came slowly, all but dragging his feet.

He was leaving her.

She barely sat behind the desk when he spoke.

"I'm supposed to kill you." Any nuance in Jase's voice was stripped away. He stood before her, a firm grip on his knife, showing he knew what to do with it.

Raven tensed as he padded toward the desk.

Then he very deliberately set the knife on the wooden surface and retreated to the middle of the room.

That's all he said.

He stared at the wall, waiting for judgment. His silence, the bruises, all made sense now.

"What do you think should be done?"

He swallowed hard. "Disloyalty is punishable by death." His voice broke painfully.

Raven lifted the knife and circled the desk. "See, now that's the problem. As far as I see it, you were loyal to your pack."

Jase's eyes snapped toward her.

"Loyal to me." She held out the knife, handle first. "What more can I ask?"

He made no move to take the weapon. "I don't understand."

"I'd like you to stay. You've proven yourself loyal and resourceful. I can use someone like you." She walked up to him, pausing inches from his face, so close she didn't even think he breathed. "Next time you run across a problem, come to me sooner."

"But the rogue will come after you. Not only did you challenge his rule in front of his men, you took three people from his pack. He can't let it go unanswered."

A smile stretched her face, nothing remotely friendly in the gesture. "Let him."

"But—"

"He wanted me dead before the challenge, before you came to us. You're only an excuse." She gave a wry smile. "Unless you would prefer not to stay. This isn't the safest place."

Jase studied her for a full minute then tentatively accepted the knife, the awe in his eyes so painful to witness, her throat closed.

"My life is yours."

Raven watched him leave, a spring in his steps that had been missing.

It felt good to have at least one thing go right tonight.

She mounted the stairs, distracted by the case, when an unnatural silence crept over her. She measured the distance to the study where her weapons laid and gauged if she'd be able to close the distance in time. London entered the foyer. He spoke, but she heard nothing.

Magic brushed against her, heavy, invading her body with each breath. It drifted down from upstairs like a net to capture all within its grasp.

To hell with waiting.

## Chapter Twenty-nine

**R**aven took the remaining steps three at a time. London nearly overtook her. She shoved off the wall and ran full tilt toward Aaron's room and the heavier pull of magic.

She threw open the door. Jackson stood like a sentinel at the window, fighting two shifters while trying to shove a third one back over the windowsill.

London pointed left before charging into the fray to help Jackson.

Aaron was on the floor, barely holding off the blade angled for his throat. Raven swung back her leg, her boot catching the large shifter square in the face. Bones gave, the face caved and the body launched backwards.

All without sound.

It was unnerving to fight without the added element. She hadn't realized how much she'd come to rely on her senses.

Blood pooled around Aaron's leg where he'd taken a hit. Another wicked wound carved along his forearm where the skin pulled away from flesh.

When he tensed, her attention flashed up to see the shifter on all fours. Even as she watched, his teeth lengthened, his claws pushed from his fingers, creating large notches across the floor.

Anger took over. Raven yanked off her gloves and lifted her hand toward the wall. Electricity teemed in the wires and arced into her outstretched palm, closing the foot gap. The surge of power bowed her back, but the sharp pain was more delicious than crippling, and she soaked up all the beautiful current.

The shifter's eyes widened at the display. Sensing his prey was about to be snatched away, he charged.

Raven launched herself into him headfirst.

Bodies collided.

Her back crashed to the floor. They slid a few feet, her shirt riding up her back, and she lost a layer of skin on the carpet as they grappled for purchase. Teeth tore viciously into the fleshly part of her shoulder, the pain stealing the air from her lungs. She lost hold on one of his arms and ribbons of agony slashed down her side.

Raven gave up trying to fight fair. She laid her hands on bare flesh, one around his throat and another over his heart to complete the circuit.

The charge immediately leapt into him.

Fangs and claws receded.

Her palms heated, but she refused to allow him to retreat. If she lost her hold, he would go for Aaron again.

Only when burnt flesh filled the room did she relent.

He had enough.

But when she tried to pull back, the creature she harbored flexed her talons, refusing to be denied their prey.

A snarl of rage worked up her throat.

She would not be used.

Raven tried to wiggle away, put distance between them, but his weight pinned her beneath his bulk.

Blood trickled from his eyes and nose. His jaw clenched so tight his teeth cracked. Bile rose in her throat as she watched his blood slowly boil him from the inside out.

Horrified by the sight, she arched her back, twisting until they rolled. Scalding blood poured over her at the action.

Sputtering, Raven scrambled away from the shifter. Her back hit the wall, and she frantically swiped to get the gore off her face.

The taste of his blood lingered in her mouth. A fierce satisfaction spread from the center of her chest, the cold beast at her core staring out in pride at her work.

The shifter crawled to get away, dragging his body behind him to escape. Aaron limped forward, the knife in his hand gleaming. Raven tried to speak, but the damn spell wouldn't release her.

Aaron calmly sliced the throat of the shifter that had been sent to kill him.

Death shrouded the room. Despite the destruction of all four would-be assassins, magic continued to swirl in the confined space. She tracked the source, the spell rising like a poisonous gas from the corpse nearest London.

Launching to her feet, Raven rolled the body onto his back. A necklace rest over his chest, all but glowing with power. She yanked until the chain came away in her hand. Her creature hissed at the contact. The magic began to feed off the energy around her core now that the shifters fueling it were dead.

She couldn't shut down.

The one comfort with her power was that she'd always been the one in charge.

But she wasn't now.

The knowledge that she could be controlled, used against her will, both terrified and infuriated her.

Raven sent a burst of raw electricity into the amulet, the source of the threat. Only to have the medallion eagerly soak up the charge. Panic slithered into her gut before she could squash it, eating up precious seconds, when a reckless idea began to take root. Not giving herself a chance to think, she quickly followed the current into the necklace.

It dropped her into the spell.

She found herself staring down at a man sleeping peaceful, his form almost indistinguishable to the darkness around him.

The creature at her core charged, slashing at the image, and she saw the man's cheek slice open. He swore, jerking upright. He immediately spotted the connection. He chanted a few words she didn't recognize, and their link shattered like a pop of a light bulb.

Raven landed on her ass, completely exhausted. Sounds whooshed back into the room, loud after such a long absence. The amulet lay blackened in her fists, the weight heavy as if it still carried all that magic locked inside.

Her creature growled, circled what remained of her core like a mother with a nest before curling around it.

Leaving her without an ounce of spark.

"What is it?" Jackson reached for the chain, and Raven jerked it away.

"A spell, but with a nasty parting gift if we managed to kill the attackers. It's best you don't have any contact with it until we know it's completely dead." And it was her only connection to the mystery man.

Aaron came to stand before her, his pant leg and shirt stained with blood. He held her gloves out to her and formally bowed. "Thank you for saving my life."

* * *

Raven stood in the shower long after the blood had washed down the drain. Despite the hot water, she shivered, remembering the bitter cold as the specter of death hovered over her attacker, ready to consume him, and she'd been helpless to do anything about it.

She wanted to take the easy way and blame the necklace for everything, but it wouldn't be the complete truth.

The creature had craved vengeance.

She slammed her palm against the wall. She'd thought she'd been getting better.

"You can't stay in there forever. Your wounds need to be treated."

Taggert stood in front of the sink, sorting through the abundance of first aid products. Conceding defeat, she shut off the water and wrapped the towel around herself. Her shoulder and side ached, though she barely registered the pain. "The bleeding has already stopped. I'll bandage them."

Taggert stepped toward her, and her back thudded into the wall. She hadn't even been aware of moving away from him.

"You will not hurt me."

He sounded so damn confident.

"I nearly killed that man."

Taggert only shrugged. "If it had been any of us, we wouldn't have hesitated. Very few shifters would be strong enough to stop when their pack is threatened."

Then he very deliberately held out his hand to her.

Daring her.

Her fingers twitched when she lifted her hand and placed her fingers in his. She watched his face, ready to bolt at the least bit of reservation or fear.

Other than a crackle of static, nothing happened.

Taggert hauled her closer, propped her ass against the sink, and assessed her injuries.

"You can't just assume that I won't hurt you."

"You don't give yourself enough credit. Your power knew what it was doing. It wouldn't destroy something it's already claimed. If you doubt me, talk to Digger." There was no reproach in his words, just gentle chiding.

"You assume it thinks and feels."

"Don't you?" Taggert peeled down the side of her towel, preserving her modesty so only her back and side were exposed. Her shoulder had a bite mark that displayed a full set of uppers and lowers. The puncture marks from the fangs were jagged, but at least she hadn't lost a chunk of flesh.

Taggert sprayed antibiotic on her shoulder and bandaged it. He bent to view her side where four claws sliced down her ribs, narrowly missing her soft underbelly. "The slashes are too close together. Any stitches will pull at the wound and pucker the skin."

But he didn't stop inspecting her side. "What is it?"

He pointed to an area just above her hipbone. "The skin around this area appears bruised, but it's unlike anything I've ever seen."

Raven glanced down at the fist-sized spot. "I must have knocked into something during the fight."

But she couldn't recall. A sickening feeling of dread surged through her, a terror so deep she slammed the door against it before it could take hold.

She had to be wrong.

She ran a finger lightly over the area. Coldness met her touch, the surface hard. Her fingertips picked up subtle ridge details, and she could almost detect a pattern if she concentrated hard enough.

Then the placement hit her.

It rested directly over the void, a dead spot where her body could no longer hold current. She'd burned herself out, and it had never healed properly.

Unwilling to share her worry until she had time to learn the truth, she lied through her teeth. "I'm fine. Why don't you head off to bed. It's going to be a long day tomorrow."

Taggert recognized the brush-off but relented without a word at whatever he saw in her expression. He might have allowed her to fob him off for now, but he wouldn't forget.

Once alone, she dropped the towel and wrapped her ribs. After an hour of pacing, Raven worked up her nerve and headed downstairs to see if Digger had made any progress.

The basement was silent, the only sounds were of machines whirling. Without shifting his attention from his work, Digger waved her closer. "The drugs are absorbed into the system by placing a tab on the tongue. The chemicals dissolve almost instantly, the delivery system fast enough to affect shifters."

His explanation made sense. "This drug grants some shifters alpha characteristics for a few hours but it kills others."

A frown wrinkled Digger face. "Small doses shouldn't be lethal."

"But?"

"A resin had been added in the drug to overcome our high metabolism. The resin suppresses oxidation, so the drug remains in the system longer."

"So a timed release."

"Shifters run hot. Some too hot. Our natural temperature can cause the resin in the drug to breakdown too fast and form formaldehyde. And since rogues are closer to going feral, they run hotter and are the most vulnerable.

"Once formaldehyde binds to their system, there is no way to flush it out. Shifters have a low tolerance, so once they reach the saturation point..."

"Kaboom."

Digger nodded, a troubled expression marring his face.

"Are there any symptoms?"

"Headaches, burning sensations in the mucous membranes, but by then, it's already too late."

That explained when the guy at the diner grabbed his head and the couple in the car. The urgency of the situation ratcheted up another notch. Raven curled her hands into fists, feeling useless. "The deaths won't just stop even if we warn everyone. They crave the chance at freedom too much. The more they use the drug, the more the chemicals will build up in their systems."

Raven shook her head at the worst-case scenario and focused on those she could help now. "Since we have a handle on what we're dealing with, will any of that help Jamie?"

"He will be fine, well past the point his body would've reacted to the chemicals. The small percentage in his system slowed his healing. All we can do is wait for him to mend. A day or two more at the most."

Raven gazed at the bed in question. His wounds were smaller, but still not where they should've been.

"You aren't harming him."

Raven's head snapped up.

She couldn't speak.

Couldn't move.

"Taggert, I mean." Digger glanced up from his desk. "I'll admit that he is adapting, changing, but that's not a bad thing. In Taggert's case, it might be a blessing. You are making him stronger and that's something he needs to survive in this new world."

Raven blanched at the doctor's grim explanation. To hear her worst fear confirmed. "Is there any way to reverse what has been done to him?"

Digger studied her for a minute. "I wouldn't suggest it, nor would I advise halting whatever you're doing. You think you're harming him. In fact, I would say the opposite. You are the only thing keeping him alive. He is a weak shifter without anything to offer. Whatever you're doing to him has strengthened his bond with his wolf."

"What about the long term effect or overexposure?" As she knew from recent experience, it was very easy to kill a man.

Digger shrugged as if the choice was up to her, but it had gone far beyond that. "Only time will tell, but we know what will happen if you stop. He could very well lose his wolf."

A death sentence to any shifter.

## Chapter Thirty

**ENCLOSED CONCLAVE: FULL MOON**

The recent attack had more consequences than Raven could've ever predicted.

Her animals had yet to return.

In fact, she couldn't feel them at all. In their place was a coldness that she couldn't shake. It invaded her bones like all the warmth had been sucked out of her.

She had one guess by what.

Her core had been damaged by the magic, and the damn creature was stealing every spare ounce it could grab.

Raven kept to her rooms until it was time to leave for the conclave. She wasn't hiding, but she feared if the others found out how defenseless she really was at the moment, they would forbid her to attend.

Nothing would stop her from claiming Jackson tonight.

She would be walking into a room full of the most powerful shifters without a weapon. She just hoped none of them could tell that she was virtually defenseless. The vulnerability of being so exposed was not a comfortable feeling.

If Scotts and other *normals* felt that way around paranormals, no wonder the distrust remained so rampant between the races.

She opted not to arm herself. It would be seen as weak and draw attention, but she did grab her badge. She wore a slim fitting black outfit, knee-high boots, gloves and her necklace.

With a few more twists to hide her distinctive hair, she was ready to go. Downstairs, Aaron waited for her, and she pulled up short. His hair was trimmed and spiked, like when they'd first met, his clothes pressed. Every inch of the alpha's son. She hadn't realized how relaxed he'd become from the uptight teen he'd been not so long ago. That's when she understood.

"You won't be returning, will you?" It surprised Raven how much she would miss having Aaron near and more than just for the blessing of his gift.

A small smile kicked up the corner of his lips. "After I pass the test, my place in the pack is unassailable. Any personal attack on me would be constituted as an attack on the pack and will be dealt with accordingly."

She couldn't detect even the slightest injury he'd sustained. "Will your wounds affect your presentation?"

He brushed his hand down the front of his chest, slightly uncomfortable looking in his old role. "No. If anything, the change will speed the healing." He wandered closer, every inch of him alert and on edge, the way he was before he'd arrived. "If I don't get a chance to say it later, I want to thank you for taking such good care of me. I'm honored that you've allowed me into your pack, if only for a few days. For saving my life. If you need anything, don't hesitate to call upon me."

The last part sounded like a formal pledge. Raven bowed her head. "It was a pleasure. You know where to reach me if you need me."

But instead of answering, Aaron continued to stare at her.

"What?"

"You would have helped me even without the offer of Jackson." It wasn't a question.

Uncomfortable under his regard, Raven shrugged. "Who can say."

"A word of caution, then. Don't let the conclave take advantage of you. Don't let them ruin the good of what you're doing."

Jackson entered through the kitchen before she could reply.

The brightness in Aaron's eyes dimmed, returning to normal.

Even Jackson was dressed for the occasion, suppressed energy swirling around him. "Ready?"

Raven wasn't sure anymore. Her pack was coming together, but her power and animals were failing her when she needed them most.

She couldn't keep her pack safe without them. "As I'm ever going to be."

The ride to *Talons* was made in silence, all of them edgy, waiting for one last attempt from Vivian. She studied the shadows for any signs of attack.

Everything appeared blessedly calm as they parked. The rumble of the engine died. Before they entered the club, she put her hand against the door to prevent them from going further. "I want to make sure this is something you want."

Jackson shot to attention as if poked with a cattle prod, and Raven wondered what faux pas she'd bumbled into now.

Instead of answering, Aaron walked up to her and gave her a quick hug, ignoring the way she stiffened. "I'll be fine. My alpha is on the other side of the door waiting for me."

Feeling awkward, Raven followed Aaron and Jackson inside. And indeed, Kevin was waiting. He didn't look anxious or tense. Not that anyone would notice. It wasn't until he spotted Aaron that she saw the stress drop away.

He rose to his feet, along with three of his people. They cleared a path through the crowd, which consisted of a mixture of alphas, enforcers and so many teenagers, it felt like the rave all over again. There was a hushed excitement and expectation in the air. And surprisingly, a slight undercoating smell of fear.

"So many."

Aaron scanned the crowd. "Most are here to watch and offer support. Two others will be changing with me tonight. A shifter only gets three chances to crest. The alpha chooses when you are eligible, when they think you have the best chance at the change.

"A shifter has until the age of nineteen to complete the last two attempts."

"What about Jase and the boys?"

"They won't have to go through the public version unless they find a pack. Rogues usually crest early, but being around the pack will slow their progress. Just being in the house will give them a few months."

Raven cast him a cursory look, marveling at his confidence. There was no doubt in him that he would crest tonight.

Aaron gave her a nudge, silently telling her not to worry.

Kevin came to stand before them. "It's good to see you." Though he spoke to her, all his focus was centered on his son.

"You, too, though I thought I would find more resistance."

Kevin's face darkened, and he smiled in a rare show of emotion. "After it came to my attention what my lovely mate had orchestrated last night, I planned my own entertainment for her."

There was no doubt in Raven's mind that whatever he'd had in store for Vivian wouldn't be pleasant, not if his smile was anything to go by. He was not the type of person she wanted on her bad side.

"Do the terms of our agreement meet with your satisfaction?"

"Yes." Kevin held out his hand to his enforcer, then pulled Jackson in close and thumped him on his arm. "I'm going to miss your company, old friend. If you've changed your mind..."

Jackson pulled away and shook his head, the suppressed emotions on his face dropping years from him. "I can't serve two masters."

Kevin was all alpha when he faced her. "I release my claim. From here on out, he's yours." Then with a nod, he disappeared back into the crowd. Aaron flashed her one last mischievous grin before being swallowed by the mill of young people.

Without Aaron or Taggert as a buffer, there was an awkwardness between her and Jackson. He stared at her with an unwavering intensity that made her want to check to make sure she hadn't put her underwear on over her clothes.

Though weak, a cord of current licked under her skin, awakened as if her power couldn't wait to claim him, either.

A commotion at the other end of the room drew her attention. Eager for the distraction, not ready to face the expectation on Jackson's face, she searched for the source of the unrest.

"Did you want to stay longer?" The repressed hunger in his voice snagged at her heart.

He had his freedom now.

He could go anywhere.

"Are you sure this is what you want?"

"No." Jackson moved closer, narrowing the space between them until only they existed. "Want is too tame of a word."

Raven's spirits plummeted then rose so quickly, she was left lightheaded. He wanted her to claim him. To have a man like Jackson select her, after she had nothing for so long, made her feel precious.

"I'm sorry for the interruption, but Raven, may I speak with you in private?" Raven whirled, having so completely fallen under Jackson's spell, she'd forgotten they were in public. It took her frazzled mind a few seconds to recognize Durant.

Then she slammed back to earth with a nasty thump as their surroundings intruded. Trouble brewed in Durant's eyes. When she looked back at Jackson, Durant held out his hand. "It's important."

His agitation ate away at her composure. Beneath the surface, his cat twitched, his eyes glowed before ruthlessly repressing both. Something disturbed him so thoroughly it broke through his phenomenal control.

"Go. This can wait. I have no intention of going anywhere."

Raven squeezed Jackson's arm, still hesitant to leave. This wouldn't be like last time. Jackson would be waiting for her when she returned.

Durant had no such qualms. At Jackson's permission, he snatched her hand and dragged her into the crowd

The atmosphere of the club had changed, harsh whispers pricked her ears.

Piercing stares were directed her way.

Some judging, others suspicious.

"What's going on?"

"You need to see this." His grip tightened painfully. "Be careful. They want someone to blame. Don't let them corner you into anything."

"Blame?" Then she smelled it.

Blood and a lot of it.

No longer needing to be pulled, she shoved her way to the front. People parted reluctantly.

The council members stood outside of the bathroom. The unnerving part, they stopped talking the instant she came into view.

It only took a quick glance into the red-washed room to know what had happened. Raven cursed her luck to have a woman die at the conclave. Bad enough the death was brought here but female shifters were considered sacred.

No one could allow the murders to go unanswered any longer.

Blood dripped from the ceiling. Pulp slid down the walls. There were no signs of clothes except for a few scattered pieces of a skirt. Raven couldn't smell the blood anymore over the raw scent of meat and bile.

"Lock down the club. Don't let anyone leave. Detain anyone who tries."

"This is the case you've been working on?" Durant sounded appalled.

The older wolf on the council inhaled sharply, his eye gone yellow. "And you brought this here."

Raven narrowed her eyes, offended by the implications. "Of course not. I warned the council that this could happen."

"Well, you didn't do a very good job stopping it, did you?" The old man bared his teeth, completely convinced she should be held responsible.

Donaldson raised his hand. "Now you have our complete attention."

That was so not what a person wanted to hear from the leader of the conclave. "There is a new drug on the market, a twin of the one out a few weeks ago. This one allows a shifter the characteristics of an alpha."

"Impossible." The wolf looked down his nose at her, dismissing her without bothering to listen to proof. The old curmudgeon.

"But the drug reacts to some shifters," she nodded to the bathroom, "that way."

"Why would she take the drug?" Donaldson sounded skeptical. "Females have their own power. Being an alpha for a few hours won't gain her any standing in the pack."

Only one reason came to mind.

"A mate." Raven whispered the revelation, staring into the small room. A shattered mirror littered the room like diamonds shining amongst the gore. She made no move to enter. "I'll need to call the cops."

"We have our own ways to handle these things." The cat leaned against the wall, but there was nothing lazy in his pose. She had no doubt that he would love to be one of the people to hunt for the killer.

Anger simmered in her gut. "This could've been prevented if anyone had bothered to listen sooner. As much as I want to agree with you, this is not something that we can just pretend never happened. The police—"

"Don't know our ways. They will turn this around and blame us." The vampire's eyes had washed black, but she didn't think it had anything to do with the large quantity of blood pooling on the floor so near.

"The council had their chance. You voted for the new force. How will it look when it's discovered that you didn't let them do their job? You will ruin any future chance for humans and paranormals to work together."

"Do they treat you as an equal? Do they give you the resources to extract our justice or their own sense of it?" The cat slowly straightened, retribution battling his alpha duties to do what was best for his people.

Raven couldn't argue with what they said. Not when she was having the same doubts. "We have to give their way a try first, and that means I'm bound by the law to report this crime. I'll minimize human interaction as much as I'm able."

"Do you really think they will try to find the killers since the crimes are only perpetrated against shifters?" Donaldson appeared honestly curious, his expression grim.

"A human was killed—"

"My understanding was her being there was an instance of wrong place, wrong time." Like the human's death was just incidental.

Raven continued as if the older wolf never interrupted her, hating that they sorted the importance of death by race when death, itself, should be the focus. They were no better than the humans. "I have every intention of hunting down the criminal and bringing him to justice any way I can. It's either me or some human. Your choice."

Donaldson held up his hand when the other two would have continued arguing. "We thank you for all your work. We'll add our own services to you as well in support."

A shiver of apprehension tightened her gut, already knowing she wouldn't like what he had to say.

"Randolph will accompany you."

"The police will object." She just wished she could as well. Now that she was an alpha, she was part of the shifter world. That meant she must conform to their dictates.

He waved away her comment as if her protests were no concern of his. "Then you and he will have to make sure that it doesn't become a problem."

As if calling his name had summoned him, Randolph appeared at her side with a bland smile. The non-descript man shouldn't have made her flesh crawl, but she knew what lurked beneath his benign surface.

A stone-cold killer that enjoyed his job a little too much.

And he was her partner.

A headache began to pound at the base of her skull. Once an order was given, no matter how couched in pleasantries, there was nothing she could do to change it.

Aligned with them for one day and already her whole world had altered. If she didn't follow their decree, she wondered if they had the power to revoke her status or if they would devise of another way to make her pay.

She grabbed her phone and headed toward Durant's office for privacy. The phone call to Scotts went about what she could've expected.

Wanting to keep as much distance between the *normals* and shifters as possible, she entered into the club with the mind to clear as many of them of suspicion before reinforcements arrived. The music had stopped. Durant's men had prevented anyone from leaving. Most of the shifters were seated or standing by their alphas. They all held themselves rigid, expressions grave as they mourned the loss to the pack.

Thank goodness the kids and their sponsors had already left for the cresting. That only left her with about a hundred people to question.

She didn't need to whistle to get everyone's attention because all eyes were already glued to her.

No one even blinked.

Creepy.

Whatever anonymity she'd managed to retain all these years was well and truly gone.

"Does anyone know the victim?"

No one answered.

"We know that she is a shifter. She was female."

Still no answer. Damned stubborn shifters. The council's gaze landed on her like a weight, casting judgment and found her lacking.

Raven refused to concede defeat so easily. She gathered a small cord of energy, wrested it from her creature in a game of tug-of-war that left her chest burning in agony. She released a small burst into the room, praying they mistook her power as her alpha ability.

A few vampires jerked straight when hit with the power, their eyes washing black. The shifters reacted differently. The alphas pushed back, the ones strong enough to protect those with them.

A few snarls erupted in the room at her heavy-handed method, but a wild response from one shifter made him stand out from the rest. "You."

The male, who couldn't be more than twenty-five, stood half-hidden in the shadows of a curtain. "You knew this girl. What's your name?"

The atmosphere in the room took on a decidedly deadly overtone as everyone turned toward the kid, the threat making the air in the room thick to breathe. When the man stepped forward, she'd half expected him to be a rogue, maybe even feral.

"My name's Neil. We came together." Then the shifter raised his chin. "She wanted to put in a claim for me before the conclave adjourned for the night."

Then the last thing he would've wanted was to harm her. But that just brought out more questions. "What brought you here? She only needed her alpha's permission."

"I—"

Then things clicked into place. "Your pack denied the union."

The shifter's composure crumbled, the stench of his grief crashing into her. "I told her we could go on the way we were, but she wanted a mate all to her own."

"So you got the drug for her."

"The rogue assured us it would be safe. Otherwise, I would've never let her try it." Pale and shaky, the man looked ill himself.

"She was only supposed to take one hit, but she took them all." His voice wobbled, still shaken by the loss, and he spoke faster. "It worked, but after a while, she began to get sick."

With each word, the room took on a darker tone. The mood turned volatile when a couple shifters rose and slowly closed in on the boy.

In reply, the kid bowed his head.

He had no intention of defending himself.

Alarmed, Raven placed herself between them. "Halt! Do not harm him. We need him to find where the drugs are manufactured. It could lead us to who is killing shifters."

One large lion cracked his knuckles, sounding like he'd crushed all the bones of his hands. "I'll make him talk."

Raven scraped every bit of electricity she had to spare to surface until the air around her crackled with static. It was pathetically little, but thankfully, enough. The shifter's eyes didn't just splinter, but changed to pure yellow.

They stared at each other.

Just when she thought he would lunge, he gave a slight bow with his head. He conceded dominance and backed away. The rest of the room grew so quiet, she could all but hear their heartbeats.

Shivering at the attention she'd brought onto herself, she turned toward the young shifter. "Who is your contact for the drug?"

Instead of being pleased at her interference, the man appeared bitter at being spared. "No one, mistress. I was told to meet them and was given directions."

Raven narrowed her eyes. "Then you will show us where you picked up the drug, and we'll track them."

It wasn't a question. He nodded, and his face hardened. "As you wish."

The rest of the shifters seemed appeased, their grumblings at her interference diminished. At the pause, sirens could be heard in the distance. She had not doubt if the police didn't solve this case tonight, many shifters would take it upon themselves to protect their packs in any way necessary.

It would be a blood bath.

With a sigh, Raven rubbed her brow. This was going to be a long night. "Anyone who does not want to be present for the police, I suggest you leave now."

Almost everyone stood. Some rushed toward the exits, while others leisurely rose to their feet and departed. But in minutes, the room was emptied of all but a fraction of people, mostly workers and those in charge.

Scotts was the first to enter the club, the door having been propped open for them. He gazed around cautiously, his hand on his service revolver. When he spotted her, he gave a nod and stepped into the room.

"The body is in the bathroom." Three people entered behind him, one cop and two forensics with their collection kits. "If you're ready, I'll lead the way."

They remained in the bathroom for nearly two hours, scraping samples from every surface. Scotts had hardly said a word since entering. The strain on their relationship pricked at her nerves. "What is your problem? I'm either a cop or I'm not. Are you pissed that I did my job? I want to make sure I understand."

"We're supposed to be partners." His voice exploded out of him in a harsh whisper. "You shared more information with me when you were a consultant."

"Are we partners? I thought you were my boss. Wasn't I voted to be a Regent to handle the paranormal cases and free you up for other things?"

"Then why don't you catch me up on this case. No more hiding. No more lying by omission. There are too many bodies piling up."

Raven refused to flinch at his accusation. "Like you've shared everything?"

Scotts grunted at the direct hit. "Then maybe it's time that changed."

His concession shocked her. He was a hardcore human advocate, but he was also a cop to his very soul. If anyone could tuck away their prejudice, Scotts could if it meant justice would be done.

"I believe the killings are incidental, a side effect to a new drug out on the market. They are calling it the Alpha drug, because it gives the shifters the ability to become an alpha for a few hours."

"So it's not some sort of war between vampires or humans trying to kill shifters?" Scotts rubbed a hand down his face in relief.

"Not that I can find."

"But why kill themselves? It makes no sense."

It was her turn to hesitate.

"Come on, don't bail on me now."

"Shifters are very organized. They have their leaders. Where you fall is all based on how much power you hold." Raven glanced up at him. "So what if you could take a drug that could land you on the top of the pack?"

Scotts gave a silent whistle, understanding for the first time the danger the drug posed. "If everyone took it…"

"All shifters would become overly aggressive with no one to rein them in." She refused to let that happen.

His eyes narrowed abruptly. "I know that look. You wouldn't have told me anything unless you have a plan. You're not leaving here without me. Not this time."

## Chapter Thirty-one

**FORTH DAY OF THE CONCLAVE: WANING MOON**

By the time they'd reached her house with the police in tow, midnight had come and gone. London unfurled the map of the state forest out onto the table.

People gathered. Scotts took one side, his bulk taking up more than his portion of space, and he wasn't sharing. She and her pack stood to the left of the table, taking care not to leave their backs to any door. Randolph stood on the opposite side. No one seemed inclined to join him. He gave a little smirk of amusement, making no effort to study the map as he scoped out her house.

He was a voyeur, watching her people too intently for her comfort. Raven felt exposed and violated in her own home. Taggert passed between them, breaking the eye contact, serving food and coffee. Knowing from experience that she needed to keep up her calories, Raven accepted the sandwich he offered.

"Tell me you have an idea where to search?" Scotts accepted a cup of coffee.

There were thousands of acres on the map. They would never be able to cover that amount of ground.

"Vaguely. That's why Neil is going to show us where he picked up the drug." Raven nodded toward the lone shifter at the other side of the room.

Ignoring everyone, Neil studied the map and pointed to a small clearing. "Somewhere here."

The area he indicated consisted of a ten-mile radius.

Scotts rocked back on his heels as if understanding. "You're going to have them chase the scent."

*Them* meaning her pack. Raven didn't deny it. "Yes."

Scotts took a sip of his coffee before speaking. "You will not abandon us in the forest while you hunt."

"Not abandon." Raven had to make Scotts see reason. "We're searching for other shifters. Rogues. During the full moon, they're more dangerous and unpredictable than normal. It would be best if you and the others stay back while we take the lead."

"This is a police matter." Scott's didn't back down one bit.

"And I am the police." Raven clenched her teeth in frustration.

Randolph ignored the rest as he stared at her. "They will slow us down."

Raven understood. The cops would be an obstacle and a handicap when it came to fighting. Randolph was more of a cleanup crew, not an apprehend and arrest type of person.

"Then we will be slow." Scotts wasn't stupid. He knew the most likely outcome. He very deliberately set down his cup and placed his hand on his gun. "What is it? That's the third time you looked over my shoulder."

Raven shook her head, astonished he'd noticed when she was barely aware of the action herself. "It's too quiet. Has anyone seen either Dominic or Griffin?"

Jackson straightened. "I've been shadowing Aaron. I hadn't spent much time outside the house."

All the rest shook their heads.

"How about anyone listening by the door?"

There was a couple seconds of quiet, then a few hushed whispers. "We haven't seen them either."

"Something's wrong." She pushed away from the map. "We need you in here, Jase."

The young wolf wore a pinched expression, but she knew he had nothing to do their disappearances. She gave him a nod when he stood next to London.

"Where have the rogues been camping?"

He pointed down at the map. "The rogues move their base every few days, but they've been avoiding this area here. The alpha said it's off limits."

Everyone studied the twenty-mile area on the map. The location was within five miles of the clearing Neil had pointed out.

"I'm going to call in the paranormal SWAT. They can be here before morning."

Raven shook her head. "We don't have a few hours to wait. They probably already know we're coming. Their operation will be gone before your team will arrive."

Because she knew it would needle him, Raven continued. "Every shifter on the street could be a ticking time bomb. You might not be concerned about the shifter casualties, but think of all the humans that could be hurt. One shifter in a crowd could take out dozens of humans."

Scotts scowled at her. "Don't think I don't know what you're doing."

Maybe it was unfair of her, but he pandered to human bosses whose first concern was human reactions. "We're all you got."

"Fine." He gulped the last of the coffee as if everything was decided. "We'll take Neil and head out."

Taggert walked to her side, leaned his hip against the counter, not pulling off casual in any way. "You will need me as well."

Scotts' scowled deepened. "We don't need two shifters."

"There are hundreds of trails out there. The rogues have been here for weeks. Neil might get you to the meeting place, but I'm the only one who's able to sort the older trails from the more recent."

"I go as well." Jackson didn't glance up from his study of the map. "If you run across trouble, you're weapons will do nothing but enrage a shifter hyped up on drugs."

That left six of them including Randolph.

"I called a few men in for backup." Scotts squinted at the clock. "They should be here shortly."

"If the humans are going, I am as well." The door thudded open at those words, and Jamie hobbled into the room. His battered face was a pasty shade of cottage cheese, and he practically swayed on his feet.

"You're awake." Her relief to see him alive was short lived at his declaration. "You can barely stand, you need to rest."

He shook his head and tottered into the room. "There are too many rogues out there. I will not have them be mistaken for the threat and killed."

The words stung. She didn't care to be lumped as a killer. "I wouldn't—"

"There is also the fact that they trust me. My presence will give us free passage through the forest."

That wasn't something she could argue with.

"That leaves London and Jase to protect the house in case anyone thinks to double back."

A knock sounded on the door, and Scotts straightened. "That would be my men. Suit up. We leave in ten."

\* \* \*

Raven headed toward her office, conscious of Jackson a few steps behind her. She stopped by her desk. Her hand hesitated over the gun and Taser, but she knew that neither were going to be of much help.

She stared at her hands, or more precisely, the gloves she wore, then pulled them off and laid them next to the gun. She flexed her fingers, shocked by how vulnerable they looked without current.

"Claim me before we leave."

She turned and held up a hand to ward off his demand then slowly let it drop. The last time she had a chance to claim him and hadn't, she'd nearly lost him. A frisson of nerves danced along her spine at the thought of her mouth on him, tasting him so intimately.

She licked her dry lips. "Are you sure this is what you want?"

In answer, he pulled off his shirt and strode toward her. Breathing stopped being important when his naked chest halted inches from her face. She expected the moon's heat.

This was something more.

This was attraction on a personal level.

He reached past, never taking his gaze from hers. When he straightened, he held her letter opener in his hand. He laid the edge right below his collarbone. The gold shimmering against his skin startled her out of her daze. "What are you doing?"

"Making the bite easier on you." Without giving her a change to protest, he sliced the metal across his upper chest. The edge wasn't sharp, and he had to force it to pierce his skin.

She sucked in a harsh breath, watching a trickle of blood lazily trail down his torso. He didn't so much as flinch. When she made no move toward him, he cupped the back of her head and pulled her closer.

He bent his knees until they were on eye-level. "You are what I want."

The seductiveness of his voice and body lured her closer. She shivered at the heat of him, her skin stinging as his warmth soaked into the coldness that seemed to be so much a part of her now. She placed her hands on his chest, marveling at the texture of man. Her fingers brushed across the line of chest hair, allowing herself to be drawn forward of her own accord.

The first taste of him exploded through her. Jackson sucked in a breath, his body trembled, his arms banding around her, inviting her to take more. Instead of being repulsed, his blood tasted of power.

Like she'd gulped vodka straight from the bottle, heat burned along her cold body. A brush of fur rubbed against her mind, and she saw the stunning yellow eyes of his wolf peer back at her. When the heat hit her center, the darkness there unfurled, and the creature all but licked her lips.

Her nails dug into Jackson's shoulders to prevent her prey from escaping. Raven tried to shake the creature's grip on her mind, but she wouldn't be dismissed Talons sank into her chest in retaliation for fighting back. After what felt like eons, the creature released its hold.

Raven jerked back, horrified to find herself cradled on Jackson's lap, her knees pressed on either side of his hips like some lover's embrace. Like she hadn't just tried to kill him. He sat with his head tipped back, the long column of his throat exposed in surrender.

That was until she got a look at his face and the very pleased with himself smile. His obvious pleasure eased some of her terror, allowed her mind to settle enough to organize her chaotic thoughts. Raven trembled, hating that her legs wouldn't hold her. Hated the way she couldn't run away from what happened. "Is it always like that?"

Jackson ran a hand down her arm, tangling his fingers with hers. "Not like that. Never like that."

He made it sound like a good thing. The fool. "I could've killed you."

Jackson only shook his head. "Your beasts knew me. They've accepted me before. You wouldn't have hurt me."

Raven didn't hold back this time and smacked him. "I can't feel my beasts anymore. All there is left is that thing. I felt its hunger. It could've killed you before I would've been able to stop it."

When she scrambled away from him, Jackson straightened and sighed as if she ruined the special moment for him. "It's the way of being an alpha. To be claimed, we lay ourselves bare and wait judgment. A few cases of death occur each year. We know the risks going into it."

Raven backed away. "I didn't."

He stood, his jeans riding low on his hips. Dried blood was still smeared on his chest. Her teeth marks on his skin mocked her. She curled her fingers into fists to resist reaching for him and confirm for herself that he was all right. As if he craved her contact, too, he grabbed her wrist and flattened her palm over the recent wound. He shuddered as if her touch, alone, stole his breathe.

"Usually the exchange is made by the alpha male. He holds the pack. The bite heals in a few days as the bonds form."

"But not mine. You will always bear my mark." She hated the pleasure that spun through her at the announcement.

He brushed the back of her hand with his fingers when she would've spoken.

"This mark claims my status as your mate. It gives me equal status as Taggert and Durant." He took a fortifying breath as if preparing himself for a difficult conversation. "There are things you need to know about female alphas. There are less than a handful of females in the world strong enough to hold their own pack. The bonds between them and their pack are different. There is no way for a female to take blood without her enzymes binding them together. Their bite is a sign of possession deeper than any claiming."

"You're talking about mating." This conversation made her nervous. Raven didn't want to hear more, but her feet refused to budge.

"It's considered a great honor to be chosen. Most display their scars with pride. But you need to know that there are other ways for an alpha female to claim a male into her pack without the mating bonds.

"You can select one or two mated male to hold the bonds of the pack for you. It's dangerous. The bonds aren't nearly as strong as in other packs. You'll periodically have to take blood from them to keep the connections stable. If anything happens to these males, you would lose your pack."

"Why the hell did no one tell me sooner?" Betrayal frosted along her skin, the cold burrowing into her soul. She stared at the fresh wound on his chest, horrified what she'd done. And no matter how hard she battled herself, the creature was pleased at the turn of events.

Jackson would be forever hers.

He ran a hand through his hair, never once taking his eyes from hers. "Because I'm a selfish bastard. Also, because the pack will be stronger if you claim the best of us directly."

"Then why tell me now?"

"So no one can take advantage of you."

Another horrible thought crossed her mind. "Do the others know?"

"Doubtful. Female alphas aren't known for sharing their secrets. Vivian did extensive research, but she never developed enough ability to hold a pack. Once she realized that, she settled on Kevin as second best. I was able to access her research."

"Why would you take this choice away from me?" She couldn't remain in the same room with her hurt so close to bubbling over.

"I did what I had to do."

"Did you?" Raven stopped with her hand on the knob, her shoulders straight and brittle. One more betrayal and she would crack.

"The mating bond was the only thing that would tie us together permanently. I wouldn't survive another separation from you."

Raven shook her head, surprised that she could sense the truth to his words. Another reminder that the benefits of the mating bond went both ways. He honestly believed what he said. She glanced at him over her shoulder. "You could have tried asking."

With that, she escaped outside. Jamie, Randolph, Taggert and Neil stood off to the side. Scotts and his two members were waiting ten feet away. She didn't say a word to Scotts on his choice of men, not when she had her own army.

All three men appeared older, dressed in plain clothes. From the way they held themselves, experienced in combat and knew how to protect themselves. They were also armed to the gills. She could see no less than five weapons on them, so she would guess there were at least that amount still hidden.

The shifters were a stark contrast. No one was armed.

They *were* the weapons.

And better equipped than the humans could ever be.

No one spoke, the tension enough to drown a person. Too much time has been wasted already. "Let's head out."

Taggert and Neil took the lead. As they neared the forest, a roar reverberated in the air. One of the cops whirled, pulling his gun, staring at the darkness around the house. "What the hell was that?"

Raven gave a little smile. "That would be our send off."

She could tell the instant the soldier spotted London in his animal form. The man stared blankly down at his gun then holstered it when he realized a bullet would only piss the animal off. "A fucking bear."

## Chapter Thirty-two

Once Neil led them to the small clearing, everyone milled about waiting for Taggert to pick up the scent. He stood next to a tree, his body perfectly still as only a shifter could. He closed his eyes, sorting through the many trails. Shadows danced across the forest floor in the moonlight. If it wasn't for the absolute silence around them, the area would be almost peaceful.

One of the officers spoke, mirroring her thoughts. "Why isn't there any sound?"

Jackson answered, not looking at the officer as he searched the area for any hint of trouble. "You're in an area where large predators hunt. Everything has either been killed or moved to safer territory."

"You're just lucky we haven't decided to run as a pack and hunt more challenging game." Jamie smiled, his teeth gleaming in the pale light, making his meaning clear.

The officer swallowed, but Raven would give him credit for not flinching. Scotts picked his men well, one's who wouldn't be spooked into reacting first. She just hoped it didn't get them killed.

When she turned, it was to find Randolph studying her. He was too quiet, his silent presence freaking her out. The only good thing about the situation was if he decided to take her down, he would take a direct approach.

He'd want the challenge of a fair fight.

"Do you ever wonder why the rogues chose this area?"

"What do you mean?"

Randolph tsked and gave her a pitying look. "Haven't you even suspected that they were drawn here because of you? Your gift is a magnet for paranormals."

Raven clamped her jaw tight until her muscles ached. She would not let him goad her into giving away any information.

"I mean no harm." Randolph immediately backed down and lifted his hands to show he was harmless.

Her lack of response seemed to disappoint him, and she realized that he was trying to engage her in conversation.

Trying to befriend her.

The thought frightened the crap out of her.

"Why did you really come tonight?"

Randolph appeared surprised by the question, like the answer was obvious. "You intrigue me."

His curiosity was so not a good thing.

"Your gift is almost the opposite of mine. You can give all that wonderful energy you absorb to help others survive, while I must take. I wonder what would happen if we joined our energy. What more we could become."

Raven knew and the results had nearly killed her. He could never find out that their combined power could bring the dead back to life. Even if she somehow survived the procedure, which was doubtful, the damage would be extensive and irreversible.

"I don't know about you, but I'm not willing to test that theory. I doubt that either one of us would fare well if our gifts were destroyed."

"I found something."

Raven nearly sagged in relief at Taggert's words. Although Randolph accepted her summation at face value, she didn't make the mistake to think the subject had been dropped.

"They went this way."

"They?"

"You're sure?"

Scotts and Raven spoke together.

"There is a main path where more than one scent leads off in the same direction."

They took off, Taggert leading a leisurely pace. Well, for a shifter anyway. She wasn't in too bad of shape, clumsy in comparison to the shifters...nearly human. Until you saw how far the police force lagged behind.

A vicious snarl echoed in the trees. A slither of fear snaked down her spine, sending icy chills through her body. The enraged sound did not come from any animal remotely sane.

The shifters halted instantly, crouched and ready to spring into action, while the cops pulled their guns.

Then she heard links of chain, metal clanging against metal.

"There." She smelled the blood first, sensed him more than saw him.

Jackson grabbed her arm. "That's close enough. An injured animal can inflict a lot of harm without being aware of what they're doing."

But she stopped hearing him when she got a look at the big black wolf that barreled toward her. She straightened abruptly, something about his shape so familiar that her breath caught.

The wolf didn't slow his charge. If anything, he picked up speed. The thick chain clamped around his neck pulled his feet right out from under him. He slammed into the ground with a thud that reverberated under her feet. He laid stunned, his chest bellowed for air of one completely exhausted. "Dominic?"

The world dropped out from around her to see her friend so cruelly captured and left tied to a tree to die. She had no doubt that he wasn't meant to survive, three partial bodies that weren't quite hidden in the foliage around the base of the tree were proof.

A rustling came from one of the still forms. She stared, her mouth agape, as a naked form pushed up from the ground. Muscles rippled across the lean male back. Dirt and leaves rolled off his body to reveal deeply etched wounds scored down his spine.

Chains, clamped around his throat, clanked as the man moved.

Horror darkened her mind when Raven realized the two chains could overlap just enough that they could tear into each other if they worked at it.

When the man turned, the wolf lunged. Even though he was out of reach, the man flinched and fell on his ass.

That's when she got a good look at his face. "Griffin?"

Bloodshot eyes met hers as he lifted his head. He slowly wrapped the chain around his fists, preparing to defend himself.

In the trees above their heads were two bright red bows. The bastard had left Dominic and Griffin like presents for her to find.

"Raven, don't. They're drugged."

Raven rounded on Jackson and shoved at his chest, nearly sending him sprawling. "I can't just leave them here. Damn it to hell, anyway. I ordered them out here."

Jackson wrapped her in his grip, and she hit him again. It did nothing to alleviate the guilt. "They've been here the whole of last night, killing to survive, and I didn't even know it."

"You have to focus on what's important." Jackson bent until they were eye-level. "They're still alive."

The words were a balm to the nerves simmering so close to the surface that her skin felt ready to crack.

"Get me out of these fucking chains."

Raven whirled at the raspy voice to see Griffin leaned heavily against a tree as he fought the effects of the drugs.

"No way in hell." Scotts strode forward as if to put a stop to her thoughts. "Look at those bodies. We can't just let them free to come after us or someone else."

"The drugs are wearing off." Then Griffin stared down Scotts. "And human, you have much more to worry about than just us."

He stopped any further conversation by turning toward her, sensing she had the command to do what he wanted. "I'll be a liability to you right now, but I can take Dominic and Jamie with me to prevent more of the weaker rogues from getting slaughtered. We can cover your back."

"Release him." Randolph spoke, his voice bored. "We need to keep moving."

Raven didn't believe Randolph's indifference for a second. A fire heated his cold green eyes as he recognized Griffin. Randolph saw him as a challenge, a branded rogue strong enough to escape death for years. Griffin was the closest thing to a prince that the shifter kingdom could boast.

A prize to be hunt.

"Head toward the ranger station. Five miles northwest." He lifted a hand to touch the collar, frowned and dropped his arm. "Circle the ridge. If you head too far north, you will run across his little playground.

"He's managed to put the drug in dart form. If you're tagged, it will drop you on the spot. Most don't survive the increased dosage." He curled his hand into the chain that dangled from his neck. "Be careful. This man honestly believes that all shifters should be freed from the oppression of the pack. Nothing will change his mind. If you get in his way, he will have you eliminated and completely believe it was the best decision."

## ɞ Chapter Thirty-three ʚ

The moon had crested in the sky, the pale rays making those around her glow. If it was silent before, it was more so now. From one step to the next, the sound just shut off.

With each tree she passed, she expected to see the station house take shape out of the darkness. Taggert stopped as if he slammed into a wall.

"I lost the scent."

"What do you mean? How can you just lose the scent?" Scotts marched ahead, slightly out of breath at the pace they'd maintained.

"I can't smell anything over the dead bodies."

That shut down Scott's outrage. "Where?"

Taggert pointed north. "From the stench, I would guess more than one, and they've been there for a while."

They climbed the ridge single file. When they reached the summit, a gaping hole revealed a mass grave spread out below them, like the earth couldn't contain the horror and spit out the bodies. Raven peeked over the edge and a gust of air slammed the perfume of death right in her face. Her stomach lurched.

There were at least thirty bodies in various stages of decay, tossed over the ledge and left to tumble the twenty feet into the pit below.

"God help us all." A slight tremor shook Scotts' voice. One of the cops backed away without looking, and she couldn't blame him.

A sound came from behind.

Raven whirled, but too late. She took the hit low to her hip that launched her and her attacker into the air over the chasm.

Gravity took hold.

She twisted to land on top, but the grip on her was too strong to escape. She plowed into the pile of decomposed corpses. The bodies shifted beneath her weight. Bone snapped, the shards scraping her body. With each move, splinters pierced her skin like a swarm of bees. For a panicked moment, she feared she'd brought the corpses back to life. Cold flesh clawed at her like the dead were trying to pull her in the grave.

Raven stumbled to her feet to escape the grasping hands. And found a large bone had pierced her thigh, sticking out at an odd angle. It wasn't her own. She carefully pulled on it, gritting her teeth to keep from screaming. The large bone slurped from the wound as it finally slid free.

A slim man stood in the more dominant position on top the pile of bodies watching her. There was an ungroomed quality to him. A rogue, the missing alpha, if the power he threw off was any indication.

Wild shots rained down on them.

The rogue didn't even flinch.

"Stop or you'll hit her. It's too dark to get an adequate shot." A small scuffle from above ensured, but she trusted Jackson to keep her safe.

Training took over.

Raven shifted to take a defensive position. The rogue bared his teeth in a maniacal smile, reveling in the thrill of the battle to come, and charged.

His movements were much faster than she'd expected.

Seconds before he slammed into her, she smelled what was becoming a familiar odor.

Overdose.

The man was hyped on the drug.

Then he was on her.

Her mind shut off as he launched her into the air. She slammed into the side of the pit. The black dirt softened the impact. Musty earth spilled over her head, invading her eyes and mouth.

A bright burst of pain slashed her side, and she glanced down to see a large femur had torn the flesh along her ribs.

"Raven, hold on. We'll be right down." Jackson's reassuring voice called down to her.

Raven struggled to keep her feet under her as bones crunched and bodies collapsed. She spit the dirt out of her mouth. "No. You'll only get in the way. He'll use us against each other."

She pulled herself free of the bone pinning her to the wall like some insect on a board, and clutched the bloodied spear in her fist.

"If you don't join us, you'll enjoy the special show of me ripping your girlfriend apart, piece by lovely piece." The rogue didn't twitch, didn't move, salivating as he stared at her.

But she didn't need help. The last blow might have knocked the stuffing out of her, but it also gave a jolt to her creature. It slowly uncoiled and calmly observed the rogue through her eyes.

The cold encasing vanished.

When he moved, she countered and the grace and speed of her creature took over. She was almost clumsy, not used to having her body respond so swiftly.

"You should have minded your own business." The rogue hunched over, arms dangling loosely at his side. His fingers twitched, those sharp nails of his clicking in excitement.

Half insane by the drug, there was no reasoning with him. But maybe she could use that to her advantage. "What did you expect would happen when you started killing people for money?"

"We're saving lives."

She noted his word choice and instantly knew he wasn't the one behind the whole scheme. He said the words, but he wasn't a true believer. He might like the money, but revenge motivated him more.

Revenge on the pack that had rejected him and forced him rogue.

"What? Weren't you good enough? Do you think this drug will really change anything?" The taunt had the desired effect.

He charged.

He moved so incredibly fast she had no way to evade him. Raven threw herself to the left, protecting her injured side. She took a hit to her hip that sent her crashing to her knees. A half decomposed face of a kid no more than fifteen peered up at her.

Something was off about the boy, but she couldn't place what bothered her. She rose to her feet, careful to keep her grip on her only weapon.

The rogue watched her, showing no rush in finishing her off.

He'd been sent to delay them.

"I'm going to enjoy killing you slowly."

Raven snorted. "Yeah. Good luck with that."

Raven had a habit of not staying dead. There was only a small problem with that. With her power currently on the fritz, she wasn't sure there was enough juice left to bring her back if she lost this fight.

She nodded to the bodies. "He's using you as a cleanup crew."

"Don't think I don't know what you're doing." A sly smile curled his lips. He circled her, having no trouble traversing the field of corpses. "Nothing you can do will push me over the edge like these fools."

That's when she realized what was wrong with the bodies.

More than half of them were whole.

"These people didn't die from overdosing, did they? Too many bodies remained whole. They didn't disintegrate like those under the influence. They died fighting for their lives."

The man shrugged. "Dominance is the way of pack life."

"And you're still weak, still taking orders, pretending that you're important. We both know that's a lie. You're just like them."

The cheerfulness drained from his expression. "My pack—"

Raven laughed. "Do you mean the rogues? Where are your people now? They're supposed to be here, aren't they?"

"You don't know what you're talking about." He glared at her, pacing in agitation.

Raven tightened her grip on the bone, slowly lowering it at her side. "Did you know that Griffin didn't die? That Jamie didn't die? You wanted them both removed, didn't you? They were challenging you and you knew you wouldn't be able to fight either of them and win."

"Shut up." His pacing increased.

Raven shifted over to stand in a two-foot section of earth and firmly planted her feet. Blood trickled down her ribs. Her shirt stuck to her torso. The wound in her leg wasn't in much better condition, her thigh having long since gone numb.

What the hell happened to her creature? The damned thing wasn't content to steal her animals and power. No, it wanted everything, sitting back on its haunches and observed while her life hung in the balance.

Looked like she was on her own on this one.

"You know where they are now, don't you?"

"No." The man repeatedly scratched the back of his head as if bugs were crawling inside of his skull.

"Why your pack isn't here? Because they found someone else to follow. Someone stronger."

"No." The man roared and launched himself at her.

Raven dropped to her knees, and brought up the bone shard.

The rogue looked startled and began to flail. There was nothing to grab but air as momentum propelled him forward.

Directly onto the bone of one of his victims.

He gaped at her, shock written all over his face.

Warm blood poured down over her hands as his own weight was used to slowly impale himself.

He grabbed for her, his nails digging grooves along her forearm. "Bitch."

Blood bubbled out of his mouth as air rattled in his chest.

Hatred darkened his face as the last of the life drained from him.

"Raven?" Jackson's voice came out as a frustrated shout.

"Get me the hell out of here."

\* \* \*

The soft sides of the pit made extraction difficult. Jackson had eventually dropped down into the pit. She took a running start, stepped on Jackson's waiting hand, using him as a springboard to launch her up into the air.

Taggert easily caught her wrist and hauled her up.

The injuries on her side screamed in agony, but she refused to let out a sound. She needed to find the real killer, and that wouldn't happen if they found out the severity of her injuries.

"I'll get a crew out here—"

Raven shook her head. "This was too easy. He was a decoy. The person who created the drug wouldn't risk his life by taking it until he had a chance to perfect it. That man doesn't have the brains to organize this operation."

Scott's ran a shaky hand over his face, taking in her bloodied clothes. "That was easy?"

"We need to keep searching."

"If that was the damage one shifter could do, we'll need the SWAT. We are too unmanned to continue further."

"No." Raven whirled on Scotts, ignoring the pale hue to his normal cocoa complexion. "The noise alone probably alerted the real killer. We need to push toward the cabin now if it's not too late already."

Scotts stormed toward her, standing toe-to-toe. She waved away Jackson when he would've intervened. "I will not risk my men. Some of those people in that pit were in pieces. We don't stand a chance against that."

"That's what I was trying to tell you, but you wouldn't listen. You're treating them as human, applying human laws to them. If we wait, more lives will be lost. This is our only lead. Even now, they could be eradicating every trace."

"What you say may be true, but we need to apprehend them using the right tools. We just don't have the manpower."

Raven reached into her pocket and pulled out the badge she'd only just received. It seemed like such a long time ago.

She fingered the cold metal, the symbol of all the hope and promise between two races, and held out her arm. It felt like she was choosing sides and handing over her humanity. She just hoped she made the right decision, one that would keep her pack safe. "I can't accept that."

Scotts made no move to accept the badge. "You said the laws need to be changed. We need people like you to do that."

"Not at the cost of lives." She nodded toward the graveyard a few yards away. "When you saw the bodies, you saw tortured people first, not shifters. For the first time, you saw them as people, not monsters."

Scotts glanced away. "We're too vulnerable."

"Not all of us."

A fierce frown marred his face. "We need you here."

Raven reached out, turned over his hand and placed the badge in his palm. "I can't be your Region, your symbol of justice, and be restricted by the laws. I can be of more help on the inside." She held up her hand when he would've spoken. "You even said it yourself. I was more valuable to you as a consultant.

"But we both know someone who would make the perfect candidate. He has no allegiances. You've worked with him before. He's devoted to saving shifters. The job will keep him safe. He's handsome enough for the humans to forget about his background and has enough control that he would never slip. He'll have my nomination and yours. Push Griffin through the system."

Then she very firmly stepped back from him. She knew she made the right decision when he didn't protest. She turned and entered the woods with her men, doing her best not to limp. She'd swear she heard the moans of the dead urging her to take vengeance.

## ❧ Chapter Thirty-four ✥

They followed Griffin's directions this time and circled the ravine. When the few remaining insects in the woods fell silent, Raven knew they were nearing the location of the cabin.

Death clung to the air almost like a presence pressing against her, warning them away. She slowed her step and everyone instantly followed her lead. After two more yards, a building took shape in the trees, the shadows clinging to it like a shroud.

The station wasn't any larger than a one-room cabin. The emptiness of the place echoed around her even across the distance and frustration struck.

They were too late.

Boards echoed hollowly as they crossed the porch. Rays from the full moon filtered into the one window, illuminating a lab of some sort. And from the equipment, they had interrupted them before they could box up everything and vanish.

A sheet of plastic lay on the far counter, the thin film of liquid pooled on top, set out to dry.

Randolph and Jackson entered behind her. They ate up the oxygen in the room, turning the one small room into the size of a glorified outhouse.

"He's near."

Randolph nodded, but it was Jackson who spoke. "Are you able to sense him?"

Ever since her creature had wakened, Raven had been reluctant to call her power for fear of discovering she had nothing left. "I'll give it a try."

She sank her fingers into the electricity hovering under her skin.

The creature clenched her talons, resisting the pull. Raven pushed harder until her stomach rebelled under the strain. The air became thick in the cabin, movements slowed as if through molasses, the creature fighting her every step of the way.

It was hording the power for itself.

That was unacceptable, not when the life of her pack was at stake. Raven took every pathetic bit of power she could gather and threw it all at the creature.

Demanded a response.

With a huff, the creature finally relented, and the power broke free.

Current built under her skin, gaining momentum like a wave about to crest and drown her. Unable to hold it back, the energy broke free and shot out across the forest floor like a shockwave from a blast. The weak plywood floor of the cabin bucked under their feet. The strength of her power nearly knocked everyone in the cabin to their knees.

Raven ignored their stares, ignored the slight bitter taste of fear and awe, concentrating on the information feeding to her. She dismissed the hits she'd received from the group, followed the curl of energy, but something niggled at the back of her mind.

Then she knew.

There was one too many people.

"He's outside."

And coming up right behind Taggert.

Raven's eyes widened in alarm, and she shot out of the doorway, her fear allowing her to move faster.

"Taggert!"

She ran and leapt off the porch, her injury throbbing in protest. Slowing her down. Taggert's form was silhouetted against the stillness of the trees.

Safe.

But the tension riding her didn't abate.

"Taggert—"

He straightened but too late. A man looped his arm around Taggert's neck, shoving something that looked like a gun at his carotid.

No, not a pistol, a dart gun.

"Come any closer and I will inject your friend with the latest version of my serum."

Raven skidded to a stop with less than ten feet separating them. "Professor."

How could she not have made the connection sooner?

She only had her own stupidity to blame. She'd been so focused on her dislike of Vivian and fighting with the rogues, she was blinded to the true killer.

Though he issued the threat to everyone, he hadn't removed his gaze from her as if she were the biggest threat.

Which made no sense to her at all.

Taggert didn't appear concerned at the turn of events.

That was okay.

She was frightened enough for the both of them.

On edge, waiting for the slightest opening, she watched Professor's thumb on the trigger. If he moved, she would fry him. Professor knew it, too.

"It seems we're at a stand-off." She circled to get a better angle.

His grip tightened, his finger tensing on the trigger. "Ah-ah. I wouldn't do that. I would hate to have an accident."

Going against instinct, Raven stilled. She kept her body lose and ready to react the instant he let down his guard. "You don't seem too shocked to see me."

Professor shook his head. "The rogues' alpha hadn't the skill to kill you. You've defied all his attempts. He was a fool and underestimated you."

Implying that Professor wouldn't.

"You used him to do your dirty work, turned him against his own kind."

"No, I just gave him the opportunity. He did all the rest on his own." He twisted, using his shoulder to push up the corner of his glasses. "I have the brains. Sadly, I lack the brawn to make people listen and obey."

"So you promised him power and money in return for his cooperation." Raven shuffled closer. "Did he decide that I must die on his own or did you give him a little help?"

The slight man shook his head. "That was him. All he cared about was not allowing anyone to stop his petty pursuit of revenge. He couldn't see the bigger picture."

Raven raised a brow, not believing him completely. "And it didn't matter all the people you had to kill to perfect your drug. But it isn't perfect, is it?"

"You sound like that fool at Pak Pharmaceuticals."

Kevin.

Somehow, she wasn't surprised.

"We were at the testing stage. A few people died, so he shut us down despite all that we could've gained. He thought he'd destroyed my research, but I had backups."

Raven gritted her teeth knowing that all of this could've been avoided if protocols had been followed. "How do you think this will end after all the people you've murdered with your experiments?"

The bespectacled man smiled. "I'll be a hero. And you're going to help me. You burst into the shifter world, disdaining the old ways. You're not like the others. You understand what I'm trying to do."

Raven calculated a dozen ways to free Taggert while Professor babbled and dismissed them all. The percentages were too high.

Professor nodded to his lab, fervor lighting his eyes. "Together, we can create an equal world, no more rogues, no more alphas to rule us."

He didn't seem to realize that most of her actions had been made in ignorance to protect her pack. "There are rules in place for a reason. The way rogues are treated is atrocious, but there is dynamic in the pack beyond just control and power. An alpha keeps the pack in line and prevents them from falling into chaos."

The man's face fell. "They already got to you. Filled your head with their lies."

She tracked Professor's every gesture, shuffling closer. "You think drugging and killing shifters is the answer? You're no better than the humans."

"Only the weak," he shouted, his face turning red from the insult. The barrel of the gun pressed brutally against Taggert's neck until he winced.

Raven tensed at his outburst.

Taggert waited for her signal to run or duck. The complete faith in his eyes sent a sharp thrust of panic to her gut.

She couldn't risk him.

A twist of fear sent her heart rattling against her ribs. Talons flexed in her chest, ripping up her insides in the need to act. She needed to distract Professor from his anger, or she'd loose Taggert. "A pack cannot function with all alphas."

"That's just it. We won't need packs anymore. Each of us would be strong enough to hold our own. No more need to rely on anyone else. No more slaves. No more pack war."

At one time, Raven might have agreed with him. "You talk of peace, but you have no clue what it's like to be an alpha." She swallowed hard. "We saw the bodies. They killed each other as they battled for dominance. If this drug ever got out, no shifter would be able to remain in the same city. We'd hunt each other to extinction."

Professor waved away her words, her stubbornness at not seeing things his way beginning to wear thin. "No, you're purposely looking at it wrong. I just need to adjust the drug to weed out the aggression."

"You want to change us. The humans will view us as monsters again. You'll destroy everything that we've built in the last ten years." With each word, rage swelled in her chest, spreading heat in its wake.

"Don't say that. My work is the next step in evolution."

Raven understood then that no amount of reasoning would change his mind. The only way out was to make him mad enough to shoot her, giving Taggert the chance to run. "When we first revealed ourselves to the human world, they experimented on us. They acted out of fear. You're just a coward desperate to escape your fate as a rogue. You would never amount to anything in the pack."

A deathly pall washed over his face, a calmness to him that sent a shiver up her spine. "You're wrong. I'll show you."

Raven tensed to leap, but realized her mistake too late. She surged forward, only able to watch in horror as Professor's finger flexed on the trigger. Taggert flinched, grabbed at his neck even as he crumbled. She fell to her knees, her injured leg giving way when tried to catch him.

Professor raised the gun. She braced to be shot, but he only held it level at her.

"Stop, not any closer. We can't risk anyone else being infected. You know what happens when two alphas fight."

They would battle to the death.

Raven jerked the dart from of Taggert's neck, heaving it into the woods. She watched Taggert on his hands and knees, chest heaving as the toxins coursed through his body. Blood rushed in her ears as she waited. She half expected to see Taggert shredded before her very eyes.

"You've killed him." Sorrow nearly swallowed her whole. Raven waited for wrath or hatred to overwhelm her apathy and take control but guilt left her incapacitated.

She brought him to this by involving him in her cases.

"On the contrary, I saved him. With this new mix, his body would've reacted by now." Victory reflected off his face. "I granted him a gift. He will know what it feels like to be a true alpha."

She reached out with trembling fingers to reassure them both, only to have him snap his teeth at her.

The rejection stung.

Never in her wildest nightmares had she ever anticipated that reaction.

The truth of his words reflected back in Taggert's yellow eyes. Instead of the need for belonging she normally saw there, possessiveness bordering on cruelty, gazed back at her.

Raven retreated and stood. Taggert growled and mimicked her movements. He inhaled as if he could smell her then licked his lips.

Randolph studied her reactions like a bystander. Her lips tightened, her anger growing at his passiveness while her people suffered. Neil ignored the scene unfolding, his attention unwavering as he stared unblinking at the Professor.

"Tell me doctor, what happens to all the women in your grand new world? They will be fought over, hunted down and slaughtered. No more pure lines. Our race will die out. Do you think the humans will allow us to steal their women when none are left?"

Professor shrugged. "It's no better for them now, bartered like cattle."

"They are protected by the pack. They are our future." Anger heated her chest, her outrage nearly making her step toward him.

Taggert's muscles bunched, and she froze.

One more step and he'd be on her.

Shifters always carried their beasts close to the surface. She had no idea how much control the human side of them exuded to remain in charge. How much more she had yet to learn. The drug had ripped away Taggert's filters, leaving her with a wild animal.

Nothing of him remained.

"You're smart, but you forgot one thing."

A frown creased Professor's brow, and he slowly shook his head. "I can assure you that I have not."

"You've discounted the strength of pack." Raven lifted her chin, staring at Taggert in challenge.

His lips pulled back, revealing sharp, canine teeth. Her pulse fluttered, but not in fear of his threat. The fear came from what she had to do to save them.

She had to show dominance.

Normally, not a problem, but all she had left was the creature.

There was no choice.

She couldn't lose Taggert.

Raven slowly dropped the shields she'd spent a lifetime building. The talons in her chest flexed at the new freedom, and Raven surrendered to the pull. The creature immediately dropped into the pure energy.

Cracks spidered along the edges of her core before it slowly crumbled. Heat sizzled through her, speeding along her veins as if someone injected her with acid. Pressure built until her body felt too small to contain it.

The cold that had followed her dissipated and delicious warmth took over.

Raven lashed out. Her hand gripped Taggert's throat, and she dragged him near. A growl rumbled up her throat, angered that he'd dare test her. She fought against the need to rip into him and teach him a lesson.

Taggert dropped to his knees and offered his throat. The yellow eyes splintered to chocolate brown, an alpha recognizing himself as prey to the creature she harbored.

At his recoil, she managed to pull herself back from the edges of her rage, but her power would not be tucked away.

Never again.

Her hair fell about her, swirling in the current only she could see. The silver tips shimmered in the dimness, the color spreading up the darker strands, slowly consuming her.

Raven didn't look at anyone. Didn't want to see the rejection. The revulsion.

Her secrets were well and truly exposed.

She was a monster even amongst the monsters.

"That's not possible."

Raven raised her head at Professor's voice. Her vision sharpened until she saw each pore on his face, counted each follicle of hair. His scent turned sour, and she watched him stumble away from her, his face ashen.

"What the hell are you?" Horror made his voice hoarse. He lowered the gun, stumbling over his own feet in his haste to get away.

At the opening, Neil leapt, a snarl twisting his lips. Professor lifted the gun, automatically pulling the trigger. Four darts whooshed through the air until all she heard was an ominous click.

Each dart struck dead center of Neil's chest. They kid moved forward uncaring, his focus on bringing down his target.

Chemicals bloomed in the air, clogging her nose.

"What have you done?" Professor's voice squeaked in panic. He scrambled backwards, but Neil would not be denied vengeance. The kid closed the distance between them in a brutal tackle.

Their bodies landed with a heavy thud.

Professor ripped into Neil, a desperate animal trying to escape his own trap. Claws rented through the body like cutting paper, fangs ripped out large chunks of flesh from the kid's shoulders and neck, but Neil refused to relent, not even bothering to defend himself as he held onto his prey.

Then the realities of what he'd done slammed into her.

What the kid sacrificed.

"Everyone down!"

Jackson blanched.

Instead of listening, he ran toward her...directly into the blast zone.

## Chapter Thirty-five

**LAST DAY OF THE CONCLAVE: WANING MOON**

Raven ran toward Jackson, determined to protect him, all the while knowing she would never make it in time. Hands grabbed her from behind. Though she recognized Taggert's hold, she struggled to move forward.

He couldn't die on her, not now.

"Damn it. Get down." Taggert tightened his grip.

Randolph solved the problem for her by tackling Jackson at the knees, and they both went sprawling. The trained assassin stared at her with real fear, as if the pieces had finally settled into place.

He knew her greatest secret, one she'd never spoke out loud and secretly prayed had died in the labs.

That awareness stopped her cold.

There was nowhere left to hide.

Taggert took advantage of the moment. He spun and shoved her down, protecting her body with his own. A gurgled scream rented the air, brutally cut off a second later.

Raven didn't hear the blow. Bits of blood and gore exploded through the air and pelted them.

Her gaze landed on Taggert. He grunted. Color slowly drained from his face. His grip flexed on her hips, but he didn't waiver.

"You're hit." Taggert reached up to her face.

Raven felt nothing. She couldn't say the same for him. She grabbed his wrist to prevent him from moving and sending the shards deeper. Bone splinters stuck out of him like a dartboard, some shallower with the protection of clothing, but there were hundreds of them all along the line of his body.

Tears crowded her eyes as blood began to trail down his skin in rivulets. His pulse stuttered under her hand, and his breathing followed suit.

Raven allowed her mind to sink deeper until she saw the damage to his aura. Each injury was like a pinprick of darkness where his body had been pierced.

So much darkness.

Even as she watched, it spread to consume the rest of him.

His wolf wasn't strong enough to heal the massive injuries.

Death was stealing him from her.

But the fear never came. Raven leaned over until her mouth hovered over Taggert's. "You do not have permission to die on me."

She slammed her lips against his and kissed him. Power pulled up from her bones, passing from her to Taggert. The drugs still lingered in his systems, and she drew upon it, forcing him to become alpha.

Forcing him to heal.

He trembled, his wolf slowly pushing the shards out of his body. When he wasn't healing fast enough, she pushed the animal to his limit by calling him to her.

Even dying, a shifter couldn't refuse the call of their alpha.

His scent wrapped around her.

Her mouth watered in hunger.

She shuffled closer, drawn to his wolf and the ravenous need to taste. Raven flinched, realizing the intense hunger wasn't hers, not completely, and no matter how she tried to curb the craving, it lingered at the back of her tongue.

She dropped her hold on him, terrified of her reaction and what she might do if her control slipped even a little.

Taggert collapsed.

Her mind screamed to help him, but she couldn't risk touching him again. The darkness around him had lessened. He would survive, but she wasn't sure in what condition after the things she'd done to his wolf.

Without his touch, the hunger receded. Blood dripped from her hand, and she couldn't be sure if it was her own or his. She stood, legs trembling, and stepped back, hoping to ease the urge to snatch him back up and take.

She reached for her core to help stave off the hunger.

Only to find nothing.

The power had soaked into her body. There was no turning it off. As if her thoughts triggered it, tingling rippled down the left side. Her flesh knitted together.

All but the void spot.

It burned cold like frostbite under warm water.

She lifted up her shirt. Her pale skin shimmered like silver in the moonlight. The bruised area had grown in size. She probed her side and encountered a hardness that was not her own flesh.

Raven dropped her shirt. Things have progressed too far. Being around her pack put their lives at risk. She couldn't be trusted around them, not until she learned what the hell was happening to her. She refused to believe that she could be cresting.

She had to leave.

The devastation nearly crippled her.

Her gaze landed on what remained of the two bodies, the destruction pushing home the truth. The five-foot radius looked like someone had dropped a can of paint, but the pool of blood and shattered body parts belied the image.

Only pieces remained of the stupidly brave kid who'd saved them all. His body, what was left of it, would barely fill a Ziploc bag.

Professor had died much too quickly for her vengeance to be appeased. Most of him remained intact...if you discounted the holes that made him nothing more than a glorified flyswatter.

A hazy mist lingered over the bodies like steam. When she squinted, she'd swear she recognized Neil's features before the fog dissipated in the darkness.

Her breathe trembled in her chest. Part of her wondered if all the dreams she had of the dead were really dreams or someone reaching for her from beyond the grave.

"You're hurt." Jackson reached to touch the uninjured side of her face, and she flinched away from his probing fingers. He couldn't discover how close she was to snapping. Discovered the horrible truth about the creature that has taken root inside her very soul.

"I'm fine." Her lips were numb as she spoke the lie.

Jackson dropped his arm, muscles flexing to prevent himself from reaching for her. "The police should be here shortly. Are you strong enough to stand their interrogation?"

Raven studied his face, afraid it would be for the last time, her chest too heavy to breathe. "It would be best if I left."

The words sounded flat to her own ears.

Jackson's eyes narrowed. He heard it, too. The finality. "You're not going back to the house."

It wasn't a question, but it demanded an answer all the same. "I have to return to *Talons*. I gave my word to the witches as part of my deal for Taggert. Let me borrow your phone."

"But that's not why you're going." He could stop her. She saw the desire in his eyes. He pulled out his phone, handed it over, but didn't release it. "What about your pack? What about the rogues?"

"Take care of them for me."

When she said nothing more, he finished her sentence. "Until you return. If I didn't know better, I'd swear you were cresting."

Jackson paused, worry written on his face, waiting for her to confirm or deny his charge. They both knew she didn't have the ability to shift. Any attempt to change would kill her outright. "Promise me you'll be safe and come back to us."

"I'll do my best." Raven swallowed hard, carefully grabbed the phone without touching him, and walked away from the only family she'd ever known.

She pressed the buttons by rote, her heart thumping as the phone rang.

"Raven?"

"It woke."

There was a heartbeat of silence then he inhaled sharply. Since vampires didn't need to breathe, it spoke to how much her revelation had disturbed Rylan.

"You gave your promise that if anything happened—"

"Not until we know."

She feared it was already much too late. There was no going back, no more sleep, not when it had tasted freedom.

"One week." She had to keep herself together for seven days. "I must fulfill my promise to the witches first."

"I'll meet you at the club." Then there was only dial tone. It took her a few seconds to lower the phone, and another few to press the button to disconnect them.

She had one week to learn control or force Rylan to fulfill his vow to eliminate her before she became a risk to others. They both knew the dangers of this creature. It was what allowed them to escape the labs, but not before destroying everyone and everything in its path.

It couldn't be allowed free.

As Raven walked away from the scene, she caught Jackson rapidly speaking on the phone, never once removing his grim gaze from her, no doubt scheming and plotting, not even bothering with the courtesy to wait for her back to be turned.

She knew he'd given up too easily.

He'd be trouble.

He'd throw up roadblocks. Try to prevent her from doing the right thing.

She couldn't allow that.

Raven ran. The ghosts of her past chased hot on her heels. She'd never escape, but maybe if she pushed hard enough, those around her could. As the crime scene faded behind her, she wondered if it wasn't already much too late to save any of them.

## THE END

## ❧ Sneak Peek ❦

### *Electric Storm*

### *Book 1 : A Raven Investigations Novel*

**A** commotion at the other end of the room erupted. The boy. She knew it even before she saw his face. Five women surrounded him, heckling and caressing him. He stood there, a frozen smile plastered in place, tolerating the touch. Tolerating but not enjoying.

Then he flinched. His smile became strained, the women's laughter more wild. The boy's eyes hardened but he kept still, enduring the obscene fondling and cruel taunts.

She scanned the crowd. A few people snickered at his discomfort, a few looked away, pity leaching the life from their eyes. But no one protested.

Then the man who had accompanied the boy stood to his full height. The muscles of her back loosened, and she eased back into her seat, unaware she'd half risen to her feet. The big man would keep him safe. But instead of rescuing the boy, the Ogre turned his back and pushed his way to the bar.

A lump grew in her throat at the unwanted attention the boy endured. Memories of similar situations from her past cut into her mind, blurring reason until fury burned along her face.

Stillness settled inside her, burying everything but the need to do something, the need to prevent the past from repeating itself. Before she knew what she was doing, she moved.

The closer she came, the more she sensed his unwillingness and his resignation. She stopped outside the circle of women. Their gazes collided. Recognition sparked, and his gaze latched on to hers.

Pleaded.

It was a mistake coming here tonight, but she couldn't leave without knowing he'd be safe. Couldn't stop herself from rescuing him.

"He's mine." She reached through the circle of women, clamped down on his wrist and pulled him to her side. He came without a word of complaint, his head lowered, a small smile on his lips that barely lasted a second. His body trembled slightly before he controlled himself.

"What do you think you're doing?" A blonde in strappy, three-inch heels stepped forward, drink in hand and a determined expression on her face. A woman who always got what she wanted.

Raven wasn't impressed. "We're leaving."

As she turned, herding the boy in front of her, the woman's talons dug into her arm.

Reacting on instinct, Raven spun and thrust out her palm, slamming her hand into the blonde's chest, releasing some of the pent-up power that swirled inside in response to her anger.

The impact lifted the woman off her feet. She sailed over the table, one heel flying. Her mouth dropped open in moue of surprise, while her drink spun and sprayed her friends.

Conversation slowed, people turned. No one touched the woman as she staggered to her feet. Raven braced herself and scanned the crowd.

No one stepped forward to detain her or the boy.

"Is there a problem?"

Tiger.

He broke through the wall of people who circled the small group. Broad shouldered, lean but roped with muscles, he easily drew attention to him and it had nothing to do with the elegant clothes or wildly untamed mane of hair. The combination should've looked ridiculous but only succeeded in making him appear all the more dominant.

It gave him a dangerous air. An aura of bored arrogance seeped from him, but Raven knew differently. Power thrummed beneath his skin at his annoyance for being disturbed. The beast roamed close to the surface even in his human form.

"No, sir. The lady here claimed me, and Miss Jackie objected."

"A challenge?" The tiger's eyes sharpened in the muted light, his attention never leaving her face. He brushed against her shields, then shoved against them as if surprised to find resistance. The intensity increased, seeking a weakness. Her eyes narrowed. Usually only vampires or very powerful alphas had such strong mental ability.

Protocol dictated certain rules, and he broke them by probing her without permission. They both knew it if his sudden, impudent smile was anything to go by. If he pushed harder, she'd retaliate. She refused to let him enter her mind, refused to let him harvest all her secrets. It was too dangerous for either of them.

When he persisted, she twisted a strand of energy around his shields, using tremendous control to surround him instead of breaking through. Then she slowly tightened her hold. She let it rest there, let him feel her perusal, the threat. Her fingers trembled. Her stomach flopped like a fish out of water. It took everything she had to hold back more power and ignore the dangerous lure to crush the threat.

Then his aura fluctuated, rubbed against her own shield in a way that sent a shiver down her spine in a very pleasant way. Her blood heated, and she could almost swear she felt a purr from her core. From the startled look and the aroused flush to his face, the reaction wasn't something he'd anticipated either.

Then he relented and retreated, bowing slightly in deference. "Please forgive my rudeness. I'm Jeffrey Durant, manager of Talon's."

She reeled in the string of energy, suppressing the unholy need to curse. A formal greeting. Rules of the pack dictated she reply in kind, supply her name at the very least, and the bastard knew it. She had to work with shifters. She couldn't piss in the pond just because she didn't want to do something. "Raven–"

"Do you know who I am?" Like a yippy little dog, the blonde charged forward, red blotches of anger coloring her face. Her eyes shimmered a yellowish-green with her emotions, but quickly reverted back to mud brown.

Part shifter.

A weak one.

Most males could shift no matter what percentage of animal DNA they possessed, but the women had to be at least half shifter for their animal to take form. That meant Raven could take this little dog.

Raven adjusted her stance, keeping the kid at her back and met the threat, damning herself for being a sucker. "I don't give a shit. I know all I need."

"Oh, do tell." The rumpled blonde crossed her arms and smirked. "This should be good."

"You're too weak to be a pure blood. Not even quarter, if I had to guess. You surround yourself with people who are weaker so you have someone who looks up to you. You enjoy abusing the very people you're supposed to be protecting."

A fist flew at her face, and Raven caught it mid-air. Anger allowed her to easily lower the blonde's arm. She lifted her chin, relieved to know she'd guessed right. If the woman had been a true shifter, her jaw would've been crushed. "Are you issuing a challenge?"

A slight murmur went through the crowd. It was the only thing she could think of to get them out of there fast. A challenge meant more than possession of the boy, it meant pack position and a fight to the death. Jackie would die. Raven would see to it. Although she relished a certain poetic justice if she let the little wolf live. It would force the bimbo to the bottom of the pack, where she'd have to earn her place in the hierarchy. And something told Raven it wouldn't be so easy to step over the very people she'd been treating like servants.

Fury darkened the woman's eyes, the brown splintered and specks of yellow appeared, then vanished as fast as they came.

"No." She spit out the one word, a promise of retribution for this humiliation dancing in her eyes.

Giddiness trickled through Raven. Her unique gift remained secret. She'd been foolish to risk it over a boy. The need for fresh air pressed heavily against her, effectively caging her without the use of bars. She faced the tiger and raised a brow, doing her damndest to exude a calm she wasn't feeling. "Then I believe I'm free to leave?"

A charming smile curled his lips, but the intent stare reminded her of his animal form. He was hunting.

And she was his prey.

"There's no rush." He edged closer.

Raven countered quickly, pulling the boy close to her back. "Nor is there a reason to stay."

The beautiful way he moved drew her gaze, hypnotic and beguiling.

"Except to get to know one another." The tone of his voice was deep and soothing. So inviting. The beasts at her core inched forward in curiosity.

A movement in the crowd snapped her to attention. The Ogre. Then the tiger's words registered, leaving a trail of cold in its wake. Clever kitty. She'd bet he lulled many people the same way, using that luscious voice, subtle movements and just the lick of wildness to lure them to him.

"I think not." Though she tried to rein it in, power burned along her arms at the thought of being held against her will. The beasts retreated, leaving all that power behind along with the dangerous urge to release it. The leather she wore usually protected those nearest her, but direct touch couldn't mute the effects. Not even wearing gloves kept those around her completely safe when her dander was up.

The boy sucked in a sharp breath, and she quickly dropped her hand from him. She refused to look behind her, but she didn't need to. She could see everything in the tiger's reaction. The way he tensed slightly, the way his eyes flickered back and forth between her and the boy.

The crowd drew closer, pressing in on her from all sides, stealing the air around her.

She needed to leave.

The music grew louder, the lights brighter.

A bulb popped, glass shattered. Three more blew in rapid succession.

She took off at a run, dodging through the crowd, ignoring the shouts. The tiger quickly closed the gap between them. She could feel his breath against the back of her neck. Desperate for space, she thrust a burst of current into the crowd. A mass of confusion ensued as everyone received a nasty shock and started shoving one another.

Lights flickered, plunging them in darkness. Electricity lashed out of the floor and up into her feet, the charge filling her with power.

She slammed into the door, out into the night and took off at a dead run. She should've known better than to be seduced into entering a slave auction by some innocent needing her help. She had a hard enough time staying out of trouble without the need to borrow someone else's. She just prayed no one could tie this whole, rotten evening back to her or there would be no end of trouble to land on her doorstep.

## ✥ Sneak Peek ✥

### *The Demon Within*

Blood trickled from a gash, coating the rough surface of stone beneath Caly's fingers. Warming it. Pulling her arm back, she ignored the cut and parted the vines.

And caught a glimpse of stone.

Spreading the vegetation further, she stilled when powerful thighs filled her gaze. The voices of the men arguing disappeared in the background as she tilted her head back and looked up.

A black beetle so large it had to be on steroids paused climbing the statue and flicked a perturbed glance at her. With a little hiss for disturbing him, the little critter launched itself in the air with a flutter of wings. She flinched, bowed backwards to miss being hit in the face.

And met the open-eyed stare of a statue, a man forever captured in time. All thoughts of bugs vanished. Caly's lips parted, her eyes widened and her breath stuttered out of her mouth.

There was a God.

The man—and from her view kneeling on the moss covered ground, he was most definitely a man—was absolutely gorgeous. Not in the normal sense, not by Hollywood standards. Prominent cheekbones, a full, sharp nose and a strong jaw kept his face from being too feminine.

Desire twisted through her, and a deep yearning tightened her chest. A bubble of hope swelled. This was a man she could depend on to not let her down. When she looked at him, the chaos inside that defined most of her life settled.

She felt normal.

Reality crashed over her, settling heavily on her shoulders. Desire for a damn statue. How ironic she could be attracted to stone when live men left her cold. But here, in the middle of nowhere, she found a man who turned her on like nobody else, and he wasn't real. It was enough to make her cry.

Little details filtered into her brain. A thrill of excitement thrummed under her skin. The answers she sought about her condition were stuck in the past; she only had to uncover the clues.

This was why she came here, what quieted her protests against the mission, all for the chance to learn if there was a possibility for her to be human again. To find a way to finally destroy the demon infection that had taken root and flourished in her body. Each time the darkness opened up in her, the harder it became to fight. The more she wondered why she fought it at all.

The mission forgotten, Caly took her time to catalog each odd detail, a dark thrill brushed against the edge of her awareness. The statue wasn't what she'd come to expect from this region. Instead of native garb, the grey stone man had chiseled, close fitted pants. Two inch carved straps crisscrossed his chest, appearing to almost dig into the stone. His long hair, wild with waves, was tied back from his face.

Her fingers twitched to run her hands over him. Though his complexion was tinged green with age, the fierce expression drew her gaze instead of repelling her. The turn of his lips was anything but sensual, yet their full form made her think of sex and what a man could do with a mouth like his.

Strong shoulders led down to a lean, sculptured chest. His open shirt did little to disguise his physique. The statue shouldn't have impressed her, but it was as if the stone called to her. She had to curl her fingers into a fist to resist touching him. A streak of light filtered through the canopy, wavered a moment then illuminated him like an offering. Something just for her and no one else.

As she watched, she swore his chest moved to breathe. It took a physical effort to pull her gaze away, regulate her breathing, and longer to tuck away the desire to stake claim. The weird light faded, and her focus came to rest on a knife strapped to his right side. The fifteen-inch dagger rested close to his body, the curved handle arched up, wrapping along his ribs. What drew her interest was the intricate design etched along the outside of the scabbard and handle. It was too detailed for any stone crafting of the time. Or it should have been.

Absorbed in the discovery, she leaned forward for a better look. It reminded her of something important, but she couldn't put her finger on it.

A heavy hand landed on her shoulder, jolting her attention back to her surroundings, leaving her guts in her throat.

"Did you find anything of interest?"

Oscar.

Shit.

"No." The protest rose automatically to her lips. Her fascination with the statue triggered her unease again. Especially the way it so completely made her forget her surroundings and the mission.

It took more force than she liked to drop her hands to her sides. A hand she hadn't even known she'd raised. The vines swung inward, the statue disappeared from sight, and her stomach dropped. Caly honestly didn't know if her reaction was due more to the fact she messed up or because the statue was no longer under her watchful eye.

She had an awful, sinking feeling it was the latter.

"Nothing of interest." Guilt caused her to flush, but she didn't want the old man to find the statue, feeling protective of the stupid thing. She tried to tell herself she was overreacting, but her mind didn't agree. She held her ground, waiting for him to move away.

The contest of wills broke when, with his usual vigor, Oscar leaned past her and yanked on the vines. Vegetation shredded, bruised leaves drifting abandoned to the ground. Bold and savage, her statue faced forward, a sentinel frozen in time, waiting to be awakened.

She swore that Oscar instinctively knew what she wanted and made sure she never received it. In her peripheral vision, she watched him circling the stone, but once he disappeared from view, he disappeared from her thoughts as well.

One step forward, then two, she stood only inches away from temptation, her palms itching for just one touch. She stole a quick glance at the statue from under her lashes, then forced herself to turn away and put him...it out of her mind. The urge to linger pulled at her sense of duty. The simple task to turn and walk away was surprisingly hard, especially since she'd dedicated her life to her work.

"You know what it is." Oscar's low growl didn't have its normal bite, yet the tone stiffened the muscles of her back.

Caly refused to face him, refused to let him see the fear in her eyes. Fear for the stone man. She swallowed past her painfully dry throat. "A statue."

"Don't be a fool. You know it's a demon, one of the cursed guardian statues. Just pray that your blood isn't human enough to wake him. If the blasted thing wasn't mounted in granite, I'd have it smashed."

The lash of his words stung, but the threat to the statue sent a surge of terror through her. And that pissed her off. She opened her mouth to protest when a jungle cat's roar rang out and echoed in the treetops.

Caly whipped her head around, her eyes narrowing at the undergrowth. At first she didn't see anything. After a moment, two eyes blinked lazily, staring back at her as a big ass cat licked its muzzle. A chill crept down her spine. A twitch of muscles betrayed her abhorrence of the creatures.

There was nothing behind those eyes but pure predator. No hunger, but a need and desire to kill for the pleasure of it.

"Skins!" Possessions were when a demon took over a body. Skins were when demons forced the actual soul out of the body and used them as indestructible suits that only a beheading would free the demon and allow it to be killed.

Even as she bellowed the warning, the guides screamed like kids and took off. A streak to the left broke her concentration, and she saw another animal, a black panther, bound after the two men. Their bloodcurdling screams were cut off abruptly, leaving no doubt to their fate.

The other panther slowly slunk out of its hiding place, its eyes locked on her.

A sound to her right had the big cat's head swing in that direction. "Run!"

## ❧ Sneak Peek ❧

### *BloodSworn*

Trina wasn't aware what woke her, but she wanted to kill them when the warm, sensual dream faded. She held still, half-able to feel those hands linger on her body, but the outside world refused to bow to her wish.

Sounds seeped in first.

Or the absence of sounds.

No tweeting of birds. No people coming or going. She groped for her weapon and sighed of relief when her fingers encountered cool steel.

The image of the sexy man, bound and determined to bring her pleasure, vanished like a wisp of smoke, and she nearly whimpered.

Then she became aware of the soft surface beneath her and not the hard lump of the makeshift bed she'd created in the shed. She cracked open one eye, uncertain what to expect.

The Den.

Merrick.

He was the Leo. Of course he was. How could she not have known? And how the heck did she get his attention or more importantly, how did she escape it now that she was his concubine?

Memories of yesterday flittered through her head. One thought rose to the forefront, like how she fell asleep on the couch and ended up on the bed.

Half-afraid of what she'd find, she stretched out, shivering at the feel of silk against her skin. She was spread-eagle on the bed, nowhere near the sides, when she realized she was alone. Relief and disappointment struck in equal measure, and she hated that she felt both.

The dream teased the back of her mind. She felt haunted by her phantom lover's touch, the aching need when he kissed her. She was devastated by the loss, the realization he wasn't real.

She befriended humans, but had never committed to a relationship for the simple fact that any boyfriend she chose would always be in danger.

She'd avoided the paranormal as well for fear of discovery. But the man in her dream was different. He knew about her past and could protect himself.

What hurt the most was it would only ever be a fantasy.

She rubbed her eyes, banishing the dream as best she could. She had work to do. Sunlight streamed through the room, and she was surprised at how deeply she'd slept. A few more nights rest like last night, a couple of meals, and she'd be back to normal.

But first she had to do her job.

She scooted to the edge of the mattress and found that her feet dangled nearly a foot from the floor. She dropped down, the plush rug warm under her toes. She walked around the bed to grab her pack, probing her ribs, taking measure of her injuries.

Or where her wounds should've been.

She ripped off the bandages, wincing at the tug of stubborn tape. Deep bruises made the whole side of her body sensitive to even the slightest touch, but the open lacerations she'd sustained last night had closed. Smooth skin met her fingertips. Though she was thankful, the rapid healing didn't bode well for her.

It meant the bindings were weakening. How much longer before they broke all together? A small part of her, the little girl who'd lost her powers just as she found them, cheered at being able to defend herself. The adult trembled.

What did she know about magic?

If she reversed the process and stopped her magic from unraveling, she could buy herself some time. She was halfway bent down to kneel and grab her bag when she saw him.

The same man from her dreams.

A very naked man.

Merrick.

Her mind rebelled. She couldn't have had a sexy dream about the man who might very well destroy her. Vampires had been inside the Den not a day ago. She couldn't forget that, no matter how much her body wanted to be worshiped by him.

Merrick lay stretched out, dwarfing the extra-large couch. He didn't look comfortable, but that wasn't what captured her attention. The sun highlighted the golden color of his skin. It was just how she imagined his animal would appear.

The only thing blocking her view was the sheet draped haphazardly over his slim hips. Her brain short-circuited at the thought of him completely nude.

Him sleeping within a few feet of her and all without a stitch of clothing on struck her dumb, and her emotions jumbled at the conflicting emotions.

She swallowed hard and fanned her face. No matter how much she might have wished it, there was no way that image would ever be far from her mind. Every time she saw him now, she would picture him stretched out as if for her pleasure.

It didn't matter that she was a doctor, that she'd seen hundreds of naked bodies. She knew layers of skin and bone, but nothing in her studies had ever shown a man structured quite like him, with muscles quite so defined and begging to be stroked.

Doctor.

She shook her head at the reminder, as if she could banish the impulse so easily. She needed to get a closer look at him to decide what was the best course of action...for medical purposes she told herself sternly when her pulse betrayed her and sped up.

She just didn't know if she'd survive it.

One thing would help...getting him clothed.

But she couldn't tear her gaze away from that sheet. Or more precisely, what it hid. Where was a gust of wind when you needed one?

Her fingers itched to explore all that exposed flesh, but she feared it had nothing to do with science. Her body urged her to touch, while the sane, sensible part of her mind seemed to have taken a vacation.

Then she saw the lines of strain, the stiff way he held himself even in sleep. She needed to see his back.

"Merrick, roll over."

Trina found herself sprawled across the floor with a lion, in all but animal form, half sprawled over her with his face just inches from hers.

She hadn't even seen him move.

Was it her imagination or were his teeth sharper, his body larger, and his eyes shaded just this side of golden?

She gave a tentative smile, knowing better than to try and escape. "Hello."

"Are we under attack?" He blinked as if confused, finally recognizing her. His sleepy expression sent her heart thumping hard against her ribcage. The rumpled appearance only made him more attractive, more approachable and more touchable than was good for her.

Especially when she felt the sheet tangled around her feet.

No matter how much she told herself not to do it, it was too late. Her eyes flickered downward.

Yup, naked.

And such a nice naked backside, too.

It was her turn to blink when she felt his arousal.

"Attack?" It sure felt like it, and she was unarmed.

# ABOUT THE AUTHOR

Stacey Brutger lives in a small town in Minnesota with her husband and an assortment of animals. When she's not reading, she enjoys creating stories about exotic worlds and grand adventures…then shoving in her characters to see how they'd survive. She enjoys writing anything paranormal from contemporary to historical.

### Other books by this author:
BloodSworn
Coveted


### A Raven Investigations Novel
Electric Storm (Book 1)
Electric Moon (Book 2)
Electric Heat (Book 3)


### A PeaceKeeper Novel
The Demon Within (Book 1)


### Coming Soon:
Citadel
Electric Legend (Book 3.5)
Electric Night (Book 4)

Visit Stacey online to find out more at **www.StaceyBrutger.com**

Printed in Great Britain
by Amazon